Praise for *New York Times* bestselling author Lori Foster

"Foster is a master at writing a simmering romance, and *Fast Burn* is no different."

—*USA TODAY*'s *Happy Ever After* blog

"Hot enough to start a fire!... A delicious and dangerous tale that proves why Foster is one of the best in the genre."

—*RT Book Reviews* on *Fast Burn*

"Teasing and humorous dialogue, sizzling sex scenes, tender moments, and overriding tension show Foster's skill as a balanced storyteller."

—*Publishers Weekly* on *Under Pressure* (starred review)

"Best friends find hunky men and everlasting love in Foster's latest charmer.... Her no-fail formula is sure to please her fans."

—*Publishers Weekly* on *Don't Tempt Me*

"Foster brings her signature blend of heat and sweet to her addictive third Ultimate martial arts contemporary."

—*Publishers Weekly* on *Tough Love* (starred review)

"Emotionally spellbinding and wicked hot."

—*New York Times* bestselling author Lora Leigh on *No Limits*

"Storytelling at its best! Lori Foster should be on everyone's auto-buy list."

—#1 *New York Times* bestselling author Sherrilyn Kenyon on *No Limits*

"Foster's writing satisfies all appetites with plenty of searing sexual tension and page-turning action in this steamy, edgy, and surprisingly tender novel."

—*Publishers Weekly* on *Getting Rowdy*

"A sexy, believable roller coaster of action and romance."

—*Kirkus Reviews* on *Run the Risk*

"Steamy, edgy, and taut."

—*Library Journal* on *When You Dare*

Also available from Lori Foster and HQN Books

Body Armor

Under Pressure
Hard Justice
Close Contact
Fast Burn

The Guthrie Brothers

Don't Tempt Me
Worth the Wait

The Ultimate series

Hard Knocks
(prequel ebook novella)
No Limits
Holding Strong
Tough Love
Fighting Dirty

Love Undercover

Run the Risk
Bare It All
Getting Rowdy
Dash of Peril

Edge of Honor

"Ready, Set, Jett"
in *The Guy Next Door* anthology
When You Dare
Trace of Fever
Savor the Danger
A Perfect Storm
What Chris Wants
(ebook novella)

Other must-reads

Cooper's Charm
Tucker
(ebook novella)
A Buckhorn Baby
Built for Love
(ebook novella)
A Buckhorn Bachelor
(ebook novella)
A Buckhorn Summer
(ebook novella)
All for You
Back to Buckhorn
(ebook novella)
Heartbreakers
Charade
Up in Flames
Turn Up the Heat
Hot in Here
Animal Attraction
(ebook anthology)
Love Bites
All Riled Up
The Buckhorn Legacy
Forever Buckhorn
Buckhorn Beginnings
Bewitched
Unbelievable
Tempted
Bodyguard
Caught!
Fallen Angels
Enticing

LORI FOSTER

DRIVEN TO *DISTRACTION*

HQN™

Recycling programs
for this product may
not exist in your area.

ISBN-13: 978-1-335-00625-7

Driven to Distraction

This edition published by arrangement with Harlequin Books S.A.

For questions and comments about the quality of this book, please contact us at CustomerService@Harlequin.com.

www.HQNBooks.com

Printed in U.S.A.

To my son, J.Z. Foster,

First, after having you live in South Korea for eight long years, making do with twice-yearly visits, FaceTime, phone calls and emails, it's amazing to have you back home in the States! My daughter-in-law is absolutely wonderful and I adore my granddaughter so very, very much. It's a true blessing to expand the family in such a beautiful way.

Second, oh, how I *love* having another writer in the family!

I'm incredibly proud of your talents and I'm thrilled for your successes. Even though we're in two different genres—me with romance and you with horror/urban fantasy—it's still super fun to discuss authorly experiences, compare notes, share promo and such.

I love you, J.Z. Thank you for being you!

Your mama,

Lori Foster

Dear Reader,

Back when I started the Men of Honor series, I didn't plan for it to overlap through a secondary character to the Love Undercover series. But it did. And I didn't plan for the Love Undercover series to trickle over to the Ultimate series through another secondary character but again—it did. AND (are you detecting a pattern?) I didn't expect "extra" characters from the Ultimate series to demand yet another series, but...they did, so I wrote the Body Armor series.

You, dear readers, are the reason why that pattern happened, because when you write and ask about stories for other characters, it's like a kick to my muse, making me turn secondary characters into heroes. Not always, but obviously, quite often. I loved writing all those series, and I loved all those characters, from Dare to Rowdy, to Armie to Brand. But oh, how I love, love, *love* writing all-new characters in an all-new setting. (Insert happy authorly grin!)

This brings me to *Driven to Distraction*, the first book in my Road to Love series. Brodie Crews—*swoon*. What a guy!

I've got my fingers and toes crossed that you adore reading him as much as I adored writing him. He's a man who can swing a punch as hard as he can steal a heart, loves his family without question, does his utmost to understand women (especially the heroine) and never takes injustice lightly.

He's also deliciously flawed, rugged in a most basic (very sexy) way, and he has this big-boned, slobbery, crazy-lazy dog that he rescued. Yes, I adore him. I think he's my favorite character ever and since I've written over a hundred stories, that's saying a lot.

If (when!) you read this book, do let me know if you agree.

Lori Foster

PS: All of my books stand alone. You never, ever need to read them in order to know what's going on. BUT...if you prefer to read in order, my books are listed by series on my website here: lorifoster.com/connected/.

CHAPTER ONE

Mary Daniels huffed as she continued to climb the rock path on the hillside, her briefcase in hand. Had she known that the Mustang Transport courier service was inaccessible unless a person planned to hike, she wouldn't have worn one of her nicest blouses. Or a skirt. Or the low-heeled shoes that were now starting to rub her heels raw.

Being short and excessively curvy made it difficult to find clothes that fit in a way to play down her proportions rather than emphasize them. She thought she'd succeeded, but now...

She had the awful suspicion that she'd started to sweat.

Worse, as she looked around at the not-impressive surroundings, she very well might be overdressed.

Tendrils of her hair, always a little frizzy, began to spring loose from her topknot. With the late-morning July sun full on her face, no doubt her freckles showed stark against her flushed skin.

Misery.

But finally, finally, a building came into view. Granted, it looked more like a garage with an office attached than an elite business, but she went where she was directed, conducting the business assigned to her, with the people her employer chose.

She reached level ground—and froze, stunned.

The building sat to her right, but to her left stood a man, his naked upper body under the hood of a junker as he worked on...well, something. The engine maybe. He wore ridiculously faded jeans that almost fell off his hips, with work boots. Muscles flexed in brawny arms and his broad back glistened in the sunshine.

No man had ever left her breathless, but she'd never seen a man like him before. Suddenly her clothes felt too tight and her lungs seemed to have stopped working.

Behind him, a woman tickled her fingertips down the groove of his spine to those low-slung jeans, across his butt and...

Mary gasped as the woman reached under him for a bold fondle.

A big lazy gray dog, which she hadn't even noticed, lifted its head and gave one vaguely interested "Woof."

The man didn't appear to notice being sexually stroked in the light of day, out in the yard, while working on a car—but with the dog's bark he glanced at her and away—and quickly came back for another, more assessing look.

Good Lord. Her heart stalled, then shot into a gallop.

Slowly, he straightened. His dark brown eyes, framed by crazy thick lashes, locked on her. Grease streaked parts of his broad, hairy chest, down solid abs, even across a flat stomach bisected by that same downy hair...

It suddenly struck her *where* she was looking and she ripped her attention back up to his face.

Though his mouth curled in a sign of amusement, his granite shoulders flexed as if in anger. Without releasing her from his stare, he cleaned his hands on a rag, then swiped a wrist across his forehead beneath a bandanna he'd tied around unruly brown hair.

The woman, a stunning blonde in a barely there sundress, stepped in front of him to ask her, "Who are you?"

Mary stiffened. The woman's suspicious tone made it clear that she'd intruded on an intimate moment.

An intimate moment, out in the yard of a business, in broad daylight.

Struggling to focus on anything else, Mary noted the dirt racetrack beyond the people. Adjacent to that property she saw a drive that probably wound around the hill and to the main road below—which meant she had parked below and climbed those awful stone stairs for no reason.

Well, really, they needed a sign with some directions for customers.

Movement in the building drew her gaze and she spotted an attractive man—a clean man, fully dressed—stepping out from behind a desk.

Thank God. "If you'll excuse me," she said to the woman and hurried to the door.

The gentleman from inside beat her to it, opening the door with a smile. "May I help you?"

"Yes, thank you." She wanted inside—away from the caveman, the model and the grueling heat, but he stood there, inadvertently blocking her way. He was as tall as the caveman, not quite as bulky but still very fit, wearing a polo shirt and khakis.

Attractive, yes, but not overwhelmingly so like the other one. "I'm here to discuss business with Brodie Crews."

The man smiled. *He* didn't look like a Neanderthal. *He* wasn't covered in grease. And best of all, *he* wore a respectable amount of clothes.

But he said, "I'm Jack Crews." Looking beyond her, he said, "Brodie?"

Oh. Oh *no.* Dread crept over Mary. No, no, no.

The scent of grease and heated male alerted her to his nearness before a rumbling deep voice said from right behind her, "I'm Brodie. What can I do you for?"

★★★

At his deliberately misspoken question, little Red whirled, her expression aghast. She looked ready to faint. Or maybe scream.

Odds of her running away were high.

Brodie grinned—then winced at the pain in his head.

Her mouth opened, but nothing came out. She closed it again, breathing deeply from flared nostrils.

Gorgeous mouth, he noticed. Full lips that looked a little pouty when he doubted this woman knew how to pout. As he stared at her, more freckles appeared over the bridge of her narrow, hoity nose. Her eyes were vivid blue, like the midday sky or sapphires or… Hell, he was too hungover to pinpoint the exact color of her eyes.

Her hair, though, he could nail that: fire red. And curly.

His gaze swept over her body quickly, but a glance was all he'd needed to realize she was stacked and doing her best to hide it.

Jack cleared his throat and the woman jumped as if his brother had goosed her. She looked back at Jack with longing, then at Brodie with distaste. "You're Brodie?"

Never had a woman said his name with such disappointment. True, he wasn't at his best, but still…

Just then, Gina's boobs smooshed up against his sweaty back as she draped herself over him, trying to stake a claim.

"Brodie," she whined in his ear. "About tonight?"

There'd be no shrugging her off, so he said to Red, "'Scuse me a sec," and turned to walk toward the car. After a smug look shot at Red, Gina came along.

He hadn't gone far enough away not to be heard, but it was his best stab at compassion. He shoved his hands in the back pockets of his sagging jeans. "I already told you no. No for tonight, no forever. Let it go, okay?"

"But—"

"No buts. Jack and I share a lot, but not that."

He heard Red gasp again, heard Jack growl, and then the office door opened. Brodie glanced their way in time to see his brother escorting the scorched redhead inside.

Why the hell did that bug him so much? *Because she came here for me.*

"Jack was a mistake. I want you, Brodie."

He rolled his eyes. Now she was insulting his brother? Did the woman not know his feelings on family?

Apparently not.

"This isn't a carnival. You don't get a ticket for all the rides." Her pout was deliberate and perfectly practiced. If she hadn't screwed his brother, he might've been interested. "Go home," he said, a little more gently. "We're not happening."

Without bothering to look at Gina again, he turned to Howler. The dog had sprawled in the scant shade of the Mustang, catcher-mitt paws in the air, junk on display, one loose lip drooping down to touch a floppy ear. "C'mon, boy. Let's go cool off."

Howler opened one eye, grumbled and closed it again.

"I'm going to get lunch."

That got his attention. The dog's long bony legs flailed in the air as he frantically struggled upright, lumbered to his feet and ran over with a "Woof."

Quiet voices reached him as Brodie stepped inside; Jack's calming, Red's rushed denial. The brush of cooled air played over his fevered skin, drying the sweat on his body and tightening his nipples. He went past Jack's office, glancing in only long enough to say, "Be right back."

He saw Charlotte—his and Jack's secretary, who was more like a little sister since they'd known her forever—fetching cold bottles of water.

He leaned in to whisper, "Don't let her flee, okay? I gotta wash up but I'll only be a minute."

Brows up, Charlotte snorted. "I'm not your pimp."

Brodie cocked one brow. "She wants to hire me, brat."

"Not anymore, she doesn't. She's doing her best to convince Jack to take the job instead." With a wink, she sidled past him and down the hall to the office with the drinks.

"Son of a bitch," he muttered to her back, apparently not low enough.

Red leaned out the door to frown at him, but was guided back inside when Charlotte entered.

He heard Jack doing introductions. "Ms. Daniels, this is Charlotte Parrish, our assistant."

"Their *everything,*" Charlotte corrected. Then the little witch shut the door so he couldn't hear anything else.

Howler gave Brodie a look, then pivoted to trot after Charlotte, knowing she was the real source of food.

Annoyed, Brodie shoved into the bathroom, but wished he hadn't when the door hit the wall and his head tried to crack and fall off his shoulders.

After digging aspirin from the crooked medicine cabinet, he washed them down with water from the tap, scrubbed his hands with the special soap to remove as much grease as he could and splashed his face and chest.

One look in the mirror and he knew he hadn't improved things much. He still looked like hell. He thought about getting his shirt from his car...

Fuck it.

He rapidly dried off and sauntered to the office, opening the door and stepping inside just as Red was making her argument.

Charlotte blew him a kiss on her way out.

"Yes, my boss requested Brodie specifically, but that was based off internet research. I'm sure he wouldn't be opposed to hiring you instead—"

"No." Brodie turned a chair to face her profile and slouched into it, his sprawled legs only inches from touching her small feet.

As Red inhaled, her extraordinary chest swelled, her chin

tucked in and her brows came down. It was an impressive show of anger and control.

If he wasn't such a dick, he might have felt chastened.

She slowly turned her head to pinpoint him with her brilliant blue-eyed disdain. "You look inebriated," she stated, her voice a little louder than it needed to be.

"Cuz I was. But that was last night. Now I'm just suffering a hangover." He winced theatrically. "Have a heart and talk a little softer."

"Why," she asked, her voice not one iota quieter, "are you working in the sun if you're—"

"How else will I learn?" Keeping his face straight wasn't easy, but her expression made the effort worthwhile.

Her brows smoothed out, then lifted. "Pardon?"

Jack laughed—and since he was a loving brother, *he* at least moderated his tone. "Brodie is a big believer in self-discipline."

"More like self-castigation," Charlotte muttered as she returned with a tray of sandwiches and chips on paper plates. "If he suffers the ill effects of his decisions, maybe he'll make better ones."

Brodie saluted her with his water bottle, then took half of his sandwich and offered it to Howler. The dog gulped it down in one big bite, then waited hopefully for another.

"Damn, man. You seriously gotta learn to chew."

Ears up and alert, the dog licked his loose lips.

Red blinked quickly.

Brodie blinked back at her. Mocking. Taunting.

Why, he didn't know, but it just happened.

She rolled in those soft, plush lips and turned away, her curvy little body stiff. "Mr. Crews—"

Jack and Brodie both said, "Yes?"

Her spine straightened even more. Her gaze stayed only on Jack. "I'm quite sure my employer would be pleased to—"

"Jack's not available." Brodie bit into the other half of his sandwich.

Her hands fisted in her lap. "I haven't yet said when I need him."

When she *needed* him? Smirking, the wheels already turning—

Jack glared a not-too-subtle warning at him, cutting off the joke he so badly wanted to make. Yeah, he got it. They needed the job.

He swallowed the bite and asked, "What're the specifics for the job?"

Somehow, the little prude managed to stiffen even more. She looked ready to break—and damn, how he wanted to see that.

Her attention only on Jack—or so she wanted them to believe—she pulled out a manila folder from the soft briefcase she held in her lap.

Tilting his head, Brodie studied her shapely calves and trim ankles beneath a knee-length skirt. Her skin was pale, her legs smooth, her feet small.

Hell, he'd known plenty of small smooth pale women, so why was he getting so twitchy?

"The job is immediate." She slid the folder across the desk.

As she did so, the skirt grew taut over her sexy rump and rounded thighs.

Yeah, he noticed. Hell, no amount of alcohol or morning-after headaches would keep him from seeing something that luscious.

Little red ringlets, curled from the humidity, stuck to her delicate nape and dangled around ears decorated only with pearl studs.

Realizing he was taking interested inventory, Brodie lounged farther back in his seat and gestured for Jack to open the folder and peruse the contents.

First, Jack set aside the enclosed business card, then looked over what Brodie assumed to be a proposed contract. After a few seconds of reading, Jack asked, "Marigold, Kentucky?"

"A very small town that borders Tennessee. I've estimated it to be a single-day job. Five hours to drive there, an hour to retrieve the item my employer has purchased, then the drive back." She nodded at the papers. "Sign and you're hired."

Jack turned the contract so Brodie could see it, but spoke to the lady. "This says five thousand dollars. For a *day* job?"

Brodie nearly whistled. That was some serious cash. "What are we picking up? A dead body?"

Soft lips pinched. "Of course not."

"A *live* body?"

She swiveled her head to glare at him, cobalt eyes trying to cut out his heart.

"Hey, I've seen *The Transporter.*"

She inhaled, making her breasts strain the front of that damp, thus sheer, blouse. "What my employer has purchased is very important to him. He wants to ensure its safety…and it needs to be delivered to him by end of day tomorrow."

"Does the contract say what it is?" Brodie asked.

"Does it matter?" she returned.

Jack and Brodie shared a look, but hey, five grand was five grand. If he got there and it was anything shady, he could deal with it then.

Decision made, Brodie enjoyed telling her, "Well, Jack's out."

"True," Jack said with sincere apology. "I have a previous commitment that can't be changed. But Brodie—"

"Your *first* choice," Brodie chimed in.

"—is absolutely available."

Her eyes narrowed.

Knowing he'd gotten his way, without quite knowing why it mattered, Brodie put his arms back in a relaxed pose, his fingers laced behind his neck so he could pop out some tension without being obvious about it. He really did feel like shit.

Yet the day rapidly improved.

Miss Priss glanced at his armpits, scrunched her face in disapproval and turned back to Jack with a plea. "But—"

"I'm sorry," Jack said.

She disapproved of *armpits*? Everyone had them, even prissy redheads. Brodie smiled. "I can leave at 5:00 a.m."

After prolonged hesitation and, he guessed, some teeth grinding, she finally nodded.

Thwarting the lady felt so good, it even took the edge off the drumbeat in his temples as he watched her averted face. "Just give me the address and the name of the person I'll be seeing, whatever other info I need, and I'll get it done."

Silently, she closed her briefcase, slid a long strap over her shoulder and stood.

Jack came to his feet, too.

Brodie didn't. He tipped his chair back on two legs and watched the frustration play over her face. She wasn't a real beauty, but she was certainly pretty. The hair was a showstopper. Those eyes, so damn blue they defied description, would always draw attention. And that mouth, even while compressed in annoyance, could inspire fantasies.

Here in the cooler air, her freckles weren't as noticeable.

Shame. They were kinda cute. Maybe sexy even.

All that with curves galore in such a small package, and it was no wonder she affected him.

"Ahem."

Brodie forced his eyes off the lady long enough to cock a brow at his brother.

Jack's scowl sent a message loud and clear: *if you lose this job by being an asshole, I'll make sure you regret it later.*

Knowing Jack, he'd probably take advantage of Brodie's diminished state. Sighing, he decided to attempt some gentlemanly behavior.

But Red beat him to it.

"I'll have all the pertinent details, as well as half the payment, with me tomorrow before we leave. We can finalize the contract then."

His chair dropped forward with a clatter, making his head nearly explode. He squeezed his eyes shut and clenched his jaw to contain his brain, which seemed to be doing aerobics between his ears. When it finally eased up he cracked open one eye.

Both Jack and Red watched him, the first with pity, the second with annoyance.

"We?" Brodie rasped, unsure he'd heard correctly.

"It is my responsibility to ensure the safety of my employer's purchases." She looked down her nose at him. "You are merely the transporter."

Merely the transporter? Indignation brought him to his feet so that he towered over her. Her haughty little nose barely reached his collarbone, but did she back up a step?

No, not this ballsy lady. Instead she tipped back her head and met him glare for glare.

Brows drawn together, Brodie pointed a finger and opened his mouth.

But she wasn't done.

"Be sober tomorrow."

He almost sputtered at that flat demand. "I don't drink and drive!"

One brow arched up. "No hangover, either." Her stern gaze dipped over his body, and then she dismissed him as she turned away—with a last cutting remark. "And, Mr. Crews?"

He waited.

One hand on the doorknob, she glanced over her shoulder. "If you truly want the job, you must be fully dressed."

With that edict, she marched out of the office and toward the exit.

Brodie stepped out to the hall to stare after her, watching that well-rounded behind barely sway at all as she went through the door and into the dusty yard. Well, damn.

Joining him, Jack put a hand to his shoulder. "I like her."

"You would," he grumbled. But honestly, he liked her, too. The lady was a fireball. He started to grin.

"No," Jack said. "We need the money, so don't fuck it up or I'll demolish you."

"That's the thing with you," Brodie complained with good humor. "You only look like the civilized one."

Mary cursed herself for the hundredth—maybe the thousandth—time as she sat on the bed, her laptop open before her at three in the morning. Her eyes burned and she couldn't stop yawning, but then she hadn't slept much through the night.

She put the blame for her sleepless night squarely on the boulder shoulders of that scruffy-faced, rude, provoking cretin that Therman insisted she hire. When he'd first named Brodie Crews as the courier he wanted, she'd thought nothing of it. Their last transporter had relocated and hadn't been that reliable anyway. Twice he'd been unable to accept Therman's assignments, and that had left them scrambling for a replacement. If Brodie Crews worked out, Therman wanted him on retainer.

But then her boss, Therman Ritter, an eighty-six-year-old eccentric sweetheart, didn't have to be around the man. No, Therman stayed tucked away in his million-dollar retreat, collecting his "valuables" and avoiding society.

It was Mary's job to socialize, to make human contact and to ensure the acquisitions happened without a hitch. She always accompanied the courier to guarantee Therman's interests were respected—and kept private.

She should have had Mr. Crews sign the contract yesterday, but at that point she'd still been hoping to talk Therman out of hiring him.

And she'd wanted to get away from the man as quickly as possible.

In some indefinable way, he threatened her peace of mind

and her carefully crafted persona. A first for her, and damn him, she didn't like it.

Looking over all the research she could find on Brodie, she marveled that Therman had chosen him. She couldn't find one overwhelming reason to explain why her unusual boss had focused on that brother instead of the other, but she did know now that Jack wouldn't have been accepted. Therman had been very clear on that point.

Thank God Brodie had insisted, because Therman had been very displeased with her efforts to switch up brothers. Her descriptions of them, her comparisons, hadn't mattered at all.

Therman wanted Brodie, and only Brodie.

It wasn't the Mustang Transport website that had convinced him. It was still being built and contained only the basics. It wasn't Brodie's bio, either, which mostly mentioned his history as a courier and dedicated work ethic. Nor would it be his stellar driving record, because that was expected for his career choice.

No, the one thing that had won over Therman was Brodie's rescue of that oversize, long-boned dog. Therman had read a lot into it: compassion, determination, duty, honor... The list went on and on. That single heroic incident had convinced him that Brodie was the perfect person to complete the job.

Frustrated, Mary sat back against the pillows and read the too-brief article again. Brodie had found the dog chained to a stake in the broiling sun near a junkyard. No food, no water. Signs of abuse.

Mary swiped away a tear, furious with the idea that anyone would ever mistreat any animal. In many ways, it was the same as mistreating a child. One couldn't speak, and the other was often too afraid to tell.

Brodie must've been furious, too, because he found the owners and offered for the dog. In doing so he'd apparently stumbled onto a drug deal in progress. Guns were drawn, shots fired—and somehow Brodie had come out of it whole hide, with three men wounded. He'd taken the dog home, rehabilitated him and given him the cushy life.

That was a year ago, and while Mary did consider it incredibly heroic, it had absolutely nothing to do with transporting Therman's valuables.

Knowing she couldn't put it off any longer, she closed her laptop and got up to shower and dress. It'd be a long drive, requiring professional yet comfortable clothes. Knowing things didn't always go as planned, she carried an overnight bag with an outfit change and other necessities, just in case. In the past she'd been caught in downpours, had food or drinks dumped on her, and once she'd slipped on a muddy hill.

Since she detested her freckles, she also packed her makeup for touch-ups.

Today, she would not let Brodie rile her.

She wouldn't deliberately breathe in his earthy scent, either.

Or admire his body... The way those massive shoulders flexed with each small movement, or how his muscular frame tapered into lean hips, and how that damp, curling body hair teased down his torso and into the loose jeans that hung so low...

Mary stifled a small groan. Ungluing her feet from the floor, she rushed into the shower, vowing that she definitely wouldn't notice that.

Given her instructions on his presentation, namely that he be fully clothed, it should be a little easier.

She'd never known a man like him, never experienced such casual rudeness and disregard for propriety, never met a man so, so...unashamedly masculine.

She'd never felt the ridiculous magnetism.

Mary covered her face, whispering aloud her shameful truth, "Physical attraction." She was hotly, keenly turned on by a goon, a brute, a man who flung his maleness out there for all to gawk at.

And gawk she had.

Over and over again the scenario in the office played in her mind. The way he'd slouched in his seat, uncaring that his legs had sprawled out, his big feet in the rough boots almost touching her chair, those solid thighs straining the worn material of his jeans.

The soft bulge behind his fly nearly impossible to ignore.

He'd positioned those thick arms behind his head, exposing his underarms as if it were a casual thing to display himself in front of a possible client. The pose had flattened his impressive pec muscles into solid slabs over his chest, while bulging his biceps and tightening his abs.

And she'd looked. Against her will, against her usual comportment, against every proper behavior she'd always adhered to, she'd been unable *not* to look.

It was as if all decorum and civility had been stripped away from him, leaving only hot, raw man and she, as a woman, had instinctively reacted.

But that was yesterday and this was today, and today would be different. She'd see to it.

By the time she headed out of her apartment to her silver Ford, she'd donned as much armor as she could.

Subtle makeup covered her freckles.

Her wild hair was tightly contained in a knot at the top of her head.

She wore a long loose gauze skirt that skimmed her ankles, with a snug-fitting tank, topped by a blouse for extra coverage in case his car's air-conditioning made her too cool, and comfortable slip-on sandals. She looked neat and professional, but not stuffy.

And best of all, her overblown curves weren't that noticeable.

After stowing her briefcase and small overnight bag in the back seat, she checked her phone one more time to ensure she hadn't missed any messages. Therman often had last-minute instructions, but today, with Brodie, he remained silent.

Ignoring the tiny thrill zinging through her bloodstream, she set off for the Mustang Transport office.

She had a feeling today would be quite the adventure—because Brodie Crews was quite the man.

CHAPTER TWO

The offices were empty, the air heavy and still, only Howler's snores breaking the silence.

Brodie glanced at his phone screen to check the time, then returned it to his back pocket. Red was two minutes late. He folded his arms. What if he'd scared her off? What if she'd found some other courier to take the job?

They could use the money both to make repairs to the existing office and to expand the business. But that was only part of the reason he wanted her to show.

Yesterday he'd been in a fog of discomfort, so he wasn't sure if her impact on him had been as sharp as he remembered. Red hair, blue eyes, a full rack and a handful at the rear… Nice, yes. Sexy, sure.

But altogether, did she really pack such a lusty punch to the libido, or had he only been weakened by the hangover?

He kept picturing her with her frowns and derision, contrasted with that rockin' bod, and why the hell that'd make his cock jump, he had no idea. But even now he felt it, the brief stirring, the pull.

Fuck that.

Today, he decided, he would play it cool. He'd be business-like. Circumspect. Calmly polite.

If she showed.

Damn it, he should have gotten the contract signed yesterday. If he hadn't been so busy pricking her temper and enjoying her reactions, he might've thought ahead to do it.

Jack, who hadn't been nearly as fascinated with her, should have seen to it. But no, that dick just let him wallow in his bad manners with only the occasional glare.

Why the hell hadn't Charlotte made it a priority? She had enough experience, along with a real head for business, to know it should've been done. Why had they let a financial catch like Mary Daniels slip out with no more than a verbal commitment?

Suddenly Howler perked up one ear. That was followed by one eye opening. That single eye searched the area directly in front of him—because Howler wasn't getting up just out of curiosity. As headlights flashed over the track, the big dog managed to lift his head enough to issue a single "Woof."

That done, he stretched out again.

"What a good dog," Brodie said in the voice reserved only for Howler. He knelt and stroked the animal's neck. "You're the best guard dog ever. Yes, you are." Howler's tail thumped at the praise. "Contract first," Brodie told him, though he suspected Howler was back asleep. "Then we'll go."

At that particular word, the dog bounded up in a clumsy rush and circled his car, looking for a way to get in.

"Not yet, boy. Patience." Waiting for Red to reach him—which, given her snail's pace, could take a while—Brodie leaned against the fender and crossed his arms. Anticipation prickled along his spine.

Why, he didn't know, but there you had it.

Per her request, aka demand, he was clearheaded this morning, freshly showered and dressed in jeans and a T-shirt. The thick morning air settled dew on everything, including him. On the ground beside him, a packed cooler waited with a thermos of coffee leaning against it, lidded travel mugs on top.

Her car, a pristine silver Ford, rolled up behind his. Through the dim light of the security lamps, he watched her put the car in Park. She opened her door and out came one small foot, adorned in a white sandal with a fluttery floral skirt drifting around it. Her toenails were painted a shiny color that closely matched her skin.

Not looking at him, she stepped out and brought her seat forward so she could retrieve a few things from the back seat.

Her briefcase and…an overnight bag? Interesting.

Down, he told his baser instincts. *We're not spending the night with her.*

Noticing that she didn't have a cooler, Brodie suppressed a smile. He could behave and still have some fun. Perfect.

After locking her doors, she finally glanced up at him, her assessing gaze going over him as if looking for signs of dissolution.

Brodie spread his arms wide. "Do I pass muster? Got enough covered up to spare your delicate sensibilities? I don't need a hat, do I?" He ran his fingers through his messy hair, then down over his throat. "A muffler? It's damn hot for a muffler but if throats shock you—"

"You'll do," she cut in, her tone calm and controlled.

Too controlled, damn it.

Sapphire eyes clashed with his, then she sniffed and looked away. "A shave wouldn't have killed you."

"How do you know?" He scratched over his scruffy jaw, hearing the rasp of a two-day shadow. "I shave every other week. That's enough torture for any man."

Her widened gaze came back to his. "Every other?"

"Week," he filled in for her since she seemed too appalled to manage the last word. Every muscle in his body flexed with interest. Insane. She wasn't wearing anything sexy—the opposite, in fact. She didn't make any overt gesture toward him. And her poor hair—she'd drawn it up so tightly it made his temples sympathize.

"And in the meantime?"

He'd been so busy thinking about liberating her hair, it took him a second to catch her meaning. "In between shaves, I have whiskers. Not a big deal, you know. Men are hairy. People—" he silently mouthed, *You* "—should learn to deal with it."

Hostility tightened her jaw. "So you won't have to bother grooming yourself?"

"Hey, I'm groomed. Mostly anyway. I showered, brushed my teeth, sort of combed my hair—"

"Sort of?"

He wiggled his fingers. "Works as well as a comb." Before he forgot that he was supposed to be polite and nice and all that other sugary shit, he swiped a forearm over the narrow trunk space and the low spoiler at the back of his Mustang to remove the dew. "Contract?"

"Oh." As if coming out of a daze, she withdrew papers and looked toward the office.

"Still locked up. Charlotte won't get here till nine, Jack is gone for the day, and we should have headed out five minutes ago." A subtle jab while withholding a last bathroom break. *That's what you get, Red, for your constant criticisms.*

She frowned. "I'm only a few minutes late, and only because I wasn't familiar with the road that came up here. Yesterday I climbed those grueling rock stairs and I didn't want to have to do that again."

"I run those bitches like Rocky, but yeah." He dropped his gaze to her hips, then to her ankles and those shiny little toes. "Guess I'm a little more muscular than you."

"A little," she said, her tone prim.

What an understatement. At about five-two, she was at least a foot shorter than him and no doubt a hundred pounds lighter, with most of her weight being tits and ass. But whatever. She might've lacked brute strength, but she made up for it with attitude and confidence.

At a loss as to how to reply to that, she just looked at him.

He gestured at her briefcase. "Contract?" he said again, but what he really meant was: Check?

"Of course." She approached the car and, with reluctance, laid her briefcase against the trunk with the contract on top. She handed him a fancy pen that probably cost more than a tankful of gas.

After quickly reading it over, he saw that it was a standard agreement except for the amount paid and the stipulation that he had a very short time frame to deliver. Interesting that Mary Daniels was listed as an agent to contact for any issues and all communication related to the delivery service.

It meant he still didn't know who he worked for, only that Red was employed to see the job done.

He twirled the pen. "So who are we delivering to?"

"It's not a secret, so don't look so suspicious."

"Time's tickin' away here, Red."

"Mary," she corrected, going rigid as the rebar used to reinforce concrete. "I'm employed by Therman Ritter." Her stiff smile was more like a baring of teeth. "If you sign the contract, you will be employed by him as well."

Brodie sighed. "Fine." He scribbled his name at the appropriate place.

She handed him a check, careful not to touch him. "Half now, half once we deliver." She folded her hands together. "There's one more thing."

Before she could say something that might make him rethink the deal, he tucked the check away in his wallet.

Easiest money ever made—so far. With that done, he looked down at her.

Even in the dim dawn, her hair shone like a beacon, picking up each and every beam of available light. God, how he'd love to see it down.

Not like that'd happen anytime soon, though.

She really was a little thing. And those expressive eyes, those plush lips… He drew a breath. "What's the other thing?"

"If this exchange goes well, Therman is interested in putting Mustang Transport on retainer."

"No shit?"

"Er…"

"Like he'd use us exclusively?" How many high-end deals did this guy make a year? A month?

She nodded but then corrected, "More specifically, he wants to put *you* on retainer."

"Huh." Should he be flattered or wary? Unsure, Brodie squinted across the landscape at the rising sun. "How about we discuss that on the road?" He needed to ensure the success of *this* transport before planning the future.

"Certainly." She glanced around. "Where's your car?"

Keeping his smile inside, he opened the driver's door, pulled the seat forward and whistled. Howler, who'd been sitting not too patiently, came alive in that clumsy, rushing way unique to him and his too-long limbs. In one big leap, he shot through the slim space into the back seat. Sitting much like an old man with his head and shoulders stooped forward, knobby knees up, and expectation on his long face, he took up every available inch of room on the seats.

Brodie closed the door, circled to the passenger side and with an absurd flourish, opened her door.

At first she didn't move. She appeared to be taking in the obvious with disbelief bordering on horror.

Finally she closed her mouth and found her voice. "*This* is the car you're taking?"

"Yup." He stroked along the roof. "She's the girl that never lets me down."

Red struck a militant pose, her arms stiff down at her sides, hands fisted, jaw tight. "Does this car even run?"

He put on a face of affront. "Of course she runs."

"*She's* rusted."

"No, she's touched up with primer because soon she'll be—" he looked at Mary's hair "—*red*. I would think you'd know the difference between falling apart and a trip to the salon."

Blue eyes flared, then narrowed severely. In a dangerous purr, she asked, "You think I deliberately made my hair this color?"

Hmm. He would have teased her more, but he detected a hint of hurt in her tone, as if she didn't like her hair. Hard to imagine since he thought it was sexy personified, but he'd tackle that in a bit—after the steam stopped coming out of her ears. "I think it's hot as hell out here and my dog will roast if you don't get a move on."

She fumed a few seconds more, then seemed to catch herself. Her lashes lowered as she took a deep breath that swelled her chest, and when she opened them again, he saw the banked ire as well as that iron control.

Admirable. There were a lot of facets to the lady's personality. He'd never been that fond of puzzles, but damned if he didn't want to figure her out.

"You were working on her—" she shook her head "—*it*, yesterday."

Nose in the air, he stated, "Her name is Matilda." At that bit of nonsense, Red looked ready to stomp.

In fact, she *did* stomp—on her way to the car. She shoved the overnight case onto the back seat. As she slid in, she muttered under her breath, *"Matilda."*

Brodie let himself grin as he said, "Buckle up." Then he circled around to the other side of the car and did the same with Howler. "That's a good boy," he crooned to the dog. "Good dog. Yes, you are."

As if in slow motion, Red swiveled around to ogle him.

He kissed the dog on his wrinkled forehead, which earned him a big sloppy tongue kiss, right up his chin to his left eye.

Using his shoulder to wipe away slobber, he grimaced. “You’re the only dude I’ll let do that, bud.”

Red was still giving him that look of incredulity as he moved her case to the floor, away from Howler. He even helped block it with the hard-sided cooler, then poured himself a coffee.

One look at her face and he huffed. “Howler is in a perpetual state of teething. If I hadn’t moved your case, he’d have gnawed on it the whole trip.”

“That dog is not a baby.”

“Try telling him that.” Brodie shrugged. “Next to sleeping and eating, his favorite activity is chewing.” Pretty much everything—except for the chew toys he had in abundance.

“Thank you, but that’s not what I meant.” Her right eyebrow rose. “You baby-talk your dog.”

“So?”

“So you and that particular tone are a very odd mix.”

“Howler likes it.” And that was what mattered. Before she could ask him how he knew that, he offered, “Coffee?”

Catching her bottom lip in her teeth, she hesitated.

Mmm. He wouldn’t mind biting that lip himself. It was plump and soft, rosy and wet, and he’d bet his left nut she tasted really good.

“You have another cup?”

His gaze jumped up to hers. Was she afraid to share with him? Thought he might give her cooties? Somehow every damn thing she said managed to offend him.

Or turn him on.

Mostly turn him on. “I don’t give my morning coffee to just anyone, so yes, I have another cup.”

“Then thank you.”

“I have cream and sugar packets if you—”

“Black is good.” She took it from him, sipped and murmured,

"Oh, that's so good," in a husky whisper that tiptoed down his spine. Lashes at half-mast, she held the travel mug close to her stubborn little nose and breathed in the aroma.

Brodie stood there, a little dumbfounded that she could make drinking coffee look and sound so sexual. "Anyway." He poured another cup, snapped on the lid and put it in the console holder between the seats, then got behind the wheel. "You don't mind Howler going along?" Here he'd been all prepped for her arguments and she'd surprised him by not giving any.

"Not if he's used to going along. Since he has his own car restraints, I assume he is."

"Yeah, he hates to be left behind. Breaks my black heart to hear him whining, so he goes where I go. I had to make the restraint, by the way, because they don't make them big enough to fit his—" he glanced at Howler as if worried he might offend "—bone structure. But it's definitely necessary." With the turn of a key, the engine rumbled to life, purring like a kitten.

Maybe a pissed-off kitten, but still a kitten.

"Howler loves to ride, but if anything spooks him, and just about everything does, he crawls into the front seat and tries to get on my lap. Brought me close to wrecking a few times, so now I buckle him in."

"It's clever." As he pulled away, she shifted to see the restraint again.

Brodie had to admit it wasn't as pretty as something store-bought, but it got the job done. He'd designed it to attach to the seat belt buckle and to the harness that Howler only wore while riding. For extra stability, he'd expanded the usual single strap to two so it latched on both sides.

Howler had a tendency to topple on turns.

"You love him a lot."

That particular soft voice from her could be lethal to his libido...if she said anything else. Why the hell would she use that word? Did the woman not date? Did she not know that men like him and that particular word didn't mix? Any mention of love, even in relation to his dog, set off warning bells. Too many women had tried to go down that road, but unlike his dad, he'd wait to settle down until he was damn good and ready.

He wasn't ready yet.

"He's mine and I take care of what's mine."

"He wasn't yours when you rescued him."

Pushy, that was what she was.

He felt her watching him, but he concentrated on the road.

"You've had him ever since?"

Not a story he'd go into with her. Though it was a full year ago, thinking about it still put him in a dangerous rage. Talking about it left him exposed. So he switched topics. "What about you? Any pets?"

"No." Turning to stare out the windshield, she held her coffee in both hands and sipped. "I'd love a dog or a cat, but I'm not home enough and it wouldn't be fair."

Something in her voice drew him. "Did you have pets as a kid?"

Her humorless laugh broke off quickly and she sipped again. "No, no pets."

Hmm. That edgy laugh put him on alert. "Ever?"

"Let's talk about future employment and what it'd mean to be under a retainer."

No one would ever mistake him for a gentleman. In fact, other than family, those who knew him would call him the exact opposite—and worse. But he knew how to read women, and this woman's desperate grasp for a new subject meant something about her past, maybe her upbringing, had left her emotionally bleeding.

Jerk or not, he would never deliberately hurt a woman, any woman. But for some bizarre reason that basic, bone-deep urge to protect suddenly burned extra hot.

If Red knew he was feeling territorial, that he wanted to

shield her, she'd probably give him hell. She could take care of herself, he didn't doubt it, but that didn't matter to his baser instincts. He never fought the inevitable.

Nodding his agreement, he took the ramp onto I-71 South. "Lay it on me."

For about an hour, Brodie was somewhat pleasant, causing Mary to change her initial assessment of him. He'd shared his coffee with her until they'd finished off the entire thermos. As they did so, they'd spoken amicably about a retainer agreement, with him accepting the requirements without complaint. Overall he'd acted like a relaxed, competent, albeit rough-edged man.

So she decided to give him a second chance.

After all, having a hangover could have thrown off anyone. Plus she'd obviously caught him by surprise with her visit.

And granted, with the heat of the day and the embarrassing way she'd reacted to him, part of their adversarial byplay yesterday was her fault.

They passed another exit, and Mary squirmed. She glanced at Brodie's profile, wondering if she should ask him to stop.

Smug satisfaction curved his mouth into a smile.

Oh, it was small. Barely there, even. But she saw that little curl to his sensuous lips, the crinkle at the corners of his lushly lashed eyes.

That was when she started to wonder just how wicked he might be.

She'd made the early trip to his office—which had been closed. Then after sharing his coffee—the whole blasted thermos, most of which she'd drunk—he'd asked her to get them each a bottle of water from the cooler. Unsuspecting at the time, she'd politely accepted, and though he'd only taken a few drinks of his, she'd finished off her bottle.

Now they'd been on the road for a little over two hours, two and a half for her, and he showed no signs of stopping.

She was deeply regretting her beverage choices.

How difficult would it have been for him to unlock the office? And why, after their initial confrontation yesterday, had he gone out of his way to share with her this morning?

As they were passing yet another exit, he pointed out—with a twinkle in his dark eyes—that they were right on schedule, making great time...unless she needed a pit stop?

The man was diabolical.

Well, if he thought she'd cry uncle, he'd be sadly mistaken. Pressing her lips together, she vowed that he'd give out before she would.

He turned on some music. "Feel free to nap."

Impossible. She crossed her legs and glanced at Howler. The big dog slumped sideways, his head drooped against the window where he'd started out watching the passing scenery but had since fallen asleep and begun snoring. All hope that the dog might need a pit stop died.

"Don't worry about Howler," Brodie said, as if he'd read her mind. "He sleeps more than he does anything else. Usually only *f-o-o-d* can rouse him."

The dog cracked open an eye, making her smile despite her need for a bathroom break. "I think he can spell."

"He catches on quick," Brodie agreed.

After a long sigh that sounded amazingly like disappointment, Howler's eye sank shut again and his snores returned.

Mary had a hundred questions about him, but she didn't want to chance stirring Brodie's curiosity again.

Her past was strictly off-limits.

The music, a mellow country tune, drifted in the air. She was more of a rock-and-roll woman, but she appreciated the sight of Brodie moving ever so slightly with the music, his fingers tapping against the steering wheel.

If a boulder could be relaxed, she'd say he was just that. Yet, while his expression seemed peaceful, his shoulders stretched his dark T-shirt and his biceps bunched and flexed with each small adjustment.

How exactly did a man go about getting a body like that?

"Do you work out?"

Mouth kicking up in amusement, he glanced at her. That dark-eyed gaze flashed over her before he returned his attention to the road. "You realize that's a pickup line, right?"

Oh Lord, his eyes were…well, amazing. And hot. If it wasn't for the unfamiliar lick of heat that intense look caused, she might've been embarrassed. Instead, her reaction threw her off.

Oh, she had her fair share of male attention, but usually it left her indifferent.

Not so with Brodie Crews.

Her MO was to steer clear of interested, or interesting, men, but really, what harm would it cause to look? She'd see him during this ride, then not again for a while. For that reason, she'd looked her fill—without being obvious.

His profile fascinated her, the way those thick, dark lashes shadowed his eyes, the high bridge of his strong nose and the curve to his mouth. His dark, thick hair held a slight wave, and no matter how many times he tunneled his fingers through it, it fell forward over his brow. The growth of whiskers on his jaw made her curious to know how it would feel to her fingertips.

And her lips.

"I'm just wondering," she said, trying to play it off as idle chitchat. "You're muscular for a man who makes his living driving a car."

"I also work on cars." He slid her an intimate smile. "As you know."

The reminder of her first sight of him sent another flush over her skin. Coolly, she replied, "Is that what you were doing? I got an entirely different impression."

"Because of the way Gina groped me?"

He said it without an iota of shame, making her jaw loosen and her mouth fall open.

Obviously, she was out of her league.

Brodie chuckled. “If I hadn’t been struggling to stay upright, I’d have shaken her off sooner, but Gina can always sense weakness. She thought she’d sneak in there while my defenses were down.”

“Your defenses?”

“I’m not at my best after a night of drinking.”

“Then why did you do it?” Personally, she’d never seen the draw. She sometimes had wine on very special occasions, which were few and far between. Drink, drugs… They caused a loss of control, leaving you not only vulnerable, but oblivious to all that really mattered.

“I’ve turned her down more times than I can count.” Brodie’s mouth went sideways, then he scratched the top of his head. “She’s persistent, I’ll give her that.”

“Is she in love with you?”

“Ha! No, not even a little.” Laughing, he shook his head. “Gina likes me okay, but that’s it. Mostly she wants bragging rights to say she’s banged Jack and me both.”

It took all Mary had not to drop her jaw again.

“The lady has a healthy sex drive. Unfortunately she also has a mean competitive streak.”

“A…” Mary cleared the frog from her throat. “A mean competitive streak?”

“Yeah, you might not have noticed, but our business is in a small town. Small as in minuscule. Everyone knows Jack and me, and vice versa. My mom worked in the cafeteria at school, and Dad was known for his stunt driving.” He rolled one shoulder. “Guess it’d be a coup to tag us both.”

In a scandalized whisper, Mary asked, “At the same time?”

He looked stricken. “You know, I never thought to ask. If that is her preference, I doubt she gets her way very often. I know a lot of the guys she's been with and I can't think of any who'd go for that."

"And now she wants you and Jack?"

He shrugged. "The lady's doomed to failure, at least where I'm concerned." His grin flashed. "Years ago, she and Jack spent a few hours together, and that puts her at the top of my no-go list. But over the last year, she's decided I'm next...or something. Maybe I'm just the only game in town now."

For some reason, this whole conversation got her annoyed. "So if she hadn't been with Jack, you might have—"

"Doubtful. I guess I've known her too long, you know? Grew up with her older brother, and she was the nagging little sis who wouldn't leave us alone. Doesn't seem to matter that Gina's a knockout now. Uninhibited, fun, isn't clingy—"

Mary snorted.

Humor crinkled the corners of his eyes again. "Should I have been more specific?" Before she could answer, he said, "I should've. I meant she doesn't get emotionally attached. Physically, yeah, she's an octopus, but in a good way, you know?"

No, she didn't know and didn't want to know. "Does it bother your brother that she's coming on to you?"

"Nah. They had a hookup, not a date or anything."

Such a cavalier attitude made her stomach roil—because she knew she wasn't the norm. For her, sexual involvement had always meant so much more than quick release, convenience or a lost hour. Too much more.

Keeping his eyes on the road, his voice neutral, Brodie asked, "You don't hook up?"

She started to shake her head before she realized how inappropriate their entire conversation had become. How had she let it get that bad? To cover her faux pas, she blurted, "We need to stop for a break."

"Thank God. I was beginning to think you were a camel."

Almost immediately he glanced in his mirrors, then switched lanes until he could take an exit to a rest stop.

Suspicious, Mary narrowed her eyes. "If you had to go, too, why did you make me ask?"

"To see if you would?"

That he said it like a question made her seethe. "So it was a game?"

"Or maybe just for the hell of it." He steered into a parking spot. "Who knows how my mind works?"

"That's the most—"

"Did it kill you to ask? No, it didn't," he replied before she could. "Count it as something new that you've learned."

"I've learned you're a jerk!"

"Maybe," he agreed with a small smile. "But I didn't bite, right? So while we're together—"

Her eyes widened.

"For *business*, feel free to tell me when you need something." He paused. "Even when it's *not* business, just…tell me. Okay?"

Mary was trying to think how to reply, but as he turned off the car, the dog woke with a flurry of activity.

"Hang on, bud," Brodie said to him. "You're first on the agenda, I promise."

The urge to rush from the car and hurry to the building with the restrooms was difficult to suppress, but she managed to leave the car in a leisurely manner. She even waited while he attached a leash to Howler's harness.

Right there at the curb, Howler relieved himself. Then again on a garbage can. And once more on a bush lining the path to the vending machines.

"Dude, we're not in the pet area yet. Contain it, will you? People are looking."

Mary didn't mean to, but the laugh bubbled out. "You're the one who made him wait so long."

"You got me there." He looked down at her, those dark eyes

first teasing, but slowly warming with awareness. "You don't have to stay with us."

"Yes, well..." Every time he looked at her like that, it felt as if he'd physically touched her. Her breathing deepened. Her skin warmed. Her blood seemed to rush...

Abruptly, she turned away.

The rest area wasn't crowded, but there were enough people to convince her she should hurry before she got caught in a line. "I'll be right back."

As she walked away, she felt his gaze tracking her, and it made her feel so funny inside, in a way she'd never really felt before.

Annoyance, she decided. He was too bold, too deliberately provoking, and he annoyed her.

That was all it could be. She wouldn't let it be anything else.

While in the restroom, she took the time to freshen up. Her hair was still in the topknot, so she didn't need to do anything to that, but she did touch up her makeup and chew a mint.

When she came back out, she found Brodie sitting in the picnic area at a wooden table under a tree. Howler stretched out his leash to sniff every blade of grass. He found a bug and ran a circle around it.

Mary checked the time. They were ahead of schedule and she was starting to get hungry. "Want to take a turn?" She indicated the restrooms. "I can hold his leash."

"Thanks." He handed it to her, then dug out a dog dish and walked off at an easy pace.

She realized she was watching his behind when Howler frantically tried to follow and pulled her halfway off the bench.

As if he'd expected it, Brodie turned. "Stay. I'll be right back."

When Howler sat, she felt safe in assuming Brodie's order was for the dog.

Howler kept his attention glued on Brodie, a low, groaning whine coming from his throat.

Poor baby. Mary stroked his muscular neck. "You love him,

don't you?" She, at least, didn't use baby talk. "He won't be long. You'll see." Howler glanced at her, gave her hand a quick lick and went back to waiting.

Luckily Brodie returned in only minutes, balancing the dish, now full of water, which he set in front of Howler. The dog was too busy greeting him as if he'd just returned from war to take a drink.

When Brodie took the leash from her, she said, "I think I'll grab something from the vending machines—unless you had other plans?" Whenever possible, she tried to defer to the driver's preference.

"You said you always ride along with the drivers?"

"Yes. Therman insists that I be there to protect his interests." A breeze carried her skirt against her legs, and she tipped up her face, eyes closed, to enjoy the shade and the scent of fresh air. After the long drive, it felt heavenly.

When Brodie said nothing else, she opened her eyes and found him studying her.

The probing intensity of his gaze made her breathless. Their eyes held for a few heartbeats before she managed to find her voice. After clearing her throat, she dragged her attention to Howler. She tried to sound casual, but knew she failed miserably. "Why do you ask?"

After a few more seconds of perceptible scrutiny, he replied with a shrug in his tone, "Just wondering what it is you usually do for meals."

"I'm easy." The seconds the words left her mouth, she blanched. She knew without looking that Brodie now wore a smirk. She felt it, damn him.

What was it about Brodie that rattled her so badly? She'd dealt with drivers for three years now. Some were indifferent, some too anxious, some complete professionals.

None of them had been as explicitly sexual as Brodie.

None of them had made her too warm with just a look.

Gathering her wits, she explained, "By easy, I mean that I leave it up to the driver. Some like to grab fast food, some want to stop and stretch their legs at an actual restaurant."

"You adjust accordingly, huh? Nice. Gotta love an agreeable woman."

Everything he said screamed of innuendo, which made everything *she* said the same.

Gritting her teeth and barely repressing a snarl, she stated, "The contract stipulated that your expenses are covered. You saw that, correct?"

He nodded, then produced the cooler from under the table.

Howler jerked around so fast he tripped over his own feet. Eyes wide, his tail swinging in the air, he looked hopefully toward the food source.

"Take a seat," Brodie said to her as he withdrew cloth napkins first. "I packed enough for two."

"You packed food?" That seemed so incredibly domestic, which was in direct contrast with his carnal manner. "For me?"

He gave her a wicked grin as he produced wrapped sandwiches. "It's bad enough having Howler salivate over my food."

And now teasing?

She really wished he'd settle on one mood long enough to allow her to adjust to it. "I wouldn't have salivated." But her stomach growled as he set out two containers and more bottled water.

Before he unwrapped the food, he opened one bottle, took a drink, then pretended to put it in the water dish.

Howler ignored it.

"First you drink," Brodie said, his tone firm.

The dog looked at the bowl, back at Brodie—who hadn't moved—and back at the bowl. Finally he drank it all, his broad tongue slinging water everywhere.

Brodie refilled it with the bottle, then got out another dog dish.

On alert, Howler tracked his every move.

He opened a can of dog food—and pretended to eat some, even making a few "Mmm, mmm" sounds. Howler got to his feet, body tense in anticipation, and when Brodie put the food in the dish and gave it to him, the dog ate it so fast Mary couldn't hold in her laugh.

"I know, right?" Brodie turned on the bench to face her, his mouth twitching. "He has to think I'm giving him people food or he doesn't want it. 'Course, that's not healthy, so I fake it when I can."

"You two are hilarious."

"You find spoiled dogs funny?" He unwrapped a sandwich, then passed it to her.

"Guess I do." She looked at the loaded croissant. "What is this?"

"Chicken salad." He bit into his own with an expression of ecstasy that nearly stopped her heart.

Was that how he'd look during sex? Or would he appear more feral?

"My mom makes the best there is."

With a flush of embarrassment, she wrenched her gaze off his mouth and up to those dark eyes. His lashes cast shadows over his cheekbones as he watched her.

He looked as if he knew exactly what she'd imagined.

Mary cleared her throat. "Your mom?"

"You thought I was hatched in a lab?" When he peeled back the lids on the other containers, she saw dill pickles and potato chips. He gestured. "Help yourself."

"I've never before had a picnic with a driver." But here, under the tree with the sun shining bright and Howler still licking his lips, it felt completely natural to accept his offer. She took a bite of the sandwich, and agreed with him. "Mmm. This is delicious." Far, far better than anything she could have gotten from the vending machine or a fast-food drive-through.

"Told you so." He grabbed up a few chips. "So you usually

keep it all stuffy and professional with the couriers, even though you're stuck in the car with them for hours?"

"It's easier than you think when I can sit in the back seat and do work along the way."

"Ah. But Howler has the back seat and there's no room for you." He nodded with what looked like pure satisfaction. "So I forced your hand on that."

Mary tipped her head. "In a sense." It was her job to understand the courier, to determine their reliability, their loyalty, but she wasn't sure a lifetime around Brodie would help her to understand him. "Was it important to you to 'force my hand'?"

"For the sake of my sanity, yeah." He ate half a pickle wedge in one big bite.

There he went, confusing her again. "Your sanity?"

"Yeah, I can't do uptight." He gestured with the remaining bite of pickle. "Bugs the hell out of me. If you want me on retainer, you're gonna have to loosen up." He gave her a wolf's grin. "Might as well start today."

CHAPTER THREE

Brodie watched the wariness creep into her eyes seconds before she angled her face away. He could almost hear the gears turning as she dissected what he'd said, and how she wanted to respond.

Probably searching for a professional reply.

He snorted.

Her gaze darted up at the rude sound. "Excuse me?"

"Stop weighing your words. Forget what's appropriate and what isn't. You have real reactions, Red." He held out his arms. "Lay 'em on me."

As if in slow motion, her shoulders went back, her gaze became direct and her eyes narrowed.

Bad time for him to notice that the outer corners of her eyes slightly turned up, that her lashes were thicker there, giving her an erotic expression even in anger.

Cat eyes, that was what she had. Very blue cat eyes.

"So far," she said, "absolutely everything with you is inappropriate, from our initial meeting where you behaved horribly, to our discussion of your friend Gina, to this cozy little picnic."

"It is cozy, isn't it?" A hapless bee got too close to her, and she nearly punched it away.

The lady had a fiery temper that for unaccountable reasons tweaked his interest.

Good thing the bee was quicker than her swing. He enjoyed getting a rise out of her, maybe because then he saw the real *her.* "You might as well know, if I'm your guy, it'll be picnics all the way." And he was pretty sure, given her boss's preference, that he was her guy.

"Therman chose you, yes. But when I give him my report—"

It was Brodie's turn to straighten. "Your *report*?"

Smug, she reached out and chose a pickle. "Once the job is complete he'll want an evaluation before he makes a decision on the retainer."

Well, hell. "You're *evaluating* me?" Again? Still?

"You do like to stress words, almost like reports and evaluations spook you." Her smile was deliberately mean, as was her casually spoken "I wonder why."

He felt like snatching that pickle right out of her hand. "And to think I shared my mother's chicken salad with you."

Red surprised him by snickering. At his affronted expression, she covered her mouth with a napkin, but the laughter came through, and finally, bending, with both hands over her face, she gave in to honest, loud, natural guffaws.

Brodie couldn't keep his own lips from twitching. Damn, she was pretty when she laughed. Looser. Softer.

Fucking sexier.

"What?" he asked, just to keep her going.

Wrapping an arm around her middle, that napkin still crushed in her hand, gasping breaths, she managed to say, "Your face!"

"Most ladies like my face." Shame she didn't like it more. He could easily imagine wrapping up this trip with a good hard ride—in bed. His imagination took off without his mind's permission, envisioning those heavy breasts bare, her gorgeous hair loose, her parted thighs cradling—

"Even when you're dumbstruck?" Gingerly she wiped her eyes, still grinning hugely.

"Yeah, even then." Damn it, he was half-hard. If she noticed, she'd be thinking he didn't have any control at all when control hadn't been a problem since his teenage years.

Propping his elbows on the table, arms folded, he studied her. Humor added a whole new dimension to her demeanor. A more approachable dimension.

It dawned on him that other women didn't leave him dumbstruck. Huh.

They didn't fascinate him, either, but Red did, in a dozen different ways.

Reaching beneath the table, he adjusted himself. Luckily she was still patting her eyes, trying to remove the tears of hilarity without smudging her makeup. "So what will you put in that report?" Before she could answer, he added, "It better include my generous nature, and how I can make you laugh."

"Oh, definitely," she teased. "In fact, if we remove yesterday morning from the equation, I'd say it'd almost all be accolades."

"Almost all?"

She pointed the pickle spear at him. "You did ply me with coffee and water just to deny me a bathroom break."

She didn't sound at all irate over it.

Damn, but he couldn't stop marveling over her, and how ridiculous was that?

Brodie made a presentation of crossing his heart. "My motives were just to get you to bend a little. I mean, how prissy can a woman be when she has to pee?"

Red choked, then glared.

"Seriously?" Brodie did his best to hide his amusement. No pretty blushes for Red. No, instead her face turned blotchy and it cracked him up.

Perversely, it made him want to tease her even more.

"The mention of *pee* has you blushing?"

"You're ridiculous."

"Me?" God, it was fun, riling her. Fun, and far too easy. "You're a mature woman, for crying out loud. Sedate, sure, but you have an important job, and no one would accuse you of lacking confidence."

"Am I supposed to thank you for pointing out the obvious?"

"Why not? They were compliments." One minute she was laughing almost hysterically, and now she was miffed again. "How old are you anyway?"

"Thirty," she growled as she came to her feet and began gathering up her garbage with hard, jerking movements. "Not that age matters when you're being deliberately crude and trying to—" The tongue-lashing died a sudden death as her gaze went past him to the parking area. Surprise replaced umbrage. "Someone's looking at your car."

Brodie jerked around and sure enough, two men were hovering near Matilda, one even crouching down at the back, out of sight. "Stay here with Howler." Already on his feet, he headed for the lot. All his focus was on the men, two of them, dressed in dark T-shirts and jeans, sunglasses hiding their eyes, *GQ* haircuts.

His instincts screamed and he strode faster, harder. Once he was close enough, he called out, "Can I help you?" which was the universal "nice" way of asking, *What the fuck are you up to?*

The upright man grinned. "Sweet ride. '05?"

"Yeah." Brodie circled the car until he stood over the bastard crouched by the back fender. Saying nothing, he stared down at him until the man warily regained his feet.

Both of them were big, but not as big as him. They were slick, too, but not like Jack, who Brodie likened to a polished rock. No, these dipshits had a veneer of shine over cheap plastic.

Leaning against the back of the car, Brodie crossed his arms and eyed both men. They looked to be in their early thirties, just a little younger than him. He'd run across plenty of men like them, but he'd be willing to bet they hadn't encountered another like him.

Because he'd gladly kick both their asses if they were up to anything shady. And hey, he already sensed that they were.

"Rather than fidget around like virgins at prom, why don't you bozos tell me what the fuck you want and what you were doing to my car?"

"Doing?" Cautious now, they glanced at each other.

In an almost choreographed move, they pushed up their sunglasses.

The one who'd been behind the car tried a laugh as he held out his hands. "I wasn't doing anything, dude. Just checking her out."

"Uh-huh. And your dipshit friend wasn't a lookout, either?"

The friend bunched up. "What's your problem, man?"

Do it, Brodie silently urged, staring the man in the eyes. *Make a fucking move.* "Other than having to deal with idiots, you mean?"

Hands bunched, shoulders tensed, the two stepped forward together.

Anticipation sizzled along his skin and Brodie gave up his relaxed pose on the car. His smile taunted. And—

"Are you ready to go?" Breathless, her tone ludicrously jovial, Red joined them as if there wasn't a conflict going down. She struggled with the dog's leash wrapped firmly around one hand while hauling his cooler in the other. She had trouble staying on her feet as Howler did his best demon-dog impression, quietly enraged, straining at his harness, his loose lips pulled back to show sharp teeth, muscles in his shoulders rolling.

Red must've packed up at Mach speed.

Before she lost her footing, he relieved her of the dog's leash, shortening it in his fist so Howler couldn't get too close to the men.

He said to her, "Wait for me in the car."

Though her smile didn't slip, her tone grew a little more strident. "No, I don't think so." She plopped down the cooler and, despite his narrow-eyed warning, came to stand beside him.

Like they were a fucking team?

Brodie stared at her, but then so did the other men.

Wasn't every day you met a lady like Mary Daniels.

Oozing innocence, she smiled. "The car will be stunning after she's painted, but even wearing primer, she's beautiful. Do you like Mustangs?"

The men appeared just as boggled as Brodie. The lookout dumbly nodded.

"You were admiring her, right?" Like a freaking caress, she ran a hand along the car. "I'm not much of a car aficionado. Is there something in particular about her rear that you liked?"

Brodie choked.

Red peered down at the car, her nose scrunched. "All I see is a fender and a muffler." She stroked those teasing fingers along the trunk lock—and the men all tracked the progress as if they, too, could feel it.

"Mary—" he started.

"Does she have something special going on back here?"

The two jerks looked at Brodie as if unsure whether to laugh or run.

"Do you prefer the rear?"

He almost groaned.

"She has some excellent curves up front as well."

Predictably, the goons dropped their gazes to her magnificent chest.

Brodie wanted to annihilate them both.

"Do you gentlemen have a preference?"

"Don't answer that," Brodie growled at them, and then to her, he said, "Damn it, Red—"

Expression angelic, she smiled up at him. "I can go on all day, or we can get in the car and leave." She patted Howler. "There's no reason for you to upset your dog."

Good God, she'd done it on purpose, talking sexually shaded nonsense just to defuse the situation. *Hard for me to kick ass when all three of us are now thinking about women's behinds.*

She folded her hands in front of her, that contented smile not budging.

Scowling, Brodie warned her, "We'll discuss this later." He turned to the mute men. "This is your one and only warning. Don't touch my car."

They wisely took advantage of Mary's interference and backed away until they reached a black SUV.

"Clichéd fucks," he muttered.

"Beg your pardon?"

"Hired thugs should at least try to *not* look like thugs, right?" After Brodie watched the car drive away, he went to his knees to study the fender, the undercarriage, the tailpipe. He felt around the license plate and the back tires. "Nothing."

"Did you expect a bug? A booby trap?"

"Something like that, yeah."

"Because you believe them to be *thugs*?"

"You don't?" he challenged.

"Well, if I'd had doubts, Howler convinced me." She hugged the dog's neck. "He paid no mind to anyone else, but with those two, I do believe he wanted to draw blood."

"He'd have mangled them." Brodie straightened, wondering what he'd missed.

Stepping back to do her own survey of the car, Red touched her chin thoughtfully. "Hmm. The only thing of interest back here is your license plate. If they have the right connections, they could track you down with your license number, right?"

Brodie stared at her. "You're a genius."

"Smart," she agreed. "But not that smart. If I was, I'd know why they wanted to identify you."

The urge to swing her up, maybe even kiss her, must have shown on his face because she turned quickly for the passenger door. “We should be on our way. We don’t want to be late.”

Brodie went along with that plan, getting Howler buckled in and storing his cooler. But once on the road, he decided it was past time he knew what Mustang Transport was getting into.

“You know this has to be related to whatever we’re picking up.”

While texting a message, Red nodded. “Possibly, though it’s doubtful they know what it is.”

“So what are we fetching?” he pressed.

“I can’t tell you that.” She finished her message and tucked away the phone.

He did not like mysteries. Well, other than Red. He wouldn’t mind putting together that particular puzzle. “At least tell me if it’s legal.”

She gave an exaggerated sigh. “Of course it’s legal. Therman Ritter is an upstanding, honest man—and he regards loyalty very highly. He’ll be pleased to know you continued on despite your nervousness about a threat.”

Nervousness? Of all the idiotic… “Who’s nervous?” Insult hung heavy in his tone. “I’m not *nervous*.”

She gave him a *Yeah, right* look and then continued, “Personally, I’m not worried, and I just told Therman as much.” She relaxed in the seat. “There are a lot of rivals for unique collection items.”

Unique collection items. Like severed heads? He had to wonder.

“At times it can get ugly. We face the occasional confrontation and, yes, attempted theft. It’s why Therman doesn’t have his purchased items mailed.”

“Too risky?”

“Mail can be intercepted.” She half turned in the seat to better face him, one leg slightly drawn up. “What would you have done if I hadn’t interrupted?”

"Gotten some answers." He still wanted them, damn it. He felt primed for violence.

The only good substitute was hot, hard sex, and while he felt the interest surging between them, Red was doing her best to ignore it. Given they could really use the income from future jobs with her well-to-do employer, he should try to let it go, too.

Easier said than done.

She tipped her head at his statement. "Just like that?"

He didn't have any illusions about his ability. "Intimidation goes a long way. Neither of those clowns wanted a fight, so odds are they'd have spilled their guts quick enough." He shot her a look. "If you hadn't ruined it."

Her expression sharpened. "Let's cover a few things now that I might have been remiss in mentioning at the onset."

Brodie hated that she was back in prim and proper mode. "Yeah, let's."

"First, I'll remind you that I don't work for you. We each work for Therman Ritter and the hierarchy places me above you, not beneath."

Oh, the things he could say. One look at her pinched face and he wisely decided to play mum. Didn't stop the images in his brain, but at least he didn't say something that'd get him maimed.

She appeared suspicious over his control. "Also," she continued with a bite, "Therman does not condone violence if there is any other alternative."

"I was using intimidation, not violence." Though violence could have easily followed. Hell, given how he felt now, he wished it had.

She nodded once. "Since I'm not familiar with your tactics, I'll give you the benefit of the doubt. In the future—if there is a future—I'll try to trust your judgment...as long as you understand that violence is a last resort."

"Got it." Determined that there *would* be a future, he promised, "No cracking heads if it's not absolutely necessary."

Frown stern, she said, "It would rarely, *very* rarely, be necessary."

Did she have to beat it into the ground? Did she think he ran around looking for excuses to swing his fists? He was a peaceful man. A *nice* man, damn it. "I said I've got it. Move on already."

"Fine," she snapped right back, then sucked in a breath. And another. Calmer now, she said, "My name is Mary. I thought you'd completely forgotten it, but you did say it when those men were there."

"Respect."

Her brows shot up. "What?"

"I would never disrespect you in front of goons by using a nickname." Brodie popped his neck to the side, disgusted to find he was now tense. Getting lectured by Red had a very muscle-tightening effect on him.

It left him feeling anything but nice.

She aggressively angled her body back toward him again. "How about you don't disrespect me at all, ever?"

Was that what she thought? Was she so damned strict, she couldn't indulge in conversation with the hired help?

Or had he inadvertently hurt her feelings?

That idea bothered him a lot. In many ways, he could tell that Mary was different from other women he'd known.

Hell, from *everyone* he'd known.

He had the suspicion that she used her formality as a barrier against the rest of the world.

But why? That was what he wanted to know.

CHAPTER FOUR

Brodie knew he should let it go. Accept the job, the money and the prestige that the association would bring to Mustang Transport. Depending on the frequency of the jobs, they could make a lot of improvements to the office. Jack could fix up his house, and Brodie could sock some money away in the bank. Lend some financial help to his mom and Charlotte.

Don't rock the boat, he told himself, but it was advice he couldn't take. Something about Mary's prickly defenses made it impossible.

Somber now, he asked softly, "Have I been that bad?"

"What?" Genuinely surprised, she shook her head. "No, of course not. But nicknames are too—"

"Familiar?" Sure, he might have started out teasing in a not exactly respectful way, but that was when she had condemnation written all over her face. It felt different now. Friendlier. "Why can't we be? Familiar, I mean. If we're going to be working together—"

The way her eyes widened in alarm kept him from finishing the thought.

She looked away, her gaze aimed out the passenger window. She breathed faster and she locked her hands together in her lap.

Knowing he'd hit a nerve, Brodie debated on how to proceed. She almost seemed guarded, making him wonder if he scared her somehow.

Or maybe it was that throb of sexual tension that had her shying away. His nostrils flared on the thought.

No, he sternly told himself. *She's off-limits.* The rational part of him understood that. But the more primitive part felt driven to show her how good it'd be.

Luckily for all concerned, he'd quit letting his dick make decisions a long time ago.

"I don't like to be called Red."

So most of her reaction was over a nickname—a nickname, he reasoned, that suited her perfectly given the vivid color of her hair. "Want to tell me why?" Was it because, as she'd claimed, it was disrespectful, or because she was touchy about her incredible hair?

"Not particularly."

Hmm. Looking at the way she'd tortured it into a tight knot at the top of her head, minimizing it as much as she could, he didn't need her confirmation that it was the latter.

Should he delve, or let it go? Maybe a compromise would be best—not a hard push, but a gentle opening for her to share. He wasn't ineffective with women. He could be charming when he put his mind to it.

He flashed a glance her way, but charming or not, her expression wasn't promising.

Screw it. "I'm guessing some asshole used to tease you or something?"

Incredulous, she glared at him.

"I hope it's not still bothering you, because your hair is..." He trailed off, at a loss for the right description.

Ripe with suspicion, she asked, "My hair is what?"

Brodie shook his head. "I was trying to think of the right words, but I'm as far from a poet as a guy can get. Let's just say it's stunning."

"Stunning?"

He gave a sharp nod. "And not to overstep my lowly employee status—"

She made a rude sound.

"—it's also sexy as hell."

Lips parting, her hand lifted to her hair, but she stopped short of touching it. Her chin firmed. "It's red."

"No shit. Smokin' hot red." His hands tightened on the wheel. "Like I said, sexy."

Her hesitation pulsed in the air, then she said primly, "It makes me look cheap."

The incredulous laugh came before he could stop it. "Cheap? With the way you carry yourself? How the hell do you figure that?"

She started to speak, but rethought whatever she would have said and instead pointed out, "You, along with a lot of other people, assumed I dyed it that color on purpose." In a lower voice, she added, "As if."

"Hey, I'm not a beautician or anything, but I can tell it's real." All those different shades picked up by the sunlight were too remarkable to be faked. At various times he saw gold, auburn, brown, burgundy and scarlet. The hair around her face was a little lighter, sort of a strawberry blond, and it looked really soft. "That was just me joking, maybe getting a little payback."

Her lashes swept up in an expression of surprise. "Payback?"

"Now, don't act surprised." Feeling more in his element, Brodie smiled. "You want to talk respect? How about the way you looked at me like I was a bug on your shoe when we first met?"

Her brows came down in a ferocious frown. "You were hungover."

"So? Newsflash, people are allowed to drink. Besides, it was my day off and we weren't expecting you. If I'd known you were going to show up, I'd have been better prepared."

Testing him, she asked, "If it was your day off, what were you doing there?"

"Working on Matilda." Gaining traction on his argument, he went on to say, "And how do you know I didn't have good reason to get hammered? Maybe I was dealing with something monumental. Something tragic. Did you think of that?"

White teeth caught that plump lower lip as she studied him with concern.

Did she know how that affected him? He doubted it. She seemed extremely unaware of her own appeal.

In a small, concerned voice, Mary whispered, "Were you dealing with something awful?"

He took perverse pleasure in saying, "Nope."

Breath left her and she demanded, "Then why did you insinuate it?"

"Just to make a point."

Bristly now, she crossed her arms. "Being?"

"You started it."

She huffed, sitting back in the seat. "Okay, fine. I did make assumptions and I was probably rude first. I'm sorry. But once you knew I was a potential client, you should have been more professional."

"Probably." Brodie grinned as he shook his head. "But the way you looked at me felt like a challenge, and I admit, I'm not good at backing down." He reached out with his right hand. "Truce?"

After thinking about it for far too long, she put her small, cool hand to his.

Fuck me, I will not get a boner over a handshake.

It was the female to his male that spiked a heated reaction. He brushed the pad of his thumb over her delicate knuckles. Her skin was so smooth, soft and warm. He knew she had a backbone of iron, yet she felt incredibly fragile. He cradled her hand in his, very aware of the sexual charge arcing between them.

She probably didn't like it.

He savored it anyway. Hell, he couldn't remember the last time a simple touch felt like so much more.

When she lightly tugged, he let her go, and she retreated to the corner of her seat, getting comfortably settled with her legs crossed under that frothy skirt.

As if she hadn't just made him edgy with awareness, she gifted him with a warm, sincere smile and said softly, "I'm glad you didn't have anything tragic going on."

God, he had it bad. When was the last time he'd fumbled this badly with a woman?

Since Mary Daniels, obviously. She'd breezed in, leveled him with her contempt, cut him with her authoritative manner and left him half-hard, all at the same time.

Neat trick, Red. *Dangerous* trick.

He'd have to stay sharp around her.

"Yep, me, too." Needing the distraction, he glanced in the rearview mirror, and sure enough the SUV still followed.

He'd noticed it right away, but hadn't yet said anything. He didn't want to alarm Mary.

"So why did you get drunk?"

Good. If she pried, he could pry in return, and that suited him just fine. "Actually, life is pretty damn good, so it was sort of a celebration. Hanging with friends, playing cards, drinking, yukking it up. Old school–style, ya know? Reliving the good times."

"Getting drunk and suffering a hangover the next day is what you consider good times?"

"Sure." He glanced in the mirrors again, saw the SUV and switched lanes. "Ever tried it?"

"No, thank you."

"I wasn't inviting you to a drunken revelry, Red…er, Mary."

He shook his head. To him, she was already Red and remembering to call her Mary would take some adjustment. "Though if you ever want to give it a try, let me know. I'll be your designated bodyguard and driver, so no one takes advantage and to make sure you get home safely. Deal?"

She circled a finger in the air. "Let's rewind this a bit."

Knowing he'd smothered her anger with nonsense, he grinned. "Sure."

"I'll agree to a more relaxed relationship if you stop deliberately riling me."

"But it's so fun."

Though her lips twitched, her brows pinched together, almost making him laugh. "You'll just have to find your amusement elsewhere."

When she fascinated him? Okay, so he needed to tone it down. He could do that… "On one condition."

"You don't get conditions."

Ignoring that, he said, "Tell me why you dislike that glorious hair."

"No." Mary drew her phone out of her briefcase and started texting.

"C'mon," he cajoled. "You can tell me."

She continued working on her phone.

Disappointed, he shook his head. "The old tried-and-true silent treatment, huh? I thought you'd be more unique than that."

"If you must know, I'm prioritizing. Therman likes to be kept apprised of what's going on during our trips."

No way. He flattened his mouth. "You're telling him that I'm curious about your hair?"

"What? No, of course not," she said in exasperation. "Therman wouldn't care about that."

He didn't relax. Not yet. "Then what?"

She looked up at him as if he were a dunce. "I'm letting him know we're being followed." She finally put the phone away and turned to glance out the rear window. "I think it's the same SUV the men in the rest stop were driving. They must have circled around."

Floored, he felt his jaw slacken. "You knew they were there?"

One eyebrow rose in disapproval. "You didn't?"

"Of course I did." As the driver, he paid attention to everything. "They've been tailing us for a while now, staying about five cars back."

"You don't have to sound so snippy about it."

"Snippy?" He'd never been *snippy* a day in his life.

She shrugged. "You didn't let on."

"Neither did you!"

As if soothing him, she said, "I didn't want to alarm you."

That was so absurd that Brodie was forced to laugh. "Figured you'd somehow deal with it all on your own, rather than bother the driver who's twice your size?"

"I'd have told you eventually. After all, we don't want them following us the entire way. At some point, you're going to have to lose them. But we have some time."

Brodie grinned when he glanced at her. "You surprise me, Red." He waited a heartbeat, then corrected, "Mary."

She rolled her eyes at him. "Red Mary is worse than just plain Red, so pick one please and then stick to it."

Her capitulation thrilled him. It was like she'd just given him more, much more, than the use of a nickname.

Regardless of what name she went by, he looked forward to knowing her better.

"Well, Mary, hold on tight. With your approval, I'll lose them now rather than later."

She smiled at him and, in that prim voice that was starting to sound sensual instead of annoying, said, "Yes, please."

As he wove them seamlessly through the traffic, off an exit ramp, along a short drive through a commercial area, then back onto the expressway again, Mary had a revelation: everything about Brodie Crews was over-the-top.

His rugged good looks.

His teasing manner.

His frank way of speaking.

And now, she had to add, his skill at driving. He maneuvered with ease, weaving through traffic without speeding, seeming to find his way in and out of communities instinctively, all the while being completely relaxed.

In fact, if it hadn't been for seeing his anger at the men who'd approached his car, she would wonder if Brodie Crews took anything seriously.

For the rest of the drive, she helped keep watch but she didn't spot the SUV again.

Finally, she could relax, too. "I think you lost them."

He shot her a look of comical indignation. "You had doubts?"

Not really. And for some absurd reason, she was proud of him. What would he think if she told him that? He'd probably make a few more jokes, laugh it off and continue being outrageous.

Belatedly, she answered him, "No."

"No?"

"I didn't have any real doubts."

"Good. Because my guess is that they'll somehow catch up to us on the way back. I mean, if they're following, the whole point would be to steal from us whatever your boss bought, right?"

That was always a possibility. There'd been other times where she and a driver were waylaid, the goods stolen and she'd had to go back to Therman empty-handed.

She would avoid that as best she could. "Yes, it's possible."

Cavalier, somewhat cocky, he said, "Hey, don't sweat it. I'll make sure we make the delivery, and on time, too."

Mary appreciated his confidence because it boosted her own—especially as they left the highway for the less traveled roads that would take them to their destination.

Giving up her vigilance, she watched Brodie instead. His relaxed posture belied the alert way he took in his surroundings.

She realized that he knew trouble could happen, but also believed that he could handle it.

Astounding.

She'd never known a man so convincingly capable. She'd call him arrogant, except that he was so big, so powerful and formidably hard all over, it was easy to believe he could handle just about everything that might come their way.

Thinking that warmed her and she slipped off her button-up shirt, leaving her in the thin tank top, her arms exposed to the cooler air-conditioning. That helped, but not enough.

Especially when she knew that Brodie noted her every movement, even though he wasn't obvious about it.

More heat uncurled from deep inside her, making her breasts feel heavy, her inner thighs tight. It was an unfamiliar heat, but she recognized it for what it was—base lust.

For Brodie. Insane. Ill-advised.

But apparently unavoidable.

Before she did something stupid, it seemed wise to distract herself by ensuring Brodie understood every possibility. "They could have been following us for another reason."

"Yeah?" He pulled up to a red light and, after checking the traffic in every direction, turned to look at her. "What's that?"

Having that dark, direct gaze aimed at her didn't help to redirect her thoughts. His eyelashes were almost girlie, they were so thick and dark, but Brodie was more elementally male than any man she'd ever met.

He quirked a brow. "If we were anywhere else, I'd take that as an invitation."

As if coming out of a trance, she blinked. "What?"

"The way you're looking at me?" His voice was deep, a little rough. "That usually means—"

"They may just want to rule out what Therman is getting,"

she blurted, cutting him off. *Dear God, she had been staring at him like a starving woman.*

She almost considered putting her button-up shirt back on, just to make sure he didn't misunderstand. But maybe that would be even more obvious, displaying her uncertainty in situations like this.

"They?" he asked, his supercilious brow still up.

"The men following us." She jumped on the topic, hoping to talk past her own embarrassment. *She wanted him, really wanted him, and it didn't make any sense at all.* She tried for her confident smile. "There are several collectors who want the same items. Usually, whoever is willing to pay the most comes out the victor."

He grinned. "Sounds like some serious sport."

"Oh, believe me, collectors take it very seriously." Needlessly, she checked her hair, smoothed her skirt and overall squirmed over her own revelations.

She'd been forever without a man. Why now, and why him?

She didn't have any answers; she only knew that he was off-limits. *Damn.* "Some want an item enough to go bankrupt over it."

"Or to steal it?" he asked, his attention now on her...mouth?

She drew a breath. "It happens." A distant memory intruded. "Back when I first started working for Therman, he lost out on an item, but he said it was okay." Despite her inner turmoil, she kept her voice steady. "The seller gave it to another bidder for a lesser amount because, according to him, it meant more to the other man."

"Huh." The light changed and Brodie eased the car forward. "Guess some collectors have an odd code of honor."

"Yes." They were close to their destination now, but Mary felt no threat. She didn't know if that was a sixth sense speaking to her, or her comfort level at being with Brodie.

She was starting to understand why Therman had chosen him.

A few minutes later, a moderate home, white-painted brick with black shutters, came into view at the end of the lane. All the houses in the community sat on quarter-acre lots with mature trees spaced around tidy sidewalks.

When Brodie pulled up at the curb and turned off the car, Howler came awake with a jerk, his jowls trembling. Bleary-eyed after his long nap, he gave a lazy "Woof," then yawned widely and looked around.

"I have to let the dog do his business first, then I'll walk you in."

After pulling on her shirt and doing up most of the buttons, Mary opened her car door. "Not necessary," she said in her most officious voice, hoping to cut short a disagreement. "You can wait here. I won't be long."

Brodie got out before her. "Like hell."

At being left behind, Howler whined pitifully and strained against his restraints. Brodie looked back at the car, the muscles in his arms flexing as he fought himself.

The man was very dedicated to his dog.

She knew he was torn and took advantage of that. "Brodie," she said with gentle insistence. "You're the driver, not my bodyguard."

He scowled.

Brisk now, Mary pulled the briefcase strap up and over her shoulder. "Take care of Howler, but please be discreet. We don't know how the seller feels about big dogs using his lawn for a toilet."

With soft steel in his tone, Brodie stopped her. "I have a question before you go."

"What?" she asked, the single word clipped.

"Just a second." He leaned into the car and leashed Howler.

Mary folded her arms and made her impatience loud and clear.

As he led out the now contained dog, he asked, "Am I relegated to outside because I can't see what Therman is buying?"

"In part." She turned away.

"Is the other part your independence?"

Mary paused, then looked at him over her shoulder. "What do you mean?"

"You want to make sure that I, and maybe everyone else, know that you don't need help."

He'd nailed it, and that surprised her. Brodie was fairly perceptive—and damn it, that only added to his appeal. "I don't need to prove anything to anyone."

"No, you don't." He moved with Howler as the dog smelled a tree, watered it, then moseyed on to a bush. "Last question."

"You're stalling, Brodie, and I'd rather get this over with."

His attention was on the dog when he asked, "Do you believe in instincts? Gut feelings?" His gaze lifted to hers. "Intuition?"

Because she'd learned the hard way to trust herself and her feelings, she rarely did anything that made her nervous. "Actually, I do."

"Great. Because my gut is telling me this is a bad idea. If I sit out here, I'm just going to worry, and you should know, I'm not good at it."

She turned to fully face him. "Meaning?"

"God only knows how I'll react when worried."

Her shoulders stiffened. "Is that a threat?"

Some emotion softened his expression. "C'mon, Red. I would never, ever threaten you."

Damn it, she believed him. Her mouth flattened as she considered how to handle him—then she realized she couldn't.

Who could possibly handle a boulder?

Temper frayed, she snapped, "I'll leave the front door open and I'll stay in the living room. If anything terrible happens, you'll hear me call out."

Gracious, he smiled and said, "Thank you, Mary."

Did he use her name on purpose to soften her up? Deliberate

or not, it worked, wringing a sigh from her. "Try to behave. I won't be long."

Before he could detain her any longer, she marched up the walkway and knocked on the front door.

While waiting, she noted that the house needed some attention; weeds overgrew the outdated landscaping, grime obscured the windows, and the front stoop looked as if it hadn't been swept in years. Up close she saw that patches of paint peeled from the bricks.

She had Therman's payment in her case and wondered if it would be put to good use. Since being hired, she'd met wealthy men with unusual interests…and she'd met people who gave up nearly everything to add one more piece to a valued collection. At times collecting seemed harmless enough.

Other times, it was like an addiction, or a sickness.

A woman answered the door in a rush, then nervously glanced behind her. She asked, "You're Mary Daniels?"

"Yes."

She didn't invite Mary in. "You have the payment?"

So they were going to conduct business here on the stoop? That should please Brodie. Mary didn't mean to, but she glanced back and saw him leaning against the front fender of his car, Howler next to him, both of them alert.

"Of course." Mary withdrew the payment and showed it to the woman.

Her eyes gleamed at the amount before she gave another furtive look into the house. "Let me have it."

Ignoring the burning touch of Brodie's interest behind her, Mary returned the payment to her briefcase and held out a hand. "May I?"

"You have to hurry," the woman insisted, thrusting the box at Mary so she had no choice but to take it.

It was lightweight, flat, about the size of a sheet of paper but an inch thick, with the lid taped shut. Mary inspected it, looking for the easiest way to get it open. Delicate items could be damaged if a person didn't use care when unsealing.

Some collectors encased their treasures in display cases for all to see.

Others, like this collector, kept them hidden away in everyday containers to fool possible thieves.

Carefully peeling back a piece of tape, Mary asked, "The papers are also inside?"

"Yes," the woman hissed. *"Hurry."*

Mary got the lid loose and lifted it off. Inside, a lock of black hair rested atop the stack of papers. She quickly perused the photos, articles and other forms of documentation that would prove the authenticity of the hair.

Just as she returned the lid, a roar sounded from inside the house.

Shrieking, the woman held out a hand, shaking it urgently. "Give me the money!"

"No!" A heavy man dressed in an undershirt and sagging jeans came barreling from the hallway. "Eunice!" His gaze shifted from his wife to Mary and back again. Horror turned his voice to a rasp. "What the hell do you think you're doing?"

Mary stepped back, out of the way of his anger. "Mr. Graveson."

"You!" His attention zeroed in on Mary, then dropped to the box she held. His face paled.

He was an intimidating sight with his eyes bloodshot and a growth of whiskers on his bloated face. At one time, before health issues had stolen his livelihood, Mr. Graveson had been a mortician to the rich and famous.

Now all he had left were the remaining bits and pieces of his collection.

Clearly Mr. Graveson didn't know what his wife had planned. Was Therman aware that the woman sold the coveted lock of hair without her husband's permission? If so, he apparently didn't care.

Mary hastily slid the box into her briefcase and held out the check. "Here you go, Mr. Graveson. The agreed-upon amount."

"I didn't agree to shit," he growled, followed by a roared demand. "Give it back!" He started forward. Eunice grabbed his arm, which didn't slow him down much.

"It's a lot of money," Mary said.

"I don't care. You have no right!" He got nearer, but then his gaze moved past Mary and he halted, his chest heaving, his lips thinned.

She had to convince him to go along with the arrangements, and also defuse his anger. In contrast to his shouts, she kept her tone soft, gentle. "Therman was generous, Mr. Graveson."

He put his head back, eyes squeezed tight.

"He's been working nonstop," Eunice said to her, then she pleaded with her husband. "We need it, babe. You know we do."

Mary blinked at the endearment. Mr. Graveson was a rough beast of a man, overweight, currently unkempt—and apparently also well loved.

"But my hair..." he groaned.

"Not *your* hair. Just hair. *Only* hair." Eunice drew a breath and tears glittered in her eyes. "You're supposed to be taking it easy and instead you're working yourself to death. For what?" She gestured at Mary's briefcase. "To keep that? Old hair that doesn't really matter?" Eunice put a hand to his chest. "*You* matter. *We* matter."

Mr. Graveson put his hand over hers, whispering, "You don't understand."

"I do," his wife whispered back. "That's why I chose your least important piece and negotiated a better than fair amount. We'll both be able to take a little time off." She put her forehead to his shoulder. "We can enjoy life."

Mr. Graveson didn't look like he cared about any of that,

but he relented—grudgingly. With his arm around Eunice, he snarled to Mary, "Give her the goddamn money, then, and get out before I change my mind."

Relieved, Mary handed the payment over to Eunice. The minute the woman had it, Graveson slammed the door in her startled face. She heard the lock click.

Well. Overall, she'd handled that perfectly, if she did say so herself. Though her heart was hammering in her breast and her hands trembled, she had Therman's coveted addition to his collection, plus she'd avoided any violence.

Satisfied, she turned—and almost ran into Brodie.

Silently, his expression implacable, he stood right behind her, a large, immovable wall of hard muscle.

The truth slapped against her pride: she hadn't defused the situation at all.

Mr. Graveson had given up because of her driver.

CHAPTER FIVE

Fury, as well as hurt, overwhelmed Mary.

Brodie hadn't trusted her, hadn't respected her enough to follow her directions. He'd interfered when she'd specifically asked him not to.

She set her mouth and concentrated on the anger. It was easier to deal with.

Howler sat beside him, ears up, teeth showing as he continued to stare at the closed door. Both males looked dangerous.

Mary lifted her chin and stalked around them.

"You okay?" Brodie asked as she passed.

Mary barely refrained from curling her lip. Did he think a closed door had somehow wounded her? Did he think her so weak? "You should have stayed by the car as I instructed."

He silently trailed her. All she could hear was Howler panting.

Fine. Let him stew. Going around the hood of the car, she opened the passenger door and, ignoring the wave of heat that escaped, sat inside.

The sun beat down on the car in suffocating waves. She waited for Brodie to get in, but all he did was open the back seat to get Howler's water dish. He set it on the curb and filled it.

Howler drank and drank some more, then piddled another dozen times.

By then, Mary felt the dampness on her skin. Sweat beaded on the bridge of her nose and under her eyes.

Obnoxious man. Was he trying to make her melt?

To distract herself, she got out her phone and texted an update to Therman.

All went well. I have the purchase. We'll be heading back now.

An immediate reply popped up on her screen.

Excellent. Any problems? How did Graveson take it?

Using a judicious choice of words, she texted, Annoyed, but he didn't fuss too much.

There was a pause, and then, Did our driver get involved?

No.

No?

Therman always knew when she left out a detail. Mary locked her back teeth and replied, He refused to stay at the curb.

Because he had voice-to-text capability, Therman's question came quickly. Graveson let him in?

Mary grabbed a tissue to blot her face and throat while she thought of how to answer. She settled on, He didn't invite either of us. The exchange was made on the front stoop. Crews waited behind me.

Therman stated, Ah, backup. Smart.

Mary didn't see it that way. No, she saw it as interference and an implied doubt in her ability to handle matters.

I want to meet the driver. Bring him in when you arrive.

She nearly dropped the phone. Therman rarely wanted to meet the couriers. Why did he have to choose Brodie to get curious?

With her pulse tripping, she texted, Are you sure?

Bring him in.

Having just broken a cardinal rule—questioning her employer's decisions—Mary knew she couldn't push any further. Yes, sir.

She waited, but Therman said nothing more. He was used to giving orders and having them followed. Period. Hopefully he wouldn't remind her of that in front of Brodie.

She slipped the phone back into her briefcase and rested her head against the seat. A drop of sweat slid between her breasts and her thighs were starting to stick together. No air stirred from the open doors. It felt like she sat in a sauna.

She was just about to demand the keys so she could start the air-conditioning when Brodie got the dog secured in the back seat, then slid behind the wheel.

She opened her eyes, but otherwise didn't move. Her body had glued itself to the leather seats.

"Sure is hot today."

Other than narrowing her eyes, Mary didn't acknowledge him.

He started the car and turned up the blower, then surprised her by aiming the vents directly at her.

Heaven.

"You're flushed," he said in that soft, rough voice.

This time she *was* giving him the silent treatment, because if she spoke, she just might start cursing.

As he pulled away from the curb, he asked, "Should I apologize?" When she didn't answer, he nodded. "Guess I should."

Perfect. When he humbled himself with sincerity, she'd tell him to shove it. The nasty words hovered on the tip of her tongue as she waited.

Only...he denied her by not saying another word.

God, he was annoying!

Without moving her head, she slanted her gaze toward him. His large hands loosely held the steering wheel. She knew from their earlier handshake that his fingers were rough, his broad palms warm.

Thick wrists led up to steely forearms dusted with hair, then to smooth, incredible biceps that bunched and loosened with even the smallest movement. Was his darker skin tone natural, or did he often work out in the sun?

He glanced at her and she turned away.

Still, he didn't say anything.

Howler, apparently feeling the tension, leaned his great head over the seat so that his snout rested on her shoulder. His worried eyes looked back and forth between them.

Mary idly stroked his downy ear. "It's not your fault, honey. You're a good dog, I know that."

Brodie snorted. "In case you're wondering, Howler led me to the door. I couldn't hold him back."

"Such a good dog," she continued, then had to dodge a big tongue when he tried to lick her face. "You know how to behave, don't you, baby?"

Brodie's jaw tensed. "If by behave, you mean drag me after you, yeah, he knew how."

Mary inhaled but still didn't address Brodie. "I can't believe he's trying to blame you. Next time he tries to sweet-talk you—" she lowered her voice, whispering to the dog "—*bite* him."

Howler whined.

"Shame on you," Brodie said in good humor. "Trying to corrupt my dog."

After one hot glare, she turned to look out the window. The landscape rolled past without much notice from her.

"You're going to make me do it, aren't you?"

If he meant to apologize—

"It's impulse, you know." In case she didn't understand, he explained, "To defend and protect, I mean."

"Odd," she muttered, her gaze still aimed away. "That sounds nothing like an apology."

Silence, and then a tentative "Does my job depend on me apologizing?"

Unfortunately... "No." She knew Therman had already made up his mind and even if she wanted to, she couldn't influence him.

"Good." Brodie turned a corner. "Then you'll know it's sincere when I say I'm sorry."

She slanted her gaze his way. "*When* you say it?"

"Well... I just did." He held up a hand as she turned more fully to glare. Sounding of ill humor, he said, "But hey, I don't mind spilling my guts again."

Mary curled her lips, waiting.

He made a big show of inhaling and exhaling, then growled, "I'm sorry."

It wasn't very pretty, was in fact grudgingly given, but it did sound genuine, so she nodded.

His big shoulders relaxed and he gave a tentative smile. "Does that mean we can talk again?"

Had her silence bothered him so much? If so, good. "What did you want to talk about?"

"Hair."

Oh, for the love of—

"Did we seriously drive all this way to buy a freaking hank of hair?"

"Yes, we did. But I'll point out that you wouldn't know what we bought if you'd—"

"Waited by the car as you ordered me to. I know." He checked his mirrors but didn't seem concerned. "I meant it when I said it was Howler's idea. He's sensitive to angst, and that lady was oozing it. Then when the big guy showed up—roaring, I might add—I agreed with Howler. We were already there, but still."

"You have way too many excuses."

"Hey, they're all legit." He reached up to give the dog a pat. "By the way, your situational awareness sucks. How did you *not* know we were behind you?"

Turning on him with disbelief, she snapped, "I was focused on getting what we came for!"

"Sure, but we'd had those yahoos following us, right? What if it'd been them, instead of Howler and me? You might've lost the prize—and gotten hurt in the bargain."

The logic of what he said only notched her temper higher. "You were *right there* by the car."

Half under his breath, he muttered, "If you had your way, that's where I would've stayed."

"Exactly!"

"You 'bout done giving me hell? Howler's getting stressed with all the shouting."

Mary almost threw up her hands, but damn it, she had gotten a little loud—and maybe a little shrill as well. Poor Howler indeed looked upset. Contrite, she stroked his nose and found it as downy as his long ears. His short fur was very soft and sleek.

Drawing a deep breath, she let it out slowly. "Okay, I'm going on the record right now: if I'm ever being physically attacked, please, feel free to lend a hand. But until then—"

"Does that mean I get to stick around awhile?"

"Yes." She hated to admit it to him, but figured she might as well get it over with. "Therman would like to meet you." She tensed, waiting for his reaction.

"Okay."

Blinking, she said, "That's it? Just okay?"

"Should I sing hallelujahs?"

Would he ever do the expected? Probably not. She sighed in frustration. "Maybe you don't realize it, but Therman doesn't meet just anyone. It's a big deal."

Brodie grinned. "So I'm getting the red carpet, huh? Sweet."

Time to get serious. "Brodie, listen to me. You have to—"

"I like when you say my name."

She blinked at him, thrown off course.

"Just saying." He shot her a glance. "Your voice is nice."

"My voice?"

"Well, mostly your mouth, but I figured you'd consider that inappropriate, so I concentrated on your voice."

He liked her mouth. It made her want to bite her lip self-consciously. "Thank you."

"Welcome."

She almost smiled. Yes, for him to mention it was very inappropriate, but still, she enjoyed knowing… No. *No*, she could not be thinking things like that!

Ruthlessly, she brought herself back on point. "Therman is very selective," she said in her most bureaucratic manner. "The only time I know of him meeting a courier is when the man got hurt. Therman wanted to ensure he was okay."

"And that he wouldn't sue him, right? Am I right?"

Likely, but she wouldn't confirm it for him. "We'll both walk in when we deliver the item."

"Hair." He rolled one bulging shoulder, saying with disgust, "The item is hair."

"When you speak to him," she continued, forging on despite his nonsense, "you will be respectful."

"No shit, Sherlock. He's the boss, so of course I'll show him respect." Appearing disgruntled, he grumbled, "I'm not an idiot."

The look she gave him clearly indicated that she wasn't yet

convinced. He could be so crass, crude and often obnoxious, that she didn't want to leave it to chance.

But he likes my mouth…

She shook her head, chasing away that thought. "For my peace of mind, will you promise to be on your best behavior regardless of how you're greeted?"

"You're making me think this Therman dude is an ogre." He held up a hand when she started to speak. "But sure. I'll be so good you might mistake me for a choirboy."

"Ha." Not likely.

He drew a fingertip in an X over his chest. "Cross my heart."

Hmm. At least he planned to try, so Mary nodded. "Thank you." Regardless of how he'd be greeted by Therman and the others, he did need to make an impression.

"Now that we're past that, let's talk about hair."

"It's only a part of Therman's collection, and no—" she cut him off "—I'm not going to discuss it with you. If you're interested, ask Therman and he'll tell you whatever he wants you to know."

Now that they were openly chatting again, Howler moved back with a grumble and got comfortable. In minutes he was snoring.

Mary smothered a yawn. She hadn't gotten much sleep last night, and now the heat and long trip worked against her, making her drowsy.

Brodie's gaze drifted over her in a way that she actually felt, warm and intimate. "Put your head back," he suggested quietly. "Doze if you'd like. I'll wake you when Howler and I are ready to take a break."

"I couldn't." But it sounded so nice. She yawned again, this time so widely her eyes watered.

Brodie's mouth curled. "One thing before you nod off."

"I won't."

"Uh-huh. But in case you do, there's something you should

understand." He switched lanes as they neared the on-ramp. "I really am overprotective. My mom gives me hell about it all the time. Charlotte, too."

"I notice it's only women—" she started to say.

"Even Jack," he continued at almost the same time, then he realized she was talking and said, "Hmm?"

Leaning back in the seat, Mary shifted to face him. "You try to protect your brother?"

"No, I didn't mean that. Jack can take care of himself. But," he added with emphasis, when she started to roll her eyes, "he's two years younger than me, so I stuck up for him a lot when we were growing up."

"And now that he's an adult you figure he's fine on his own, yet because I'm a woman, you think I need you looming behind me."

"I didn't *loom*," he objected. "Not on purpose anyway. And here's a newsflash: in identical circumstances, I would have backed up Jack the same way I did you. Trouble is trouble, and I can't ever ignore it when I see it coming."

"You don't think Jack could have handled it on his own?"

"You did, so yeah, he probably could've, too. But that's not the point."

His confidence in her went a long way toward making her feel better. "No? Then what is?"

"Backup is never a bad thing." He nodded at his own assertion. "You know I'm right."

With a tilt of her head, she conceded the point, but still decided to test him. "What if our roles had been reversed? If I'd stepped in as *your* backup, would you have complained?"

"Uh..." Shifting, he rubbed the back of his neck, glanced at her, then away and finally blew out a breath. "Everything I said was valid."

"Yes." She waited.

"Okay, so sue me. I'm old-fashioned when it comes to protecting anyone smaller than me, at least with a physical threat." He drew down his brows. "And before you start on another tangent about men and women, yes, if you were a little dude, I'd have felt the same in that situation."

Mary arched her brows. "If I were a 'little dude'?"

He grinned. "Okay, so I wouldn't admire your mouth, even though it inspires—" He glanced at her again, then frowned at the road. "Well, never mind what it inspires, okay? I wouldn't notice everything else, either, if you weren't a woman."

Everything else?

"But since you're half my size I would feel protective, so score one for me."

He sounded so reasonable, sure of his convictions, that Mary wondered if she'd misunderstood. "So it's only in a physical confrontation that you'd feel the need to intercede?"

"Yeah, sure. Not like you'd need my help to shred someone with your disposition or your smarts." He playfully grumbled, "You've shredded me enough times for me to know you've got that covered. Not complaining—I had it coming, I'm sure—just saying I have firsthand knowledge of your ability there." He gave her a boyish grin when he finished, which on him looked wickedly sexy.

Odd, but she believed his explanation. After all, he'd rescued a dog in need, so it stood to reason that he would never stand idly by if he could help those in need. Maybe she'd gotten offended for no reason. She could be touchy about proving her worth—more to herself, than anyone else. Not that she'd discuss it with him.

That *everything else* comment he'd made, though…she'd like to know if he was as attracted to her as she was to him. It seemed unlikely. Brodie Crews was an unequivocally sexual man, whereas she tried not to think about sex.

But with him, she couldn't help herself. It seemed every reaction he'd gotten from her was extreme, up to and including lust.

For now, it was enough to know he admired her hair and her lips. Actually, it was almost too much.

She really needed to regroup before verbally sparring with him again, so she said, "If you're sure you don't mind, I think I will rest my eyes."

"Don't mind at all." He turned on music, turned down the blower on the air and smiled at her, his dark eyes mellow and warm and…sensual.

Or maybe that was just her.

It was after 5:00 p.m. when Brodie drove his Mustang down the long private lane. He watched for the grand entry Mary had described, but it took a few minutes before he finally spotted it. Yeah, definitely grand. Like…holy shit grand.

He pulled into the long, wide, tree-lined drive and blinked. The entry was nothing compared to Therman Ritter's mansion. Luckily Red was too busy fussing with her makeup, a small round compact mirror in her hand, to notice the way he gawked.

The man's house was big enough to be an apartment complex, but way fancier. After seeing where the other collector lived, the poor schmuck who'd nearly cried over selling a snippet of hair, Brodie hadn't expected this.

Yes, he'd figured on the boss having a nicer setup. He employed Mary and a courier, so he had to have some serious dough. But still… "How many people live here?"

"Just Therman and a few of his companions."

As she spoke, she slicked some pale gloss over her lips, and Brodie forgot to listen.

Mmm, that mouth…

He'd already compiled a list of fantasies based around those soft, plump lips. Her hair often factored in, too. She'd have it loose, spilling over her small shoulders and perfect tits while that sinner's mouth moved over his skin.

He almost groaned. Much more of that and he'd be meeting the boss with a boner. Not cool.

It took him a second to remember what she'd said. He no longer cared that much, but still he asked, "Companions?"

"He doesn't like to call them employees because they've been with him so long. There's the housekeeper and the cook and his personal assistant."

"Do they all live here?"

"Now, yes." She put her makeup away and began smoothing out her blouse, doing up a few more buttons so that she all but concealed herself.

Shame that. She had a body made for showing off, whether she realized it or not.

"Therman is eighty-six. The head housekeeper and her husband, the cook, are both in their sixties. Vera—she's the housekeeper—she told me that she and Burl didn't move in with Therman until a few years ago." As if someone might hear them even though they were still in the car, she explained in a lower voice, "Burl had a stroke and Vera almost lost him. As soon as he recovered, Therman insisted they move in with him. They live in the downstairs of the house now."

Sounded like Therman was a good guy. Since Red worked for him, Brodie was glad. "And the personal assistant?"

Instead of answering, she said, "Park over there," pointing to the right of the six-car garage, where a skirt extended from the immaculate drive.

Given the elegance around him, Brodie knew his car looked even more like a junker than usual. He glanced at Mary, but if it bothered her, she hid it well.

When she started to open her door, he caught her arm just below her elbow. She was so damn fragile, his fingers overlapped and a primitive sort of emotion clashed with his innate manners. She looked at him with a question in her eyes. The urge to kiss her was so strong, he almost forgot what he'd wanted to say.

Then Howler propped his head over the seat and whined, and that brought him back around.

"What do I do with the dog? You know I can't leave him out here."

Those sweet lips of hers curled in a genuine smile that licked over his nerve endings and made him think things very inappropriate to their circumstances. "We'll take him in with us, of course."

Given the country-style castle where her boss lived, Brodie didn't see any "of course" about it. "He'll need to drain the pipes first." All around them was pristine landscaping. "Where do you suggest we do that?"

She patted his hand. "I'm sure Howler will have a few ideas." She opened her door and circled around the hood, reaching his side of the car just as he'd leashed Howler. The dog bounded out to greet her with a wagging rump, then dragged Brodie to an unspoiled bright green lawn where he did his business.

In fact, it was a good ten minutes before the dog decided he'd marked enough territory and they started up the grand entrance of the place.

Everything was done up in stone, just like a castle, two towering stories tall with fancy slate roofs. It swept wide, balconies and a half turret supported by pillars. Interesting curves and angles added to the impression of wealth. Brodie didn't know architectural terms, so he wasn't sure what most of the extras were called, he only knew they didn't come cheap.

Mary used a code to enter by the massive double front doors. Howler was as uncertain as Brodie; the dog took short, halting steps, his head slewing in every direction.

Once inside, Mary pressed a buzzer on a panel beside the front door.

A plump woman with salt-and-pepper hair and squeaky shoes showed up a minute later. As she wiped her hands on an apron, she beamed at Howler. "Oh, such a beautiful dog." Then she turned to Brodie and paused, looking at him over her half-glasses.

Mary said, "Vera, this is Brodie Crews, the new courier. Brodie, meet Vera, the housekeeper."

Brodie leaned toward the woman and stuck out a hand. "Ma'am."

She twittered, took his hand and said, "My, you're unexpected." Without explaining that, she turned to Howler. "Is he friendly?"

"Very," Brodie promised. He was aware of Mary watching him in surprise. Because he behaved? Well, she'd be shocked senseless before the meeting was over. He did have manners—they just seemed to flee around her.

A robust man dressed in jeans, a T-shirt and apron came around the corner. "Mary." He held open his arms and Mary embraced him.

They were like a big friendly family. Brodie found himself smiling, liking them all already.

When the man let her go, Brodie stepped forward. "Burl, right? It's nice to meet you."

"So Mary told you about us?"

"I had to grill her, but finally got enough info to identify you."

All eyes went to Mary. She shook her head. "He exaggerates." She stood with one hand on Howler as if to reassure him.

"You want a drink?" Burl asked her. "Something to eat? It was an all-day trip, right?"

"Yes, and thank you. I'll wait to see what Therman wants to do, though."

"Therman," came a new voice, "would like you to join him for dinner."

Only then did Brodie hear the heels coming down a grand staircase. The woman was tall, almost as tall as him, very thin with a straight back and long neck. She wore a trim black dress with low heels, her white hair styled atop her head.

"Perfect," Burl said. "There's plenty."

"While we wait," she continued to Mary, "he'd like to meet with you both in the library."

Mary nodded. "Of course."

Brodie guessed the woman to be in her seventies, and though she was attractive still, he'd be willing to bet she'd bowled men over in her younger days.

Burl said, "Twenty minutes, Jolene. Then I'll have everything ready." He turned and left the room, and if he'd ever had a health scare, it didn't show in his easy stride now.

Mary properly introduced him to Jolene, Therman's personal assistant—though Brodie would bet she was more than that, too.

The way Jolene held out her hand, Brodie wondered if he was supposed to shake it or kiss her knuckles. He settled on a gentle squeeze and a nod. "Nice to meet you."

She smiled. "I see that you've already met Vera and Burl."

Brodie noticed that only his first name was given, which made the introductions less formal and gave tacit permission for him to call each person by name rather than include titles. Apparently Therman liked to keep things casual.

"There are others who work here, of course." Vera frowned at a speck of dust on a dark wood table. She used the edge of her apron to quickly whisk it away. "Landscapers, maintenance crew, pool cleaner. Eventually, you'll meet everyone."

Brodie nodded even as he wondered if there was a reason he needed to meet everyone. So far, no one in the fancy house fit his expectations.

Curious about the odd welcoming committee, he glanced at Mary and saw she watched him with bright eyes full of laughter. So she'd known how it would be, huh? She could have warned him, but as her lips twitched, he realized she'd wanted to see his reaction.

And here she'd lectured him on being respectful, the tease. Maybe Therman would be different, more ceremonial, but he was starting to have his doubts.

Poor Howler fidgeted about, first standing, sitting and then standing again.

Smiling at the dog, Jolene lightly stroked his head.

Howler tipped up his face and closed his eyes as if in bliss.

"Therman loves animals," she said. "He'll enjoy meeting your pet."

"Thank you for including him. If I'd left him outside, he'd have worked himself into a pitiful mess."

"He's very well behaved." She turned away. "I'll let Therman know you're here."

As she left, Vera said, "Come along. I'll take you to the library to wait."

Brodie found himself walking with Howler and Mary down a long hallway wide enough for them to be side by side. Instead of the tile of the foyer, Howler's nails tapped on polished wood flooring. Gone were the towering two-story ceilings in the entrance, but these ceilings were probably still eleven feet high. With everything so oversize, it should have felt cavernous, yet didn't.

Vera pushed open large double doors and they stepped into an immense room with a different, richer wood on the floors in a herringbone pattern, wood panels on the walls, and even on the ceiling, all of it with loads of trim. With several sets of French doors on one wall, plenty of light filtered in, saving it from feeling dark.

One set of doors led out to a parklike enclosure with fountains bubbling and flowers everywhere.

Vera touched several wall switches and overhead lights slowly brightened the room even more.

"Make yourself at home," she said. "If the dog needs to go out, feel free to use those doors." She gestured toward the park setting. “If you need anything else before dinner, Mary can buzz me.”

As soon as she was gone, Mary started snickering.

Brodie gave her a mock-severe look. “You think it’s funny, huh?”

She put a hand over her mouth, but the giggles came through. “Sorry,” she managed to say, not sounding sorry at all. “I don’t know what you expected—”

“Yes, you do.” Her whole face brightened when she laughed, making her drop-dead gorgeous.

She nodded, chuckling more. “Yes, I do.”

Damn. “You’re sexy as hell when you laugh.”

She blinked. “What?” As if she hadn’t heard him, she laughed again.

Drawn to her, to those glittering eyes and that sweetly smiling mouth, Brodie took a step closer. “When you laugh, it makes me want to kiss you.”

Now her eyes were big, soulful and uncertain.

“It affects me,” he said. “Keep it up and I’m going to look indecent when I meet the head honcho.”

A rush of heat painted her face, her gaze dropped down his body, and she bit her bottom lip.

In anticipation of seeing him hard? He had a little more control than that—but not much. Not with her. “Mary—”

“This is interesting.”

Brodie turned fast and found a small man in a wheelchair, his body frail but his expression alert. Well, hell. If he didn’t miss his guess, he’d just met Therman Ritter.

Busted.

CHAPTER SIX

Brodie waited, for what he wasn't sure. All the man did was study Mary through one squinted eye with a bushy gray brow lowered over it. His still-thick hair, precisely cut, was more a steel gray than Jolene's white hair.

Wearing jeans, sneakers and a casual button-up shirt with the cuffs of the sleeves turned up, he looked comfortable in his chair. His gaze shifted to Brodie.

Age might have weakened his body, but a keen intelligence showed in those shrewd gray eyes. "You nailed it," Therman said.

"Head honcho, you mean?" He'd already been caught; no way to back out of it now. "I figured."

Beside him, Mary quietly groaned.

Therman tapped his fingers on the chair arm. He murmured, "And you're Brodie Crews," as if taking his measure.

Unable to fully judge the man's mood, Brodie said, "Guilty." He stepped forward, bringing Howler along with him. "It's a pleasure to meet you, sir."

Given his smaller size, Therman's grip was surprisingly firm.

Releasing Brodie, he sat back in his chair and smiled at Howler.

Was everyone here an animal lover? Brodie had a feeling a large part of his warm welcome was thanks to the dog.

"Aren't you a handsome fellow?"

Yeah, Brodie knew that definitely wasn't for him.

Surprisingly, Howler went straight for Therman, nosing against him gently.

The old man grinned and cupped the dog's large head in both hands. "Call me Therman."

He assumed *that* part was to him. "All right."

Howler sat beside Therman, his head over his legs, and let out a long sigh.

Resting a hand on Howler's neck, Therman asked Mary, "You have it?"

She immediately withdrew the box from her briefcase and brought it to him.

He opened it with near reverence. "Ah." Those calculating eyes slanted toward Brodie. "You know what this is?"

Brodie shrugged. "Hair."

"She didn't tell you whose hair?"

"Told me it wasn't any of my business, that if you wanted me to know, you'd tell me."

A wide grin split his wrinkled face. "Mary understands me well." He glanced at her. "Would you mind seeing what's keeping Burl? I'll starve to death before he calls us in to eat."

"Oh." Her gaze bounced from Therman to Brodie and back again.

Brodie could tell she didn't want to go and he grinned. Yeah, let her wonder what he'd say and do. Served her right for misleading him.

Since she didn't have much choice with Therman waiting, she relented. "Of course." The quick smile that curved her lips never quite reached her eyes. Flashing a quick glance at Brodie, she warned, "I'll be right back."

He was still grinning when Therman said, "She's afraid you'll insult me."

"If I do, it wouldn't be deliberate."

"Be yourself. It's not a problem." Putting the box across his lap and taking Howler's leash, Therman turned his chair. With a small control, he wheeled it toward a set of inner doors. "Come on, boy."

Brodie had no idea who he meant that time, but he followed them both anyway. "I haven't always been on my best behavior with her. I didn't meet her under ideal circumstances and—"

"She told me." Therman waved off his explanation. "I got a good laugh out of it."

Thoughts jumping, Brodie stepped around him to open the door. "All of it?"

Therman laughed. "She tried to talk me out of hiring you. Wanted me to take on your brother instead." They entered a connected room built in a semicircle with floor-to-ceiling windows. The same wood flooring continued, but the walls were painted a light cream color with a variety of displays situated everywhere—musical instruments, pictures, paintings, clothes. "I insisted you would suit better."

Great, Therman liked him—but did Mary still regret being stuck with him instead of Jack? If he got bored, maybe he'd ask her, just to see what she'd say.

She might get all severe and lecture him, or she'd start laughing again.

Odd that either possibility excited him.

Realizing he'd been quiet too long, Brodie said, "I appreciate the confidence." He looked around at the eclectic collection, grouped in a way he couldn't identify, yet somehow everything seemed to belong.

Therman shrugged. "I'm told I can be demanding."

"Yeah?" He wondered if it was age, illness or an accident that had the man rolling instead of walking. "Who tells you that?"

"Mostly Jolene." Therman's bushy brows bobbed comically. "No one else would dare." He moved toward the back of the room. "If you agree to the terms, you might need to take off at a moment's notice. I try to avoid holidays, but it's not guaranteed. Nights, weekends, during inclement weather—none of that factors in when I have to act quickly on a piece that's become available."

Brodie eyed a display of morbid drawings. One was ink on a stained napkin, another marker on a torn piece of cardboard. Weird. Still studying them, he said, "Barring any emergencies with my family, it shouldn't be a problem."

Therman rolled up to a pair of blue suede shoes, laces neatly tied, sitting on a grand display pedestal with an accent light aimed at it. Carefully, he placed the lock of hair over one shoe. "Want to guess whose hair that is?"

Bemused, Brodie tugged at an ear. "You shitting me?" He glanced at Therman. "Sorry, I meant—"

"Not shitting you, no. The guitar is his, the suit, signed album and signed school yearbook." He rubbed his hands together. "It's an impressive collection, isn't it?"

"Very." Brodie looked at the lock of glossy black hair. He supposed the importance of it now made sense, at least for a collector. He shook his head and glanced around again, this time with new perception.

"Our Mary is a special woman."

Our Mary? Brodie shoved his hands in his pockets so he wouldn't bump anything and, trying to act like Therman hadn't just thrown him a curveball, asked, "Oh?"

"The others here… They're friends who offered help when I needed it, and now they've become like family. Their loyalty is the same as you'd have for your brother."

Brodie figured that was more valuable than anything Therman could add to his collections, but he didn't say so.

"Mary, though, she came to me as a stranger when I placed an ad for an intelligent, motivated, savvy businesswoman who could, as I explained to you, be ready on a moment's notice without complaint or excuses." Therman rolled to another display, this one of abstract images created with light, thick paint. "You agreed to those terms with the caveat that a family emergency would take precedence. That's as it should be."

"I'm glad you understand."

Therman rolled again. Howler patiently followed until they stopped before a display of small figurines on glass risers. Quietly, Therman said, "Mary had no caveats before she accepted."

The meaning of that stopped Brodie in his tracks. Therman didn't look at him, but then, he didn't need to. The tension in the man's shoulders, the way he held his head, told Brodie that this was an important topic for him.

Our Mary.

It was weird, but Brodie felt his heart go heavy.

In sadness?

Sympathy?

He wasn't sure. Whatever the hell caused the uncomfortable sensation, he wasn't used to it. Not with women unrelated to him.

There was a lot of meaning in the conversation, so Brodie didn't take his usual out using sarcasm or jokes. Instead he came to stand beside Therman. "How long's she been with you?"

"Three years." While petting the dog, Therman peered over his shoulder. "She's as loyal as the others, but not from familiarity or a long-standing bond. Her loyalty is from respect—and gratitude."

"Gratitude for what?" A woman like Mary Daniels could have her pick of jobs. Probably her pick of men, too.

"She's never missed a day," Therman continued without answering his question. “Not a single day. Not in three years. She’s never balked at picking up and running at a moment’s notice. Never complained about a driver, either.” Those steely gray eyes pinpointed him. “Until you.”

Well, that sucked. “I don’t…”

Half under his breath, Therman muttered, “Had a few who were real pricks, too.”

Umbrage dug into his shoulders, making him stiffen. “I hope you fired them.” It annoyed Brodie, on Mary’s behalf, naturally, that she might’ve had to deal with jerks.

Jerks other than him, he meant. *Shit.*

“Didn’t need to. Mary managed them like a teacher with an unruly third-grade class.”

A reluctant grin caught him. “Yeah,” Brodie said, relaxing just a little. He had to remember that Mary Daniels was a force to be reckoned with. “I can imagine that.”

“I’ve never known her to date.”

Another bomb dropped unexpectedly. What the hell was Therman getting at? “You expect her to report her personal life to you?”

“No, but she’s here a lot,” he groused. “I think I’d notice, whether she mentioned it or not.”

“Hmm.” Maybe he’d ask her that, too, Brodie thought. Then he shook his head, unsure if he wanted to hear her mooning over some dude. Instead, he reassured Therman, “A woman like her, I’m sure she’s kept busy.” What guy could resist? If it wasn’t for the job, Brodie would have already tried his hand—

Mary burst back in, then paused as her gaze scoured over him critically, probably looking for telltale signs of monkey business. When he winked at her, she caught herself and, shoulders back, walked sedately toward Therman.

Which also put her close to him.

Brodie looked her over with new appreciation. The woman was all abundant curves and take-charge attitude in a sedate package that teased his senses. He noticed that a long tendril of hair, glossy and red, had escaped her updo. It draped over her shoulder, the curling end licking at her left breast.

Damn.

He must have made a sound because when she reached the back of Therman's chair, she paused to glance at him, one supercilious brow raised. "What?"

Crazy that such a simple thing could thicken his blood...and his cock. Struggling to get it together, Brodie asked, "Did you run?"

A little breathless, she replied, "No, why?"

Fibber. He reached out and fingered that silky hank of hair between his fingers. The backs of his knuckles brushed beneath her collarbone. Even through the blouse, he felt the warmth of her skin. Seeing the pulse beating wildly in her throat deepened his voice. "You're coming undone."

Their gazes held.

A sudden "Harrumph" intruded.

Mary jumped away from him, yanking her hair when he didn't let go quickly enough. Wincing, she turned her back on him and jabbed the hair back into that hideous bun.

Therman didn't turn to see them, but he did say, "If you young people can zip it up for now, I'd like my dinner."

Embarrassed heat splotched her cheeks, but Mary said calmly, in that strict authoritative voice that Brodie found hot, "Burl has it ready. Would you like me to take Howler?"

"I've got him." Therman turned his chair and with the dog keeping pace, rolled out of the room. Mary stuck close to him, but while she pressed her pretty mouth with anger, her gaze repeatedly strayed to Brodie.

The interest was there, for both of them.

The big question now, at least from Brodie's perspective, was what to do about it.

★★★

Mary knew she walked stiffly, but holy smokes, she might have caught fire when Brodie touched her. Right there, with Therman present. She wanted to fan her still-hot face but didn't.

She also wanted to ignore him—and couldn't.

Against her better judgment, her gaze repeatedly flicked his way, and each time she found him watching her. He was an irreverent person, often mocking, always baiting, yet now he seemed incredibly somber.

Why did he look so different?

Why was he looking *at her* differently?

Therman talked to the dog as they made their way to the formal dining room, telling him what a strapping lad he was and praising him for his manners as if the dog understood every word.

"I used to have a dog." Therman tipped his face up to Mary. "A little yapper, no bigger than this one's head." He stroked Howler from his ears to the base of his scruff. "My wife, God bless her, got him five or six years before she passed, but he was never really her dog. No, he took to me right off."

Mary said, "Vera told me about him." She knew he'd loved the dog, and maybe that was why, in all the time since, he hadn't gotten another.

"Never met a more temperamental creature, or one that adored me as much." Therman grinned at some memory. "He was always on my lap and used to bite anyone who got within reach."

"That amuses you?" Brodie asked with his own grin.

"He couldn't really hurt anyone, but he'd give a mean pinch." Therman cocked his bushy eyebrow and admitted, "I used to lure people over to me, just to see them get nipped."

"I guess you being you, no one got mad?"

Mary wasn't sure what that was supposed to mean, but Therman seemed to get it.

"Oh, I'm sure they did, but they hid it." Sounding disgruntled, Therman complained, "Respect is one thing. Cowardice is another."

"I'll keep that in mind," Brodie said.

Therman snorted. "I can't picture you swallowing your ire, so don't spin that yarn on me."

He gave a short, rough laugh. "No, I won't."

Eyeing him, Therman said, "You wouldn't have gotten mad at the dog, either."

"With you egging him on? I'd know where to put the blame."

Therman grinned.

It amazed Mary that they already got along so well. In one respect, she was relieved, because their friendliness would make her job easier. But in another, she almost felt...left out.

Like a third wheel.

The friend who got taken along out of pity, but never truly belonged.

For Brodie, it seemed simple to just fit in. She imagined most men liked him. And most women probably wanted him.

She did—even though she knew she shouldn't.

They'd be working together for the foreseeable future. Somehow she had to insulate herself from his appeal. It wouldn't be easy, but then, little in her life had been.

Two weeks later, Brodie dragged himself into the shop in time to see his brother preparing to head out. First things first, he decided, yawning as he made his way to the coffee machine. God bless her, Charlotte always fixed a pot first thing, and she knew to make it strong.

Jack poked his head out of the office and asked, "Late night?"

Brodie poured the mug full. At least three times a week, Therman sent him and Mary out. It was more than he'd expected, but with the amount of money he made he didn't have any complaints. The work was easy and there wasn't anything he'd rather be doing—especially since he enjoyed spending time with Mary, even though she'd retreated into professional politeness.

For now, he'd let her have her way. Eventually she'd loosen up again—he hoped.

"Actually, I got in by six," Brodie said. "It was a short trip."

Sauntering out of the office, Jack asked, "So why do you look like you haven't slept?"

Because he hadn't. To stall, he drank a gulp of coffee, and burned his mouth.

While he grimaced, Charlotte breezed in, looking extra pretty in a simple yellow sundress, her curly brown hair in a long loose braid.

Her blue eyes were lighter than Red's, he noticed, as she looked him over with humor. "Our boy, Brodie, isn't used to being around a woman who doesn't fall at his feet."

Jack, the dick, lounged against the wall, arms folded. "Seriously? She isn't begging you for it?" Dripping sarcasm, he asked, "It's been weeks now. What's wrong with the lady?"

"She's smart," Charlotte sang, while patting Brodie's shoulder. "*And* she's a professional."

"Meaning she can't sleep with the hired help?" Jack tsked.

"Don't you have someplace to be?" Brodie asked him.

"I have at least fifteen minutes to heckle you."

"In that case, fuck off," Brodie said to Jack, and then to Charlotte, "You used to be such a nice girl, but you're developing a real mean streak."

"It's from being around you two." She sashayed past on her way to her own small office.

It was a teasing statement, but it hit Brodie like a brick. He looked at his brother and saw Jack was just as poleaxed.

They stared at each other.

Jack spoke first, saying, "We probably are a bad influence."

"No probably about it." He swallowed more coffee, this time welcoming the burn.

"She's twenty-five now, not fifteen."

"Which just means she's ripe for picking, and what if someone like me goes after her?"

Jack choked and, like a loyal brother, asked, "What the hell's wrong with you?"

"You know."

They thought Charlotte couldn't hear, but she leaned out of the doorway and smiled. "You're perfect, Brodie—just not perfect for what I want."

"Which is?" he asked, half-afraid to hear the answer.

"Marriage that lasts. A battle-free home. Two babies, a boy and a girl. Happy-ever-after." She waved a hand. "All that."

He opened his mouth but shut it again. She'd answered without hesitation, completely stumping him. He turned to Jack. "I got nothin'."

Jack scowled, but said only, "Pretty sure you can't dictate the sex of your babies, hon."

That made Brodie a little green, thinking of Charlotte, who was his little sister in every way except blood, giving birth.

"I can do anything I set my mind to. You two taught me that."

Brodie rubbed the back of his neck. "Well..." Charlotte waited, her expression patient and expectant at the same time. "It's just that you're setting some impossible goals."

"Men aren't perfect," Jack explained.

Brodie nodded.

"Overall, we're really imperfect."

"Assholes, even," Brodie added.

Jack shot him a look. "Speak for yourself."

"I think he was." Charlotte laughed, bringing their attention back to her. "When I find the man I want, which I'll do without any help from you two, thank you very much, he won't be like either of you."

Jack straightened. "What'd I do?"

"You schmooze," she accused.

He drew himself up in indignation. "I do not."

Snickering, Brodie said, "Yeah, you do."

"And you," she said, pinning Brodie in her gaze. "You're too full of yourself to know a good thing when you see it."

"If by *thing*, you mean Red—"

"See," Jack interrupted with a sneer. "He's not too stupid after all."

"She never said I was stupid!"

Jack opened his mouth, but Charlotte beat him to it. "No, I didn't. And I never would. You're both wonderful. Smart. Caring and considerate."

Brodie watched her warily.

"But you two can be so incredibly dense."

Jack tried to speak.

Charlotte wasn't having it. "And yes, I meant Mary." She shifted to Jack. "You hold women away with distant politeness, and Brodie drives them away with mockery." She put her little nose in the air. "If I didn't love you both like crazy, I'd call you cowards. But that would be mean, and I'm never mean."

Brodie snorted.

Jack glanced at him. "She's been insulting us for ten minutes and she doesn't think that's mean?"

"She must've taken a few lessons from Mom."

The outer door opened and Mary stepped in, Howler on her heels.

Brodie shook his head. The dog rarely bothered to stir himself for anyone, but he adored Mary and followed her around like a lovesick pup.

She stopped when she saw them all in the hallway, Jack outside his office, Brodie near the coffeepot, and Charlotte lounging in her office doorway.

Jack and Charlotte grinned at her.

Brodie refilled his cup.

Howler plopped down to his butt and leaned against her legs, almost throwing her off balance.

"What's going on?" she asked. "Am I interrupting?"

Today she wore a sleeveless navy blouse with peach-colored capris that should have clashed with her hair, but instead made the red more intense. The shirt was long and loose, draping over her full breasts like a tent, blending into her rounded hips in a way that totally hid her waist. If he was a blind man, or as stupid as Jack accused, he'd think she was shapeless.

But the opposite was true: the more she covered, the more he saw, and damn it, the more he wanted her.

Those vivid blue eyes went from his face, to Jack's, to Charlotte's as she waited for an answer.

"Not at all." Charlotte shifted away from her lounged position. "Come on in. Coffee?"

"Thank you."

"No problem." Charlotte looked pointedly at Brodie. He rolled his eyes, but turned to fetch the cup. Looking away from Red, even with her still in proximity, would give him a few seconds to get it together.

All night he'd thought about her—mostly in the sexual context. Not since he was seventeen had he suffered so much unrequited lust. It sucked.

Couldn't be healthy. Hell, he'd never believed in blue balls, but if he checked out his own, he'd probably find them in some shade of misery.

Behind him, he heard Jack ask, "Where are you off to today?"

Mary said, "Indiana. We'll only be gone a few hours."

"Short notice again?"

"That's usually how it works. A collector decides spur of moment to let something go, and whoever jumps on it first gets it. Sometimes there are auctions so it goes to the highest bidder, but for the most coveted items, all the serious bidders are already aware of who has what. Odds are they've already been making offers in hopes of striking the right number."

"Brodie said your boss is a great guy."

"He is."

Charlotte piped up. "He's invited you both to dinner—what now? Three times?"

"Yes. Therman likes to get firsthand accounts, plus he likes to know the people working for him. Talking during dinner gives him a chance to get more familiar."

Bringing the coffee to her, Brodie said, "Like one big happy family." Except that Red still kept herself apart. He could sense it, and so could Therman.

Why did she do that? Why cut out people who cared?

Her fingers barely brushed his as she accepted the cup, and he felt the jolt clear down to his suffering balls.

He watched her mouth as she sipped, saw her lick those fantasy-inspiring lips—

Jack's shove caught him off guard and he damn near ran into the wall before whirling around, seriously thinking of shoving back.

Jack's grin and Mary's alarm halted him.

Brodie pointed at his brother. "Soon."

"Pay no mind to them," Charlotte said. "They're always threatening to kill each other, yet as you see, they're both still here."

"I wasn't going to kill him, brat. Just bloody his nose."

"If we're comparing noses," Jack said, not the least bit worried, "anyone can see yours is the one that's been broken."

Mary gasped, then scowled at Jack in accusation. "You broke his nose?"

"Not me, no," Jack quickly reassured her. "He got it smashed playing the hero."

It took a second for her expression of anger to clear before Mary asked with exasperation, *"Again?"*

Brodie started to deny it, but everyone conspired against him.

Charlotte said, “That’s our Brodie, always jumping to the defense of helpless maidens, innocent dogs and even the occasional outnumbered man.”

“It was the last,” Jack explained, “that left his nose bent.”

“That’s enough.” Brodie glared at Jack, and for once he took the hint and shut up.

Unfortunately his glares didn’t work on Charlotte, and she turned into a Chatty Cathy.

“See, there’s this sweet guy in town who everyone knows isn’t a fighter. In fact, Willard is a little slow, if you know what I mean. Anyway, one night in the bar where he works as a server, he accidentally bumped into this jerk who decided to go apeshit over it. Willard would have been annihilated, so it’s a good thing Brodie spends much of his free time there.”

Brodie choked on his coffee. Oh, great. Now Red would think he was a drunk!

“The jerk grabbed Willard by his collar,” Charlotte said. “He had him on his tiptoes, yelling into his face, threatening him.” At this point, she beamed. “Then Brodie stepped in.”

Red’s eyes were huge with interest.

Jack took over the story. “Brodie told him to knock it off while also squeezing the guy’s wrist—which got Willard loose real quick. When he’s pissed—and he was—Brodie has this low lethal voice that only an idiot would ignore.”

“That would have been the end of it,” Charlotte continued. “Except that the bully wasn’t alone, so Brodie ended up taking on four of them—”

“Might’ve been five,” Jack mused.

“—and Brodie got in his fair share of hits, but he also came away from it with a few bruises—”

“And a bloody nose.”

In a flourish, Charlotte finished, “But overall, he kicked their asses.”

With her lips slightly parted in awe, her eyes now brightened with fascination, Mary stared at him.

"For the love of… We're going to be late, Red." A second passed and Brodie corrected himself. "Mary." He stalked for the door, but on his way out, he added, "And it was only three, none of them fighters." If his brother and Charlotte kept it up, she'd start thinking he was a brawler—a *drunken* brawler—without enough sense to avoid a fight.

Just as he stepped out, he heard Jack ask, "Why does he call you Red Mary?"

He let the door close behind him.

Steamy air enveloped him and he paused in the dirt yard, hands on hips, head tipped back to draw in a deep breath. He needed more coffee, damn it.

He needed to get Red naked and agreeable. But even more than that, he wanted to get to know her, the *real* her. No one other than Charlotte would call him considerate, but that was what he was trying to be. Ever since Therman talked to him about Mary, he'd been plagued with the need to understand her, to get inside her head and find out what made her tick.

Coming on to her wouldn't accomplish that, but then, he wasn't sure what would. Indecision was not his forte. He was man who liked action.

Action with Red… Yeah, that'd work.

The door opened behind him and he heard Howler's panting breath as he and Mary caught up to him.

She touched his arm, which brought him around to face her, and she demanded, "*Only* three?"

Obviously, she was still stuck on that. "They weren't fighters, just idiots." Dark clouds offered a brief respite from the morning sun. In this light, her blue eyes looked velvety. Her brows were pinched together, that incredible mouth firm.

He slowly inhaled, absolutely racked with pulsing need.

Unaware of his struggle, she folded her arms. "If they weren't good at fighting, how did you get a broken nose?"

She looked incensed for him, making him chuckle despite his absurd state. "I got shoved from behind and literally ran into a fist, otherwise I wouldn't have." He turned and opened the car doors to let out some of the accumulated heat.

"But *three*." She persisted. "And if you knew they couldn't hold their own, then why did you brawl with them?"

Brodie threw up his hands. "See, I knew you'd look at it that way." He reached in and started the car to get the cooler air going. "What those two tattletales failed to mention is that I *tried* to settle things without it getting physical. I told them Willard was a gentle guy and that I didn't want to fight."

"I take it that didn't do it?"

He shook his head. "The guy still took a swing, I blocked it and all hell broke loose." Howler looked between them, then plopped down to nap until they settled things. "At least Willard wasn't drawn into it. Jack made sure of that."

"Jack was there?"

"Charlotte, too." He stared down at her, annoyance creeping up his neck. "You don't think I recounted all that nonsense to them, do you?"

Mary shrugged.

"And just so you know, we were there for a damned fund-raiser. The bar is where almost all the fund-raisers are held. Hell, my mother was there. So don't start thinking I'm a drunk." It was bad enough the way they'd first met; he didn't need his family to shore up that impression.

Her lips twitched. "Charlotte did imply—"

"Charlotte is like a little sister and sometimes her favorite thing is to give me shit."

"And Jack?"

"What about him?"

The corners of her lips lifted, fascinating him. "If he was there, why didn't he help you in the fight?"

With an offended frown, Brodie said, "I didn't need help!"

And that set her off. She gave that sweet, silly giggle he'd heard before, which quickly escalated to a chuckle. Hugging herself, she started to outright laugh, and when she looked at his face, she hooted with hilarity.

For Brodie, it was the tipping point.

The happiness on her face, the twinkling of her bluer-than-blue eyes, the dropping of all her barriers...

Her shoulders felt small and frail in his large hands as he eased her closer to his body. Her breasts brushed his chest and her laughter died. Instantly startled and very aware, her gaze locked on his.

But she didn't pull away.

"It's so fucking hot, the way you laugh." He put his mouth over hers. A closed-mouth kiss suitable to a schoolboy, and still it made his cock stir.

Lingering there, his lips pressed gently to hers, he breathed in her warm, unique scent. *Goddamn, she smells good.* Like sunshine and flowers and...woman.

He wanted to eat her up, and thinking that made him groan.

Slowly, he urged her flush against him, her body so deliciously rounded in all the right places. Her arms unbent, falling loose at her sides. Her head tilted back to keep the contact of their mouths.

All in all, she rested in his arms, not fighting him, but not actively participating, either.

And it maddened him with lust.

"Mary?" Her heart thundered against his chest, her breath coming fast and hot. *Nothing passive in that.*

She leaned closer and made a small sound of need.

He didn't know enough about her, why the kiss felt so special, or why she seemed so surprised by it. In good conscience, he couldn't proceed until he had some answers.

Getting them wouldn't be easy, but he figured Mary was more than worth the effort.

As if waking, she slowly opened her dazed eyes, her lashes fluttering. That particular look would be good for his ego, if only he wasn't so worried.

He kissed her once more, quick and firm, then stepped back to give her room to breathe. Deliberately breaking the spell, he asked, "You're not going to slap me, are you?"

She swallowed and, still mute, shook her head.

"Should I apologize?" Damn, he wasn't sure what to do. He sensed the moment was incredibly fragile—he just didn't know why. "If I did," he continued, "it'd be a lie because I'm not sorry."

Her gaze skipped away and she drew a long, shuddering breath. When she looked at him again, her eyes were clearer even though a rosy flush still stained her cheeks.

Arousal, not embarrassment. Nice.

"No, you don't need to apologize." She cleared her throat and the next words were a little stronger, less husky. "But we should get on our way so we're not running late."

Though it felt like a reprieve, Brodie didn't like it. Already she'd started around the car to the passenger side. Howler realized what was happening and bounded up and into the back seat, taking his position in front of the harness.

The drive wouldn't be as long as some, but Brodie had a feeling it'd be strained—and he didn't care. All he could think about was kissing her again.

Longer. Deeper. Wetter.

Mouths open, tongues playing, lots of heavy breathing…

Damn. Unless she insisted otherwise, he'd be taking care of that at the first opportunity.

CHAPTER SEVEN

Mary needed a distraction, and she needed it fast. They'd been on the road for over an hour without much conversation. She could breathe again, thankfully, but keeping her thoughts off Brodie wasn't easy.

The way he'd kissed her, so...sweetly. It had shaken her more than a carnal encounter would have. It was sensual, definitely, because Brodie was walking, talking sensuality.

Everything about the man seemed designed to make a woman melt into a puddle of need.

But he'd kept all that hotness leashed while moving his mouth so carefully over hers.

She'd felt his warm breath, the rasp of whiskers against her sensitive skin, the tempered strength in his hands on her shoulders.

Shivering anew, she clenched her hands and tried not to think what it would be like to open herself up to him.

Dangerous. To her plans, her feelings. To her very soul.

Brodie didn't bring up the kiss, and for that she was thankful since she had no idea yet what she wanted, but he kept pawing the steering wheel as if he could barely restrain himself.

From that simple kiss?

She'd like to think so, but she knew she was far more affected by it than he'd been. After all, she hadn't been touched by a man in a very long time, and the last time she had...

Ugh. Disaster. Her own fault, of course, because she knew better, but... No. She definitely didn't want to think about that. Not now. Not ever. Lesson learned...or so she'd thought.

Before Brodie Crews.

It took her a few minutes more to think of a benign question, and then she asked, "Where do you live? Does it take you long to get to the office each day?"

His dark eyes glanced her way, then over her—almost as if he could see through her clothes. Or like he was trying to.

Her nipples tightened, her lungs constricted and a sweet ache settled low in her body. If she could, she'd walk away, but the job required that she be closed up in the car with him and, God, today it was excruciating.

The memory of that near-chaste kiss combined with the hungry look he'd just given her sparked her every nerve ending with sensation.

Pleasurable sensation, which was nice.

Brodie was just that kind of man.

With a strained frown that she knew was directed inward, not at her, he gave his narrow focus back to the road. "I live at the office."

"You live..." She hadn't expected that. The idea that he might be impoverished helped to blunt some of the chafing lust.

"Behind it, actually."

Her brain went blank.

"I'm not living in a garbage bin, Red. I have an apartment there." He shifted, his shoulders bunching and flexing, his thick thighs opening a little more.

Of course she noticed the bulge there. A fresh rush of awareness feathered through her bloodstream. She struggled to get her brain off his anatomy—impressive as it might be—and back on the conversation. “An apartment?”

As if he, too, needed a distraction, he gave a sharp nod. “When we were younger, my mother raised us there. Dad ran the shop, that is, when he was around and willing to play family man, which wasn’t all that often. She kept it going the rest of the time.”

Mary tried to picture the office building in her mind. Yes, it was long, all one level, and she’d only been to the front of the building for the office. Where the rest of the building led, she didn’t know. She hadn’t ever considered it, yet she couldn’t recall seeing anything that resembled living quarters. For one thing, only dirt and gravel circled the building. That made sense for the cars.

But for children? Some of the concern must have shown on her face, given how he responded.

“Now, Red, don’t get all maudlin. Mom made sure we had everything we needed, so it wasn’t bad.”

The way he made light of it squeezed her heart in sympathy. She’d needed a different focus, and this worked better than most. “What did you mean about your father?”

“Dad’s a runaround,” he said without any shame or condemnation. “Always has been. Mom got fed up with it when I was an early teen and booted him to the curb, not that he was around a lot before that.”

“I didn’t realize.”

“No reason you should have.” He rolled up to a red light. While there, he looked at her again. “Mom had plenty of reasons to run him down to us, but she never did.”

“He cheated on her?”

“Among other things.”

Gradually, the rigidness left him, so she kept the topic going by asking, “What other things?” Talking would help put them back on an even keel, and besides, she wanted to know more about him.

Brodie shrugged. "If you asked Dad the color of the sky, he'd say green. Ask him where he'd been all night, he'd sure as hell make up a story. For whatever reason, he's a habitual liar."

"That must have been..." She didn't have the words. "Rough?"

"Like I said, Mom made up for whatever Dad did."

What would it be like to have a mother that attentive, that caring? Brodie obviously loved the woman, and to Mary, that said a lot about her.

Almost as an afterthought, he added, "When Dad was around, he was a good dad. He enjoyed playing with us, coddling us. That's what Mom always pointed out."

No doubt his mother had pointed it out for Brodie and Jack's sake, so they wouldn't feel neglected.

The light changed and Brodie drove forward.

It wasn't at all the same thing. Not even close, thank God. Yet Mary felt an affinity for Brodie and his relationship with his father. "What about when he wasn't around?"

"That's as often as not. Still." He gave a quick shake of his head. "That's just him, the way he's made. Mom feels sorry for him. She says he hangs on to his youth out of fear. She could be right."

"So you and your father don't get along now?"

"Sure we do." His mouth lifted in a crooked smile. "Mom taught us to appreciate the good times and ignore the bad. Overall, that's what Jack and I still do."

Comparisons were a terrible thing, weighing heavily on her shoulders. Would she ever be able to ignore the bad times? There were so many...with only a handful of good times to balance it out.

Mary studied his handsome profile, the heavy brows and dark bristles on his jaw.

That sensuous mouth that had touched her own.

It was impetuous of her, but she couldn't stop herself from reaching over and lightly, with a single finger, touching the slight bump in his once-broken nose. "If Jack hadn't told me, I wouldn't have realized." Her voice sounded softer than she meant it to, but touching him, even in such an innocuous place, felt intimate.

He kept his eyes on the road as an odd stillness enveloped his usual energetic demeanor. After a moment, he asked, "The break? It wasn't bad. Not a big deal."

Inhaling slowly, she moved her fingertips to the stubble on his jaw in a very brief caress before withdrawing. Her fingers tingled and heat pooled in her belly.

How nice would it be to touch him as much as she wanted? To be free to touch him anywhere. *Everywhere.*

A tidal wave of temptation washed over her. Some very basic female instinct whispered that Brodie was the man who'd make it worthwhile. He wouldn't leave her wondering why she'd bothered.

And there would be no condemnation from him. Just the opposite, he seemed to think sex, for the sake of sex, was the most natural thing in the world.

Mary curled her fingers into her palm and rested her hand on her lap.

"Just so you know," he said, his voice as rough as gravel, "I liked that." He laughed a little. "Crazy shit, I know, but there you go."

Puzzled, Mary asked, "Crazy?"

"You, initiating a touch. Only on my face, but still… For some damn reason it felt like more."

It felt like more to her, too, and she couldn't help staring at him. *Wanting* him.

"Red," he growled low, before laughing again, a rasp of sound.

"Cut me a break, okay? It's starting to rain and I have a ways to drive to get there, then the drive home, but if you want—"

She'd never calm her heart if he finished that sentiment, so she said in a rush, "Your mother sounds amazing."

"Not what I'd usually pivot to—but okay, I'll take what I can get." His smile widened in what looked like fondness. It drove a dimple into his cheek and added crinkles to the corners of his eyes. "You'd love my mom. I'll have to introduce you sometime."

The thought of meeting his mother didn't sit right. It was enough to know his brother and Charlotte. But a mother? A *wonderful* mother? No, she didn't want to.

Besides, knowing his family would make their association too cozy, too familiar.

The business relationship she could handle.

Even sex might be doable—once or twice, to get it out of their systems. But anything more would be ill-advised.

Hoping he wouldn't notice her unease, she feigned a smile. "She doesn't live at the office anymore?"

"Nah. Jack and I bought her a house. Man, she bitched about it for weeks on end, but after we moved all of her stuff there, what could she do, right? Her bedroom, family room, all her dishes... We took away her choices."

"You forced her to move?"

"We made it easier for her to accept." Brodie cast her a look. "You're full of curiosity today, aren't you?"

Still trying to picture him relocating his mother's belongings without her permission, Mary said, "I, um—"

"Charlotte helped us out by moving in with her. Mom's at her best when she has someone to take care of. It's win-win with them. Charlotte deserves a little coddling, and Mom was born for it."

Mary wanted to know more about Charlotte, but she'd save that for later. "And Jack?"

"He has his own house that he's remodeling in his spare time." They turned onto a narrower road, and he slowed accordingly. "Any other questions?"

A million of them. Brodie and his family dynamic fascinated her. She'd never heard of anything like it.

She'd certainly never experienced anything even remotely close. Her childhood had been one of loneliness, shame, fear and regret.

Brodie seemed to pick up on her mood. "I don't mind, Mary. I was just teasing you."

She wished he'd make up his mind on what to call her. "Are you happy to live at the office?"

"In an apartment behind the office," he corrected, "but sure. It's more room than I need, really. Small kitchen, family room, two bedrooms, one bath." Those impressive shoulders shifted. "It's just me, so it's not like I need a lot of space, and I only have to walk out the door to get to work."

Mary knew he was in his midthirties and she suddenly wondered about his ambitions, what he wanted out of life and when. "Do you want a house of your own?"

"Eventually, sure. I'm saving up for it so I can build it the way I want. I already bought the land. Eight acres behind the house we got for Mom. It's wooded with a creek dividing the property. I like the idea of being close to her, you know? But not too close. We'd both have our privacy."

She couldn't remember a time when she'd wanted to be close to her mother—and now it no longer mattered.

"What's wrong?"

How did he read her so easily? Most people couldn't, when they bothered to try. Therman, for example, along with his family of friends, had been trying to dissect her awhile.

She'd always been polite, even friendly, but she'd never been tempted to open up.

"I was just thinking." Mary assumed that privacy was more

important to Brodie than to his mother, especially given his carefree lifestyle. Brodie probably had many late nights out, and she imagined when he was home early, he had a woman with him. "It's nice that you and your mother are so close."

"She's my mom," he said, as if that explained it.

Mary, better than most, knew motherhood didn't bring any guarantees.

The rain started, hitting the windshield in a steadily growing downfall until the wipers worked overtime. Brodie turned on the defroster and slowed to a near crawl on the rain-washed streets.

"Is your mom big like you?"

He snorted. "She's probably only a couple inches taller than you. Jack and I were towering over her by middle school." He pulled up to a stop sign at a busy four-way intersection. "Mom claims she'll never marry again, and since she won't even date, I believe her. Charlotte's twenty-five now, so who knows how much longer she'll be content to live there." He frowned. "Charlotte's a looker, damn it, smart, too. Some clown is bound to win her over sooner or later and then Mom will be alone. The idea bothers me."

It would've been easier, Mary thought, if she could hang on to her initial assessment of Brodie as an indulgent, heavy-drinking, irresponsible runaround—but she couldn't. Each trip she shared with him chipped away at her misconceptions and reinforced that he was a responsible—although outrageous—man dedicated to his family. The love he felt for his mother was as obvious as his strength, and it made her yearn for someone she could love that much.

Foolish dreams.

She'd level those dreams eventually. It was pure irony that while Brodie would eventually build his house, Mary wanted to demolish hers.

As he pulled forward, he said, "If Mom knew I was saying

any of this to you, she'd smack me. She hates to be perceived as weak in any way." He twisted his mouth to the side, then teased, "Reminds me of someone else I know."

She ignored that to ask, "What kind of house will you build?"

"I've got a few designs in mind. I'm mostly concentrating on the yard, though. I'd put in a track for test-driving the cars I've rebuilt, and maybe a big garage for working on Matilda."

Mary rolled her eyes at the continued use of a name for his Mustang. "You and that car."

"Hey, we've been together a long time." He laughed, and the remainder of the tension seeped out of his big muscled frame. "Dad got me the car when I was twenty-one. That's his shtick, ya know? He showed up with a gift for my eighteenth birthday, even though it was months after I'd turned twenty-one."

"That's..." *Terrible.* "A little late."

"A little." He shook his head as if amused by it. "He did the same for Jack, only Jack was twenty-four when he got the car."

"Had he really lost track of your age?"

"I doubt he ever knew it, so how could he lose it?" Tapping his fingers on the steering wheel, he added, "When I was eight, he gave me a BB gun. Mom had a conniption, saying I was way too young, and come to find out, Dad thought I was twelve."

Mary stared. "He made a four-year error?"

"Mom was ready to explode. She was so pissed, but she always managed to keep it together around us." He laughed as if his father's disinterest was funny. "She put the gun away and I didn't get it until years later, and then only after she'd taught me to shoot it and lectured me endlessly on being safe. After that, every week or so, she'd take Jack and me out to this big target she built and she'd sit with us while we shot cans."

Brodie made it all sound nice, idyllic even, as if having an awful absentee father was a lark.

She wished she could look at it the same way.

Was her absentee father a nice man? More likely not.

"Now, Red," he said, switching up her name again. "Don't act like it's a big deal. Jack and I were used to Dad missing birthdays and every other holiday. Mom more than made up for it. When Dad did show up, she encouraged us to enjoy the time with him. She said that Dad's life wasn't great and he came around when he needed us."

"Your mother must be a saint."

His mouth twisted in wry humor. "Meet her before you make that judgment. On any given day you're liable to see her giving Jack or me hell."

"But not your father?"

"Guess she considers Dad a lost cause. God, I used to feel so sorry for him. It was easy to see that Mom was right, that he had missed out on so much and that he was always… I dunno, chasing something he couldn't get. Like lost youth. Lost opportunities." He glanced at her. "Family."

"He has family." She felt angered on Brodie and Jack's behalf. No parent should ignore children, walking away without knowing if they were cared for.

Or if they were loved.

Her hands tightened.

Brodie shook his head. "We're strangers he occasionally visits when he starts to think about how alone he is. It lasts a week or so, sometimes a month." As if it really didn't bother him, his voice stayed neutral—he could have been reciting the weather. "Once he hung around for a whole summer. In the end he always finds some young thing to boost his ego and he's off again. His relationships never last, not with the ladies, and not with us."

"But he must love you," she protested. He hadn't left them completely.

Brodie grunted. "He doesn't know my middle name, hon. He doesn't know my birthday." His mouth quirked, not with hurt but with irony. "He has no idea what interests I have other than cars. He wasn't there to see any music programs in grade school, or when our football team won the championship, or when I went to state for wrestling." He flashed her a small smile. "That was all Mom."

Tentatively, she asked, "Do you love him?"

"Sure, but only because Mom taught us to accept him, faults and all, and not to expect more than he could give. She used to say asking Dad to be an attentive father was like asking a cat to fly. No matter what you said or did, it wasn't going to happen."

Was that true for her mother as well? Had she expected things that the woman couldn't give? No. It was different, because while Brodie had a mother to make up the difference…she'd had no one at all.

Before her thoughts got too heavy, she shifted to face him, one leg drawn up in the seat, and asked, "What is your middle name?"

"Now, Red," he murmured. "One kiss doesn't give you the privilege of knowing that."

She drew back, surprised that he'd bring it up after everything else they'd discussed.

He continued as if he hadn't taken her by surprise. "Give me a second kiss, a *real* kiss, and I just might spill my guts." His searing gaze cut her way, but only for a second. "You can let me know when the curiosity gets the better of you, okay? Until then, I won't pressure you."

So it was all up to her? She had to initiate things? A little stunned, Mary sat there, wondering if she dared, imagining how that second kiss might be…

"What's good for the goose is good for the gander, right?"

That statement intruded on her imagination. "What?"

"All your questions have me feeling nosy, too," he explained. "Tell me, where do you live? Instead of you driving to the office every time, it might be easier, and quicker, for me to pick you up."

She mentally scrambled, trying to think up an excuse not to tell him. Nothing came to mind.

"I won't drop in uninvited, if that's what you're worried about."

No, she wasn't. What did worry her was the idea that if Brodie picked her up, he'd also have to drop her off. Thinking the things she was thinking right now, having her apartment, and a bedroom, right at hand might be far too dangerous.

"Relax, Mary." He glanced in the rearview mirror before turning down a narrow gravel road. "I don't want you to break anything with all that heavy thinking, so forget I asked."

There were very few houses around and those she did see were set way back, often behind large, mature trees. "Is someone following us?" She looked over her shoulder to peer out the rear window, and saw only the long stretch of road, barely visible through the rain. Had she missed something?

"Nope."

"But you checked the mirror."

"Just making sure, since we're getting pretty far off the beaten path." He leaned forward to check the address on a crooked mailbox they passed. "What kind of driver would I be if I didn't keep checking?"

She sighed. Now he sounded insulted, maybe even hurt, and that bothered her. He'd been so open, chatting easily about his life. Was it fair for her to deny him everything?

Decision made, she admitted, "My apartment is about a half an hour away from Therman. It seemed like a good idea to be near to him since he often hires drivers within the area."

"Makes sense. Being near to him means being near the drivers."

"Usually." With Brodie, she had to concede, "You're farther out than most." The problem wasn't so much the distance, but that much of the driving was rural, in and around the small town. That added time spent in her car, but it wasn't a big deal.

"Your address?"

She saw no reason not to tell him. It'd still be up to her whether they met at the office or at her apartment. She recited the street address, and since he couldn't write it down, she figured he might not even remember.

He nodded with satisfaction, saying, "Thanks."

Mary had the odd feeling that he'd just committed it to memory.

The houses eventually disappeared and the gravel road became bumpier with puddle-filled holes. Weeds and scrub bushes grew along the sides, nearly hiding a ditch.

She checked the directions, but Brodie hadn't erred.

"This is getting weird," he said.

Mary agreed.

A few minutes later they reached the designated address, not on a mailbox but rather on a wooden marker. Buried in a heavily wooded lot with no discernible driveway was a cabin. Beyond that, she could barely make out the shoreline of a large lake.

With the car still idling, Brodie stared toward the rustic little shack and scowled. "I don't like it, Red."

No, she didn't, either.

"I'm not buying that anyone lives here."

No reason he should. "Therman mentioned that we'd be meeting at a neutral location, I just didn't expect…" *This.* She definitely hadn't expected this.

The thick cluster of trees combined with the cloudy sky cast the area with ominous shadows.

Brodie turned an incredulous look on her. "Who the hell meets in the woods?"

Pretending nonchalance, she shrugged. "Some sellers don't want their locations known."

"Thieves, you mean. People who are selling stolen goods."

He could be right, but she said only, "I seriously doubt that's the case, but it's Therman's business, not mine and not yours."

Brodie had gotten into the habit of standing beside the car with Howler, keeping watch as she did the exchanges. He was always near enough to intercede if necessary, but not since that first day had he imposed by coming closer.

There'd been no reason.

Today felt different. The entire scene sent a warning screaming along her nerve endings. Seeing the cautious way Brodie surveyed the area, she knew his instincts were sparking as well.

Mary had to remind herself that this was her job, that she'd handled other seemingly treacherous exchanges with no issue at all. Past experience, combined with current weather conditions, made up her mind: there was really no reason for them all to get soaked.

Shoring up her determination, she turned to Brodie. Over the seat, the dog watched her, ears perked up, expression vigilant.

"I won't be long." She idly patted the dog's neck to reassure him, but the muscles straining there told her she failed. "Why don't you and Howler just watch from the car? No reason for all of us to get muddy." She waited to see how he'd react to that.

Brodie gave her a long, telling look and without a word he turned off the car, opened the door and stepped out.

Impossibly stubborn! But…a small part of her was relieved. Since she had a bad feeling about things, it'd be nice to know Brodie was close.

Getting out, too, Mary immediately opened her umbrella. "Suit yourself," she said over the sound of low rumbling thunder.

"Plan to," he replied. Howler jumped out and immediately splashed into a puddle.

Shaking her head, she gave a last cautious look at that decrepit little building and started forward.

To his credit, Brodie stayed back a discreet distance while Howler lifted a long gangly leg near a tree.

Mary picked her way forward, twice getting her umbrella

snagged on limbs, once catching the toe of her sandal in a tangled root. Though she pitched forward, she managed to stay upright.

Aware of Brodie's gaze boring into her back, she straightened her shirt and continued on.

Right before she reached the door she heard a motor start. It seemed to come from the lake, probably a boat motor, and just knowing others were near helped to settle her worry. Standing to the side of the entryway, away from a thatch of prickly weeds, she knocked on the rough-hewn door and waited.

With an eerie screech of rusted hinges, it opened.

A short, heavy man, his eyes nearly hidden beneath a hat pulled low, looked her over and then searched behind her. "You got the money?"

Dark patchy whiskers covered his loose jowls, double chin and thick upper lip. He appeared oily, as if he hadn't bathed recently—but then, wearing a hat plus a long-sleeved dark shirt with jeans on such a hot, humid day could explain the sheen of perspiration layered on his exposed skin.

Despite his lack of courtesy, Mary spoke with an air of cool command. "Yes, of course. Do you have the item?"

"Money first."

Wearing the strap of her briefcase over her shoulder, Mary laced her fingers together and rested them over her stomach. "I'm afraid not."

He looked beyond her again, and she wondered if he saw Brodie and Howler. Neither man nor beast made a sound, but of course they were near.

If not, she'd have felt even more vulnerable.

Grumbling under his breath, the man stepped back and snagged a plastic bag from behind the door. "Got it right here."

A garbage bag, crudely held, did not ensure a fair exchange. "I need to see that it's authentic."

His jaw worked in defiance, but she held his gaze without flinching and finally he handed it over.

"Thank you." Juggling her umbrella and briefcase, she opened the heavy bag and found a boot box, which she withdrew. She peeked inside and saw glints of gold beneath a few papers.

"If you wouldn't mind?" She attempted to hand him her umbrella, and when he acted put out by her request, she explained, "If the documentation gets wet, it could be impossible to read, and we might not have a deal."

Eyes narrowed, he jerked the umbrella from her hand and stuck it into the air over her head. The movement brought him nearer, allowing Mary to see beyond him, where she noticed that a back door stood open.

Those warning bells blared a little louder.

She glanced over her shoulder and saw only thick trees, swaying with the furious weather.

Brodie wouldn't be far away—unless this was an ambush and someone had already gotten to him?

Her heart shot into her throat with that thought. *Dear God, what if she'd led him into—*

Suddenly the man tossed aside the umbrella. Startled, she saw the wind carry it away while a deluge of rain immediately soaked her.

"What—" she started, but his hard hands grabbed at her, throwing her off balance as he wrestled away the boot box while also yanking at her briefcase strap.

Instinctively, she tried to hold on but, with a gasp, she lost her footing and flailed, her feet sliding out from under her on the slick ground. Arms out to catch herself, she landed with a hard splash. Something sharp dug into her hip and her right forearm connected with a very prickly weed.

Shock kept her immobile for a heartbeat. She got her wits together just in time to see the man fleeing out the back door.

He had everything!

Mary scrambled upright and into the cabin. Not to give chase, really, but again, she seemed to be on autopilot, just *doing* without thinking it through.

The man was already away from the cabin, running hell-bent through the storm toward the lakeshore where a small boat waited.

The motor she'd heard.

Suddenly Howler was there, nearly airborne as he launched at the man, teeth bared and back bristling. Mary covered her mouth, watching in horror as Howler brought him down.

Screaming, the man released both her briefcase and the package as he tried to free himself. He swung at the dog, kicked and thrashed.

Howler didn't let go.

And then Brodie was there, silently fierce as he tossed aside her case, putting it out of the reach of the struggle. He grabbed the man by the front of his shirt and half hauled him to his feet.

The dog had just released the man, apparently confident that Brodie had it under control, when a gun blast echoed over the lake and mud sprayed up right before them. Howler yelped and jumped back, only to plunge forward again in renewed rage.

Mary spotted the second man standing in the boat, a gun held at the end of his straightened arm.

Her heart leaped into her throat. "Gun!" She stepped out into the rain, waving her arms to get Brodie's attention. "He has a *gun*!" She wasn't sure if anyone heard her over the ferocity of the storm and Howler's savage barking, but then Brodie scowled in her direction.

"Get inside, damn it!" He managed to hold on to the man until another blast echoed over the lake.

Brodie dove to cover Howler, holding on to him so he couldn't attack again.

Mary wasn't sure where the bullet went, but the man reached for the bag.

Brodie lunged over Howler, getting hold of it first, then caught

Howler with his other hand when the dog would have attacked again. For a single moment, he was sprawled out, both hands full as Howler dragged him a foot. Yet another shot sounded, and Brodie quickly shifted, wrapping himself around the dog, shielding him with his own body.

He didn't let go of the bag.

Good Lord, did he really think she cared about that right now?

She was about to order him to leave it when the man half scrambled, half slid the rest of the way to the shore, high-stepped into the water and dove headfirst into the bow of the small fishing boat. The guy with the gun adjusted the motor until the boat turned away. Just as easily, they disappeared into the storm.

For a second, Mary felt glued to the spot, dizzy with adrenaline, her lungs burning, her hands pressed to her mouth.

Hysteria threatened, but she fought it back and tried to get her bearings. "Brodie?"

The howling wind stole her whisper. She swallowed and tried again, saying louder, "Brodie!"

Howler struggled to be free, yet Brodie stayed locked around him, still, so very still…

Mary ran. She tripped and fell twice, once getting a mouthful of mud and fallen pine needles, but she didn't care.

Just as she reached him, Brodie rolled to his back. Blood showed on his forehead, running into his left eye.

"Oh my God." She dropped to her knees, uncaring of the sodden ground beneath her or the rain that plastered her clothes to her body. Howler snuffled against Brodie.

"Fuck."

Well. At least he didn't sound faint.

She shoved back her fallen hair, trying to see better through the rain. "Where are you hurt?" Hands shaking, she touched his face, over his nose, his cheekbone to his ear and up to his temple, searching for the source of the blood. Rain spiked his thick lashes and made the blood and mud trickle together.

"Fuck," he said again, this time with disgust but less heat as he shrugged her away. "I'm fine, Red. Quit fussing."

"You're *bleeding*," she said, feeling awfully close to tears.

"I hit my head when I covered Howler. It's nothing." He laughed—actually laughed—when he realized the big dog was trying to get on top of him. "Hey," he said in a gentle voice, "I'm all right, buddy, I promise."

Mary sat back while he took time to reassure *the dog*. He gathered Howler close and stroked him, even hugged him a little.

She didn't mean to, but the sob welled up and there was no containing it.

Mortification scalded her with the realization that she was jealous of a sweet animal. Shooting to her feet, she tried to make a hasty escape, but Brodie snatched her hand and he wouldn't let go, no matter how desperately she tried to tug free.

"Mary." Keeping her hand trapped in his, he stood up behind her.

"We're in the rain!" And that wasn't the point at all, but she didn't care.

"I noticed. Not like we're going to get any wetter." He let her go, but only to wrap both arms around her in a hug that pulled her back to his chest. Near her ear, he said, "I'm always a dick when I'm frustrated." The teasing words were a direct contrast to his comforting hold. "It's just reaction, and reaction is okay."

She stiffened, both at his gentleness and her own reactions. Wanting to lean on him, but afraid to give in to such an alien sensation, she settled on anger instead. "It's okay for you to be a dick?"

"Temporarily, yeah." Then with added meaning, he said, "Just as it's okay for you to get upset and cry a little."

"I'm not!" Crying was the most useless thing in the world.

"Everyone deals in their own way."

Now he wanted to reassure her?

She dashed her hands over her cheeks and nodded. It seemed the expedient thing to do. "We need to get out of this weather."

He kissed her ear. "Don't move." He gathered up the bag and her briefcase, then caught her hand again and called to Howler, who followed. Brodie's urgent pace kept her slipping, but he didn't let her fall again.

At his car, she balked. "I'm layered in mud."

"We all are, but we seriously can't stay here. If the bastards come back, maybe with reinforcements, I want to be long gone."

Very true. Nodding, she got in, arms folded around herself in a sudden chill, while he stuffed the bag and briefcase on the floor near her feet.

He didn't strap Howler in, choosing haste over safety, and before long they were driving back onto the main road. No one spoke. Even the dog stayed silent.

Twenty minutes more and he pulled into a gas station near a busier drag. With the car idling, he sat there, hands clasped on the wheel, muscles in his jaw knotting.

Mary knew she was a hideous mess, her hair more down than up, her makeup smudged with mud, her clothes ruined. She couldn't find a reason to care.

He could have died.

She closed her eyes and gulped air.

She heard the seats squeak and suddenly his mouth was on hers, warm and firm.

It wasn't a gentle kiss this time. He didn't test her response and ease into things.

No, he opened his mouth over hers, moving, taking...and giving.

How such a thing could happen, she didn't know, but she clutched at the wet material of his shirt, fear and adrenaline coalescing into red-hot, unfamiliar need.

CHAPTER EIGHT

It surprised Brodie when her mouth opened under the urging of his, when her tongue teased across his lips. He angled his head, accepting her participation with a sweep of his own tongue. Jesus, she tasted good, felt right.

Mary.

He tunneled the fingers of his left hand into the wet ropes of her hair, holding her close, tipping her head one way while he went the other so that their mouths fused perfectly for the kiss to go wild.

She was with him every step, just as hungry, just as lost to the moment.

"Mary," he murmured, putting his open mouth to her throat, sucking, biting a little on his way to her shoulder. Her skin was soft and sleek. He wanted to eat up every part of her.

He heard her gasping and lowered his hand to her breast.

Oh, fucking-A.

She was every bit as full and heavy as he'd known she'd be, her nipple already pointed tight, her wet shirt and bra clinging to every curve. He flicked with his thumb and she arched into him.

If it wasn't for her shivering, he couldn't say what he might have done. But she did shiver, either in excitement or from their ordeal, he couldn't know, but it brought reality crashing back down on him.

They were in the parking lot of a gas station and she'd just been attacked. *What the hell was he thinking?*

Breathing hard, he eased his hand away.

Her eyes opened, the surrounding smudged mascara making the blue impossibly brighter. Color rose high in her face and her slender fingers kneaded his chest.

"Brodie?" she whispered.

"Shh." He covered her hand with his own and lightly kissed her bottom lip, now wet and swollen, then the corner of her sweet mouth. She drew a shuddering breath, and that, just that, was damn near enough to make him lose his head again. "Any other time, Red, and I'd be so ready..."

Hell, he was ready now. Insane, but his cock had stirred the second she'd accepted his kiss and now he was full-blown hard and aching.

"Your head," she whispered, almost like she'd just awakened. Then stronger, "Damn it, your poor *head*."

"It's on my shoulders," he teased, but yeah, now that she'd mentioned it, he felt the pain.

Mary dug several tissues from her purse and knelt on the seat to dab at it. "It's stopped bleeding, but you have a cut."

The position put her boobs right there by his face and that was one temptation he didn't need, not while he was trying to do the right thing.

"I think I hit a rock when I dove to cover Howler."

At the mention of his name, the dog whined.

Brodie glanced back and Howler jumped on the attention, his butt wiggling with the wild wagging of his tail, ears down as he hung his head over the seat, snuffling and licking everything in reach.

Brodie laughed. "You held all that in while I was inappropriately coming on to Red, didn't you, boy? I appreciate the consideration, I really do."

Mary, he realized, was uncommonly silent.

He took the tissues from her, waiting until she'd reseated herself, then he twisted to stroke the dog. "Such a good boy. So fast. You were protecting us, weren't you, bud? That's my good boy."

Mary gawked at him, either because of what they'd just gone through, or because he'd used that silly baby talk on Howler again. The dog liked it. He had his eyes closed, his large head tilted up as if in pleasure at the praise.

"You need to go to a hospital."

"Hell no." Brodie pressed the tissues to the cut and pulled out his cell phone. With a quick search he found the nearest motel that accepted pets. It sounded like a dive, but if it had a shower—and hopefully a laundry—it'd do.

Her somber eyes studied him. "What are you doing?"

"We have to wash up and change and regroup. All that shit."

She nibbled her bottom lip, making him even more nuts, then suggested, "You could do that at a hospital—"

"No hospital, hon. I swear it's not necessary. Charlotte has knocked me around worse than this."

"That's nonsense."

"Only a slight exaggeration, I swear." Blood matted his hair and mud kept his clothes stuck to him. Why the hell had he jumped on Red? She had to be shaken, and the last thing she'd want was a make-out session with him.

The way she'd kissed him back, though…

"We do need to clean up." She touched her hair, then dropped her hand. "I'm wrecked."

"You're gorgeous, but yeah, the motel will be welcome." He tucked one long hank of hair behind her ear. "Okay?"

She nodded her agreement. "I have to update Therman."

"Yeah," Brodie growled, anger rising up again. "And when you're done, I have a few things to say to him, too."

Her eyes widened.

It should have been comical. After all, her gorgeous red hair hung in thick wet ropes around her face and shoulders, not really down, not really up, and she had equal parts mud and ruined makeup on her face.

Instead, she looked adorable.

When he started thinking *adorable* was so fucking hot, he couldn't say, but—

"Oh… Brodie, you can't."

He'd gotten so absorbed in looking at her that it took him a second to figure out what she meant. "Wanna bet?" He'd talk to Therman and he'd make a few things crystal clear.

Like the fact that he'd never again put Mary at risk.

She licked her bottom lip. "Talking to Therman is my job, and my job only."

He put the car in gear and, thankful no one was out and about in the rain to have noticed them, drove in the direction of the motel.

"Brodie," she said, her voice small, "I want you to remain the driver."

So she was worried that he'd get fired? Or did she think she'd never see him again if Therman canned him? Whichever, he reassured her with, "You won't be rid of me anytime soon."

She touched his arm. "You don't understand. No matter how much he likes you, you can't dictate to Therman."

"Credit me with a little sense, Red, okay? I won't raise holy hell, you have my word."

While she considered his words, her hand remained on him.

He liked that small contact.

More contact would be even better. Naked contact. Full-body naked contact.

"All right," she said. "If you promise to be circumspect."

Circumspect. She could've been killed and that was what she was worried about?

Yeah, he knew he was still being a dick, but damn. Did she expect him to just let that whole shit storm fly without voicing a single objection? He avoided making any promises by saying, "There's no way Therman thought that setup was legit."

"You don't know that for sure."

Yes, he did, but he kept quiet rather than piss her off. She'd been through enough without him adding to it.

The motel sat near the road so there was no way to miss it. Old-fashioned, with a rickety balcony that circled a second floor and a chipped, kidney-shaped in-ground pool off to the side. It appeared disreputable enough that no one would blink when he walked in looking like he'd just lost a mud-wrestling contest.

He pulled up by the door. "Stay here with the dog while I get us checked in."

"I should do it." She lifted her briefcase off the floor and opened the sturdy latch. "I have a business card for expenditures like this and—"

Brodie leaned over, caught and lifted her chin, then put his mouth to hers. He concentrated on keeping this kiss light and easy.

He was not a damned marauder. He wouldn't pressure her or take advantage of her upset.

Going instantly still, she leaned toward him, her soft lips slightly parted. He couldn't resist one small taste, teasing his tongue over her plump bottom lip.

She made a low sound of hunger, nearly devastating his intentions.

He couldn't think of any other woman who tempted him as she did. Disgusted with his lack of control, he pulled back. They stared at each other, but for the life of him, he couldn't read her expression.

Finally he exhaled a deep breath. "Think you could give me a break, Red, and just this once not argue with me?"

Her attention went to the cut on his head and her gaze softened. "All right. But I'll see that you're reimbursed."

Ignoring that, he turned to Howler. "Stay. I'll be right back."

Before Howler could test that order by crawling over the seat, Brodie stepped out and closed the door. Through the window, he told Mary, "Lock it."

Looking around nervously, as if the thought of a continued threat hadn't occurred to her, she did as he asked, then leaned nearer to Howler.

The fact that she was still so nervous ramped up his anger. Eventually, someone would pay for upsetting her. He'd see to it.

One way or another.

"So let me get this straight." Helton Reinhold's chair squeaked as he swiveled to face the two idiots standing in his office. Controlling his rage wasn't easy. Hell, nothing was easy anymore. Not since he'd gotten stuck in a fancy office wearing tailored suits, forced to temper his reactions.

He'd enjoyed life as a thug so much more.

As the prodigal son dragged back home, he had more money, but then, he'd already had money—money he'd fucking well earned with his fists.

He had added prestige, too, but it came with choking responsibilities he didn't want.

And the fucking expectations? He sure as hell hadn't asked to inherit those.

This new life was a challenge in so many ways.

Like he couldn't just dismember the bastards standing before him, expedient as that might be. Others in the office would hear the destruction and then he'd have to pay someone to clean up the mess.

No, as his deceased father's representative, it'd be better to practice keeping his cool and deal with them as any good boss would.

At least for now.

So he steepled his fingers and looked at them from under his brows. "You lost everything."

Both men stared at him. It was Lem who located his balls and replied, "They already knew our faces, so we had to hire it out."

"A royal ass fucking," Helton said as if Lem hadn't spoken. "Not only did you fail to get the payment, you lost my prize. A damned valuable prize at that." Not one he particularly cared about. Not one crucial to his departed father's legacy. Still…

He pushed out of his seat, his suit jacket open over his massive chest. Knowing it'd look evil, he smiled. "But hey, you two are here, none the worse for your failure, I see."

Lem Keller had a few more smarts than Todd Lutz, proved by the way he kept quiet and took the verbal battering.

Todd, the fool, launched into explanations. "We weren't there, Mr. Reinhold. We figured since they already knew our faces—"

"Shut up, Todd," Lem suggested, low.

Todd didn't listen. "—it'd go smoother with someone else running point—"

Helton buried his fist in Todd's stomach. It felt good, so good. Forbidden fruit that he craved day and night.

Todd, the lightweight, doubled over, gagging.

Now that he'd gotten that off his chest, Helton drew a cleansing breath. He even patted Todd's back in sympathy.

Gut punches were a motherfucker. They got a man's attention without leaving blood everywhere.

But given how Todd carried on… Helton frowned. "You puke on my floors and I'll break your neck." Yeah, he knew his punches carried an impact. Before being forced into legit business, he'd been known for cracking ribs and rupturing spleens. "I didn't hit you that hard." At least, he didn't think he had.

Sometimes he didn't know his own strength. He had hands like concrete blocks that had served him well as he'd held his own on the street.

That was before his dad had died, leaving Helton his fucking *collection*. So much time and energy put into amassing bullshit. He didn't get it, but it had sentimental value.

He grinned at the irony.

Addressing Lem—who looked wary, rightfully so—Helton asked, "You don't know for sure that they failed, do you? You're only taking their word for it?"

"Yes, sir."

"You can find them again?"

Lem's expression darkened, reminding Helton why he'd brought him on board in the first place. Lem and Todd had the successful, slick look that would forever elude Helton, but they were both deadly pricks, willing to do whatever he asked for the right price.

"I'm meeting them in a few hours. They'll be there because they think they're getting paid."

"I want them dead."

"Consider it done."

Helton cast a look at Todd. He'd finally straightened, one arm around his middle, his face pale, his expression downcast.

"Don't cower, goddamn it. It disgusts me."

Todd's chin came up.

Hell of an invitation, but he'd abused Todd enough for now. Helton walked around the desk back to his chair and seated himself with a big sigh.

"The point of this whole exercise, besides keeping the prize and the payment, was to get familiar with the driver, see if he can be bought, if we can—" he tapped his fingers together "—*persuade* him to cooperate with us when needed."

On his end, Helton was taking care of things, dealing with the other players. Unfortunately, much as he loved it, the physical grunt work was now out of his realm.

"Eventually that last piece will be offered. The best way to ensure I get to it first is to know how Therman's driver reacts, his habits, his—"

"He likes the woman."

Helton looked at Todd, one bushy brow raised in an expression he knew prompted fast explanations. There were a few things, after all, that had carried over from his previous life.

Like a puppy anxious for a pat, Todd said, "The bitch that works for Therman Ritter."

"Mary Daniels?" Helton didn't consider her a bitch. Not at all.

A worthy adversary, yes. A complication, occasionally.

A fucking mystery, definitely. He was still working on uncovering all of Mary Daniels's secrets. Eventually he'd have her figured out.

Until then, she intrigued him. "Is that so?" Helton asked with narrowed eyes. He had very few scruples but mistreating women, verbally or otherwise, topped his list. In his mind, real men pampered women, all women. Hell, whores, junkies and hookers had practically raised him when his dad had been too busy building his legacy to bother.

They'd all been gentle...when compared to his father.

"He's right," Lem said. "*Ms. Daniels* has the driver's attention for sure. He was ready to provoke a fight, but she defused it easily enough."

Todd, having caught on to the emphasis Lem put on the lady's name, cleared his throat and added, "Ms. Daniels walked up and the driver could barely take his eyes off her. I got the feeling he was possessive."

Possessive men were easily controlled. It was one reason Helton had never gotten that involved. "So maybe we can use her, but first you'll have to find out everything you can about the driver. You know where he works. Go there and dig into his files." He leveled a look on them both. "But don't get caught. I won't tolerate another miscalculation." *What a pansied way to describe how badly they'd screwed up.* "You won't like the consequences."

"No, sir." Lem recognized the dismissal, turning and nudging Todd toward the door.

Helton sat back in his seat, his size and weight making it creak. Unlike his dad, he hated wearing a tie. It strangled him, reminding him of everything he'd lost when he was called to his father's deathbed.

The Oscar had been a bit piece in his father's collection, a random addition and only valuable off the grid—except as bait. Selling the awards was frowned upon. The Academy expected to reacquire them for pennies. Officious asses.

It had been a gamble offering it up anonymously, using it as bait to see how far Therman would go to get what he wanted.

Now he knew.

Therman would throw ethics out the window, he'd race across the line, and he'd risk those in his employ.

It was something they had in common.

If only his lackeys hadn't bumbled the exchange. Now he had no money to show for it, and Therman would be crowing to the online crowd about his fucking prowess. That could set him back, but not for long.

More than the other collectors, Helton despised Therman Ritter. The man was everything Helton would never be: a perfect fit for wealth, accepting it as his due, living with ease within its cage.

He cracked his knuckles. Unlike Therman, he was an assassin, born and raised. He had respect because he demanded it. Even without his father's accounts, he'd amassed wealth because he took it. His powerful influence had nothing to do with social standing and everything to do with the ability to back up his wishes with physical might.

To others looking on, he had it all, yet every day he fought the urge to break free, to return to the comfort of the street.

He understood the rules there, how to survive, how to profit. There, he'd been a happy king in a comfortable castle.

Here, in a posh office and in the gift of his father's enormous house, he was no more than an impostor.

The car rental empire that his father had built with blood, sweat and determination felt like an ever-tightening leash around Helton's neck.

For his father, he suffered it, all of it.

For the same reason he added to that damned collection, fulfilling his father's last request.

Sentiment.

What a damned stupid thing for an angry ape like him to feel. Absurd. Fucking nonsense.

And so goddamned unavoidable.

If all else failed, he'd use Mary to get what he needed, but he'd handle it himself to ensure she wasn't hurt.

Until then, all he could do was wait.

And hope he got to the prize before Therman.

Brodie watched her remove her sandals at the door and step inside, her gaze sweeping around at the room, pausing on the full-size bed, an old TV on a dresser, a chair by the window.

She slipped the strap of her briefcase off her shoulder and carried it across the room to the other side of the bed. Even bedraggled, she walked with her back straight, her chin up.

Admiration edged in with the other turbulent emotions he couldn't quite subdue.

Brodie carried her overnight case and the plastic bag that held God-knew-what. He kicked the door shut, then realized Howler was about to jump up on the bed.

"No, you don't." He dropped Mary's things and caught the dog by the collar. "Bath first, bud."

At that, Howler started jumping around in glee.

"I take it he likes his baths?"

"Loves 'em." Brodie found himself in a quandary. "I should offer to let you shower first, but—"

"Howler needs to get clean or we'll be paying damages for this room." She smiled at the dog. "And I know not to sit on the bed until I've washed away the mud."

"Thanks for understanding." He stepped into the bathroom, saw a tub with a plastic curtain and turned on the water. Before it had even gotten warm, Howler was in the tub, sprawled out and enjoying the spray. "You were just in the rain. How is this so much better?"

Howler groaned and rolled to his back, his junk rudely on display.

Shaking his head, Brodie stepped out and found Mary standing at the window, cheap curtain pulled aside so she could look out.

They were on the second floor facing the back lot. Not much to see.

After ensuring the door was locked, he strode over to her. "You'll stay put?"

"Where would I go? The choices are slim."

"Just as well, since I want to know you're inside." Not touching her was hard, but if he started that, neither of them would get a shower. "I'll be quick."

At that she turned. "Quick at what?"

"My shower."

"I thought you were washing the dog."

"I am." The way she looked up at him stirred every primitive instinct known to man. He liked it that she didn't fuss about being a mess, didn't try to hide or repair the irreparable. "Showering with him is the easiest way to get him clean." Instincts won out, and he bent to kiss the tip of her nose, one rounded cheekbone, then the corner of her mouth. "Be right back."

"Be sure to wash that cut on your head, please."

"Yes, ma'am." After putting his phone and wallet on the

dresser, Brodie stepped into the bathroom and pushed the door until it was almost closed, but not quite. He wanted to be able to hear her if she started chatting with Therman.

He stripped off his dirty clothes, dropping them into a pile, then pushed back the curtain again. Howler still sprawled, but Brodie got him to move back enough that he could wash himself. As Mary had requested, he gingerly soaped the cut on his head. It was sore, but not too bad. He'd had enough injuries in his lifetime to know it wasn't a big deal.

When he finished, he worked on Howler. "Regular shampoo for you, bud, but just this once."

It was a good twenty minutes before he had a towel wrapped around his hips and Howler was as dry as he could get him. Luckily there were plenty of towels to go around.

Steam followed him out of the bathroom. As he knelt to put a towel on the floor for the dog, he said, "Let me rinse the dog hair out of the tub and you can have a turn."

Silence.

He glanced up—and found Mary devouring him with her gaze, one hand splayed over her chest.

Damn, her interest threw gasoline on the fire he tried to keep banked. "Don't look at me like that, Red, or this towel won't cut it."

"It's barely covering you anyway." Those blue eyes focused on his stomach, traveling down to where the towel would soon be tented, then to his thighs and very slowly up again to his chest. Her breath sighed out and she whispered, "You're lethal."

Brodie gave a final pat to Howler, who flopped back on the towel in exhaustion, and then he straightened. "Keep staring and you're not going to get a shower."

The warning jarred her out of her preoccupation. "Tempting, but I'm miserably dirty and such a wreck that getting clean takes precedence. But before I do that..." She lifted a small first-aid kit.

"What's that?"

"I'm going to bandage your head."

Mothering was not what he wanted from her. "It's fine."

"Still." Wearing a stern look, she came over to him. "Bend down a little."

He obliged, leaning close to her.

She smoothed back his damp hair. "It's bruising. Thank God it wasn't worse than it is." After opening a small tube of ointment, she dabbed it on his head with a swab, then applied a butterfly bandage, gently smoothing it into place.

With her brows together in concentration, she looked so serious that he had to fight the urge to kiss her.

Her gaze met his and the air seemed to go still. They were close, and he wore only a towel.

"There." Flustered, she stepped back. "Painless, right?" Without waiting for a reply, she hurried away from him to throw away the swab and return the kit to her overnight case. She closed it up and, holding it, headed for the john.

Brodie moved to slightly block her path. "Did you talk to Therman?"

"I texted him the details. That's his preferred method for updates."

"And?"

Her smile was tight. "I haven't heard back yet."

No shit? Seems like Therman would have replied right away after finding out they'd been set up. "Does that surprise you?"

"No."

"Then why do you look so pinched?"

Her mouth flattened. "I'm trying not to ogle you." She pushed past him and went into the bathroom, closing the door firmly behind her. He even heard the lock click.

"No faith, Red," he called out, pleased that she'd admitted, more or less, to the sexual tension.

"Right now," she said through the door, "I don't trust either of us."

He grinned, until the vision of her buck naked in the shower, her hair down, crowded into his beleaguered brain. What he wouldn't give to join her…

She hadn't invited him, though, so he'd man up and keep it together—which basically meant not getting a boner.

He stared at the towel and silently ordered his dick to behave.

Soon as he heard the water start, he went to the old handheld phone and dialed the front desk. Luckily, they did have someone who brought up a fresh pot of coffee and creamer, and left with Brodie's clothes, promising to have them back in ninety minutes or so. He wasn't in a rush, so that worked for him. He tipped the maid well and looked around the room.

Howler was snoring, and knowing women, Mary would be in there for a while yet, so he dropped onto the bed and went through TV channels until he found an old movie that might, barely, distract him from thoughts of Mary soaping up.

The coffee was good, and he'd finished off a cup when he heard a buzzing.

Sitting up, he listened and realized it was coming from the other nightstand—where Mary had left her phone.

Bingo.

Without any hesitation at all, he rolled to the side and snatched it up.

He answered with a gleeful, "Therman."

After a pause, he heard "Brodie? Where's Mary?"

"In the shower." Brodie sat on the side of the bed and stared out the window while he ordered his thoughts.

"In the…"

"Yeah, see, we had an ordeal." To put it mildly. "After being attacked, she's covered in mud."

"She told me. Is she okay?"

"Depends on your definition, right? Was she thrown around

by those assholes? Yes, she was. Did she fall into the mud more than once? Yup. Did some fucking lunatic shoot at her? That happened, too."

"She told me the shots were aimed at you."

And that made it better? "In the storm it's impossible to know." His words came out in a snarl. "Shots were fired. She wasn't that far from me." Renewed anger drove him to his feet. *"She could have been killed."*

Silence. Brodie could almost picture Therman wheeling around his big room of collections.

Voice gruff, he said, "I want you both to come to dinner tonight."

"No."

"No?" Shock sounded in the single word.

Brodie didn't care. "Not tonight, Therman. She needs a break. She needs to rest." *She needs me.* "If you want to see us, we'll come tomorrow."

"Mary would never deny me."

"Probably true, but I know what she doesn't know."

Annoyance coming through, Therman asked, "And that is?"

"You care about her." Not enough to ensure her safety, but in his own way, Therman definitely wanted to make Mary a part of his family.

It was Mary who resisted.

Therman huffed in defeat. "I do. And I'm so damn sorry about this. You'll take care of her?"

"Damn straight." The water shut off. Mary might be coming out soon and he didn't want to be on her phone when she did. "We'll see you tomorrow."

"Brodie," Therman rushed out, then explained, "It was for an Oscar."

He mentally did a double take. "What?"

"An Oscar. I wouldn't normally ask her to pick up an item under such shady conditions, but Oscars are almost impossible to get. The Academy always tries to reclaim them if one becomes available, and legally, they can't be sold. Getting it was a—"

Brodie laughed, cutting off his explanation. He looked at the bag Mary had set on the floor, barely resisting the urge to kick it.

Hell, he wanted to pitch it out the window.

"You risked her life for a chunk of gold?"

"They're bronze, plated in gold."

Brodie held the phone out to stare at it in disbelief. With it back to his ear, he said, "I don't give a shit if they're carved from kryptonite."

"I didn't know she'd be risking her life! I thought it was shady because it's illegal to sell them, not because someone wanted to inflict harm or rob me."

Pissed as he was, that sounded plausible, but Brodie didn't care. "Tomorrow, Therman. You can explain it all to her then." He disconnected and put the phone on the nightstand.

"That was Therman?"

Brodie jerked around—and clenched all over.

Mary stood in the bathroom doorway, backlit by the fluorescent light behind her. Her long hair, only towel dried, was every bit as striking as he'd known it would be. Wearing a dressed-down peach T-shirt and clinging white shorts—*no bra*—she literally took his breath away.

She watched him, her fingertips fiddling with the high hem of the shorts, maybe waiting for his reaction.

"Nice outfit," he growled, the rush of lust making his voice rougher than he'd intended.

"It's actually for sleeping, but I…wanted to be comfortable."

Her comfort made him very *un*comfortable—in a delicious way.

Because he suddenly had other things on his mind, he said, "Yeah, it was Therman," as he started around the bed, heading toward her.

He knew he should wait. He'd just told Therman that she needed to rest.

There was something in those startling blue eyes, though… "We're going to see him tomorrow."

"Not today?" She backed up a step, then stopped and lifted her chin.

"Tomorrow," he said again, slowing his pace until he stood right in front of her. Their gazes held as he stared down at her. He wanted to pull her close, and he wanted to make this last. The two didn't go together because he knew the moment he touched her, he'd be lost.

To ease into things, he asked, "Did you think about me in the shower?"

She touched his shoulder. "Yes." She inhaled. "Did you think about me while I was in the shower?"

"God, yes." He thought about her all the time, but after what they'd just been through? Knowing she could have been hurt? She was front and center in his thoughts, and damn it, he liked her there.

"Brodie?" Her fingers slid down to his chest, through his chest hair. "Do you have a condom with you?"

CHAPTER NINE

"Was that an invitation, Red?" He crowded closer, his voice rough and husky. "Because it sure as hell sounded like it."

"Actually...yes." The warmth of his skin, that fascinating chest hair, even his small dark nipples, all made discussion difficult. But this was important and she was determined to be a full participant. "If you have protection."

"I have two rubbers," he said, and his hand slid along her neck, under the fall of her hair. "You're sure? I don't want to take advantage—"

"I wouldn't let you." She'd given it plenty of thought and she knew what she wanted. What she wanted so badly. "If you keep talking, I'm going to think you aren't interested."

Those crazy thick lashes lowered and his mouth tipped in a predatory smile. "Then I'll shut up right now and kiss you instead."

Oh, and what a kiss. With one brawny arm around her waist, he drew her up on her tiptoes against him. He opened her lips with ease and then his tongue tasted her, leisurely, thoroughly, as if he couldn't get enough.

Impromptu sex in a seedy motel after a near-death experience might not be a novel thing for Brodie. For her, it was unheard of. Her few excursions into carnal activity had been sorely uneventful. Disappointing even.

Hardly worth the effort.

But running her palms over all the solid, hot flesh of Brodie's shoulders and chest, relishing the way he handled her, how he kissed her, she sensed he'd be the exception to the rule.

She trailed her hands down to his waist, then around to his back—and lower—until she encountered the towel.

It didn't take much for her to tug it away.

He lifted his mouth from hers. His eyes were incendiary, his mouth wet, and color slashed his cheekbones.

Mary stared up at him and said, "Oops. I think you lost your towel."

The corner of his mouth kicked up. "You want to see me, Red?"

She had a heartbeat, so of course she did. "Yes, please."

Arms out to his sides, without even a hint of modesty, Brodie stepped back.

So much heat infused her, she should have melted.

Brodie wasn't a bodybuilder type, but honest-to-God muscles, earned from hard work, carved a physique that made her mouth go dry…while other places got decidedly wet.

"Do I measure up?"

She gave a jerky nod. Of course she'd known he'd be incredible; she'd already seen him shirtless, and jeans didn't hide the strength in his long thighs. But without clothes…

No wonder the man was so cocky. He had good reason, looking as he looked.

Dark hair decorated his body to masculine perfection. *Why would any man wax or shave when hair was so freaking sexy?* It shaded his chest from nipple to nipple, narrowed to a thin line down his torso to circle his navel, then trailed farther down, where it got thicker around his sex.

He was bigger than she'd expected and while it made her a little nervous, it also left her body throbbing in anticipation.

"You could take off that shirt while you look."

Her gaze lifted to his. "Then you won't let me look anymore."

"Sure I will." He frowned, but it didn't appear to be in annoyance. More like curiosity. "You expect me to start rushing you?"

Because she couldn't help herself, her attention went back to his body. His torso was truly a thing of beauty. "Men definitely rush when they see a naked woman." That was her experience anyway. Not that it had mattered before, because those times she'd wanted to get through it.

Her first time, she'd only felt obligated to lose her virginity. It had been in defiance mostly, a refusal to let others influence her decisions.

That had been so miserable, she tried a second time out of curiosity, just to see if the first time had been a fluke, a case of bad luck and bad choices.

The experience hadn't improved much. When she hadn't hidden her dissatisfaction, she'd caught the blame. Truthfully, it was partly her fault because she hadn't known what to expect.

Her mother had certainly loved sex—with any man, at just about any time, for any reason. Television and movies made it out to be life altering. Books romanticized it even more.

For a long time she'd decided sex wasn't worth the bother.

Eventually, affection had motivated her to try once more, only to discover that affection was not a good basis for sex, either. It wasn't horrible, but again, was it worth the bother?

She hadn't thought so.

But none of those experiences applied with Brodie. For the first time that she could remember, her past with all its complicated, negative influences didn't factor into things at all. All that mattered was that she wanted him.

Badly.

Since the day she'd met him, he'd occupied her thoughts.

While she'd been looking at him and thinking how novel it was to really *want* a man, Brodie had apparently been stewing.

He shifted his stance, crossing his arms and giving her a narrow-eyed glare.

She blinked in surprise. "What?"

"Here's the thing, Red. You can look all you want. I don't mind at all."

"Thank you." She could happily look at him all day, but she really wanted to touch, too. And smell.

And *taste.*

"But I do mind if you start comparing me to some asshole who came up short in the sack."

Her eyes flared. "You're annoyed with me?"

His expression softened. "We're the only two here, babe. You and me. Let's leave it at that, okay?"

He was always so sure of himself. She wished she could be just as confident. A glance at Howler assured her the dog was sleeping. "He won't mind?"

Brodie rolled a shoulder—and since he was naked, she enjoyed seeing his erection bob with the movement.

Fascinating.

"I don't usually make a habit of including him, you know? But he can sleep through anything, and he's pretty zoned after his ordeal and the bath." He went to the bed to retrieve the remote, giving her an incredible view of his muscled behind, too, then he turned up the TV. "Background noise might help."

"I'm willing to try."

He grinned, rubbed his mouth, then laughed.

She should have been offended, but instead, she smiled, too. "What?"

"You look anxious, Red. Makes it hard to keep my promise about not rushing you, but swear to God, I'll somehow manage."

He could rush her a little. So far all he'd done was talk.

And display himself.

She put her hands up to her still-damp hair, pushing it over her shoulders. "I should have taken the time to dry it."

"I'm glad you didn't." Frowning now, he came toward her, but not to take over. "What happened here?" He caught her right wrist and lifted her arm, examining the rash there.

"Um…it's nothing." He was *so* close, that bare, gorgeous body near enough that she breathed in his scent. His erection, standing big and bold, almost brushed her hip.

She wanted to jump him, to take advantage of the sizzling awareness and hot excitement before it waned. So far, this interlude had been unlike anything she'd ever experienced, and was nowhere near what she'd imagined.

Barely there, his rough fingertips stroked around the ugly raised welts. "It looks painful."

"A little itchy." Because he was so serious about it—while she stood there aching for him—she explained, "I fell when that creep tried to take my briefcase. My arm went into some prickly weeds and my hip hit a rock, but I really am fine, I promise." Fine enough to get on with it.

The anticipation was killing her.

"Your hip?" He paused, and for a moment his attention zeroed in on her puckered nipples. Closing his eyes and breathing deeply through his nose, he murmured, "Are you hurt, Red? Tell me now and so help me, I'll ease up, I swear."

When sexually primed, Brodie Crews was impossible to resist. She stepped up against his body, relishing the heat and solid strength—very aware of his erection between them. "I'm not that hurt," she promised, rubbing against him. "Now, no more talk, okay? I've waited too long."

Gathering her closer still, he kissed her throat, making her toes curl, then asked, "How long is too long, baby?"

She couldn't think, so she definitely couldn't do math. "I don't know. Forever, maybe." She grabbed his face so she could get to his mouth. "I've never really wanted anyone like I want you."

His gaze heated even more. "Can't say I have, either." One big hand settled on her behind, cuddling her cheek, urging her into stark contact with his body.

A knock sounded at the door.

"Fuck," he muttered, pained. "That's some bad timing, but I guess it could have been worse." He levered back to look at her. "Could've had your shorts off you."

Mary struggled for breath. "Who?"

"Probably my laundry." He drew in a long, bracing breath, then looked around. "Hide if you want while I take care of it." He found his towel and quickly looped it around himself.

It was tented.

Her face went hot and she hissed, "You can't answer the door like that."

"Wanna bet?" He found his wallet on the dresser and drew out some bills.

The knock came again.

Unconcerned, Howler lifted his head and yawned. He seemed to instinctively know when there was or wasn't trouble, and she wondered if he picked up those cues directly from Brodie.

"Just a sec," Brodie called loudly.

Mary quickly ducked into the bathroom and closed the door, her heart hammering as she listened to the muted conversation. Dear God, he was shameless!

Shameless and sexy and *big*.

Half a minute later—meaning he'd rushed the poor person who'd returned his clothes—Brodie said, "Come put me out of my misery, Red."

Jerking the door open, she found him standing there, still in the towel, his stack of laundry folded on the dresser.

Howler stood beside him but with one look at her, he strolled into the bathroom and sprawled out on the tile floor. Incredulous, she watched him fall back to sleep.

Brodie pulled her forward enough so that he could quietly close the door. "No more interruptions."

Finally.

Launching herself against his body, Mary wrapped her arms around his neck, caught his mouth and kissed him as thoroughly as she knew how.

Brodie knew women well enough to sense a sort of desperation in the way Mary attacked him, like maybe she thought she had to grab the opportunity or it might go away.

Not likely.

He appreciated her enthusiasm. She was a soft, warm weight in his arms, big breasts cushioned on his chest, full rump filling his palms as he held her.

After so many days of her figure-concealing outfits, perfect makeup and tightly contained hair, seeing her like this, loose, unkempt and *real*, was the equivalent of hours of foreplay. He especially loved her freckles. His cock throbbed in time with his racing heartbeat.

He maneuvered her to the bed, then released her long enough to fish out the condoms and toss them on the nightstand.

Eyes bright with sensual curiosity, she licked her bottom lip. "Do you always carry them?"

"Usually, yeah. Since meeting you, definitely." He fit his hands to her waist, which nipped in from her full hips and impressive rack. "I'm an optimist and I knew from day one that I wanted you."

"You didn't like me when we first met."

"You disliked me more." He watched her as he eased his hands under her shirt, around to the small of her back, up to her rib cage…and to her breasts. "But liking and wanting are two very different things."

Her eyes went heavy. "Do you like me now?"

"At this moment, I'm crazy nuts about you."

A very sexy smile curved her lips. "Ditto."

He bent to kiss her temple, the rim of her ear, and breathed, "Can't believe you hide all this."

She didn't pretend to misunderstand, didn't fish for more compliments. She simply said, "I don't like to draw attention."

That was why she tortured her hair and wore loose clothes? "Later," he promised, "we'll talk about that." Before she could object to that plan—because Red seriously liked her privacy—he brought his thumbs up and over her stiffened nipples, back and forth, gently tormenting.

Head tipped back, her eyes closed and her long hair trailing to the mattress behind her, she looked to be an entirely different woman from her usual persona.

She *wanted* to enjoy this—and that was different from expecting enjoyment.

He'd make it so, even if it killed him.

"Let's lose the shirt, baby, okay? I want to see you."

Keeping her eyes closed, she nodded and moved as if she'd take care of it herself.

"Let me." Since his hands were already under there, it was easy to bring the material up and over her head. Mary lifted her arms to help, and rather than strip it off her, he paused with the material tangled around her wrists. Keeping her arms held high, he looked at her, at those full breasts and tight pink nipples and he groaned.

"Damn, you're perfect."

"I'm really not."

"Don't argue with a man who has a raging boner." He bent and tongued one nipple before drawing it into his mouth, sucking softly, then not so softly.

Mary struggled to get her arms free, but he switched to the other nipple, saying, "Hush."

"Hush?"

Grinning against her velvety nipple, he suggested, "Maybe

just this once?" He caught her in his teeth, lightly tugged until she subsided, then he straightened. He still had her arms trapped over her head, and the position put her gorgeous bod on display.

For *him*.

Heady stuff. Not that a nude lady was a novelty, but he'd bet the transport company that it was new and unusual for Mary Daniels and that made the moment special—for both of them.

The flush in her cheeks, the swollen lips and fast breaths all told him she was turned on.

A good start—but not good enough. He wanted her feeling as desperate as he did. He wanted to hear her crying with a hard climax, feel her clenching all over.

He wanted to taste her wetness.

Holding her gaze, he asked, "Will you trust me to make this good for you?"

That teasing tongue came out again, dampening her bottom lip. "Trust you to do what?"

"Anything and everything you'll enjoy."

She inhaled sharply, her eyes never wavering from his, and finally she nodded. "Please."

Feeling triumphant, he ran a hand up her side, over her left breast and to her arms overhead. "I like you like this. Keep trusting me and you'll like it, too." He put one knee on the bed by her thigh, nudging her against the mattress until she abruptly sat.

"Lie back." Helping, he held her shoulders until she was stretched out, her calves over the side.

"This is awkward."

Looking down the length of her body, Brodie shook his head. "Keep your arms up," he murmured, as he stretched out beside her and pinned her legs with one of his. "Let me enjoy you a bit until you catch up."

"Catch up?" she gasped, because he was again toying with her nipple, rolling it between his fingertips, pinching carefully, pulling until her back arched.

"I'm on the ragged edge, and you can still ask questions." He leaned over her to lick the other nipple, then drew her in, sucking leisurely while she squirmed under him. His cock was against her thigh and he moved against her, driving himself insane.

Driving her a little insane, too, if her choppy breathing meant anything.

He glanced at her face. She'd pressed her head back, eyes closed, neck arched.

So fucking beautiful.

With his fingertips he worried the wet nipple he'd just left, while he sucked at the other. Her body grew taut under his and her hips rhythmically rolled against him until he couldn't resist any longer.

He smoothed his hand down her body, over her hip, her stomach...and between her soft thighs.

Though she went very still, the muscles in her legs flexed with impatience. "You want me to touch you?"

"Yes."

No hesitation, not for a take-charge woman like Mary. "Here?" He traced the seam in her shorts and felt her reaction as he coasted over her sex.

She gave a jerky little nod.

"Are you wet, Mary?"

It was damn near his undoing when she nodded again.

"Let's get these shorts off so I can see for myself." He sat up and caught the stretchy waistband, pausing only a moment for her to react.

She lifted her hips.

As he slid them down, he realized she wasn't wearing panties. "Naughty girl," he growled, taking in the curve of her belly, the jut of a hip bone. "I approve."

Her pubic hair was darker, lacking the red highlights of the hair fanned out on the bed. He dragged the shorts down and off her knees, and she clumsily kicked them off her feet.

"Open your legs."

Her expression almost defiant—and definitely aroused—she parted her thighs.

Brodie stroked her, oh-so-slowly, from her knee up. "Wider."

A deep breath lifted her breasts…and she shifted her position.

It still wasn't enough. He wanted to see her, all of her, so he cupped a hand behind her knee, bending it up and then pressing her leg to the side.

Now. *Now* he could enjoy her. His vision seemed to narrow to only Mary, to her lush body and that straightforward blue-eyed gaze.

He'd never felt it before, but he recognized the possessiveness searing into his brain.

Mine.

Rather than beat his chest and do a Tarzan *call of the wild*, he traced around her sex, his fingers barely grazing her. "Do you like this?" he asked.

She readjusted. "Brodie."

His gaze lifted to hers in question.

Her eyes looked like blue flames, banked with arousal. Voice throbbing, she gasped, "I need you to touch me."

God, he loved the way she stated things. Sitting beside her, he cupped his palm over her, the heel of his hand pressing on her clit, his fingers searching, parting her slick lips.

Very wet.

Stifling a low growl, he asked, "Better?"

She breathed harder. "Some."

With his middle finger, he barely pressed into her, a mere tease as he relished her heat. Watching her closely, seeing her frustration and mounting lust, he asked, "Does that help?"

"Damn you." In a sudden flurry of movement, she wrenched her arms from the shirt, tossed it over the side of the bed and grabbed his wrist, pulling his hand more tightly to her while she lifted her hips.

As his finger penetrated, she gave a vibrating sound of pleasure. He felt her squeeze around him, and it pushed him right over the edge. Taking her mouth in a hard kiss, he fucked her with his finger until both of them were urgent with need. Forethought fled and he acted solely on instinct.

He'd told her he wouldn't lose control, but her mouth was wet and hot, her legs sprawled, her heat bathing his hand. She was ready, and yet, it wasn't enough.

Goddamn, he didn't know what would be enough, not with her.

Almost angry with his need, he moved down to her breasts, sucking her pebbled nipples, biting softly, licking. She grabbed his head, trying to hold him there.

But he needed everything.

Mouth open, he trailed down her torso to her belly. He loved the feel of her skin, her incredible scent. He felt drunk with it.

"Brodie," she whispered brokenly, her fingers tangled in his hair.

She twitched when he licked her hip bone. He stored away the knowledge of her ticklishness for another time, then, still between her legs, went to his knees over the side of the bed. His shoulders kept her legs wide-open.

The position gave him an awesome visual; he saw her slippery wet lips, swollen and so pink, and her little clit, waiting for attention. He stroked her inner thighs, relishing the sight of her, the scent of her excitement, her need—for *him*.

Groaning, he lifted her legs over his shoulders and pressed his face to her, breathing her in. His cock swelled even more, aching. He'd be lucky to last a minute once he got inside her. Hopefully, she'd be there with him.

He parted her with his fingertips, licked into her, up and over her. Feeling her tremble, he closed his mouth around her, holding her with a gentle suck while stroking her little bud with his tongue.

Because her breasts were too luscious to ignore, he stretched one long arm up and thumbed a nipple. He flattened the other hand on her stomach, trying—and failing—to hold her still.

Within minutes her movements grew more frantic, and her cries grew louder.

He loved it—and prayed it wouldn't disturb the dog.

When he felt her clenching, when her soft thighs tensed, he worked two fingers into her, pressing deep.

She came apart with raw, guttural cries that she tried unsuccessfully to muffle. Brodie stayed with her, making it last as long as he could, then eased gradually until she rested flat on the bed again, her legs sprawled, her breathing labored.

He placed one more soft kiss to her and stood. His hands shook as he opened the condom and rolled it on. Never in his life had he been this turned on. "You still with me, Red?"

"Mmm."

Aware of her watching him through lowered eyelids, her expression relaxed and maybe a little awed, he crawled up and over her body. "I'll take that as a yes."

Gazing at his mouth, she let out a soft sigh.

Nice. He'd left the lady speechless.

Positioning himself between her legs, braced on his forearms, he said, "Look at me, Red."

Her lashes lifted and he stared down into those blue, blue eyes, feeling utterly lost. It unnerved him.

She touched his face, down the bridge of his nose to trace his mouth.

Brodie nudged his cock against her, getting the head good and wet, then he pressed in. After having his fingers in her, he already knew she was tight—especially for a man of his size. But she wanted him, he could tell, and she didn't flinch as he began to fill her.

He felt the natural resistance of her body for an instant, then the slick glide as he relentlessly wedged into her.

Her lips parted.

His heart hammered.

For a few seconds, which was all he could handle, he just rested against her, *in* her, giving her a chance to get used to his size. When she finally unclenched, he shifted. "Okay?"

She nodded and whispered, "You are a gorgeous man, Brodie."

Despite the lust, he felt a crooked smile creep up on him. "Yeah?"

She didn't smile back, but she curved one small, soft hand around his neck and drew him down.

As gently as he could, he kissed her parted lips—and withdrew.

She squeezed him as he did so, making him breathe harder—and he pushed in again.

Mary put her hands on his shoulders, her nails a slight sting.

"Easy," he murmured, retreating again, thrusting back.

"I didn't expect this."

"This?" he asked, driving into her again. Up to now he'd managed to keep things metered, slow...but he'd about reached his breaking point.

"That it could feel so good."

Yeah, that did it. He took her mouth in a deep, tonguing kiss as he rode fast against her. She matched his rhythm, her legs locking around him.

Faster, harder, the bed rocking, both of them rough, both of them urgent...

He freed his mouth and put his face in her neck. He felt his balls tightening, felt himself straining—and then he heard her low moan, felt the grip of her body and the rush of wet heat as she came again. He gritted his teeth, waiting as the orgasm gripped her, and then he let himself go.

God, it was good. He locked himself to her, as deep as he could get, and came with a harsh groan.

As tension drained out of him, he sank down to rest on her, suddenly aware that her mouth was on his shoulder, her fingers sliding over his back in subtle, lazy caresses.

She hadn't expected it, didn't think it could feel so good.

A million questions suddenly crowded into his brain. Someone had disappointed his Mary. Or worse, someone had hurt her.

He swallowed heavily, fighting off a surge of protective rage.

"What is it?" she asked, her voice lazy but also curious. She kissed his chest. "Is something wrong?"

With an effort, Brodie rose to his forearms. With her cheeks flushed, the freckles showed more and he wanted to kiss each and every one. Instead, he touched his mouth to hers. "You have the most amazing eyes."

She blinked in surprise, then grinned. "Do I?"

"Yeah, especially when you look at me like that."

"How am I looking at you?"

"Like a woman satisfied."

Smoothing her fingers through his hair, she sighed. "Very, very satisfied."

He wanted to devour her all over again. "How would you feel about staying the night here?"

Her mouth curled in a slow smile and she looked around, as far as she could with his shoulders in the way. "In this room?"

Nudging against her, his cock no longer quite as impressive, he said, "Here, with me."

"And Howler."

"I'll take him out. And I'll figure out something for dinner, too. You," he said, punctuating that with a kiss, "should stay right here, naked, in bed."

Beneath him, she stretched luxuriously. "I like that idea."

"Great. I'll let the front desk know." Maybe, away from the familiar and all the responsibilities, he could get her to open up a little, to share some of her past, some of her worries and ambitions. "You're beautiful, Red."

While lightly tracing the edges of the bandage on his head, she said, "You're sweet. Thank you."

Brodie laughed. "Not a description usually put to me, but I'm glad you think so." He lowered his forehead to hers. "I'm going to have to dispose of the rubber soon, which is going to wake Howler, so before I do that, will you tell me something?"

Wariness immediately crept into her gaze, forcing out some of the pleasure. "What?"

"Back up." The last thing he wanted to do was lose the pleasure of the moment. "Before I ask, will you do me a favor?"

She huffed. *"What?"*

"Trust me?"

With her fingers playing over his shoulder, she frowned. "I do."

"To a point?"

Her gaze met his. "To a point."

"Will you try to trust me a little more?" He didn't let her answer, not yet. "Just me, Red. Talk to me, confide in me, and it'll end with me. You have my word."

Skepticism clouded her expression, but she kept her tone soft. "Because we've had sex, I should trust your word?"

That stung. Hell, it stung *too* much. "I'm not a saint, Red, but I'm also not a liar." He started to roll away but her legs tightened.

"I didn't mean it like that."

"No?" If he didn't move soon, he'd be taking a chance with her. The rubber really needed to go. "How'd you mean it, then?"

She stared at his mouth while she thought about it, but looked into his eyes when she said, "We had sex. We've both had sex before. Clearly it never meant much or we wouldn't be together now. Sex is not a reason for confidences or..."

"Or for liking someone? For softening your stance and letting down your guard?" Her pragmatic approach bothered him more than it should have. That pragmatism often defined Mary, but damn it, what they'd just shared was more intimate, more special, than anything he'd known before.

For him, it wasn't just sex.

It was so much more.

A small, almost helpless shake of her head wasn't the answer he wanted.

This time Brodie got away from her and moved off the bed to stand beside it. Feet braced apart, feeling damned defensive, he marshaled his thoughts. This was Mary, and he sensed her uncertainty—though of course she'd do her best to hide it.

He banked his disappointment—not in the carnal act, because Mary's enthusiasm had scorched him. But the cuddling and sharing afterward, which he usually disliked, was missing—and this time he wanted it. He thought about things while ignoring the way her gaze tracked over his body with renewed fascination.

"It could be a start." But he wouldn't beg her, damn it. "You just have to let it." Turning away, he headed for the bathroom. He had the rest of the day and all through the night. Somewhere in his lust-clouded brain, he'd find the right words. And if he couldn't...

Well, maybe he'd just find the right moves instead.

Mary liked sex. *With him.* Hell, he'd surprised her.

In a good way.

For now, for tonight, that might be enough. As he'd said, it was a start. If it all rolled the right way, he could build off it.

Not a bad plan at all.

CHAPTER TEN

Helton stood staring out the office window, watching the traffic go by below, when his cell phone rang. Tonight, he didn't want to do business. He'd rather change into a casual shirt, drop into a bar at the old neighborhood and maybe start shit. A fight would feel good.

He'd gotten addicted to the feel of bruised knuckles and pumping adrenaline, the taste of blood in his mouth. Like the junkie needing a new high, his skin itched with the need to engage physically.

Sex, much as he enjoyed it, couldn't compare with the satisfaction of a vicious brawl, not when he insisted on treating women with kid gloves.

He flexed his knuckles, smiling at the memory of his last fight. He'd demolished two men who'd insulted a barmaid, leaving them broken in an alley while he'd gone home with proud war wounds. He inhaled, missing it, *wanting* it…

The phone kept ringing so he glanced at the screen, then answered with an impatient, "What is it?"

Lem replied with his patented calm assurance, saying, "The men who screwed up—that situation is resolved."

Helton glanced at the clock. That was fast. "Where'd you dump them?"

"In the same lake where they'd set up the exchange."

A laugh took him by surprise. "Beautiful irony." One problem down. "Getting info on the driver is the priority now."

"Yes, sir."

"Find out if they're an item, what habits they might have, anything we can use."

"We can use Ms. Daniels."

"Last resort. Until then, get me info. I want to know Brodie Crews inside and out—his family, his friends, but also find out if he has any enemies, anyone who might like to see him brought down a peg."

"I'm on it."

"And, Lem? You don't want to disappoint me again."

"Won't happen, you have my word." He disconnected.

Helton picked up his suit coat and shrugged it on. God, how he would have loved to join in on the antics today. If only his dad hadn't kicked it, leaving him a legit business to run.

If only he hadn't died with a fanatic obsession for finishing a particular collection.

The good old days were gone, but maybe if the driver proved difficult—a hopeful thought—he could resurrect some of the perks and even get in on the action.

He had to honor his dad's legacy, but nowhere was it written that he couldn't have some fun along the way.

Wakened by the dawn light filtering in through the curtains, Mary carefully lifted her head to see Brodie. With one arm he held her cuddled against his side, her head pillowed on his biceps. His other arm was up, folded behind his head, and the position made those incredible biceps bulge even in sleep. The sight of the dark, downy hair under his arm seemed oddly intimate, even more so than everything they'd done through the night, the things he'd done *to* her, the incredible orgasms he'd given her.

Seeing him like this—unguarded, tranquil, all his vital energy at rest—made her toes curl. His dark brows were relaxed, his thick lashes casting shadows over his cheekbones. Beard stubble added enticing angles to his already rugged face. His hair, mussed from sex and sleep, stuck out in every direction.

Be still my heart.

No, *not* her heart. She wouldn't let it be her heart.

Too many times, in too many disastrous ways, she'd seen her mother hurt herself. Over and over again...

Mary squeezed her eyes shut, drew a breath and deliberately kicked the memories away. She was here, now, with the most elemental man she'd ever known, and studying him was far more enlightening than dwelling on the past.

With that thought in mind, she came up onto an elbow and looked at him again.

Around the small bandage she'd put on his head, she detected shadowy bruising. That knock on his head had to have hurt, yet he'd acted as if it hadn't. Was it a macho display for her benefit, or was he really so used to injuries?

Across the room, she heard a snuffle that settled into a snore. Howler. Through the night the dog had groaned, stretched, snored elaborately and overall enjoyed his rest.

He made her smile.

Brodie made her smile, too.

Emotions commingled, leaving her thoughts turbulent.

They could have been killed.

Therman had risked them both.

Brodie had pleasured her.

And God help her, she wanted to stay at the hotel. Another day, another week, having incredibly hot, amazing sex, being coddled as if she mattered, eating pizza in bed and watching old movies.

Like a dream, it was all so wonderfully normal, when her life had never been that.

During that very special interlude, the rest of the world had receded and now she found she didn't want to face reality. She would—she was always responsible—but she didn't want to.

Brodie shifted, sort of rolling toward her, moving one hand to her backside, the other to her breast.

"You're awake?"

"Shh, no," he said in a dark, sleep-rough voice. "I think I'm having a wet dream."

Snickering, she bent to kiss his mouth. *Oh, that hot, sexy mouth and the things he'd done with it…*

"Another," he gruffly demanded.

Obligingly, she returned to his mouth, this time teasing his lips for a five count, lingering, feeling her heart swell and her toes curl.

"Mmm," he murmured. "I love the contrasts of you."

Mary stilled. "Contrasts?"

He turned, putting her under him, his lower body pinning her down while he lifted to his forearms and stared at her chest. "These big soft tits, your prickly attitude—"

"Hey!"

"They are big and soft," he insisted, deliberately misunderstanding her complaint. "I'd like to rub my dick between them." His dark gaze locked on hers. "What do you think?"

He was so extraordinary, she didn't know what to think. Yet somehow, everything Brodie suggested sounded hot. "Maybe."

Those thick, masculine brows shot up. "Seriously? See, that's another contrast. You contradict me so often, then out of the blue, bam, you're agreeable."

She was agreeable to more sex, more orgasms, more bone-melting pleasure and in that, she did trust him. Completely. He'd already proved to be a pro in bed. "If you think I'd like it, I believe you. You haven't been wrong yet."

"Yeah?" Grinning, he put a hand on each breast, idly caressing. With a hint of mischief, he said, "Well, I think you'd *love* giving head."

Hearing him say it made her want it, so she replied honestly, "With you, I probably would."

He stiffened, then turned again, pulling her atop him. "I can't believe I'm going to say this—like, I *really* can't believe it—but let's put that on the back burner for a bit."

Feeling unaccountably agreeable, maybe because his body could so easily distract her, she shrugged. "All right."

"I promise I'll bring it up again later."

She believed him. Brodie was so sexual that it probably wouldn't be far from his mind. Unfortunately for her, they'd used both condoms last night. If she insisted on pleasuring him, it would pleasure her, too. But sex was out without protection, and the idea of getting aroused—or more aroused—without satisfaction didn't sound like much fun.

Of course, before Brodie, she hadn't realized the scope of "satisfaction." Now she did, and she would never again settle for less.

"You're so distracting." The firm column of his erection burned against her belly and she pressed against it, making his eyes close.

"I want to talk."

"Okay." She loved his chest. He had these rock-solid pecs sprinkled with hair, making that part of his body especially appealing.

Of course, his biceps were also amazing, as were his hairy thighs and his flat abdomen with that line of hair that led her gaze to his erection... She shouldn't think of that now, but Brodie had easily made her obsessed.

Sighing, she spread her fingers out over his chest, then lightly dragged them down, letting her nails graze his nipples as she did so. "What do you want to talk about?"

The swat he landed on her behind startled her more than it hurt. "Hey!"

"Quit distracting me, Red." With both hands, he massaged her butt as if that could take away the sting. "I'm going to take Howler out, and I'll grab coffee on my way back up. The bathroom is yours until then."

She badly wanted to run her face over his chest. And down his body, following that tantalizing line of hair to—

Another swat had her growling and ready to smack him back.

Brodie laughed. "I could almost feel what you were thinking, honey. I had no idea you were so wicked." He bobbed his brows. "I like it." Once more, he turned, this time dumping her to the side of him on her stomach.

His big hand settled on her left cheek, right where he'd landed that firm smack, but now his fingers were ultimately gentle.

"Damn."

"What?" She reared up to look over her shoulder at him in accusation. "Did you leave a mark?"

"'Course not. I'd never hurt you, Red." His gaze sought hers. "It *didn't* hurt, did it?"

"It smarted."

He made an "aww" face. "Want me to kiss it and make it better?"

She gave it thought… "Maybe."

Grinning, he dutifully, *slowly*, buffed his lips over her cheek. The grin vanished as he circled a spot on her hip. "You have a big bruise here."

She tried to see but couldn't. "Remember I told you I'd landed on something hard when that jerk accosted me?"

"I should have killed him." He gave her another kiss, this one to the injured spot. "If I get a second chance, I'll make him suffer. I promise."

She rolled her eyes. "Don't sound so bloodthirsty. Personally,

I hope we never see them again, but if we do, remember your promise to avoid conflicts when possible."

"Yeah," he said, his tone rife with irony, "I'll keep that in mind."

"Brodie," she warned.

"Gotta drain the pipes, honey." He strode into the bathroom, his butt and thigh muscles moving fluidly, making it a grand show.

Mary sighed and fell onto her back.

She heard the toilet flush, then water running. When he stepped back out, she hadn't moved. She wasn't sure she wanted to.

"Perfect," he said as he stepped into his jeans, his gaze caressing her body. "Only problem now will be getting zipped." He carefully got his jeans closed.

Mary smiled and stretched—which made Brodie groan.

It was so nice the way he carried on, as if she were a model or something—even though she knew she wasn't. Yes, she had a lot of curves, but they were on a short frame, which made them even more exaggerated. She didn't dislike her body, but neither was she blind to her flaws.

What she usually disliked most was the attention her curves drew from men.

Not so with Brodie. She loved seeing the heat in his intense gaze.

"Do you want any breakfast?"

The words were no sooner out of his mouth than Howler rolled clumsily to his feet, ears perked with expectation. Brodie laughed. "Yeah, for you, too, bud."

"That dog was awfully accommodating all night." She slanted her suspicion his way. "Is he often in rooms with you while you have sex?"

"Not when I can help it, believe me. But last night, with *you*,

I'm pretty sure a herd of elephants rampaging through the room wouldn't have put me off."

The odd comment, which she took as a compliment, warmed her.

Brodie pulled on a shirt. "The rain has stopped. Before we can leave, I'll need to clean the car."

True. The interior had to be covered with mud. "I can help."

"We'll see." He came over to the bed and bent to kiss her, one hand fondling her breast as if he had the right.

And she supposed, after last night, he did.

"Food?"

"I could eat."

"Then I'll see what I can scrounge up. Give me twenty minutes." With a final kiss, he straightened, leashed Howler, and out they went.

Mary took the opportunity to shower and put on makeup, not her usual full face's worth—she just plain didn't feel like it—but enough to look like a qualified professional instead of the drowned rat she'd been yesterday.

She started to pin up her hair, but feeling absurdly mutinous, she decided against that, too, and instead put it in a high ponytail.

Surveying herself in the mirror, she wasn't sure what to think. Maybe the ponytail was too much? In her own jaundiced opinion, it made her look younger. Less serious.

She exhaled, debating between what she wanted, what she felt and what she was used to. Everything felt different now. *She* felt different. But it was so new, such an unfamiliar sensation, that she didn't know if she should trust it.

Brodie, she could trust...in some things. Like sexual things. Pleasure things.

But herself? She'd made so many mistakes, especially in matters of intimacy—or rather, lack of intimacy. Would loosening up be just another mistake?

Too late. Brodie would return soon and she had to be dressed or they'd never get out the door. Much as she'd wish it otherwise, they had to leave today—no more stolen moments.

Before they did, though, she had a few things to get straight. That much she knew was important.

As she dressed in her replacement outfit, she listed them in her mind so that by the time Brodie returned, she'd be prepared.

He'd barely gotten in the door when she made the most important announcement. "You can't tell anyone."

Juggling an overflowing tray, bag and Howler's leash, Brodie paused.

Her words had landed with the impact of a rude slap. Not her intention, but she couldn't take them back.

His attention tracked over her, taking in her slightly wrinkled business attire: a boxy gray skirt that fell a few inches below her knees, flat-heeled sandals and a sedately striped, untailored blouse with a straight hem.

It made her look as if she had no figure at all, and suddenly she resented that. What difference did it make if other men ogled her boobs and butt, when she had Brodie's appreciation?

God, and didn't that make her sound like a desperate virgin anxious for a man's approval? *Never.*

She squared her shoulders and met his gaze.

An odd expression, maybe caution, moved over his face. "Tell anyone what?"

She held the door open until he got Howler inside. "About us." That made her shake her head and she rushed to add, "Not that there's necessarily an *us*."

"Pretty sure I wasn't jacking off all night." He cocked a brow in a look of irritation. "We were both there."

Good Lord, the things he said. "That's not what I meant." Being an *us* implied they were a couple, and she didn't want to be presumptuous.

"Two," he stated, "equals an *us*."

"What I meant is that this—" gesturing, she indicated the mussed bed and room in general "—should be kept strictly private."

His dark brows came together in a fierce scowl. He set the tray on the dresser and turned to unleash Howler. The dog promptly plopped down to stare at the food.

Ignoring Mary, Brodie drew two dishes from the bag. Into one he poured dry food, which had Howler scowling, too. He carried the other into the bathroom to fill it with water.

Foot tapping in growing anxiety and annoyance, Mary waited. She'd given it a lot of thought, and if anyone discovered that she'd thrown professionalism out the window, she could be ruined. She loved her job with Therman. He paid her well. It was a respectable job, proving *her* as respectable. Risking that would be beyond stupid.

So why did it feel as if she'd insulted Brodie?

Maybe because he'd uncovered a part of her she hadn't known existed, a part she'd always longed to find but couldn't. For years she'd searched…before finally accepting defeat.

She'd thought herself unemotional. Detached from physical pleasure.

Oh, how Brodie had proved her wrong.

Hand to her stomach, Mary watched as Brodie went to his knees by the dog and lifted a nugget of food. He pretended to toss it into his mouth, then fake chewed.

It was an endearing thing he did for the dog. Acknowledging his innate kindness added to her inner turmoil.

"Well?" she asked, wanting, *needing* him to say something, hopefully something that would reassure her, that would make her feel like herself again.

Howler looked skeptical, so Brodie did it again, even adding an "Mmm, mmm," then smacking his lips.

The dog gave the food a second look, bent to sniff and started to eat.

"God, he's a tough nut to crack." Getting back to his feet, Brodie asked in forced nonchalance, "What's it going to be, Red? Donut or scrambled eggs and bacon? You should know, though, the eggs are powdered and taste like shit. Howler's food might actually be better. The bacon's okay, though. Hard to mess up bacon." After all that nonsense muttering, he picked up a strip of crispy bacon and bit off half.

She heard his teeth snap together, saw the harsh clenching of his jaw as he chewed. Anger?

She searched his face and found it closed. "Did you hear what I said?"

"Yeah, I heard." He forked up some of the eggs, eyed them grumpily, then ate.

"I'm serious, Brodie."

"Yeah, I know." His gaze flicked over her. "The ponytail says it all."

She *knew* she should have pinned it up. Everyone took her more seriously when she put on her armor. There'd been times, though, when she thought Brodie saw through it.

Like now.

"Thing is," he continued, in that grating indifference, "I'm trying not to get pissed. You're making it tough, the way you keep insulting me."

Folding her arms and feeling defensive, Mary gave him a narrow-eyed look. "Because I want my private life to stay private, you're insulted?"

He rolled a shoulder and drank some coffee. "There's two ways to look at it. Either you're embarrassed to have slept with me, the lowly driver, or you figure I'll go running my mouth, bragging about what an easy lay you are."

Stunned by his asinine conclusions, her arms dropped. "It's neither of those things!" God, for a badass, he was awfully sensitive. "How could you even think that?"

That dark gaze pinned her. "How could I not?"

Her hands clenched together and her lungs squeezed. God, she was making a muddle of things, but this was all so new to her. Being thirty hadn't automatically given her the experience needed to deal with the proverbial "morning after," not under these circumstances. Not when she'd enjoyed herself so much.

Not when she wanted to enjoy herself again. *With Brodie.*

Did valuing her privacy really come off as insulting? He should know better. After all, *he* had plenty of experience.

Recalling that brought back a touch of irritation. "They're dumb assumptions to make and you know it."

The coffee cup half hid his face as he said, "Really? You're the one who's always reminding me that I'm *just* the driver."

Mary shook her head in denial. Yes, she'd given him some reminders—when he'd overstepped. It didn't make him *lowly.*

Guilt still crept up on her. Now that she felt closer to him, she realized how arrogant she'd probably been.

Huffing, as much in regret as exasperation, she said, "One, I'm not at all ashamed of what we've done, so please don't ever think that. You being the driver is an important part of the job. Very important. But as a professional, this shouldn't have happened."

As if he didn't care, he ate more bacon.

"Two," she pressed, reaching for patience that ran thin, "I have never been an easy lay. Most would say I'm difficult." Her face burned with that admission and took some of the crispness from her tone. "And they'd be right."

Brodie stilled.

"I know it's true because until now I've never…" She faltered over the personally difficult truth, but Brodie deserved to know. "That is, I haven't…"

He waited, his expression not exactly sympathetic, more like understanding. And *very* curious.

Better just to spit it out and get it over with. "I didn't know sex could be that good." *Good* was such a wishy-washy word, but she'd feel foolish saying *stupendous*, *magnificent* or *life altering.*

Actually, she couldn't think of a really appropriate description. Because she hadn't known it could be anything other than embarrassing and uncomfortable, he completely changed her perspective—on sex and, in some ways, on life. She felt changed. Permanently altered.

It was so very uncomfortable—while also being indescribably wonderful—but she didn't have the words to explain it to him.

Setting aside the coffee, Brodie shifted his posture, going more alert, less insolent. "You're saying it was so good, but you already want to ditch me?"

"I don't! God, no." Ending this, when it had just gotten started, was definitely not her intent. Hoping to show him what she couldn't seem to say, she stepped up to him and slid her arms around his waist, absorbing the warmth of his skin radiating through his T-shirt. Her palms encountered solid strength as she spread her fingers to touch more of him. The differences in their height put her cheek directly over his steadily beating heart. Near her ear, she felt his warm breath.

Crazy as it seemed, her pulse raced at the simple hug.

Was it possible she'd already missed him?

Yes, she relished the strength in his body, his heat and scent. Yet she also liked him, *him*, not just his wide shoulders and muscled thighs and...his large cock.

As if he suddenly understood, he crushed her close. "You aren't, huh?"

Now that she was touching him, Mary forgot the topic. "What?"

"You aren't ditching me?"

"No, of course not." She gave him a tight squeeze. It was dangerous to feel this way about him; she hadn't navigated the perils of a romantic relationship in a very long time.

Actually, she'd never navigated *anything* with a man like Brodie.

Because he was so boldly plainspoken, without an ounce of

pretense, it might be easier. There'd be no guessing, no worrying what he thought. Except that he was also a rock—in more ways than one. Rock-solid, rock steady.

Stubborn as a boulder.

The analogy amused her. "I want you, Brodie, very much. But I also want us to be private." Leaning back within his embrace, she smiled up at him. "I was actually looking forward to more."

He gave her a quick hug.

"The thing is, I love my job and I don't want to do anything that might give Therman a reason to fire me." Unlike her mother, she wouldn't place a man above everything else. She couldn't, wouldn't, be that person.

"I don't think he'd do that, hon."

Maybe not. Therman gave the impression that he cared about her beyond her role as an employee. Still... "Let's not test it, okay?"

Running one hand down the length of her ponytail until his hand slipped free, continuing on down her back to her bottom, he said, "We can be as private as you want, but I need something from you."

Thinking he'd name something sexual, and already excited by the prospect, she nodded. "All right."

"You have to open up a little."

"I am open." To just about anything he wanted to try. As she'd said, she trusted him to ensure she liked it. He'd been right on the money so far, much to her excitement.

"Love your willingness, Red," he said with a grin. "But I was talking about your past, what makes you the woman you are, why you hide that smokin' hot bod of yours, and where you got this crazy misconception about sex."

Her heartbeat jumped. He wanted her to... What? Bare her soul? Share every embarrassing secret? Panicked objections rushed forth, but before she could get out a single word, he kissed her, a long lingering kiss that tasted of coffee and breakfast and Brodie.

A delicious combo.

He released her and began gathering up his things. "We'll talk on the road."

Dazed, Mary watched as he quickly put the room in order and threw a twenty-dollar bill on his pillow.

See, he kept doing those things that chipped away at her barriers. A nice tip for the housekeeping staff. It was a pet peeve of hers that too many people were stingy when it came to tipping those who served. Not Brodie, though.

In fact, he had numerous redeeming qualities: he was a terrific driver, very attuned to danger—and a woman's body. Reliable, confident, funny.

Plus he loved his dog.

And his *mother.*

That last made her a little uncomfortable, reminding her why she didn't want to *open up.* "All those things you mentioned... They're not really things I want to discuss."

"Why not?" He attached Howler's leash. "So you bed-hopped with some losers? It's not the end of the world, though a woman like you should always demand the best."

She had a feeling she had the best—and his name was Brodie Crews.

They'd been on the road damn near a half hour, and Mary hadn't said a thing. He hated to prod her, but if he didn't find out the origin of her issues, how could they get around them? Sure, they'd made some headway.

But he wanted more.

"Time's up," he finally said, when she turned to stare out the window. "I need to know what's up so I don't stick my foot in my mouth, right?"

She stiffened but didn't reply.

To get her started, he prompted, "Sex before me wasn't great?" The silence dragged out until he decided she wouldn't fill in the blanks. "I'm not fishing for compliments—though they're always welcome. More compliments, I mean." Maybe joking would help ease her into conversation. "I'm already feeling like a stud. Given the way you—"

"Sex before you sucked." Shoulders hunched, she turned farther away. "It was either embarrassing or uncomfortable or both."

That sounded a hell of a lot worse than just a disappointing lay. "Uncomfortable how?"

Her small hand lifted, waving in the air. "Physically, emotionally."

Every muscle in Brodie's body went taut. "Someone hurt you?"

At his low, lethal tone, she finally looked at him—and softened. "Not on purpose."

Just to be sure… "So you're saying I *don't* have to kill anyone?"

"Definitely no murder on the horizon."

Now she sounded vaguely amused, and it was a hell of an improvement over her withdrawn uncertainty. "Okay, so I want details, but not *details*, you know?"

She gave him a blank stare.

Yeah, that had sounded pretty convoluted. "I want to know how you were hurt and embarrassed, but I'm not sure I could take a blow-by-blow report of you with some other dude."

She smacked his shoulder. "I wouldn't tell you details like that anyway."

He glanced at her. "Glad to hear it." To his relief, she was loosening up more by the minute. "What did the bozo do? Rush you? Coerce you?" He might still go after the fuck if that'd happened. "He didn't get you off?"

At the last, she whispered, "Bingo."

Ever? Brodie wasn't even sure how to ask that. *So you've never screamed and bucked and begged with anyone but me?*

Conflicted emotions dug into his brain. It'd be a rush to think he was the only guy who'd pushed her buttons that much. But a woman like Mary, a woman so warm and smart and confident, shouldn't have had any issues. Any man who'd slept with her should have made her pleasure a priority.

Clearly, some dumb fucks hadn't.

Thinking of her going home in embarrassment or discomfort, of *any* kind, bothered him a lot.

"So," he said, trying to find a way to ask without offending her, "you were with young guys? Geeks? Virgins themselves?"

"No. But I can't put all the blame on the guys."

He scowled. "Why not? I can."

Her smile made him want her again, right now, even though they were on the road with a snoring dog in the cramped back seat.

"You'd have to understand—"

"I'd love to. Explain it to me?" He waited, his breath held.

They passed an exit in silence and had almost reached another when she said, "My mother sold herself. Often."

Stunned, he stared straight ahead, doing his best not to react. He didn't want to do anything to insult her, embarrass her or stifle her.

But damn, talk about a shocker.

Brodie heard her swallow. "She wasn't high-end."

Jesus. His thoughts shot to his mother, his sweet, caring, rock-solid mother, and everything inside him cramped. He couldn't imagine—didn't *want* to imagine—anything that awful.

With his heart pounding too hard, he asked, "Where was your father?"

"No idea. Mom wasn't sure who he was, but she'd sometimes make up stories." Her gaze slanted at him, defiant and proud. "I know they were made-up because they varied a lot, like she maybe couldn't keep her own facts straight. One day he was Prince Charming, the next an abusive jerk, and a few days later, she'd say she didn't know him at all, that he'd been a one-night stand."

Brodie wasn't sure what to say. He couldn't tell her he was sorry because knowing Mary, she'd take it as pity. He already knew her well enough to know how she'd hate that. In fact, he figured a lot of what she did was to repel sympathy of any kind.

He couldn't pretend to understand, either. Few could.

She stated, "The worst part was the town. Everyone knew everyone else's business."

He gave an inner wince. "Small, huh?"

"Even smaller than the town you live in," she assured him. "Because I look so much like my mother, everyone expected me to either grow up the same as her, or to, in some way, be dysfunctional about sex because of her."

"Definitely not dysfunctional," he promised.

"Well." She stroked his shoulder. "I know that now."

He smiled, even while the muscles in his neck tensed. He tried to picture Mary older, less starchy, but no matter how he envisioned her, she was drop-dead gorgeous. He assumed her mother must have been also.

The pinned-up hair and unflattering wardrobe suddenly had new meaning. No wonder she was so concerned with being proper.

Growing up, she'd probably gone out of her way to show a marked difference between herself and her mother, yet from what little she'd said, it hadn't kept people from judging her.

It *was* pity he felt, mostly for her mother, who must have been a sick, unhappy person. *What would it be like to be raised by someone like that?*

He also teemed with rage on her behalf. How dare others view her only on the actions of her parent?

Mostly he was...proud. Proud of a woman he hadn't known

that long, but somehow already felt connected to. It was like the protectiveness he felt toward family, but with the edginess of burning lust thrown in. In other words, pretty damned special.

And she wanted to keep him at arm's length.

Wasn't that a kick in the balls?

Because he needed to touch her, to connect with her, he reached for her hand, ridiculously pleased that she didn't hesitate to lace her fingers with his.

"You make me feel the craziest things, Red." He couldn't define those things for her, not completely, so he stroked a thumb over her knuckles and asked, "Do you see your mom still?"

"She overdosed when I was twenty-four." Mary looked at him thoughtfully, as if curious of his reaction. "She was only forty."

The math jumped out at him and he whistled. "Had you when she was young?"

"Only sixteen." Mary shrugged. "She used to say she was a baby raising a baby, but she was still saying it when she was twenty-six, and then thirty-six." Her hand gripped his for a brief moment, then loosened and she pulled away. "They found her naked in bed, a needle in her arm. It was obvious she'd had sex multiple times that day."

They found her. Thank God Mary hadn't walked in on that. "How'd you find out?"

"I got a call." Her shoulder lifted in a shrug that belied all the things she had to feel. "Her house, her belongings, became my responsibility."

She said nothing else, but Brodie assumed the house was the same one she'd grown up in. There had to be conflicted emotions galore, although she'd kept her tone detached.

Was that how she coped? By separating herself emotionally?

He had the awful suspicion she'd been doing so for much of her life.

Aching for her, Brodie returned both hands to the wheel. Patience wasn't his strong suit, but he tried it on for size. Keeping his breathing even and steady wasn't easy, not with the vise of compassion now squeezing his heart. He hoped Mary would share more, and after a few minutes, she did.

It was as if she'd needed that time to formulate her thoughts, to find a shortcut to the telling so she could get it said without all the pesky names and dates.

Without the hurt.

"I'd moved away when I was seventeen." Another pause.

No one moved away at that age. What she'd meant—*how he took it*—was that she'd escaped at seventeen, and goddamn it, he wanted to hold her, to somehow soothe the desperation she must've felt.

At seventeen, his mother had still been...well, mothering him. To this day, in fact, he had that luxury.

And now he wanted to call his mom and say thank you. Thank you for always listening, always caring, always being there. He'd take care of that later tonight.

"I got a job at the local grocery mart," she explained. "I had my own rinky-dink apartment. Sometimes the heat didn't work, and the only air came from an open window." Her laugh was a soft sound of sad accomplishment. "Not in the best part of town, but I loved it. I was determined to make my life different, to do things my own way, the *right* way, you know?"

He nodded. Understanding Mary as he did now, he could almost feel the drive that had made it possible for a young lady with no family backup to get out on her own. "That took guts." Guts and desperation.

Her mouth turned down in a quirk. "I thought it would make a difference, but it was like everyone watched me, waiting to see which type of freak I'd be, if I'd follow in my mother's footsteps or if I'd just crawl into a hole and die."

"Fuck 'em."

That earned him an honest grin. "My attitude was more like *I'll show them*."

Show them how? he wondered.

He no sooner thought it than she explained.

"I tried sex, just to prove I wasn't damaged." She sighed. "It sucked, but I figured at least I wasn't a virgin anymore so everyone could stop taking bets."

His heart skipped a beat. Incredulous, he asked, "That happened?"

"Or so I heard."

She said it as if it didn't matter, but he didn't buy it. "The first time for anyone—man or woman—is awkward."

"That's what I assumed. It took me a while to work up the enthusiasm for it, but I tried again, thinking a different guy might make it better."

Already sensing the outcome, Brodie rubbed the back of his neck. "Guess it wasn't?"

"It was worse, actually."

Well, damn. "Define *worse*."

Her mouth screwed to the side, then she let out a breath. "The act itself was disappointing. Fast, sweaty and…sort of gross, if you want the truth. But the biggest problem was that I didn't hide my disappointment well enough."

"You complained?"

"Of course not. I'm not mean." She picked at a nail, her gaze avoiding his. "But I guess I was too quiet and he took offense. He went off loudly enough that people out on the street heard."

His heart wanted to break at the same time he seriously wanted to find the little prick and snap him in two. "Did he hurt you?"

"He never touched me, not after the sex."

The sex. What a terrible way to refer to something that should have been satisfying.

"When he got furious, I told him to get out, and he did."

Thank God. "I hope you ignored him after that."

"I tried." She gave up on her nails and turned to stare out the window. "Since he trashed me to anyone who would listen, I was the talk of the town for a while—definitely not in a nice way. I wasn't sure what to think about the sex stuff. My mother never turned down anyone who showed up with cash, because cash meant drugs. But..." Stress showing, Mary folded her arms around her middle and gave a sad, embarrassed laugh. "Sometimes the way she carried on, I couldn't tell if she was excited or being hurt. It was confusing."

Fuck. Brodie clenched his jaw and tried to speak softly. "That must have been awful." *I'm a master of understatement.*

Her arms tightened defensively. "We had very thin walls—not that it mattered when they seldom remembered to close the door."

The flippant words cut him. "That happened with you there?" *How else would she know?*

Mary nodded. "I always locked myself in my room. Turned up my music." Her lips quivered, then firmed. "I pretended to be somewhere else, until I was finally old enough to make it happen."

Fury spilled over, making his words harsh. "How the hell did this righteous little town let it go without doing something?" At the very least, a neighbor should have helped her out of that sick situation.

Mary rested back against the seat, but her posture was stiff, not relaxed. "The sheriff visited my mom often." She turned her head toward him, and for only a second her lips quivered. "With fifty bucks in hand."

That did it. Soon as possible, he'd find a way around her privacy edict and introduce her to his mom. Mary Daniels was in bad need of motherly affection, and no one liked doling it out like his mom.

He could almost understand why the people around her had made assumptions. The wonder of it all was that Mary had survived, even *thrived*, with only a few quirks of her own. She hadn't followed her mother's path, and she was intelligent enough to know that sex had to be better than what she'd seen and heard.

As if to prove his point, she said, "I tried again when I was older, smarter." She shook her head. "I slept with a man I liked, and I thought that would make it better, but I guess liking him had nothing to do with it. I finally decided that the town was right, and I had issues."

"You don't." He said it with firm conviction, determined for her to believe him.

Her mouth curled. "Thank you for helping me to figure that out."

"Oh, we'll do lots of equations, Red, anytime, anywhere you want. Say the word and I'm on it."

She smiled, a genuine, happy smile this time. "It's nuts, but I can hardly wait."

CHAPTER ELEVEN

Brodie had a shit-ton to say to Therman when they reached his house later that afternoon, but all his concentration seemed to be elsewhere.

The idea of his Mary, so proud and independent, having such a tragic background ate him up. The more he stewed on it, the sicker he felt. The angrier he got. The more he wanted to show her just how perfect she really was.

But he couldn't do any of that yet.

On the return drive, she'd taken that long slinky ponytail and twisted it up into a hideous bun that he seriously hated. Not because it looked that bad—he wasn't sure Mary *could* look bad, though God knew she tried—but as soon as she'd restrained her hair, she'd become a different woman.

She'd gone from being vulnerable and open to emotionally buttoned-up and almost cold.

But now, after everything she'd shared, he could see through the tiny cracks in that brick wall she'd built around herself. He still had questions, dozens of them, but he'd made some major progress.

More important, he was starting to understand the need for

the bricks. He could almost imagine her putting them in place one by one over an upbringing of shame and rebellion and hurt.

Which was exactly how he'd take them away—one by one.

For now, though, he needed to concentrate on the encounter with the boss. Making demands without getting personal would be tricky.

Not that Therman was stupid. He had a feeling the man had taken one look at him with Mary and seen the fireworks going off between them. After having them visit together several times now, Therman likely had a grasp of their relationship.

He might be older, and he might be crippled, but he was still a man.

Both Howler and Mary were silent beside him when he rang the bell on the massive front doors. In his fist he held the sadly rumpled bag that supposedly contained an Oscar and documentation.

Mere seconds later, Vera greeted them with loads of drama.

"Mary!" Arms open, she swept Mary in and hugged her briskly from side to side. "Oh my God, I was so worried."

If Brodie had ever bothered to imagine the personality and behavior of a housekeeper, he wouldn't have envisioned anyone like Vera. She acted more like a favorite aunt than the person responsible for Therman's mansion.

It was one of the reasons he liked her so much.

Behind Vera, an apron tied around his waist, Burl grumbled, "Turn her loose before you squeeze her to death." Then in explanation to Brodie, he added, "Therman told us what happened. You're both okay?" He frowned at the bandage on Brodie's head.

Before he could answer, Vera spoke again. "We expected you yesterday and then early today, and now it's afternoon and it's not like you, Mary, to not be here when Therman requested."

"I told him we couldn't." Brodie didn't explain that Mary had been in the shower at the time. Telling Therman was bad enough, and if Mary knew, she'd probably have his head.

"I kept imagining the worst." To shore that up, Vera clutched her hands together.

Burl put his arm around her. "When Therman worries, we all worry."

Damn it, Brodie grumbled to himself, how could he vent when being met with concern?

"Sorry," Mary said in a rush, one hand checking her already smoothly contained hair while her face went hot. "We should have gotten an earlier start, but...we had to clean the car before we could leave today. After the storm yesterday and everything...everything that happened..." She drew a breath and tried to calm her racing words. "Well, it had gotten pretty muddy." She smiled, a false, brittle smile.

Brodie hated that she had to explain herself in any way, that she might actually be regretting their time together. She had a right to her own time, and the right to spend it any way she wanted.

Especially when she spent it with him.

"What happened here?" Burl asked, nodding at the bandage on Brodie's head.

"It's nothing," Brodie said, and without thinking, he deflected the attention by saying, "Mary got a little bruised up."

"Bruised?" Jolene asked as she walked behind Therman's wheelchair. "Where are you hurt, Mary?"

Well, hell. They'd all converged on them so quickly, coming from all corners so that Brodie could barely keep track.

The house was just too damn big, with too many ways to sneak up.

Mary turned her hot face to Brodie in accusation.

Yeah...he wasn't supposed to know about any bruises. "Remember you said you hit your hip when you..." *Were attacked.* But she wouldn't like him saying that, either, so he censored himself with "Fell?"

"It's fine," she stated through stiff lips, then subtly tugged her shirtsleeve down her arm to hide the angry rash there.

Howler pushed around them both, tail swinging, and made a beeline for Therman.

While avoiding everyone else's eyes, Therman quietly greeted the dog.

That's right, Brodie thought, *you should feel bad.*

"Well." Jolene gestured at the hallway. "We can talk over dinner."

"Dinner?" Mary asked, still fussing with her clothes. "Isn't it too early?"

Already Brodie knew that Therman liked his routine and didn't vary it often. He really must feel repentant if he was trying to accommodate Mary.

"We assumed you'd be hungry after your ordeal." Burl smiled a little too brightly. "I hope you are because I've made prime rib with pan-seared brussels sprouts, butter-roasted carrots and baked potatoes." He sniffed the air. "Divine, am I right?"

Vera leaned in to say, "Cooking is his way of fretting. He was as worried as me."

Brodie took the hint. "Yeah, smells good." And actually, it did. Luckily Burl wasn't one of those fancy chefs who prepared snails or oysters, and he didn't dump wine sauce on everything. He made real food and Brodie hadn't been disappointed yet.

"I need to talk to Therman first."

Therman's mouth tightened. "So talk."

"In private."

"Brodie," Mary whispered beside him.

He said, "It's important."

Therman started his chair forward. "We can talk over dinner." Howler loped along beside him.

"If that's how you prefer it..." He didn't mind airing his grievances for the masses. The request for privacy was for Therman's sake.

Once everyone had gone ahead, Mary glared at him. "What are you up to?"

Brodie shoved his hands into his jeans pockets and prepared himself for her anger. "I told you I wanted to talk to him."

"Without *me*?"

His eyebrows shot up. "I assumed you'd join us." Even though he knew her presence was going to complicate things, he would never exclude her.

"Oh." She hesitated, but they were now too close to everyone else for her to give him hell. She settled on a warning glare instead.

He hadn't been paying much attention, but instead of going to the formal dining room, where he'd eaten with them before, they stopped in another room next to the kitchen. It was smaller, but no less impressive.

A wall of windows went up to the high ceiling, letting in lazy sunshine filtered by fat clouds. Along with a spectacular view of the grounds, it gave the impression of eating outside.

Burl and Vera hustled off to bring in the food.

"I chose the morning room," Jolene said as she ensured Therman got properly situated at the head of the table. "It's cozier, and after the storms yesterday I decided we should take advantage of the sunshine."

"It's nice," Brodie said. The table wasn't as big, and that'd make talking easier.

As soon as the food was set out, Therman asked, "You want a drink?"

Brodie gave him a direct look. "I never mix alcohol with business."

Expression falsely serene, Jolene said, "Today is to welcome you both home, not for business."

"I'm afraid it's going to have to be both." Brodie didn't yet sit, and maybe because of that, Mary didn't, either.

She stood beside him instead, appearing equal parts determined and appalled.

Vera and Burl shared a glance.

"Mr. Crews," Jolene softly admonished.

Which only made Brodie laugh. "So it's 'mister' now, huh? Is that your way of telling me to mind my manners?"

Her eyebrows arched. "Did it work?"

"Sorry, no." But he wouldn't debate with Jolene. This was strictly for Therman, and Therman alone. Better to get it done and over with. "From now on, Jack lays out my travel plans."

Mary gasped, but Brodie kept his gaze on Therman. Plotting the route was part of what she normally did, but he'd find a way to make it up to her later.

Sitting back in his seat, one hand on Howler's neck, Therman considered him. "Jack is your brother."

"You did your research before you ever hired me. I assume by now you'd know Jack as well as you know me. Probably Charlotte, too." After all, he'd been on the job for more than two weeks.

Therman gave a single nod of acknowledgment.

"Perfect. So you know he's qualified."

Jolene picked up her wineglass. "Mary is qualified."

Brodie appreciated her loyalty. "Yes, she is."

Therman laid his hand over Jolene's and she subsided. But it was out there now, and Brodie damn well planned to address it.

"In fact, Mary is one of the most qualified people I've ever met. She'd also do damn near anything Therman asked her to do." His gaze held Therman's. "But I won't."

A thick silence settled in the room until Burl coughed and Vera shushed him. He knew he was doing the unthinkable, and he didn't care.

Beside him, Mary stiffened. "You don't get to speak for me."

"I wouldn't even try." He stared only at Therman. "If you want to fire me, fine. That's your decision."

"I'm not firing you."

Refusing to show the relief he felt, Brodie continued. "Then destinations go to Jack, and he sets up the route. If he thinks anything looks too shady, alternate plans have to be made."

"That's absurd," Mary snapped. "Oftentimes there's a rush. I already explained that to you. Therman can't just change his plans at your or your brother's whim."

This would have gone better if he'd had Mary on his side, but he'd already known how she'd react, so he rolled with it, saying, "Obviously, Mary feels differently. You already know she's loyal to you, Therman—loyal enough to walk into an obvious trap because you asked it of her. Clearly she knows her own mind and can make her own decisions."

"*Wise* decisions," Mary stressed. Her fingers were over the back of the chair, gripping so tightly that her knuckles turned white. "I don't need you or anyone else to speak for me, or to protect me."

Brodie acknowledged that with a frown. "True enough. But I won't be a part of it. Hell, I wouldn't put my dog in danger, so I damn straight wouldn't put a woman—*any* woman—at risk."

Mary gasped. "This is because I'm a *woman*?"

Squared off, they both ignored everyone else in the room. "In part, yes. Take it up with my mother if you don't like me being protective." Without taking his gaze from hers, he gestured to the side, vaguely in the direction of the others. "I'd feel the same about Vera or Jolene."

Vera murmured, "Thank you."

Jolene actually laughed.

Bristling, Mary stated, "You're absurd."

"Actually," Brodie said, on a roll, "I'd feel the same about Therman, too." He speared the older man with a glare.

"Me?" Sputtering, Therman bounced his gaze back and forth between them. "What's that supposed to mean?"

"You're smaller, older and in a wheelchair." Brodie folded his arms. "You think I'd willingly walk you into danger? Well, I wouldn't."

"He wouldn't ask you to," Jolene said calmly, though she smiled. "And obviously he regrets putting you and Mary—and sweet Howler—into that position." She shook out a napkin and placed it in her lap. "Now, both of you please sit down so we can talk in a civilized manner. There's no reason for all the theatrics."

Mary looked ready to implode. She'd just been chastened, and it was clear she blamed him.

Brodie didn't give a shit. Did she really think he'd go through that twice? That he'd risk her twice?

Well, he *wouldn't.*

Still standing, he waited for her to take her seat, which she finally did with a huff.

Then he lifted the bag. "Where should I put this?"

Jolene again raised her brows. "What is it?"

"Not worth human life, that's what it is."

Ready to level him, Mary opened her mouth, but Therman's laughter stole her thunder.

"Therman," Jolene said, half out of her chair in alarm.

He looked at Mary's furious face, then at Brodie, and he literally guffawed.

"What?" Mary demanded.

Which only made Therman laugh harder. He hugged Howler and...howled. The dog loved it, his tail swinging in excitement.

Mary turned her confused gaze on Brodie.

Rolling his eyes, Brodie walked the prize over by a credenza and set it on the floor, out of the way. Over Therman's continued hilarity, he said, "There's some paperwork or photos or something in there."

"A photo," Mary bit out, "to authenticate it."

"You didn't look?" Burl asked.

Brodie shook his head. Honest to God, he didn't care what

was in there, only that Mary had been given the hazardous job of retrieving it.

When he returned to the table, Jolene was pressing wine into Therman's hand and he'd just about gotten himself under control. He still chuckled, and twice he wiped his eyes, but after a few deep breaths, he merely grinned.

Jolene, Burl and Vera all smiled in contagious amusement.

But Mary…his sweet, warm Mary, now felt like the brunt of a joke. He'd probably just taken a gigantic step back.

Hopefully, when all was said and done, she'd forgive him.

"Really, Therman." Jolene shook her head. "If you don't stop, Mary will be insulted."

Therman smiled at her. "My apologies, Mary."

"It's all right." She just wished she'd gotten the joke.

"That look you gave him…" His grin spread again, creasing his face in an unfamiliar way. "I'm betting Brodie doesn't catch hell from the ladies very often."

"You'd be wrong," Brodie said. "Mary gives me hell all the time."

While everyone else chuckled, Mary seriously considered stomping on his big foot. "Only when you deserve it."

"No doubt."

"I like that you'll keep him in line." Beneath his bushy brows, Therman's eyes twinkled. "The two of you make an unbeatable combination for my acquisitions."

Was that how he saw it? Incredible, because her perspective was very different.

Vera, who'd just finished passing around the last bowl of food, cleared her throat. "I hope all the excitement didn't ruin any appetites. Burl worked really hard on this meal."

Everyone watched Mary, making it clear that they wanted her to let it go, to accept Brodie's edict and enjoy the meal.

She didn't know if she could.

Indignation almost choked her. It seemed to be caught in her throat, making her eyes burn, urging her to expel it in an angry tirade.

The worst part was that her brain knew Brodie was right; it *didn't* make sense to take chances like that.

But her heart didn't care. Brodie had overstepped and he hadn't even warned her of his plans. Not really. Oh, he'd hinted about talking with Therman, she'd never guessed that he'd steal part of her responsibilities.

Was that what came from sharing sex? People assumed they could do and say things without repercussions?

He kept looking at her, and it made her want to lash out.

Or flee.

She'd really love to leave the table, call a cab and return to her apartment where she could stew all alone.

She knew how to be alone, how to deal with it, but she didn't have a clue how to deal with Brodie.

Dealing with him in front of everyone else? Impossible.

She'd lived through enough scenes in her lifetime that she couldn't bear to deliberately cause one. Lifting her chin, she said to Burl, "I'd love a drink, please."

Burl shot to his feet and readily filled her glass with red wine.

He turned to Brodie. "You're sure you won't have some?"

"Water is fine for me."

Though her expression didn't change, in her mind Mary mouthed sarcastically, *Water is fine for me.*

She wished she was the type who could use drink to help her stop caring. Damn it, *did she care*? She almost groaned...because yes, she knew she did.

Faults and all, Brodie was like a dream man, the mythical rugged, sexy guy, who sometimes made her bed—her *life*—feel less lonely.

Unfortunately, the wine wasn't likely to help. Because she seldom drank, alcohol hit her quickly, usually making her chatty. Not a good thing in her present state.

God only knew what she might say.

Then again, whatever she said, Brodie would deserve it.

Defiantly, she sipped the wine and tried to get her emotions together.

As usual, Jolene stayed attentive to Therman, ensuring his comfort before her own. After Therman was served and had started to eat, Jolene said to Brodie, "I suppose this will be a business dinner after all. I'm a precise person. If things are to be altered, I'll want them in writing."

"Not a problem." He put a bite of beef into his mouth and, in an attempt to normalize the conversation, said, "Damn, that's good."

Burl grinned as he sat again. "Thanks. It's one of my specialties."

"Because it's my favorite," Vera said.

Ugh. They were all trying to normalize things. She was the last holdout.

At first, Brodie had thought it odd that the housekeeper and cook joined them for meals, that they chimed in and acted like family. Now he accepted the arrangements the same as she did.

Close friendship surpassed their employment status.

Brodie had only met the groundskeeper once. He was quieter than the others, but of course he and Brodie had gotten along fine, so much so that by the end of the dinner they'd all been laughing. Same with the head of maintenance and the women who kept up with the indoor plants.

Everyone adored Brodie.

Mary stabbed her fork into a bite of her beef and tried not to glower at it. She wasn't hungry.

She was too irate.

"So." Therman slid his gaze over to her. "We're all okay with Brodie's brother mapping out the routes?"

It wasn't a true question. After all, *she* didn't get a legitimate vote. It was her responsibility to agree, nothing more.

Unlike the others, she'd deliberately remained a mere employee. Getting close to someone meant letting them in, and Brodie was the first, the *only*, person to manage it.

Did she now have regrets? No, not really. She might be annoyed with him at the moment, but she still had those very special memories...

"Mary?" Jolene prompted.

Rather than have it dictated to her, Mary took smug satisfaction in stating, "Why not? He's a *man* after all." There, she'd accepted semigracefully *and* scored a point.

There seemed to be a collective holding of breath.

Mary put down her fork and lifted her wineglass. Sparring, she realized, took nerves of steel, especially when sparring with a big hunk of man who'd given her multiple orgasms.

It was the orgasm part that made it so awkward. She wanted more of them.

Calmly, Brodie cut his food, his gaze on his plate. "What's important, at least to me, is that Jack has more interest in my well-being than he does in Therman's collections."

All eyes landed on her, awaiting her reaction.

Oh, that stung. Was that what Brodie thought? That she didn't care if he got hurt? Of course she did. When those shots had echoed around the area, when she'd thought he might be wounded, even killed... She shuddered.

Just remembering the god-awful fear she'd felt—for *him*—made her heart beat harder.

Slowly pivoting, she glared. "You *know* I was concerned."

"Concerned," he repeated thoughtfully, making it sound so bland. "Guess I was a little bit more than *concerned* with both of us staying alive."

He had a point...but damn him, she didn't want to see his side of things. He could have handled the confrontation better.

He could have confided his plans—and given her a chance to talk him out of it.

Though she felt childish, she couldn't hold back the words, or the baiting smile. "Maybe Jack should ride with you from now on?"

Brodie's gaze shot up to lock on her face. Frowning, he opened his mouth, but nothing came out. His frown darkened even more.

Perfect. She'd left him speechless.

"No." Therman thumped a hand on the tabletop, no longer so amused. "That's always going to be your job, Mary."

Always? He sounded so sincere that it almost felt like job security.

"You know how I trust you, how I rely on you." One eye squinted as he surveyed her. "I might've researched Jack, but I don't really know him. Not like I know you."

He didn't really know her, either, not her hang-ups or the fears carved from her past. Only Brodie knew.

Had she really shared so much with him, so quickly, all because of sexual compatibility? No, to be honest, it was more than that. Something about Brodie drew her in.

Dangerous.

Therman had tried to get closer, too, and everyone in the household worked to include her. It was often disconcerting. "Thank you." Feeling like a fraud, she drank more wine.

"I meant what I said." Therman propped a forearm on the table and tilted toward her. "Brodie's a terrific driver, gutsy, capable and best of all, willing to speak up."

Therman appreciated Brodie's boldness? She could barely credit it. He'd fired other drivers for less!

"But it only works if you're with him."

For a heartbeat she thought Therman meant *with* him, as in a couple, as in two people who'd burned up the sheets on a lumpy bed in a cheap hotel room, and she damn near panicked.

Then she realized that Therman might have taken her suggestion for Jack to ride shotgun as a threat that she'd quit.

Ha! Not likely. She enjoyed her job, relied on it too much to let Brodie chase her off.

As Therman waited, she started to give her automatic reply, *whatever you want*, but quickly rethought that. Even she had her limits and Therman really had pushed them too far yesterday.

She finished off her wine and said, "I'm sure we can come to an agreement."

"I'll give you a raise."

Shocked, Mary blinked. "A raise?" He already paid her well. So well, in fact, that during the three years she'd been with him, she'd never asked for more money.

"Both of you," Therman added, addressing Brodie now. "You've earned it."

Brodie lifted his water glass in a salute. "As long as the raise isn't to get me to accept more risk, I won't argue."

"It's not." Therman glared at him for the suggestion, then turned imploring eyes on Mary. "You're a balanced combo and I couldn't be happier. But understand, no matter who drives, I need you."

To most, his statement would seem very touching and sincere.

Mary knew better.

Therman was a master at getting what he wanted, and for whatever reason, he wanted her riding shotgun with Brodie. Maybe he thought she could temper Brodie's rowdier tendencies, somehow keep him in line. What a laugh. He'd just proved that she had very little sway in anything he said or did.

She'd *slept* with the man and he'd still stepped over her request to let her handle Therman.

Since no one else needed to know how hurt she felt by that betrayal, she said with nonchalance, "Then of course I'll remain with you."

Beside her, Brodie shifted. Oh, he probably had all kinds of things to say, but she wouldn't give him the satisfaction of asking.

The creases in Therman's brow relaxed as he smiled. "Thank you, Mary. I can always count on you." After a grateful squeeze to her hand, he withdrew…and slipped a bite of meat to Howler.

Until then, Mary hadn't noticed that he'd been feeding the dog. How she'd missed it, she didn't know. Howler put on a shameless display of begging, even placing one massive paw on Therman's thigh.

Apparently, she'd been too wrapped up in her own musings.

"You're going to spoil him," Brodie said, sounding unconcerned by the possibility.

"He deserves it," Therman countered, while he refilled her glass without saying a word. He set the bottle aside and asked Brodie, "Why don't you tell the others how you got him?"

Brodie gave her an unreadable look before answering. "He was chained up outside, obviously neglected, so I adopted him."

"Ehhh," Therman groused, shaking a fork at him. "You're not telling the whole story. Share the details."

"That's the gist of it."

Mary could see that Brodie didn't want to talk about it—not that his wants would stop Therman from insisting.

She recalled something Charlotte had said about Brodie rescuing women, men and dogs, and that made her a little curious, too.

"Why be modest now?" she asked with sugary snark.

Brodie snorted. "You should know I am *never* modest."

No, he wasn't. He'd paraded around naked in front of her without any embarrassment. *She* blushed just thinking of it, and remembering how good he'd looked.

She wanted to look again. Even being annoyed with him couldn't keep her from picturing his body in her mind. She had a feeling that image would be emblazoned there for the rest of all time.

"What do you have to hide?" The article she'd read had been necessarily brief, but they'd mentioned that Brodie had interrupted a drug deal, and that he'd taken on multiple people. "Is there more to the story than what the papers printed?"

"Always," he said, as if she should have known that. "A condensed, two-paragraph piece didn't even come close to what happened that day."

"Exactly." Therman pushed back his empty plate. "Give us a blow-by-blow."

"I'm sure Mary can find the article online for you."

Therman's expression drew tight. "I want to hear it from you."

"You don't get everything you want." Brodie ate his last bite.

So he could not only make demands and then defy Therman, he could do it while cleaning his plate.

She looked at her own food, barely touched, and wished she had his élan.

"Having money," Therman informed him, "means having lots of resources. You can try to shut me down, but I have ways of finding out anything I want, about anyone I want."

Jolene quickly shushed him, but it was too late.

Everyone looked at *her.*

Oh, they quickly averted their gazes, but Mary had already gotten the message and it sent alarm down her spine.

Checking into previous employment was one thing; she'd expected that when she'd applied for the job. But did they all know about her past? About her mother?

Humiliation squeezed her heart.

Breathing too fast, she lifted her glass and sipped. Or gulped. She wasn't sure which.

God, she felt exposed.

This was why she'd hadn't gotten cozier with them.

This was why she needed her emotional distance.

She didn't know what to do, but escaping seemed the best option.

CHAPTER TWELVE

Without being sure what she would do, Mary pushed back her chair…

And suddenly Brodie leaned forward, elbows on the table as he drew everyone's attention. "I'm calling BS."

Therman drew himself up. "What are you talking about?"

"You think you can buy the truth?" Brodie spread his hands, taunting. "Let's hear it, Therman. What did you find out with your advanced sleuthing ability? I'm betting it wasn't much."

"I know chunks," Therman insisted.

"I doubt any of it's accurate."

Therman blustered. "Of course it is."

"Because you paid good money for it?" Brodie shook his head. "If you didn't get it from me, then no, it's not likely."

Mary let out a quiet breath. By challenging Therman, Brodie had effectively taken the focus off her. Everyone now watched him, allowing her to relax again.

She could almost kiss him for that.

Almost.

Therman slid another bite to the dog. Expression sly, he stated, "You broke up a drug deal."

"Nope." Brodie sat back in his seat and folded his arms.

Did he know that was a sexy pose for him? Probably.

Therman sat back, too. Nothing sexy about that, though.

"The men were drug dealers," he insisted.

"That part is true, but no deal was going down. In fact, it was their off time apparently, because they were counting cash from the overnight sales."

Therman accepted the correction with ill grace. "Howler was supposed to be a guard dog, but—"

Brodie's snort interrupted him. He leaned forward to see Howler. "Does he look like a guard dog to you?"

Knowing he wouldn't get any more food, Howler turned three circles on the floor and sprawled on his back next to Therman's seat. He let his hind legs drop open. His tongue lolled from the side of his mouth and his floppy ears fell back like a woman's long hair.

As if he felt the attention, the dog opened one eye and his tail swept the floor.

Therman smiled. "He was chained out front."

"Yeah." Brodie frowned at nothing in particular. "I found out later that the bastards had won him in a card game."

Mary caught her breath. Dear Lord, who wagered a sweet animal in a game of chance? Whoever had done so must not have loved him much to begin with.

Poor Howler.

"It was a shit part of town—" Brodie's gaze came up to Vera and Jolene. "Sorry, but that's the best description I have."

Vera said, "Quite all right."

Jolene gave him a fond smile. "You are such a sexist, but let me assure you, if the men don't expire over a little cursing, neither will the women."

"It's not expiring that concerns me. It's the many times my mother boxed my ears." He tugged at one ear as if remembering. "Anyway, it was a terrible part of town."

"What were you doing there?" Burl asked. "I mean, if it's such a bad area."

"Buying a car part from a junkyard. I noticed Howler when I went by that morning, then when I returned, he was still there. It was hot as Hades and he didn't have food, water or shade. He was limp—not relaxed like he is now, but like he was ready to...die." Brodie's hand fisted on the tabletop. "I stopped and gave him water first."

Frowning, Jolene asked, "You weren't worried about getting bit?"

"Didn't really matter at the time."

No, of course it hadn't, Mary thought, because Brodie was that type of man, the type who would step up and do what he thought was right, despite the consequences.

Just as he'd done with Therman.

No, she didn't want to let him off the hook yet, but she'd had two glasses of wine and couldn't stop herself from saying, "You wouldn't have left him there."

Expression serious and direct, he told her, "No, I wouldn't."

Therman picked up where Brodie had left off. "So you offered for him."

"Wrong again." After holding Mary captive in his gaze a few seconds longer, he shifted his attention to Therman. "I'd already pulled that damned iron stake out of the yard and put Howler, chain and all, in my car. I even risked leaving it running in hopes the air-conditioning would cool him down." He paused, his mouth tight, his Adam's apple working. "I still remember how he looked at me through the window when I walked away, like he thought I was abandoning him, too."

Easily picturing it all in her mind, Mary whispered, "You should have just gone."

"Maybe. But I wanted the bastards to know I was taking him."

"And to kick someone's ass," Burl guessed.

"That, too." The corner of Brodie's oh-so-sexy mouth quirked with wry amusement. "Some dude answered the door with a gun drawn. It all went downhill from there."

Therman jumped in. "You fought him."

"I disarmed him," he corrected.

Peeved at all the corrections, Therman insisted, "You broke his jaw."

Surprise lit Brodie's face. "You do have good resources."

At that small bit of praise, Therman preened.

"The break happened when I disarmed him."

"Semantics," Therman argued with a wave of his hand.

"You did that much damage with a punch?" Vera asked.

Brodie shrugged his answer. "Few more guys came charging out. I found myself in a do-or-die situation and I knew if the latter happened, Howler might die, too, since someone would probably steal my car with him in it." Brodie let out a long breath. "I hadn't planned to be in there long, but it happened, so I fought."

"And won," Jolene said softly.

Mary lifted her glass of wine—what was left of it. "He's apparently good at fighting."

"I get by. *But*—" here he looked at Mary "—I avoid fights whenever I can."

Before Mary could react, Therman said, "The police showed up." He nodded at being able to supply that tidbit.

"Yeah, the elderly lady next door had called them. When I explained what happened, I was off the hook, especially after they found the cash and drugs inside." Smiling, Brodie added, "One of the cops even gave Howler his lunch."

"Thank God that woman called," Jolene said.

Brodie rubbed the back of his neck. "She came over to tell me the men were a scourge on the neighborhood. She knew about them, and she knew how they'd mistreated Howler. When I asked her why she hadn't done anything..." He trailed off, frustration and renewed anger darkening his face.

Mary wanted to touch him, to put her hand on his arm and offer comfort. Only because others were in the room, she held back.

Jolene prompted him. "What did she say?"

"That she hadn't called because he wasn't her dog." Brodie finished off his water and sat back with finality. "I told her to go to hell and left."

"Good for you." Jolene stared at Howler. "Who could turn a blind eye to that type of mistreatment?"

"Too many people," Burl said.

A pall seemed to have fallen over them all.

Burl refilled Mary's glass again, then his own and Vera's.

Therman nodded toward Howler. "You destroyed them and this fine fellow was the prize. Gotta respect that in a man."

Burl and Vera agreed.

Actually, so did Mary. But it was so easy, so natural for Brodie, she couldn't stop a twinge of envy. What would it be like to be that strong, to be able to save not only herself, but others?

She had the awful fear that she'd never really know.

Brodie wanted to protest when Mary started on her third glass. The fogginess in her eyes proved she had a low threshold. And yet Therman had refilled her glass, then Burl. Were they trying to get her to loosen up?

If so, that wasn't the way. He knew Mary better than that. If they pried personal information out of her now, she'd resent them for it.

Not that he had the right to say anything, especially with her pissed at him. But he could remove her from the situation.

Hoping to end the visit sooner rather than later, he said, "That's the end of the story, all the ugly details. Let's bury it and move on."

Therman, who didn't miss much, looked from Brodie to Mary and back again. "Yesterday was a mistake, and while I'm not making excuses..." He paused, his grizzled brows twitching until he admitted, "Well, I guess I am."

Brodie barely refrained from rolling his eyes. "Go ahead. Let's hear them." As long as they kept talking, Mary continued to stew. He needed to get her alone so he could start the process of... What? Apologizing? Explaining?

Kissing her and touching her?

All of the above.

Though the more she drank, the less likely the kissing seemed.

Elbows on his chair arms and fingertips touched together, Therman gave his patented squint of one eye. "Granted, it's hindsight, but I now realize that many transactions have the potential for danger. For that reason, an occasional out-of-the-way exchange makes sense. In the case of the Oscar, I was so eager to acquire it that I didn't even consider any consequences."

Odd, because his eagerness seemed to have ended now that he had the thing. Not once had Therman looked at the crumpled plastic bag dumped on the other side of the room. No, he was far more focused on Mary.

Score one for Therman. It might be belated, but he'd finally gotten his priorities straight.

"Many of my dealings are handled under the radar. Going forward, if anything seems shady—" Therman glanced at Mary again "—to Jack, I could send along discreet backup. A few armed guards who'd be on hand just in case either of you felt uncomfortable once you got to the location."

"That's a start," Brodie agreed, though he didn't much like the idea of people dogging his heels. "You can also tell me the name of the jerk who made the arrangements, and refuse to do business with him again."

Therman briefly looked away. "No, I can't do that." He rubbed one eye, then met Brodie's gaze again. "Because there are issues, like the illegality of selling an Oscar, that make anonymity necessary, some dealers are known only by their online handles with no real means to identification."

Jolene explained, "If every purchase was neat and tidy, a *highly paid* private courier wouldn't be needed, now would he?"

Yeah, Brodie got it. Didn't like it, but it made sense. Still, it'd make it harder to keep Mary safe when he didn't know the real threat.

For her part, Mary stared at her glass while muttering, "If you'd asked me, I could have told you all this. But no. Too stubborn, such a know-it-all, so damn bossy..."

Whatever else she said, Brodie couldn't quite hear it. He figured none of it was good.

She'd eaten very little. What was her limit? Would three glasses hammer her?

He'd bet yes.

Sighing, he looked back to Therman. "So I'm working blind, is that it?"

Therman ignored the rudeness. "As you now know, some of the items I purchase require not only competent driving for ensured delivery, but the ability to beat off the competition."

With a theatrical grimace, Brodie said, "Wording is everything, but yeah, I'll defend your purchases."

After a moment of confusion, Therman cackled a laugh.

Brodie suspected he'd laughed more today than he had in the last year.

"Agreed, agreed." Therman glanced pointedly at Mary and cleared his throat. "The violence yesterday shouldn't have happened, but I appreciate your protectiveness of my purchase."

That hadn't been his priority by a long shot, but whatever. "So if the situation warrants it, I have your approval for violence?"

"No," Mary said.

At the same time, Therman replied, "In minor skirmishes, of course. And afterward I want to hear all about it."

Mary gaped at Therman. "You did *not* just say that."

Therman's brows shot up.

She didn't seem to care as she shoved back her chair, making Howler jump up in alarm. *"He,"* she said, aiming a pointy finger at Brodie in case anyone didn't know who she meant, "is difficult enough to manage without you encouraging him."

Taken off guard, Therman blustered.

Coming to her feet, Jolene smoothly interceded. "Vera, Burl, would you please get the coffee and dessert?"

With quick agreement, the two of them escaped.

"While they do that, I'll update the contract I need Brodie to sign." Jolene paused with a hand on Therman's shoulder. "I'll only be a few minutes." Unlike the other two, she left the room with an unhurried and graceful stride.

From under his brows, Therman peered at Brodie as if he expected him to fix things.

He sighed, then said to Mary, "You don't drink very often, do you?"

Gripping the side of the table, she stabbed him with an angry glare. "As often as I please."

The smile caught him off guard. Mary always had a quick answer. That is, she had quick answers when Therman wasn't hinting that he'd dug into her secrets.

"Good thing I'm driving." He added to Therman, "She left her car at the office."

As if she'd just remembered that, Mary groaned and dropped back into her seat. "Maybe I could call a cab."

Terrible idea. "I had the impression you wanted to give me hell on the drive back."

Her mouth tightened. "I do—and you deserve it."

"I know." With Therman as a fascinated audience, he said softly, "I probably should have discussed things with you first."

"Now wouldn't *that* have been considerate?"

"You would have tried to talk me out of it."

"Yes!" She reached for her glass, then looked bemused when she found it empty.

Brodie said quickly, "If it helps, I'm sorry."

Mouth tight, she slanted an evil glare his way. "But no matter what I said, you wouldn't have done things any differently?"

"Not likely." He cared about her safety, whether she did or not.

As if she'd forgotten all about Therman, she started muttering once more. Probably to keep from drawing her ire again, Therman held himself very still. He didn't even twitch one of his impressive eyebrows.

"What do you say we take off as soon as I get those papers from Jolene?" Without giving her stubbornness a chance to make the decision for her, Brodie added, "Howler needs his rest."

A snore filled the air.

Together, they peered at the dog, still on his back, junk out for the world to see. Slobber dripped from his lolling tongue to dampen Therman's expensive rug.

"Yes," Mary said dryly, "he clearly can't rest here."

"So you want to stay for coffee and pie?" Brodie held up his hands. "Fine by me."

"It's a Bundt cake," Therman said. "Not pie."

Mary's eyes widened and her head slowly swiveled to focus on him.

Yup, she'd forgotten about him. Brodie took pity on her and said, "We're going to skip the cake, and I can come back tomorrow morning for the papers."

"No need." Jolene returned to the room and handed him a tidy manila packet. "I added in the changes but everything else is the same." She handed one to Mary as well. "If you could each look it over, sign and fax back to me right away, that would suffice."

"Will do." It took Brodie another five minutes to get Howler awake and motivated to leave while Burl and Vera took turns hugging Mary goodbye. She kept a polite smile pinned in place the entire time.

Burl shook Brodie's hand, then nodded at his head. "Take care of that injury."

Vera grabbed him next. "I'm so glad neither of you were seriously hurt."

To show Mary how it was done, Brodie hugged the housekeeper right off her feet.

Brow creased in a frown, Therman rolled along with them to the door. Just before they could get away, he took Mary's hand, earning a questioning look from her.

Brodie could have told him that hand-holding wasn't a natural thing for Mary, definitely not with her esteemed employer.

Jolene stood behind his chair, one hand on his shoulder in silent encouragement.

After clearing his throat, Therman said, "The raise doesn't cover it, and neither does my gratitude. You're a part of us, Mary. I hope you know that."

In reply, she tried to tug her hand free.

Therman not only held on, he enclosed her hand in both of his. "If you have grievances—"

"*When* you have grievances," Jolene said.

"I want you to bring them to me. You should feel as free as Brodie here does. Understand?"

Clearly she didn't, but she said, "Yes, thank you." She tugged again, but finally relented to the touch. "I love my job, Therman. Everything is fine, I promise."

"Good, good." Relieved, he let her go.

Jolene rolled her eyes at the half-hearted effort. "Thank you for understanding, both of you."

Finally, after another round of farewells, Brodie led Mary to the car. Now that they were alone, he waited for her to start chewing his ass.

Other than pinching her lips together, she kept herself contained.

Once they were on the road, he couldn't take it anymore. Deliberately provoking, he asked, "Are you drunk?"

Her jaw worked before she said, "Possibly."

That she'd admit it surprised him. "On three glasses of wine, huh? You don't drink often."

"Almost never."

"But you did today."

"Yes, and it's a strain to keep from yelling at you." She stared straight ahead. "I get chattier when I drink and I'm afraid that once I start, I won't be able to stop, so I'm trying not to start."

Brodie was pretty sure she already had.

"But God, Brodie, it is difficult. You could have warned me. And yes, you could have listened to my reasons for *not* wanting to issue ultimatums." As she spoke, she got louder. "But you didn't even take my reaction into consideration."

"Not true."

"You didn't care what I thought. You just bulldozed ahead with your own agenda—"

"To keep you safe."

"—and I could have lost my job! Then what? Did you even think that far ahead? I could have been heading home now an unemployed woman. What would I do? Where would I ever find another job as wonderful as the one I have?"

For a woman who didn't want to get chatty, she'd sure given him an earful. "Therman cares for you. He wouldn't—"

"This might surprise you, but I have goals, too, Brodie Crews. Important goals. Things I want." She flattened a hand to her breast. "Things I've been working for. Things that matter *to me*, even if no one else cares."

A lot of meaning hung in those words. "What things, honey?"

She crossed her arms and glared straight ahead. "Most people wouldn't understand, but I don't care. I'm still going to do it." Her shoulders slumped. "Eventually."

"What are we going to do?"

She jerked around to stare at him. *"We?"*

That was how he'd like it, but she sounded so incredulous he knew he'd have an uphill battle. "Why not? Whatever it is, we could do it together, right?" *You're not alone anymore, Red.* It would take time before she believed that.

The laughter burst out, quickly subdued with a hand to her mouth. "Oh, Brodie, you are so nuts."

He was starting to think so, too. What was it about her that made him want to dig in despite her resistance? He liked to think he was a nice guy, but what he felt for her went well beyond simple niceness.

He asked again, "What are we going to do?"

While he waited, hoping she'd confide in him, she stared at him, unblinking. Brodie could almost feel her wrestling with herself.

"If you weren't so damned handsome—and so awesome in bed—it'd probably be easier to tell you to go to hell."

His ego swelled. So did his dick. Hell, he was only human and she sat there, all sweet and tipsy, reminding him of how he'd gotten her off.

"You trust me, remember?" Trusted him to make her climax, but hey, he'd build off that.

After what felt like eternity but was probably no more than half a minute, she whispered, "I'm going to bulldoze my mother's house."

Bulldoze? Never would've guessed that one. "The house you grew up in?"

"Yes." Now that she'd admitted it, she leaned toward him, anxious to share her plans. "I inherited it, but it needs to go. Forever. You understand why."

Sadly, he did.

"The only problem is that it costs a ridiculous amount to do it properly. The house isn't fancy, but the foundation and all is still in good shape. When I first decided to demolish it, I thought I'd pay someone with a bulldozer to come in and just clear it all away. Easy-peasy. Gone and forgotten."

Brodie seriously doubted it would ever be forgotten, though he knew that was her end goal.

"The more I looked into it, the more I learned, and the costs for permits, waste material clearing, safety gear purchased, asbestos abatement—it all adds up." She bit her bottom lip. "The more obstacles I run into, the more determined I am."

Sounded like his Mary. "Why do you want it demolished?"

Instead of answering, she said, "You'd think they'd be glad to be rid of it, and rid of me, but they're fighting me."

"Who is?" Hearing her voice quaver alarmed him. It'd kill him if she cried.

Her eyes, still a little dazed, shifted away. "I shouldn't be telling you any of this. When I decided to do it, to get rid of the house forever, it was going to stay private, something that would die in the town and stay there. It'd be gone, and it'd take all the memories with it." She sighed. "Now I've already told you too much..."

"I'm glad." Because he needed the touch whether she did or not, he reached for her hand. "You can tell me anything."

She laced her fingers with his. "I'm going to regret this tomorrow."

"No, Red. No regrets between us, okay?" He almost added *Promise me*, but her words were slurring and he wasn't sure she'd remember anyway.

Her hand slipped from his. "Easier said than done, since I already have regrets." She leaned back and closed her eyes. "So damn many regrets."

"You drank too much. Why don't you nap? Things will seem

different after a little rest." At least, he hoped they would. *I already have regrets.* God, how those words cut him.

"It's not just the cost." She kept her eyes closed. "The town doesn't want me to knock it down. The town council fights me every step."

What the fuck? "Why?"

"I think because the land is pretty, or it could be when the house is gone. As a kid, I used to play out there while my mom... While she did stuff."

Brodie swallowed a groan. "Trees? A creek?"

"Both." Her lips curled. "I used to climb way up in a big oak until no one could see me in the branches." The smiled died. "I was there once, hiding, when Mom walked out with the sheriff. He liked her, I think, but she treated him the same as everyone else."

As a paying customer? Brodie didn't put the question to her. He half hoped she'd just fall asleep and not finish the awful story.

"He told Mom she should quit, but she said she loved sex and a good high too much."

"How old were you?"

"Twelve." Her eyes barely opened, sightless, lost in the past. "He asked her if she loved me..."

Brodie swallowed heavily, mentally bracing himself.

"Apparently not enough," Mary whispered softly, without any sign of emotion. "That's what she said."

He imagined she'd replayed those words in her mind a million times, and each time they'd hurt until finally she could blunt the pain with determination. It wasn't the house she wanted to demolish.

It was her heartache.

"Anyway." She shifted, getting cozy against the door. "I decided right then that I'd leave as soon as I could, and that someday I'd come back and level the place."

"Why does the town object?"

"Someone wants to buy it." A deep breath expanded her chest. "But I've refused."

"Selling it might be a good way to let it go." She could not only remove it from her life, but add to her bank account.

"No." Closing her eyes again, she sighed sleepily. "No one should live there. Not ever."

Brodie whispered, "Damn, Red, you break my heart."

No reply. He glanced at her and saw she was asleep.

It felt like a reprieve, a chance for him to catch his breath and consider all the things she'd revealed. A chance to recover—because the pain she worked so hard to hide left him hurting, too.

She had regrets. What if tomorrow things didn't look different to her? What if by protecting her tonight, he'd alienated her forever?

He couldn't believe that. He wouldn't accept it.

Soon as she was clearheaded again, he'd start a campaign for winning her over.

He'd always liked a challenge.

CHAPTER THIRTEEN

Mary woke with a jolt. She was still in Brodie's car, but instead of smooth driving on the highway, he'd slowed to a stop as three youths walked slowly across the street, pants hanging low, feet shuffling.

"Too cool for school," Brodie said, shaking his head.

"Um..." She felt a little fuzzy still. The setting sun painted the sky a beautiful crimson with streaks of purple and yellow. She pulled out her phone and checked the time.

She'd been sleeping for two hours? Good grief.

Flipping down the visor, Mary took a quick peek at her hair and gasped. Apparently she'd slept the whole ride home with her head jostled between the seat and the door. She had a crick in her neck and long hanks of hair looped out around her ears. She tried to tuck it in, but it didn't work, so she loosened it all and took it down, working the tangles out with her fingers.

"You snored," Brodie said.

Did she need to know that? "Thank you for informing me. You're always *so* helpful." She deliberately laid on the sarcasm while hoping she hadn't also drooled like Howler.

"It was cute."

She seriously wanted to smack him. "Too bad you weren't as forthcoming about your plans to talk to Therman."

He shot her a quick look. "I was hoping you'd wake up in a better mood."

Stalled in the middle of untangling her hair, she said, "Maybe I'd have been in a better mood if—"

"You hadn't guzzled a bottle of wine?" he asked innocently.

"—*you* hadn't tried to sabotage me with Therman." Remembering annoyed her all over again.

And yes, she'd guzzled her wine. Ugh. Her head was still a little fuzzy and her mouth tasted sour. She didn't need to banter with Brodie right now.

She yanked on a knot and winced at the pain in her scalp.

"I love your hair, Red." Dead serious, he added, "And I would never try to sabotage you. You gotta know that."

"You pretended I wasn't there." Giving up on her hair, she checked her makeup. Ack! Even worse.

"Relax. You look hot."

She snorted at that nonsense. Her mascara now smudged around both eyes.

"Like you just got laid," he added in a gruff voice. "It's a good look for you."

Oh no, she would not let him distract her that easily. Never mind that her bones seemed to be melting and that her thoughts jumped right back to that little hotel room…and Brodie naked…and his hands, his mouth…

"I'm always aware of you, Red. Know that much at least." He pulled up to a stop sign, this time waiting while an elderly woman pushing a grocery cart full of cans crossed in front of him. "If it felt like I was excluding you, it's because you wanted everything kept professional, right?"

"Professional means courteous." Why were there so many people out tonight? How ridiculous would she look if she put on her sunglasses?

"Sometimes, sure. But if I'd been all solicitous and shit, you don't think Therman would have seen through that and known I was personally involved? That I was worried for you?" As he pulled forward again, he growled, "That I wanted to rattle his damn wheelchair for putting you at risk?"

Her heart softened at the idea of personal involvement, even as her brain froze up in fear. She liked Brodie, way too much, but she had a lousy track record with relationships.

"You didn't have to do the whole man-to-man thing with Therman, as if the little lady didn't have an opinion."

"Seriously? You gave your opinion, Red—or don't you remember?"

Yes, she remembered and it was starting to make her stomach hurt. She'd not only contradicted Therman, she'd made her annoyance known. Instead of being professional, she'd blown it.

"Cut yourself some slack, honey."

When had he started calling her that?

"We'd had a hell of a day, in case you don't remember. Therman owed us—*both* of us—an explanation, along with some assurances that it wouldn't happen again. You had a right to be annoyed."

Another stop sign had her ready to hide. Especially when a familiar face left the curb and walked around to the driver's side.

With a low muttered complaint, Brodie rolled down the window and greeted Gina. "Hey, what's up? Everything okay?"

Smiling, Gina leaned down to brace her crossed arms over the bottom of the window frame, showing off a lot of cleavage in the process.

She was just as attractive now as when Mary had first met her...draped all over Brodie's back. Although, granted, dressed in jeans and a V-neck T-shirt, she showed less skin now.

"Wow, you have a carful," Gina said, spotting Howler in the back seat as he came awake and yawned.

She ignored Mary.

Just as well, Mary thought, since she was a wreck, still a tad off from the wine, and not in the best of moods.

"Been working, huh?" She reached in and boldly brushed the backs of her fingers over Brodie's cheek. "I see you still hate to shave."

Women, Mary told herself, *should support other women, not eviscerate them.* Never mind that harsh words teetered on the end of her tongue.

"I shaved a few days ago."

"You're such a man. It's sexy." She lowered her voice. "I think of you all the time, Brodie."

Am I invisible? Mary looked down at herself, but no, she was right there, taking up space on the seat. She wanted to say, *Yoo-hoo, I'm an unwilling witness to this come-on.* But she didn't. *Women should herald other women for their confidence, not ridicule them.*

"We're holding up traffic, Gina."

Shiny lips curled in a sensual smile. "There's no one behind you." Her gaze dipped to Brodie's mouth. "Though I wouldn't mind having you behind me."

Women, Mary reminded herself around choking amusement, *should not laugh at other women who were desperately trying*—no use. The snicker escaped, and of course, that drew Gina's attention.

Pressing her lips tightly together, Mary tried to suck it up, but the laugh squeaked out anyway. "Sorry." She flapped a hand, choking on her humor. "Carry on."

The woman's eyes narrowed. "What the hell happened to you?"

Mary touched her hair to smooth it, and before she even realized what she would say, Brodie's description slipped out. "Wild sex?"

Gina jerked back so quickly, she smacked the top of her head on the way out.

"You okay?" Brodie asked.

Mary allowed herself a smug, malicious smile. Fine, so she'd embellished a bit, but Brodie *had* said she looked like she'd gotten laid. It was better than admitting that a few glasses of wine had knocked her out and she snored all the way home.

Actually...could she blame her nasty behavior toward Gina on the wine? Yes, that was what she'd do.

Breathing hard, Gina glared an accusation at Brodie. "You're screwing *her*?"

He wisely stayed mum.

"I like his whiskers, too," Mary offered, trying her best not to laugh again.

"We should go." Brodie fought his own smile. "Howler needs to visit his favorite grassy spot."

"Bye, Gina." As he carefully pulled the car around her, Mary waved. "It was good seeing you again!" Once they were out of range, a touch of guilt hit her. "That was mean of me."

"You enjoyed it." He maneuvered them through the crowded area.

It was terrible to admit, but yes, she had. "I don't know what got into me." She cleared her throat, then tried out her excuse. "Too much wine maybe?"

He slowly nodded. "Probably."

Glad that he'd so easily accepted that, she started to relax.

Then he said, "But here's the thing, Red—you said you wanted to keep things between us private, and admitting to Gina that we're mattress dancing is a guaranteed way to get it blabbed all over town."

"Oh." The gravity of that sank in. She didn't yet care all that much, but she knew by tomorrow she would.

Hard to care when she was still savoring a minor victory.

So catty. Where had her good manners and business sense gone?

Two older women, busy chatting, stepped out in front of Brodie. If he hadn't been paying attention, he might have hit them.

The two women looked up and waved.

He waved back.

"At least your town seems friendly." Hers had never been. Not with her mother, and by extension, not with her. "I've enjoyed driving through here. It surprised me a little every time."

"Yeah, Red Oak is a constant source of amusement," he said in a wry drawl. "In the mornings you can see the farmers working the fields at one end of Main Street, and at the other is Freddie's, the local bar." He bobbed his eyebrows at her. "You meet a lot of interesting people staggering out of Freddie's at 6:00 a.m."

"I suppose you'd know that better than me."

One brow shot up over her prim voice. "You keep your heavy drinking to the dinner table?"

She winced dramatically. "Today was an aberration."

Grinning, Brodie said, "I know. Believe it or not, I'm not a big drinker myself. It's a rare occasion for me to close out the place, but luckily when I do, I can walk home."

Mary could picture him with friends, all of them laughing and drinking and having a terrific time together.

She had no idea what it would be like to cut loose that way, but she was willing to bet it was fun. "If you ignore the bar, you notice a lot of unique houses. The architecture is amazing." And unlike the house she'd grown up in, these houses were neat, close together and well tended.

She often saw children playing in the yard or along the sidewalk. It never failed to make her smile. All children deserved to be that happy and carefree.

"The houses are interspersed with two churches, a gas station, convenience store, furniture and tool rental, hardware store—"

"Tobacco shop and pizzeria," she finished.

"I almost forgot the pizzeria!" Putting on a serious face, he stated, "They sell sandwiches and barbecue, too. You knew that, right?"

Mary laughed. "So where do Red Oak residents go when they want fine dining?"

"You mean for like a date?"

Yes, she'd like to go on a date with Brodie…but did she dare? For her, actual dating would feel more involved than sex, so she said, "Or as a family—assuming you ever get tired of Shorty's pizza."

"Pizza *and* sandwiches, but yeah, that can only sustain you so long. When either of us wants really good food, Jack and I go to Mom's." He grinned. "But for a night out, we head north an hour or so. Lots of choices there from family restaurants to fancy dining. Actually, shopping is the same. I grab some groceries from the little family-owned place here in town, but I go a half hour south for stocking up."

"Where's the nearest dentist? Doctor?"

"For that, you go east."

She laughed. It seemed no matter what you needed, you had to travel some direction out of the town.

"All in all, it's good. Fresh air, not a lot of traffic. You know everyone and they know you."

The way he said it, he made it all sound very pleasant, rather than intrusive.

As he circled around to the entrance, she said, "You have a lot of property for the office."

"Most of the houses located off the main drag have three-acre lots. We have ten. Land here was cheap back when Mom and Dad bought it. The office was a shop then."

"Was your father a courier?"

Brodie shook his head. "When he wasn't working on cars, he raced them. For a while he was a local star, but he never made it big."

"He's a mechanic now?"

"Off and on, when he needs the money. He does bodywork, too, and interiors. It's one of the really useful things he taught me." Brodie stroked a hand over the car's dash. "Soon as I find the time, I'll have Matilda showing off her sexiness."

Mary choked.

"In fact," he said, "once she's painted and you're in the passenger seat, I'm betting everyone we pass will stop to stare in admiration."

Most people, Mary knew, would stare at Brodie. He definitely drew attention everywhere he went. "I think you're trying to soften me up with flattery."

Voice going low and suggestive, he said, "You're already soft."

Soft enough I just might melt. When he turned on the charm, the man was irresistible. "Brodie—"

"Hey, I know sexy, okay? I'm telling you, the combo of this car and you riding shotgun…" He gave a low whistle. "That'll make an impression."

Absurd compliments aside, it occurred to her that she'd stopped being mad at Brodie minutes after waking.

He *did* have a good excuse for why he'd handled things as he had. Still… "In the future, if you're going to approach Therman about something, I'd prefer you discuss it with me first."

"No problem."

He said it so easily, she blinked. "You mean it?"

"Don't sound so surprised. It was never my intent to exclude you anyway, and I definitely didn't mean to piss you off."

No, his intent had been to avoid dangerous situations.

As a grown woman she could decide what she did and didn't want to do. She didn't need his interference to protect her, *but…* the jobs involved him as well. That meant he had just as much right to refuse as she did to accept.

If that had been the only issue, she might not have minded, but given the new sexual dimension to their relationship, she knew Brodie had been largely concerned for her, and…

Yes, she'd overreacted.

She wasn't used to anyone looking out for her—not as a child and not now.

"Solving world problems, Red?"

He'd used that low, intimate voice again and she *really* wanted to kiss him. "Just considering things." Something occurred to her. "I enjoy chatting with you. You're so informal about everything that it helps me to be less formal, too." Being driven with definite goals in mind meant anything less than professionalism felt foreign to her.

Except here with Brodie.

He scratched the whiskers on his throat. "Yeah, I don't do *formal* any more often than I absolutely have to. Guess that means we complement each other's styles, right? You professional and me laid-back."

She wasn't sure what it meant, but she knew she didn't want to fight with him. "I'm not mad anymore."

His slow smile put a dimple in his cheek.

Yeah, she probably shouldn't have just blurted that out. "I, um, thought you should know."

Reaching over, he cupped her knee. "Thanks for letting me off the hook."

Needing a new subject fast, she cast around and remembered him carrying on again about Matilda. "The interior really is beautiful. You did a great job." Very *professional*—whether he wanted to call it that or not. "It looks factory new, but better."

"Soon her exterior will look great, too."

"You said you're painting her red?"

"Yeah." The smile turned into a grin and he winked at her. "Red is fast becoming my favorite color."

Brodie pulled up in front of the office, glad that the lot was clear. Sometimes Jack worked late, and other times Charlotte hung around for paperwork. With what he had planned, hovering family wouldn't have helped.

Howler had remained awake after Gina's short visit and now the dog whined. He was probably more than ready to stretch his legs and take a leak.

After Brodie stepped out and moved his seat forward, he realized Howler was anxious for another reason. A low growl vibrated in his throat and he stared beyond Brodie, toward the back of the track.

"What is it?" Mary asked.

"I don't know." Normally he'd turn the dog loose and let him run around the property a little, but tonight didn't feel right, so he attached the leash before unhooking the harness.

Howler almost knocked him over, he lunged so quickly from the car. Even after he ran out of leash, he continued to strain against it, his gaze on the track where the setting sun bathed the sky in brilliant colors, leaving the line of trees no more than a black silhouette.

"Easy now." While patting the dog's neck, Brodie studied the scene but didn't see anything out of the ordinary.

Howler gave him a worried look, stared a little more, then gave up to take a pee. "Good boy." He allowed the dog to lead him to a clump of weeds. "What'd you see? A rabbit? Deer?" *Or something else?*

Howler had a good nose. He'd once tracked down a wounded raccoon hiding behind their garbage bin. Luckily he was gentle to other animals and other than barking a bit, he hadn't hurt the already frightened critter.

Brodie had caught the thing, taken it to a wildlife rescue and later rewarded Howler with lots of loving.

When Howler finished his business, he put his nose to the ground and started dragging Brodie this way and that, and eventually toward the office.

It wasn't until then that he realized Mary was heading toward her car. "Whoa."

She glanced up, blue eyes quizzical, that patented fake smile on her mouth.

Not buying it, babe. He knew the sound of her laugh now, had seen her megawatt smiles versus a polite facsimile. He knew when she was faking it. "Where are you going?"

The question seemed to confuse her. "Home?"

Brodie jogged toward her with Howler happily loping along. "But you're still tipsy." And damn it, when was the last time he'd literally chased a woman?

He slowed his pace and approached her more casually.

He wanted her to stay. He *needed* her to stay. Now, how to convince her without looking like a sap?

With a dismissive laugh, she said, "No, I'm not," and dug in her purse for her keys.

"No?" Knowing she might spook if he came on too strong, Brodie leaned on her car with a relaxed vibe. Howler helped, plopping down next to her to stare up adoringly. *Good dog.*

Seemed he and Howler shared a similar infatuation.

"Then you meant to tell Gina that we're involved? I can assume it's okay for me to share, too?"

She paused with her hand in her briefcase, then slowly withdrew it. "I was tipsy—then."

"Ten minutes ago?" She might not be a veteran drinker, but she was smart enough to know effects didn't wear off that fast. Besides, it really hadn't been that long since her wine-induced chattiness—and she knew it.

She gave a great huff. "Okay, so we both know I wasn't."

Admitting it outright and facing her deception—yup, that was Red. He grinned. "Always so honest."

She flapped a hand. "I'm not good at lying. It gets too complicated."

"And you aren't at your sharpest now—so stay with me."

"Stay?" Her eyes widened, and she squeaked, "Here?"

Seeing her like this, uncertain and so damn sweet, made him want her all the more.

He couldn't embrace her because Howler had gone back to

sniffing the ground and it required a good hold on the leash to keep him from pulling away.

But Brodie could kiss her, and he did. Slowly. Lingering.

Around them, the sun faded away and shadows crept in. A second later a security light flicked on.

She stepped closer.

He cupped the back of her neck and angled his head for a better fit. A deeper fit.

Curling her tongue around his, she slipped her hands up his chest. Her belly pressed against him.

The woman wanted him, almost as much as he wanted her. "You have what you need in that overnight case you always carry," he whispered against her mouth, encouraging her. "Stay with me."

Dropping her forehead to his chest, she drew in long, slow breaths. Like a grave confession, she admitted, "I want to."

"I know." He kissed her ear. "Stay."

Her hands tightened, knotting the material of his shirt. "I'm not sure I should."

She rarely gave in to what she really wanted—but with him, she could, and she needed to know that. "It's been a crazy couple of days, Red." He brushed his thumb over the warm silkiness of her cheek. "Stay."

Her head lifted. "So you think I need to be coddled? Because I *don't*."

The inclination was to joke, to maybe palm her ass and tell her he'd make it worth her while. But he couldn't do that, not with her, not this time.

Instead he told the truth. "No, you don't. But maybe I need to coddle you. For *me*, Red." Now he caught her ass, mostly because he couldn't help himself. She had such sexy curves that even in moments like this, when he was trying to be real, he couldn't resist her. "Stay because I need you to."

So many emotions flashed over her face, most of them confused, a few hopeful, many in denial.

He held his breath.

Until she whispered, "No one's ever wanted to..."

"I know." And fuck them all. Her poor sick mother, and the townspeople who hadn't looked out for her, even Therman with his misguided intentions, they all owned that lost look in her eyes. "Stay for me, Red."

He'd keep repeating it as many times as he needed to.

"Okay."

Brodie didn't know if it was what he'd said, or the fondling of her butt that had convinced her. She might not realize it, but she was an innately sexual woman. Hiding it for too many years hadn't diminished her nature.

Going on tiptoe, she gave him a short, firm peck on the mouth. "I'll need to be out of here early, though, okay? I don't want to have to explain to your brother or Charlotte."

She wouldn't need to; they'd understand well enough that she'd spent the night and would never put her on the spot by questioning her about it. "No problem. Neither of them will get in before nine and Howler always gets me up before that."

Speaking of Howler, he did his circular "getting comfortable" move, ready to crash, but Brodie wanted him comfortable *inside*—so he and Mary could be inside as well.

Near a bed.

Or a couch. Or a table.

His imagination was already on the run.

They locked up the cars and he carried in her overnight case. Once he got through the door, Howler made a beeline for his food dish in the small kitchen, standing over it with an expectant expression on his long face.

After kissing Mary's temple, Brodie said, "First things first." He filled the dog's dish, going through the program of pretending to eat it until Howler was convinced to dig in.

Smiling, Mary leaned against the small bar that divided the kitchen from the living room. "That's one of your most endearing qualities."

Still down on one knee, he asked, "Fake eating kibble?"

She laughed. "Doing what's necessary to reassure that big sweetheart of a dog. I'm so glad you found him."

"Yeah, me, too." With Howler now occupied, he stood. "You want the two-minute tour?"

"Yes, please."

He looked around, then said, "Might be one minute. It's a small place." And damn it, he hadn't actually cleaned up lately. Most of the dishes were in the dishwasher, but he'd left yesterday's cereal bowl in the sink.

When was the last time he cleaned the floor?

Too late now.

He gestured. "Kitchen. The bar is where we had most of our meals. Jack and I sat on that side, our backs to the TV, and Mom sat on this side, keeping her eagle eye on us. You can't know how intimidating it is to have her looking over my homework during dinner."

"Did it cause you to get good grades?"

He shrugged. "Sometimes. Other times, it just made me squirm." Stepping around her, he waved a hand at the couch, two chairs and a few tables—all facing the big flat screen on the wall. "Living room. Small, but we made it work."

Tracing her fingers along the back of the fattest chair, she smiled. "There were only the three of you, so plenty of chairs."

"Are you kidding? We had friends over all the time. There were a lot of nights that Mom stayed in the kitchen to give us room while we filled every cushion and sometimes the floor." He looped an arm around her waist. "When Jack and I got older, we filled the room with girls. Mom had a strict rule about us even looking toward the bedrooms." He laughed with the memory. "She seemed to think we'd do things in there that we didn't do elsewhere—at least until she caught Jack out in the woods across the track when he was sixteen."

"Oh, wow." Mary's voice dropped to a scandalized whisper. "Your *mother* caught him having sex?"

"Caught him trying." He shook his head. "It was close. If she'd gone looking for him five minutes later, he'd have really been busted."

"What did she do?"

"She walked a safe distance away, then started calling him so he'd have time to zip up and the girl could get her top back on. We both got lectured then, again, about how to treat a lady." Remembering made him laugh. "Poor Jack." He looked down at Mary. "I hear the girl made it up to him later."

"Did your mother know that?"

"I'm sure she suspected. I mean, she knows us, right? She knew what she was dealing with." Detailing all the ways that his mother had been awesome might make Mary more aware of how hers had failed, but even better, it'd detail for her how a mother should be. He felt like she needed that.

Like she craved it.

When she met his mom—and she definitely would, maybe in a few weeks—he wanted her to be prepared.

Pausing by a door, he said, "Bathroom. I'm a slob, I know. So sue me."

She peeked in, seeing the overflowing hamper with a T-shirt hanging out, the open shower curtain, the towels slung over the rod, and the double sink piled with his toothbrush, razor, cologne and such.

When the hell had he accumulated so much junk for grooming?

Mary straightened his razor. "For a man who doesn't shave often, you like it all handy."

"Yeah." He frowned. "I should start putting it away, huh?"

Her lips twitched. "I'm teasing."

"Still..." He glared at the mess, then led her to the next room. "This was my and Jack's bedroom."

"Oh." She stepped in, looking around in smiling awe. "Bunk beds?"

"Original, from about the time I was five." He shoved his hands into his pockets and propped a shoulder on the wall. "Those crooked curtains? Mom tried her hand at sewing. It was pretty hilarious, but they matched the bedspreads."

"Race cars," she noted.

"Yeah." Damn, he had so many good memories that he wished he could give some to her. He pulled her close and growled, "I've never had sex in that bed."

Her lashes lifted. "Top or bottom bunk?"

"Bottom." Of course, his hands went to *her* bottom and he asked huskily, "Want to give it a try?"

Her mouth twitched again. "Maybe another day."

Meaning she'd come back? He'd hold her to it.

"Show me your bedroom, then I'd like to clean up."

In that moment, Brodie decided he would get her in the bunk one way or another. Not tonight, but soon.

He'd mark a milestone with her.

They strolled into his bedroom and, trying not to be obvious, he walked around picking up discarded socks, shoving crumpled receipts into his pockets and kicking shoes under the bed. "Growing up, this was Mom's room. That second closet has the washer and dryer in it. She used to fold everything on the bed, putting it in stacks for Jack and me, then we had to put it where it belonged. That is, until we were twelve or thirteen, then she taught us how to do all of it."

"You did laundry?"

Why did that surprise her? "Yeah..." He looked around again. "Despite the evidence, I still do. We had to take turns with chores. Dishes, laundry, cooking, cleaning. Mom said we needed to know how to take care of ourselves." He rubbed the back of his neck. "I can cook, too, but she does it better, so..."

"So you often finagle her into doing it for you?"

"She loves it." Very true. "Coddling is her game. She talks a hard line, but it was always backed up with smothering affection." Though he doubted it would ever seem smothering to Mary. "What about your mom? Was she sometimes affectionate?"

Under the guise of looking around the room, Mary turned away. After a full minute had passed, she shrugged. "She liked to play with my hair."

Now, that was a nice enough image for his brain. "She'd brush it for you? Maybe put it in a braid?" His mom had done the same for Charlotte many times.

But Mary shook her head. "She used to try out new hairdos on me." Her mouth twisted to the side. "In fifth grade, I was a Marilyn Monroe blonde—sort of. It's not easy to dye red hair white. In sixth, I was as dark as Elvira."

He shook his head. "Why?"

She shrugged. "Mom and I looked alike so she'd try things on me to see how they might look on her." Touching a finger to the dresser, she traced around the base of a lamp. "She gave me a pixie cut once, then laughed every time she looked at me."

Jesus, Joseph and Mary. He had no words.

Mary flickered a glance at him. "She told me it was a good thing she hadn't done that to her own hair."

Scrubbing a hand over his face didn't help remove the scowl, not when it came from his heart, from his very soul. Her mother had been downright cruel, whether on purpose or through ignorance, he didn't know.

But Mary's insistence on playing down her hair now made sense.

"I do remember something, though," she went on. "Something good, I guess."

"Let's hear it." God knew he needed one decent memory for her.

"When I started seventh grade, I was already ridiculously chesty."

Nothing ridiculous about it. "You have killer curves, Red. *Gorgeous* killer curves." She needed to know that.

Her lips tipped up in a slight smile—that all too soon faded away. "One of Mom's customers noticed."

Shit. Brodie tensed all over.

"After they—" she flapped a hand "—finished up, he was supposed to be leaving the house, but he…he detoured." Her gaze fixed on his. "To my room."

Brodie locked his hands to the back of his neck and walked a tight circle, trying to contain the scalding rage. A hundred scenarios raced through his brain, each one worse than the one before it.

He wasn't a man who lost his temper, but the things she told him, combined with how much he was starting to care…

Facing her, he demanded, "Give me a name."

Tipping her head, Mary studied him with fascination. "There's no need."

"There is *every* fucking need." He'd find the bastard and make him pay—

"No, you don't understand. My mother heard me yell and she took care of it."

Stilling, he drew a breath, hopeful, but no way could he relax yet. "Took care of it how?"

"She came charging in like a crazy woman, armed with a bedside lamp and swinging like a home-run hitter. I'd never seen her like that."

Like a *protective mother*, she meant, and that had him grinding his teeth. "You weren't hurt?"

She shook her head. "I thought she would kill him, she was so furious. He started by apologizing, then by accusing, and still she kept after him—until he decided to swing back." Growing quiet, she admitted, "He struck her here—" she touched her own cheek "—and she sprawled on the floor. I was hunkered down on the other side of my bed, and she landed right by my feet."

Brodie swallowed heavily, waiting for the outcome of this grisly tale.

"He told her to settle down, but she didn't. She was right back up and attacking again, and finally he ran off."

The quiet in the room was suffocating.

Brodie tried to recover, to assure himself she hadn't been hurt, but he knew it was a lie.

She'd been hurt so badly it ate him up.

At his silence, Mary said, "I've never really told anyone about that before. It's not the same as the fun stories you share. It's… Well." She chewed her lower lip. "I'm sorry."

"Please don't be."

Hand to her forehead, she turned away. "I don't know why I keep telling you stuff."

Because she trusted him. Because what they had was special. She needed to talk, and hard as it was to hear, he wanted to be the one to listen. "What did she say after he was gone?" *Please let it be soft words, motherly words of concern.*

"That it was bound to happen sooner or later and that from now on I should stay in my room with the door locked whenever men were over."

Okay, not what he was hoping for, but he could work with that. "She didn't want you hurt by her decisions."

"I assume not." She looked around the room again. "Your childhood sounds wonderful. Like an ideal upbringing."

"We had our moments of upset. Everyone does." But he'd never, not once, felt unloved.

Seeing her like this, so emotionally exposed, redirected his lust in a big way.

He still wanted her, he *always* wanted her, but he also needed to be a part of her, to hold her as close as two people could get.

She needed to know she wasn't alone. Not anymore.

"Want to catch a movie?" He'd go old-school with her, snuggling close in front of the boob tube. Given her upbringing, he was willing to bet she'd never experienced the joys of necking, of stolen feels and naughty suggestions. Brodie wanted her to know it all—with him. "Howler probably already has the couch but we could curl up in a chair together."

For tonight, being with her would be enough.

And that idea alarmed him. What the hell was he thinking? He had a gorgeous woman alone and he wanted to snuggle?

Jack would laugh his ass off if he knew. Luckily, Red saved him by saying, "Maybe later." Her sultry smile sent blood rushing to the wrong head. "I need fifteen minutes to shower and then I expect you—" she pointed "—in that bed." Her gaze moved over him. "Preferably naked."

And with that, she picked up her overnight bag and walked away.

Brodie stood there, a little in awe of her resilience…and a little bit in love.

Yeah, he figured he may as well face the truth.

He was falling for short, stacked, bossy and blue-eyed Mary Daniels. A first, but he figured he'd get used to it.

As long as he wasn't falling alone.

CHAPTER FOURTEEN

Brodie couldn't look away.

Mary's hair hung loose around her shoulders, and she wore only a T-shirt and panties when she stepped out of the bathroom, a waft of steamy air following her.

By deliberate choice, he'd made sure he wasn't in the bed and wasn't naked. He'd spent the time—twenty-two minutes, not fifteen—thinking of what he'd do and how he'd do it.

If Mary had her way, she'd make their time together about sex and only sex. Usually a plan he agreed with.

But not now, not with her.

He needed her to know it was *more.*

After he'd washed up in the kitchen, then taken Howler out again, he'd removed his shoes and socks so he wore only his T-shirt and jeans.

As she stepped into the bedroom, she set her overnight case by the door, with her purse and briefcase, almost as if she wanted everything there and ready when she decided to book.

Like hell.

She'd barely gotten both feet into the bedroom when he

pressed her to the wall and kissed her, a slow, deep, consuming kiss that had her quickly clutching at him.

Just what he'd intended.

Just what he needed.

When he trailed wet kisses to her throat, she whispered, "You're still dressed."

"Safer that way." Catching her bottom in both hands, he rocked her against him. Yes, he was already hard.

He'd had twenty-two minutes of torturous fantasizing to get him primed.

Against her neck, he whispered, "Much as I want you, it'd be too easy to jump the gun if I didn't have denim in my way." Not that the denim was helping that much. He strained the damned zipper, he was so hard. "But *you* should totally be naked."

Saying it, he caught the hem of the shirt and pulled it up and over her head. Mary helped, but then she stepped against him before he could look at her.

He felt every lush curve—but he wanted to see them, too.

"I'm a visual person," he said and gently pressed her back the length of his arms until her shoulders met the wall. Taking his time, he looked her over, starting with her face.

A damned precious face to him now, freckles included.

Especially the freckles.

She looked younger without makeup, extra small and sweet. Small in stature anyway. Her figure… He couldn't hold back a throaty growl, she was so damn shapely. And for now, she was his.

He trailed his gaze down her pale throat, her delicate collarbone, those proud shoulders that had carried so much hurt, and then to her big breasts.

As he studied her, her nipples drew tight.

"Brodie," she complained. "You've seen me before."

"Doesn't matter. I could look at you all day, hell, all *week*, and not get my fill."

She tried a sexy pout that proved pretty damned effective. "I want to look, too."

"Soon," he promised.

A lustrous hank of red hair hung down around her left breast, framing that pale flesh with vibrant color. Fucking *hot*.

Keeping one hand on her shoulder so she wouldn't move, he gathered the hair in his fingers and teased it back and forth over her nipple.

Her breath caught. "I'd rather have your hand."

"All right." He brushed her hair back and cupped her, gently kneading, marveling at her softness, at the weight of her breasts.

Mary shifted. "I'd like your mouth even more."

So would he. He bent down and licked her, all around her nipple while avoiding the tip.

Frustration had her groaning. And threatening. *"Brodie."*

"All right." He drew her in, sucking strongly until her back arched.

Her fingers tunneled into his hair and she cried, "I need you, Brodie."

"Let me see." Savoring her, he stroked a hand down to where her waist sharply nipped in, over the ripe flare of her hip, around to the slight curve of her belly—and straight into her panties.

Widening her stance, she breathed faster.

He found her hot and wet, and he eased a thick finger into her. The way she stiffened stopped him.

"Mary?" He looked into her eyes. "What is it?"

"It's fine. It's good." Her eyes were big, trusting.

"I know women, honey." He brushed his mouth over hers, his hand utterly still…but his finger still in her. "Tell me the problem."

Heat colored her cheeks. "I'm just a little sore."

Yeah, she would be. How long she'd gone without sex before meeting him, he didn't know, but she'd been so tight, gripping him like a fist… He knew it had to have been a while.

Swallowing a groan, he started to withdraw.

Her thighs closed, trapping his hand against her. "Don't you dare."

He put his forehead to hers. "I don't want to hurt you." Not ever, not in any way.

"I'm a big girl, Brodie. I'll tell you if I want you to stop."

True. So far Mary hadn't held back, not with him. Reassured, he kissed the bridge of her nose, her cheekbone, her jaw. "We'll go slow, then."

"I don't want *slow*."

"I know." The grin tugged at his mouth. Being wanted by her was the biggest turn-on of all. "But you're like a new present I want to enjoy. Patience, okay?"

"Brodie—"

He pressed his finger deeper, effectively cutting off her complaints.

"Once you've come, you'll be even wetter and it'll be easier for you. Then when you come again—"

She groaned.

"—I'll be inside you, filling you up."

She clenched around him.

He went back to her nipples, all while working a finger in her. Her legs trembled and she breathed low and deep. With the heel of his hand, he pressed her clit.

Mary held his head to her, occasionally guiding him to the other breast. He tongued each stiffened nipple, leaving them wet, then sucked again.

"I need..." She put her head back. "Brodie?"

He pulled his finger from her and, using her own wetness, teased her swollen clit.

"Ah... God."

He stroked, rolled, caught her in his slippery fingers and tugged.

The climax erupted all at once, gripping her with tension,

making her body bow and shake. He stayed with her, still playing, his heart full, his cock straining, until the last tremor had left her.

He caught her against him, smoothing her hair, crushing her close. "I'm dying for you."

Hands fisted in his shirt, her body lax against him, she released a long shaky sigh. "Then have me."

"Yeah." Turning them both, he back-stepped her, slowly, to the bed. "I think I will."

When they reached the mattress, he waited, giving her a little more time while he stroked the elegant line of her spine, the small of her back, that firm ass.

"Panties off." He ran both hands into the slinky material over her cheeks, dragging them down to her ankles.

Holding his shoulders, she stepped out and toed them aside. "I'm limp."

"I'm not."

Her lips curled. "I know." She reached for him, but Brodie turned her so she faced the bed.

"Bend forward."

Intrigued, she glanced over her shoulder. "What?"

Nudging her behind with his erection, he said, "Bend over the bed, legs wide." One-handed, he opened the snap on his jeans, then eased down the zipper. "And hold on."

She looked back at the bed, hesitating. Deciding.

He loved how Mary approached sex with healthy curiosity and a willingness to try things. He marveled that, until him, she'd only found self-serving fools, because God knew the woman was a glutton for pleasure. Any man, even those lacking experience, could have won her over with patience and attention.

Unfortunately, she'd drawn the short straw on the lot of them.

While she considered things, Brodie reached around to hold both her breasts, catching her nipples between his fingers. In her ear, he whispered, “I can get to you this way, play with your nipples or your clit while pounding away.”

A light tremor went through her. For only a moment she rested her head back against him, allowing him to ramp up her interest again. “Okay.” She stepped forward until her knees touched the mattress.

To his extreme pleasure, she bent at the waist, arms outstretched to support her, legs straight with that phenomenal ass up and on display.

Hell yeah. “Legs a little wider,” he murmured while stripping off his shirt and tossing it aside.

Slowly, a little uncertainly—which somehow made it sexier—she did as he asked.

Seeing her swollen pink sex, glistening wet, Brodie groaned. “I could come right now.” He ran his hands lightly over her, feeling the softness of her inner thighs, up to where they met the twin curves of her bottom. He palmed her, a cheek in each hand, and got even harder—which until it happened, had seemed impossible.

“Stay exactly like this.” As he stepped back, his gaze never left her. He kicked off his jeans and boxers, grabbed a rubber from the nightstand and rolled it on with practiced ease. His balls were tight, his muscles clenched, his heart hammering.

He wanted it to be good for her, always, but emotions were somehow pushing him, leaving him on the ragged edge, physically desperate, whole body burning. He’d never before experienced anything like it; it was confusing as hell, but also satisfying.

He wanted her. He needed her.

For now at least, she was here.

He stepped up to her, one hand on the small of her back, the other holding his cock as he teased the head up and down her slit. So wet. *For me.*

The Neanderthal in him whispered, *Only me*, but he ignored it as he nudged into her, barely there, watching as she opened around him. Knowing she was tender from previous enthusiasm, he did his best to go slow, but she pressed back, wanting more, those slick, swollen lips kissing him *there*, trying to draw him in.

He locked his jaw. "Tell me if I hurt you."

She groaned, "You're *killing* me."

With a firm press, he got the head in.

On a vibrating moan, she tightened, squeezing him, and he lost it.

He held her hips and in one smooth glide, buried himself until his groin pressed firmly against her plump cheeks and they were both breathless.

"I was going to take it slow and easy," he accused.

"Forget it." She arched her back, lifting her rump more, pushing back against him, that gorgeous hair spilling around her shoulders. "Go fast, Brodie. Fast and hard."

No need to tell him twice. Leaning over her, he braced himself with one outstretched arm and with the other, he caught a nipple, gently rolling as he withdrew, sank in again, dragged out, thrust deep. Over and over, quicker with each stroke until they were both close, so close. Then he reached lower, down her belly to her sex. Her hands fisted in the sheets and she cried out.

That did it for him. Feeling her squeeze him, seeing the frantic tensing of her body, hearing her uninhibited sounds of release... Brodie put his head back, buried himself in her and let himself go.

When his cock pumped for the last time, leaving him spent, he gently lowered them both to the mattress, turning so he spooned her on his side.

He still breathed deep and his legs were shaky.

She cuddled her bottom into him and gave a heavy sigh.

Trailing his fingertips down her arm, he whispered, "You're getting good at this, Red."

Her elbow came back, not hard—he wasn't sure she had the

strength in her present listless condition—but it was firm enough to make him grunt.

"Is that a complaint?" she asked with still-breathless humor.

"No." He squeezed her so she couldn't jab him again. "Just saying if we practice a lot—" he punctuated that with a kiss to her shoulder "—like at least once a day and twice on weekends, you'd be even better."

For a terrifying heartbeat she went utterly still, her body no longer soft against his…then she relaxed. "How long do you think it'd take for me to perfect my moves?"

He wanted to say, *A lifetime*, but he didn't want her freezing up on him again. "You'll know it when you get there. Until then, I expect you to apply yourself."

A thought occurred to him. Frowning, he turned her to her back and loomed over her. "Private lessons with *me*, Red. Only me."

With her skin still flushed, her freckles stood out. Those eyes—*God, he'd never get used to her eyes*—stared up at him as if trying to piece together a difficult puzzle. And her mouth, puffy and pink from their kisses, smiled. "I didn't enjoy it with anyone else anyway."

He was starting to think that was a good thing, at least for him.

She touched his jaw. "I insist that you not practice with any-one else, either."

He parroted her words back at her, with a slight twist. "I don't want anyone else anyway." How could he, now that he'd had her?

After stretching, she smothered a yawn.

"Sleepy?"

"Not really, but I'm not exactly energetic, either."

"Then let's go grab some ice cream and watch a movie with Howler. He likes action flicks best, but you might be able to talk him into a drama."

Mary laughed. It was a beautiful sound, especially so with her naked and in his bed. With any luck, he'd have her over often enough to hear it again and again.

Mary woke alone, shivering among the sheets cooled by a humming air conditioner. At first she didn't understand. Unfamiliar dawn light bled in through...unfamiliar drapes.

She narrowed her eyes; even the placement of the window didn't make sense.

Sluggishly, she sat up, her impossible hair everywhere, half of it in her face.

Naked?

Brodie.

The memory of him flooded over her like a warm tide: unbelievable sex, followed by the fun of curling in a chair together, watching a movie while he fed her ice cream, and then the comforting way he'd held her all night.

Oh, how she could get used to all that.

Used to it? She already *craved* it.

Of course, his side of the bed was empty, otherwise she wouldn't have been cold. The man gave off heat like her own personal furnace.

It took her a second to locate a clock. Only 5:00 a.m. He'd said Jack and Charlotte wouldn't be in until nine, so she had plenty of time. Good thing, since she always woke like a zombie.

Assuming he'd taken Howler out, she left the bed and gathered up her T-shirt and panties. A peek out the bedroom door showed everything dim and quiet. Literally sneaking, she carried her clothes and darted into the bathroom.

After taking care of business, she surveyed herself in the mirror. Not good. With her long hair tangled around her face and no makeup, she looked bad. Like Death had a nightmare and woke up screaming.

Coffee. That was what she needed.

She pulled on the shirt and panties, splashed the sleep from her eyes, gargled with mouthwash just in case Brodie felt amorous this morning and then crept to the kitchen.

The coffee was usually made at the office, but she had no intentions of still being around when it opened. It only required a little snooping in the cabinets to find the coffee and filters.

A little hopeful for quick morning sex before she had to leave, she made enough for two, then waited impatiently until the coffee machine finished. She'd just filled a mug when she heard voices outside.

Until then, she hadn't realized that the door wasn't shut completely.

Brodie had company? This early?

She strained to hear, and while she couldn't make out what was said, she realized that one of the voices was female.

Suspicion mixed with jealousy, and a vision of Gina draped all over him again brought on a frown.

Many times in her life she'd been jealous, but never over a man. God, no, not after her mother had paraded man after man into their home. She'd grown up seeing them as interchangeable. Necessary for sex, but not for anything more.

What she'd envied was the sight of a mother and daughter shopping together, walking in the park, even chatting. She and her mother hadn't shared many meaningful talks.

Now there was *this* jealousy, all new because of Brodie. He'd changed her perceptions on men big-time.

She tried to talk herself out of it, but her feet already had her halfway to the door. She told herself that she'd just peek out and see who was visiting.

Unfortunately, as she reached for the knob, the door suddenly swung open, forcing Mary to take a startled leap back. The mug slipped from her hand, spilling coffee on her shirt as it dropped, then broke on the floor, narrowly missing her foot.

Yelping, Mary frantically pulled the shirt loose, shaking it to let cooler air in near her skin as she jumped on one foot to avoid the spill.

"Brodie," that female voice chastised, "you should have told me you had company."

Oh no.

Inching her gaze up in trepidation, Mary found herself facing a woman with dark eyes and very lush lashes…who looked amazingly like a petite feminine version of her son.

Dear God, *the mother.*

"Shit." Brodie stepped in around the woman. "Are you all right, Mary?"

Wishing she could be somewhere, *anywhere*, other than here, she whispered, "Yes." Thankfully the mug hadn't splintered, but several chunks of glass covered the floor, along with a big puddle. "I'm sorry."

All her fault.

"Don't just stand there, Brodie," his mother said, stepping around the mess and rushing into the kitchen. "See if she's burnt." As she spoke, she ran cold water over a hand towel.

Mary turned to flee but she'd barely taken a step before Brodie whisked her up—literally!

She was so shocked she couldn't even get out a protest.

"Your feet," he said, plunking her down on the counter. "I don't want you to step on glass."

Seriously, her *butt* was on the *counter.*

In front of *his mother.*

"Here." That inimitable woman handed Mary the cold towel. "Put that under your shirt on your skin."

Well. Mary saw where Brodie got his bossiness. "Um…" The thing dripped water onto her thighs.

Without waiting for her to do it, his mother shot down the hall and into the bedroom with a purpose.

Wide-eyed, Mary stared at Brodie.

He took the towel from her and wrung it out over the sink. "Are you burnt, honey?"

No, he could not use that gentle voice on her *now.* "I..."

He lifted her shirt, wincing at whatever he saw.

Shock froze her. *He had her shirt above her boobs.* Glancing back to see if his mother was near, she slapped at his hands and tried to pull down her shirt. "Are you *insane*?"

"Around you? Maybe." The cold, wet cloth landed over her chest, stealing her breath again.

The woman returned with one of her son's button-up shirts. "Here." She tossed it to Brodie, who obligingly caught it.

They seemed to work in tandem or something.

"Help her change while I clean this up."

Mary did more staring. It was as if a plump but shapely, unstoppable whirlwind came through.

She'd sort of envisioned Brodie's mother with golden hair, a diaphanous white gown and possibly a halo.

Instead, she wore old jeans and unlaced white sneakers with a black Led Zeppelin T-shirt. Hair the same rich brown as Brodie's was caught up in a high ponytail.

The woman he'd described so many times had seemed like a fairy-tale version of what a mother should be, but this woman, the one now grabbing things from the kitchen, was all too real.

Disconcertingly so.

Taking a broom and dustpan, more paper towels and the waste can from under the sink, she said, "I'm Rosalyn Crews, by the way. Brodie's mom. You can call me Ros."

Mary kept her in her sights as she continued on behind them to get to work.

Brodie nudged her.

Right. She had a voice. Now if she could just find it. "Um... I'm Mary. Daniels. A coworker." *Coworker?*

That was the best she could come up with?

Brodie snickered—until she fried him with a glare.

Trying again, Mary said, "We work together." *And I obviously just came from your son's bed.* Her eyes closed in dismay. Apparently there were nuances to finding an engaging sexual relationship with a man.

He had family.

With a touch to her chin, Brodie brought her face around and mouthed, *Sorry*, with a smile.

He didn't look sorry. No, he actually looked smug.

Without a word of warning, he stripped the shirt off her.

Squawking, Mary tried to slide off the counter, maybe intending—very stupidly—to hide on the other side, where his mother couldn't see her. But that paragon wasn't looking anyway and Brodie already had the clean shirt around her.

All she could do was concentrate on getting her arms through the sleeves as quickly as possible. In the process, the hand towel fell to her lap.

Brodie turned to run it under cold water again. She tried to get the buttons done up, but her hands were shaking.

She'd blame that reaction on lack of coffee.

"Here," he whispered, placing the towel over her again.

"Does she need a doctor?" Ros didn't look up as she efficiently removed the mess like a pro.

"No," Mary said. "I'm fine."

"Are you blistering?"

"No."

Brodie said, "Just pink, but you're embarrassing her, Mom," as he worked on buttoning the shirt for her.

"Me? You're the one who left her here alone."

"Because you knocked on my door at the butt crack of dawn."

Chunks of glass clinked as Ros dumped them into the waste can. "It wasn't my idea to break into the office."

Wait… *What?*

Mary twisted to see her. "Someone broke in? When?"

"Last night," Brodie answered, still buttoning the shirt as if she were a toddler. "Don't worry about that now."

Ros ignored him, saying, "Jimmied the lock on the door and ransacked the place. Went through the file cabinets and desk drawers. They left a mess, but from what Jack can tell, nothing in particular is missing." She did a final swab of the floor with fresh paper towels, then sat back on her heels. "The big consensus is that whoever hassled you on your job the other day showed up looking for something."

"Mom," Brodie complained.

"She's surprised, honey, not dumb." Ros winked at Mary. "I know you wouldn't have a dumb woman here."

Mary said, "Thank you?" So the attack the other day hadn't ended after all. But why?

Wearing a smile far too familiar to her son's, Ros returned to the kitchen, putting things away and then washing her hands. "After Brodie told me everything, it makes sense that it has to be related. You'd have come to the same conclusions quickly enough."

Dignity began a slow return. "Yes, I would have." But now what? She had to let Therman know, but she also had the current situation to deal with.

As if Ros had read her mind, she frowned up at her son. "You want to let her down now?"

"Right." Brodie lifted her to her bare feet.

Flattening a hand to her chest, Mary held that damp cloth, which now made the shirt damp, too, in place.

Luckily Brodie was a big man and his shirt hung to midthigh on her, covering as much as most dresses would. Still, she tugged at it with her free hand, wishing it'd cover even more.

Like her face.

Ros brushed him aside and it was all Mary could do not to squirm when the woman held out her hand and smiled.

Unsure what else she could do, Mary accepted. "It's nice to meet you."

Ros laughed. "No, I imagine under the circumstances, it's not. Honestly, it's just bad luck that you have to meet me today, but please don't be embarrassed. Brodie asked me to wait outside, though I didn't know why. If he'd told me he had company—" she raised an eyebrow at her son "—I wouldn't have barged in."

Brodie shrugged. "It's not like you were waiting for an explanation. Plus, I was hoping she was still in bed."

With that statement thrown out there, Mary's face went as hot as her burnt chest. *"Brodie."*

"So that you wouldn't be put on the spot," he clarified. Then with a grin, "Get your mind out of the gutter, Red."

Good Lord. *He enjoyed her predicament.*

Murdering him was feeling like a real possibility when the strangest thing happened.

His mother aligned with her.

"Maybe *you* should have told her what was happening before you left her this morning. Then she wouldn't have been taken by surprise."

Brodie tugged at an ear. "Maybe."

"And then to embarrass her more on purpose?" She tsked. "Brodie Archer Crews, you should know better than to treat a woman like that."

Mary's jaw loosened. *Archer?* That was his middle name?

And his mother had just reprimanded him with it—in Mary's defense.

She didn't know what to say or think.

"You're right," he said. "It's just that Red is so easy to tease..."

"Red?"

He tugged his ear again. "It's a nickname."

Humor lit Ros's dark eyes, making them look even more like her son's. "I can see why." She smiled at Mary. "You have amazing hair. It's beautiful."

Words strangled in her throat.

"I've told her," Brodie said.

"Yes," Ros murmured, "I'm sure you have." With a squeeze, she finally released Mary's hand, but leaned in to whisper, "I know my son. He's always been drawn to striking women."

Striking? *Her?* She resisted the urge to touch her tangled hair and instead said a calm, and hopefully dignified, "Thank you."

She'd never had a conversation with a mother while wearing her son's shirt, but she knew she had to pull it together.

"You're kind." Hitching up her chin and convincing her lips to curve, she tried her best to look confident. "I do apologize for being such a mess." Had she had known this would happen, she *would* still be in the bed.

Maybe with the covers over her head.

At the very least she'd be fully dressed.

"If this is your idea of a mess," Ros assured her, "then every woman who meets you will be envious."

Behind his mother, Brodie grinned.

"You're sure you're not hurt?" Ros asked.

"Positive." Her skin felt tender, but she didn't think she'd blister.

"Brodie can get you some aloe. It'll help."

Mary nodded, but she didn't want aloe. She wanted away. Away from her own embarrassment, away from his perfect mother, away from her own awkwardness. "Thank you for picking up the mess. I'm not usually so clumsy."

"We startled you. It happens." Ros patted her shoulder. "I'm going back to the office to help Jack clean up."

Her stomach bottomed out. "Jack is here, too?" Great. Just freakin' great.

They could have a party.

"Howler's down at the office with him," Brodie explained. "I didn't want him to wake you."

"Charlotte will show up shortly." Ros gave her a direct look, and her direct looks were every bit as effective as her son's, but more intimidating. "Join us, okay?"

His entire close-knit, loving family would know she'd breached professionalism to sleep with him.

Mary had no idea what to say. "I, ah..."

Brodie put his arm around his mother's shoulders, steering her toward the door. "We'll talk about it, Mom."

"Charlotte is bringing donuts," Ros called back in a singsong voice, as if to entice her. "And there'll be more coffee."

Mary heard Brodie talking low, Ros answering the same, and then the door closed.

Immediately she pulled out the wet towel and plopped it into the sink, turned and headed for the short hall. She needed real clothes, a hairbrush...and her car keys.

Brodie caught up to her. "Sorry about that."

"You!" She whirled so fast that her hair swung out and slapped him in the chest. *"You,"* she repeated, her voice a feral growl.

"Me." Overruling her feeble resistance, he brought her close, his hand in her hair, soothing, stroking. "I'm damn sorry, Red. I swear, I tried to keep her out, but then Jack called to me, and while my back was turned, she came in."

"You could have told her..." What? She'd made him promise not to tell.

"If I'd said I had company, curiosity would have kept her hanging around the office until you left, and I knew you didn't want that. She's always nosy where I'm concerned. As to that, I can promise you that Jack and Charlotte will both be watching for you now, too. But I think if you wait another thirty minutes, at least the cops will be gone."

Her heart skipped a beat. "Cops?"

"Break-in, remember?" His thumb rubbed her temple. "I know Therman doesn't want us discussing his business, but it's getting tougher to keep him out of it."

"You didn't?"

"Not yet, no."

She could hear the unspoken *but* in his statement, and honestly, she couldn't blame him. Things were spiraling out of control. "This might not have anything to do with Therman's collection."

He skipped past that to say, "It's not a big deal that you're here. Not to them anyway. To me? Definitely a big deal. So let's give it a bit until the cops leave and then we'll go to the office together."

Together. She let out a long breath. "I don't think I want to go through that again."

"Through what?" He levered her back so she'd have to see his lopsided smile. "Was Mom that bad?"

"No, but she's your *mother.*" That in itself was enough, but according to Brodie, she was also much more. Protective, loving, attentive...all the things Mary had decided she didn't need.

Everything she'd decided *not* to want.

But again, Brodie had already changed her mind-set on so many things, and little *wants* were creeping in fast.

"I promise she's not judging you. If anything, they're all going to think I'm a lucky bastard."

Tired of fighting herself, Mary dropped her forehead to his big, solid chest. "I thought your mother would look like an angel."

He choked on a laugh. "Seriously?"

Leaning back, Mary said, "But she looks like you."

"Tell her that and she'll smack us both."

Mary couldn't help a small smile, a real one this time. "She's really pretty, just not what I expected."

"Because you expected an angel." Amusement brightened his dark eyes. "I guess that's my fault. I should have made it clear about her temper, her bossy attitude, how she always has to be in charge, how she—"

"Stop." Laughing now, Mary stepped back and brushed her

hands through her hair. It was going to take time to tame it. "She's a nice person and you know it."

"Very nice." He folded his arms and leaned against the wall. "But don't forget the bossy part. She somehow expects me to get you up to the office. If you don't go, she's going to blame me."

Mary groaned. "This is not how I expected to spend my morning after." She'd been hoping to enjoy Brodie more before leaving. That plan, however, had to be scrapped.

"Definitely wasn't on my to-do list, either."

Hand to her forehead, she considered all the repercussions. "First," she decided, "I have to get hold of Therman to update him."

At that, Brodie rolled his eyes but kept quiet.

She tugged at her shirt. "And I might need that aloe after all."

"Come on." He pushed off the wall and, taking her arm, guided her to the bathroom. "I'll take care of it."

Mary peered down the neck of the shirt. Her boobs now looked very pink. "I can do it."

Eyebrows bobbing, he said, "Let's play doctor. It'll be fun. Trust me."

And of course, she did.

CHAPTER FIFTEEN

She couldn't wear her bra.

Who knew a bra was the equivalent of armor? Or maybe Superman's cape.

She felt unprepared without it.

Everyone pretended not to notice, but Mary was painfully aware of the lack. Being well-endowed meant a bra was necessary to avoid drawing attention, so she *never* went braless.

It was even worse in the air-conditioned office, because she knew her nipples had tightened. Crossing her arms over her chest not only looked dumb, but was uncomfortable.

Besides, how could she help if she walked around holding herself? She couldn't.

After giving herself a pep talk, she'd applied her makeup, then pulled her hair into its usual tidy updo. In the need for comfort, she wore one of Brodie's loose, soft cotton T-shirts over her own skirt, creating a ridiculous outfit that didn't come close to matching.

Fashion, however, became less of a priority the second she stepped into the office.

Usually Charlotte kept the place well organized and now

it appeared ransacked. Papers dumped everywhere, desktops cleared, but thankfully, no real damage. The windows were intact, cabinet locks open but, from what she could tell in a glance, unbroken.

"Told you," Brodie said. "It's a mess."

From his desk where he stacked mixed papers, Jack glanced up, did a double take on Mary and grinned. "Cute outfit."

Mary opened her mouth to explain, but he didn't give her a chance.

"Sorry we interrupted your morning." Getting back to work, he added, "Thanks for being here."

Brodie winked at her.

True, that was a different reaction than she'd anticipated. Despite the trouble, Jack seemed pleased to see her. Of course, he'd always been nice.

She remembered how she'd tried to trade for him that first day, thinking he'd be a better choice for the job than Brodie. That idea now seemed very shortsighted.

Despite the ridiculously early hour, Jack was neatly dressed, shaved and calmly in charge—the opposite of Brodie, with his finger combed hair, dark beard growth and simmering vitality.

They were both handsome, both hardworking, but she'd take Brodie's gruff candor over Jack's polite demeanor any day.

Stepping out around the door, Ros shoved an armload of more papers at Brodie. "Here."

He had no choice but to take them. "What am I supposed to do with these?"

"Help sort them." Then she turned on Mary. "How are you?"

"Not properly dressed," she replied.

Ros laughed. "Don't be silly. Everyone knows what happened."

Oh, goody.

Leaning close, Ros whispered, "We top-heavy ladies have our

struggles, don't we? Going braless is almost impossible without showing our—"

Brodie said, "I'm *right* here, Mom, and I don't want to hear about your—"

"Then you better stop listening," Ros warned, interrupting him.

He turned a circle, seeking escape, before darting into the room with Jack and shutting the door.

"Sons can be very amusing." Grinning, Ros hooked her arm through Mary's and started them both forward. "Now, Jack's right—you *do* look cute."

No one had ever described her that way, not even when she'd been a girl. As a grown woman… Mary shrugged. "Thank you, but that's not usually the look I'm going for."

"I know. I can tell you're the modest type, so trust me, nothing is showing."

Mary found herself in the unusual position of confiding to another woman in a low voice. "I feel naked without my bra."

"You're not alone in that."

Not alone. Such a novel concept.

"Don't say anything to Charlotte, okay?"

"Oh, I wouldn't." How would that even come up? Then Mary couldn't resist asking, "Why?"

"She's a little self-conscious about not being as big up top."

"But she's beautiful!" And so tiny, she'd look like Dolly Parton if she had Mary's chest.

Ros nodded. "She's always been a petite person and I love her like a daughter. I tell her often how pretty she is, but you know how it is with women. We're our own worst enemies, finding faults no one else notices."

Mary touched her hair. She didn't know if other women did that or not, but she knew Brodie often complimented what she considered her worst flaw.

"Here we are," Ros said, walking her into the break room. "Let me get you settled."

"Settled?"

"After your hectic morning, you need to relax and eat something."

"I'm fine," Mary protested. "I thought I'd pitch in."

"That would be terrific, but you need coffee and a donut first," Ros insisted as she got out a foam cup. "How do you take your coffee? And do you want a plain glazed donut or one with icing?"

Mary wasn't used to anyone fussing over her. If Brodie had tried it, she'd have told him to back off.

But this was his *mother*, and she'd been so nice that Mary accepted the unfamiliar attention and tried not to look as awkward as she felt.

"Plain glazed, please. Coffee black."

"I like the ones with icing," Ros said. "But to each her own."

Howler had been sleeping by Charlotte's feet but now he lumbered over to sit by Mary instead. His jaws opened wide in a massive yawn and he slumped against her legs.

"Go ahead and get comfortable." Ros patted a plastic seat at the round table where Charlotte worked at sorting folders.

She wasn't good at sitting while others worked, but Howler helped, giving her something to do as she stroked behind his floppy ear.

He dropped down again and put his head on her feet.

Mary smiled. "You sleep more than any creature I've ever seen." This, at least, she was used to. Howler was very easy to adore.

Ros set a steaming cup of coffee and massive donut beside her on the table.

"Thank you. I'll try not to wear this one."

After a laugh, Ros peered at Mary's neck. "Do you need any aspirin? Your skin is still pink." She winced in sympathy.

Though her chest *was* tender, the soft shirt didn't bother her. *Except that it smelled like Brodie, making her think things she shouldn't.* "I'm fine, really."

As if she hadn't just said that, Ros continued. "Did Brodie get you the aloe?"

"Yes, thank you." He'd taken his time slowly applying it, too.

If only his family hadn't been waiting for them…

But they were and she'd decided that avoiding them would appear cowardly. Being thought a coward would be worse than any embarrassment, so here she was.

Looking not like a coward, but a slug.

"Good." Ros put a hand on her shoulder, lightly stroked, smiled and turned to go. "You eat and I'll check back on you in a bit."

No one had ever "checked on her." It was an odd feeling, almost disorienting. But she liked it. Too much.

Mary knew she was a strong person. She'd proved that to herself long ago out of pure necessity.

But did she have to be strong all the time?

"Don't mind her," Charlotte said without looking up. "Ros likes to mother everyone. It's just her way. Word of warning, though. If you don't eat that donut, she's going to start offering other things."

"Other things?"

Charlotte grinned. "If you don't want a donut, she'll assume you want a real breakfast. Or that you're ready for lunch and want a sandwich. She'll keep at you until she gets you fed."

"She does that to you?"

"Are you kidding? It's a wonder I'm still so skinny with the way that woman feeds me."

"Got it." Mary looked at the big glazed donut…and suddenly realized she was famished. How had Ros known?

She didn't want to enjoy sitting while others worked, but she did. It was…nice to be pampered.

And how terrible was it for her to think that? This wasn't her family. They owed her nothing, certainly not coffee and donuts and attention. It was a wonder they weren't appalled at the breach of ethics.

"Stop it," Charlotte said without interrupting her chore.

Startled, Mary looked up. "Stop what?"

"Looking guilty."

Was that what she was doing? "I don't know what you mean."

"It's just a donut. You have time to eat." Turning toward her, Charlotte cocked out a hip and lifted a brow. "In case it's something else bothering you, I saw Gina last night, so I already knew about you and Brodie. She was angrily blabbing to anyone who'd listen. I think she even posted to Facebook and Twitter."

"You're joking."

"Nope."

Mary closed her eyes. "Taunting Gina was *not* one of my finer moments."

"If I know Gina, she pushed you to it." Charlotte played with the end of a long braid, then flipped it over her shoulder and turned back to her work. "Hey, social media usually sucks, but it makes Gina look bad, not you. Besides, it wasn't news to us. We know Brodie well enough that we'd already seen the signs. Gina confirming it wasn't a big deal."

"Signs?" Had she been that obvious in her attraction?

"Sure. Brodie is Brodie, and you were a challenge, so..." Charlotte shrugged. "I pretty much figured you two would get together."

While Charlotte spoke, she rapidly moved papers and receipts into various folders.

A true multitasker. Mary liked her—and that was why this mattered so much.

Sitting aside her empty coffee cup, Mary stood. "I hope this doesn't affect our business association."

"Pfft." Charlotte absently flapped a hand while frowning at

a contract. "Let's be friends instead of associates, okay?" She set the paper aside. "Between Brodie and Jack, this place oozes testosterone. It'll be nice to have another woman around more."

A friend? Amid her surprise, Mary found a reluctant smile. "That sounds nice, but please don't misunderstand. I won't be around any more often than usual."

"Sure you will, now that you two are together."

"But...we aren't." Were they?

Charlotte went still, then looked back at Mary from beneath her brows. "Pretty sure our definitions of *together* must differ."

"I mean..." Mary glanced around. They were well away from Jack's desk, where the others worked, but still, she didn't want to be overheard, so she moved closer. "We're not in a *relationship*." Not in the romantic sense.

Business, yes.

Sex? A bonus.

And they *had* agreed to be exclusive. Hmm...

But they weren't committed or anything. Right? She didn't think so, though granted this wasn't her forte.

Charlotte studied her for a long moment before going back to shuffling papers. "Does Brodie know about this relationship lack? Because he's pretty transparent, at least to me, and I can tell you, *he's* in a relationship."

Mary paused—her thoughts, her heart...even her breathing. Could that be true? Was Brodie more invested than she'd realized? He was such a player, so funny and irreverent about everything that she hadn't allowed herself to make the mental leap.

Not that she'd object.

"One thing," Mary said.

"Yes?"

"You're not skinny, you're petite. There's a difference. Actually, you're perfect. If I didn't already know that Brodie thinks of you as a sister, I'd be worried."

Charlotte flashed a big grin. "Me and Brodie? I love him. He's the *best*—right up there with Jack. But even if they weren't in the brotherly category, neither of them are my type."

Mary hadn't thought about having a type, but now she knew Brodie was it. Every big gorgeous inch of him. "So what is your type?"

Charlotte shrugged. "Someone completely different from either of them."

Just then Jack walked in with another stack of folders for Charlotte. His hair, a little lighter than Brodie's, wasn't quite so neat anymore. "Can you go through these, hon? I think I got them all, but I'd like to be sure."

Without breaking stride on her work, Charlotte pointed to an empty spot on the table. "Put them there."

"Thanks." In a conspiratorial whisper—loud enough for Charlotte to hear—Jack said, "She's a tyrant about filing. I did my best, but I can almost guarantee she'll change something."

"I'm a tyrant because I'm the one who has to find everything." Pausing, Charlotte looked around. "Seriously, what was our intruder looking for? There's no method to the chaos he caused. It's not like we keep anything valuable here anyway."

"Nothing but paper trails," Brodie said as he entered the small room. His jeans were wrinkled, probably taken from the floor when his mother had knocked hours ago. He'd changed his shirt, washed and brushed his teeth, but he'd skipped any other grooming.

And damn it, she found him even more appealing like this, all raw, macho man with his unshaven face and messy hair.

Tension made the muscles in his shoulders stand out. The air nearly crackled around him. He stopped beside Jack and together they looked like mismatched bookends, one carved of granite, the other polished stone.

Their mother came in, nudging them both out of her way as if a six-foot wall of masculinity didn't faze her.

They had to move around Howler, who didn't budge from

his sprawled position on the floor by her feet. Jack stood shoulder to shoulder with Charlotte, and Brodie and Ros were just inside the door.

Mary felt out of place here, surrounded by their shared love. It was so rich, she could choke on the solidarity, the closeness and affection. For them, it was probably as natural as breathing.

Mary knew better. Brodie's family had something that was forever out of her reach. For a while, she'd wondered if any family could really be that natural, that wonderful.

Now she knew.

She witnessed a blessing and if she had the same, she would never take it for granted.

There were long-ago things she'd yearned for, things like acceptance, a sense of belonging.

Family.

Those things had stayed out of reach, so she'd compromised with her dreams and settled on professionalism and pride. They'd carried her through when there was nothing else.

Since meeting Brodie, sexual attraction had battered her professionalism. God willing, she still had her pride.

It no longer felt like enough. Yet, instead of there being a lack, she sensed...hope.

It was a fragile thing and she didn't dare share it. Not yet. Deciphering the newness of it would take time.

Her strong suit was business, so that was where she'd start.

Now that she had them all together, she needed to extend Therman's apology.

Purpose brought her forward into their mix. "Mr. Ritter, my boss—Brodie's boss—was very sorry to hear of this mess. He wanted you to know that he's never before had a problem like this. I've been with him for three years and I can back that up. There have been the occasional conflicts, of course, but never anything of this magnitude."

She sensed Brodie watching her, but she didn't meet his gaze. It was far too easy to let him distract her.

"I called Mr. Ritter before coming here, and he was dismayed, but also suspicious of one particular person. As Brodie told you, we had some recent trouble caused by this person. Mr. Ritter and I sincerely hope that his competition with this other person hasn't spilled over to affecting your business."

Ros touched her arm. "Oh, honey. This isn't your fault. Bad people do bad things. It's just a fact of life."

Mary hadn't specifically been taking the blame, but she did feel responsible by association. "Thank you." She'd only met Ros a few hours ago, but thanks to Brodie, she knew her all the same and hadn't expected a different reaction. "Still, for this to happen *now*—"

Jack shrugged. "Though it seems unlikely, it could be unrelated. There's no shortage of knuckleheaded kids looking to vandalize a property."

"Could be," Brodie agreed. "But I'm not taking that chance."

Neither would Mary. Whatever Brodie planned, she'd back him—as long as he included her. "What are we going to do?"

His brows lifted at the *we*, but he didn't miss a beat. "Install better locks, an alarm system and a camera."

So, nothing too drastic. She nodded. "I'm sorry it's come to that, but yes, the added security is a good idea."

"We probably should have had those things already." Brodie rubbed the back of his neck, making his biceps flex and bulge.

Which, apparently, only she noticed.

"The company's expanded a lot, most especially with Therman's business."

Charlotte propped a hip on the table and crossed her arms. "We've been running it like a small-time, hometown gig, but since your boss hired Brodie, we've gotten three other big contracts." She nodded at Jack. "He starts soon on a long-term gig."

"Looking forward to it," Jack said.

"I didn't realize." Mary wasn't surprised, though. Many people watched Therman and were swayed by his decisions, taking them as recommendations and endorsements. "The success is well deserved."

Still tense, Brodie looked down at the dog. "I used to let him have the run of the place. He knows his boundaries and never goes far. But I can't do that anymore. Last night he saw or heard something. I'm sure of it now. If I hadn't been thinking of other things, I'd have realized something was wrong."

All eyes landed on Mary.

She didn't mind. She'd drawn attention most of her life—the worst kind of negative or pitying attention. This, at least, was merely speculative, or in Jack's case, amused.

"I figured it was a scavenging raccoon or other critter, but Howler doesn't react that strongly to other animals." Brodie's jaw firmed. "I should have checked it out more."

Mary was grateful he hadn't. If he'd walked in on intruders, then what?

Charlotte ducked down to give the dog a kiss on his forehead. "He's a good boy. Aren't you, baby?"

The dog didn't open his eyes, but his tail gave the floor two hard thumps.

Fresh determination assaulted Mary. "If you're right, I'm glad you didn't let him loose." Howler was a big dog with a ferocious growl when agitated. The image of him on the attack at that little cabin in the woods flashed through her mind. When mad, Howler meant business.

Anyone would see him as a threat, and react accordingly.

Everyone loved the dog, Mary included. But Brodie had a very special bond with him. She couldn't bear the thought of either of them being hurt.

Right in front of everyone, Brodie reached out to cup her cheek. "Starting today, we *all* need to be more careful."

Was he emphasizing that to her? Hard to tell when his touch disrupted her thinking.

His family didn't seem to think anything of it, making her wonder if he was always this demonstrative with women in front of them.

If so, it probably didn't mean anything and that was why they barely noticed. To her, a gentle touch, especially when surrounded by his family, was still a big deal.

As if he sensed her confusion, Brodie moved to stand at her side, his biceps to her shoulder, his heat and strength enveloping her.

It was such a caring thing to do, that she couldn't help but be impressed with his awareness. Then again, *everything* he did impressed her. The way he smiled, his physical capability, the love he extended not only to his family but also his dog…

He was dangerously attractive, ruining her efforts to concentrate on business.

"We'll double up on security," Brodie continued. "Not only here, but also at home."

Focusing on those large stacks of folders, Mary asked, "Have you found anything missing?"

Charlotte shook her head. "Not so far. Nothing important anyway."

Mary put a hand on Brodie's arm. He wasn't going to like this. "What if the intruder only wanted information?"

"Personal information," Brodie said, as if he'd already had the thought.

Jack scowled. "All of our addresses are on one file or another. Phone numbers, too."

"Purchases," Charlotte said, lifting a receipt for fast food and another for supplies. "Anyone snooping would now know who we are, where we go and where to find us."

"True." Brodie showed his teeth in a feral grin. "But the bastard should also know that I live very close by, and I'll be keeping watch."

Dear God. Mary's heart plummeted. "You're at risk."

"Wrong." Clenching his hands, Brodie said, "*He's* at risk if he thinks he can—"

She grabbed his arm to turn him toward him. It was like grabbing a tree trunk; he didn't budge. "Brodie Archer Crews. What in the world are you saying?"

"Hey," he protested over the use of his name.

Ros laughed.

"Don't *hey* me. You can't mean to challenge someone ballsy enough to break in and ransack the place. That's nuts! You don't even know what type of person you're dealing with."

With a touch to the bruised injury on his forehead, he said, "I have a good guess."

Mary scowled and jerked up her chin. "No."

Brows up, Brodie leaned back. "No what?"

"No, I don't want you being..." *Reckless. Brave. Too protective.* "Ridiculous." It was awful, all of it, especially the looming menace. She felt it, growing closer, darker.

Yet none of the others seemed nearly as concerned. They took their happiness for granted. They didn't realize just how fragile it could be. But Mary knew.

Because she'd always lived without it.

"Promise me you won't do anything stupid."

He shrugged. "I'm never stupid, so sure."

"That's the weakest promise I've ever heard!"

"I agree with Mary," Ros announced. She hooked one arm with Jack, the other with Charlotte. "I'm not willing to risk any of you."

"I said I'd take care of it." Brodie gave her one last scowl then headed up the hall to Jack's office. "It'll be done within a day."

"Way to give him hell," Jack said with a grin.

"She worried and you razz her?" Charlotte rolled her eyes,

then plopped a big load of folders into his arms. "Come on. You can help me put these away."

Still bristling, Mary watched them go. Now that only Ros remained, she had enough room to pace.

"I like how you did that," Ros said with barely suppressed humor. "Using his name like that." She nodded. "Good touch. I've always found it added something special."

Mary pinched the bridge of her nose. "I'm sorry. I didn't exactly mean to give him hell." This relationship was complicated.

"It's good for him, especially when he's acting like King Kong. It's not what he's used to from women, so...go you!"

Surprised, Mary looked at her. "Go me?"

"I'm on your side." Ros let out a breath. "Just don't look so worried, okay? The boys have it covered."

That earned a reluctant grin. Only a mother would call those two *boys*.

"Better," Ros said as she gave Mary's shoulder a squeeze. "You're too pretty to frown."

The compliment made her choke on a laugh. She knew she was an utter mess whether Brodie's mother would admit it or not. "And you're too nice."

"I'm honest. Now." She gestured for the hallway. "Let's see what we can do to help out."

Even as Mary left the room ahead of Ros, her thoughts churned. How could these people possibly like her? She, with her insistence to trust Therman, had brought this on them.

In her defense, the job had never been like this before.

So why now?

A part of her insisted she shouldn't get too clingy with Brodie's family, but another part, stronger and more determined, wanted to hold on tight.

That part was winning.

She wouldn't let *any* of them be harmed, not if she could

help it. But to protect them, she needed to get more info from Therman.

Not for a second did she believe it had anything to do with a dusty old Oscar. This was something more than a competitor's rivalry. This was serious.

And so was her growing attraction to Brodie.

Whatever they had might not last, but it wouldn't be because of her.

CHAPTER SIXTEEN

Helton wasn't the impetuous sort, but once he got the report from Lem and Todd, he couldn't make himself stay away.

The small hick town of Red Oak, Ohio, looked nothing like the urban area where he'd grown up, but it wasn't far from where he ran the business he'd inherited.

Close enough to indulge a whim.

He'd first located the Mustang Transport offices. They were off the beaten path, situated on several acres with a track around the area. He couldn't get too close without drawing attention, and he didn't want that.

He needed to conduct his business without anyone knowing his identity.

It fascinated him, this little family-run organization with all the various characters. Yes, he knew them now, each of them. Names and numbers led to easy research. It hadn't taken more than a few hours to learn everything about them, but they'd been an entertaining few hours, for sure.

Brodie Crews was a brute. Not as much of a brute as Helton, but then few were. Given a chance, Helton wouldn't mind seeing how they matched fists. It wasn't often he respected another man's ability.

With ridiculous ease, he'd discovered quite a bit about Brodie.

For one thing, he liked people and they liked him back. Early in his research, it became quickly obvious to Helton that Brodie didn't associate much with social media, but that didn't keep others from tagging him, mentioning him.

Bitching about him.

He was one of those guys who stuck up for the underdog, even when the prick didn't deserve it. He was also the type who pissed off sexy little blonde bombshells who in turn blasted private information all over Facebook and Twitter.

Brodie was banging Mary.

It surprised Helton. He'd been aware of her since Therman hired her; even before inheriting from his dad, he'd made it a practice to collect information on people. But in all that time, he'd never known of Mary getting involved, definitely not with another employee.

Helton wondered if Therman knew, and if he did, would he care? It was dangerous to let lackeys get personally involved. Their loyalty shifted, and Helton wouldn't tolerate that.

But Therman? Who knew.

Brodie's brother, Jack, was slicker than Brodie. Helton shook his head. No, *slick* wasn't the right word.

More *refined*. Yeah, that worked.

And the little lady… Helton taxed his brain before he remembered. *Charlotte.* The photos Lem had taken of her dainty, slanted handwriting made him think of flowers, the thorny kind. She was cute but serious. Maybe too serious.

And then there was the matriarch. Sexy broad in her midfifties. Casual, stacked, happy, and he had to assume she had guts to have raised her sons alone. If Helton had a type, she'd be it.

But today, he had the bombshell on his mind.

Thanks to her detailed postings, he knew she'd closed out

the bar at two thirty, then drank with friends a few hours more before crashing at a diner next door.

The friends had eventually gone home, but he didn't think she had.

Helton located Freddie's easily enough. It was a high point of the town with its colorful signs and gravel parking lot. With his background he could practically sniff out the bars, not that he needed to with Freddie's on the main drag and the town so tight.

Right next to it was the little diner from where she'd last posted.

A bell chimed as Helton opened the door and stepped inside. The air was cool and quiet with only the sounds of prep from the kitchen and the muted voices of two customers.

There, in the back corner, was the little lady.

A night of anger-induced drinking had taken its toll. Half slid down in a booth, her head back and her mouth partially opened, she looked more like a crack whore than the beauty from her Facebook profile pic.

Catching the eye of the waitress, he nodded toward the blonde's table. "Two coffees."

She followed his gaze and nodded.

With a touch of pity, Helton approached the booth. Maybe because his father had used up so many women, Helton had a soft spot for them, all of them, but especially confused little girls like this one. Wouldn't keep him from doing what needed to be done, but with any luck, it'd teach her a lesson or two.

When Helton slid into the seat opposite her, she stirred, opening bloodshot eyes and getting herself more or less upright. "Who are you?"

It sounded like "Who'r'ooh?" which told him she hadn't yet slept it off. Too bad. For *her.*

"A friend," he lied. He didn't have friends. Didn't want them, didn't need them.

As if holding a bowling ball, she cradled her head. "Get lost, grandpa."

The words were so slurred, he barely caught the insult. It amused him. Even under the effects of alcohol, she had grit. "Afraid I can't. See, you just won the lottery."

Her red-rimmed eyes rounded. "I did?"

The coffee arrived and Helton pushed one cup toward her. "Drink up and I'll explain."

Defiance pursed her mouth, but she didn't have it in her to argue. She dumped three packets of sugar into the coffee, then three little plastic tubs of creamer before sipping. "Mmm."

"Coffee helps everything," Helton agreed, drinking his own black. He never understood why people fucked up coffee so badly. With that much sugar, she might as well pour it over pancakes.

"So what'd I win?"

"You have to be sober before I can tell you."

"M'sober." She weaved in her seat, then stilled by gripping the edge of the table.

He almost laughed. "Two cups of coffee first, okay? I'll explain everything to you after that."

Bleary eyes met his. "You sure yer not jus' hittin' on me?"

"You're not my type." Too young, too silly and far too slender.

Now, Rosalyn Crews, that was a woman he could strap on for a night. Good decision or not, if he ever got the chance, he might have to take it and damn the consequences.

But until then, he had to put the screws to her son, so he could put the screws to Therman.

And little Blondie was just the tool he needed to make it happen.

As he cleaned the mirrors on his car, Brodie told himself not to chase Mary. He'd never chased a woman in his life and he didn't want to start now.

Except that Mary was different.

Everything about her.

Everything about the way she affected him.

She tempted him to do things he'd never done...because she made him feel things he'd never felt.

Damn Therman, if only he'd call for a job, Brodie would have the excuse he needed to see her without actually pressuring her about it. Mary would never neglect the job.

But Therman didn't call, and now it had been three days since the break-in, three days since Mary's plan to keep their relationship private had gone all wrong—at least from her perspective.

Three hellishly long days since she'd helped put the office back together before telling him she had to go. There in front of his family, she'd given him a perfunctory farewell—like they were pals or something.

He knew they were more, a lot more, but did she? According to Charlotte, Mary was in denial about it. Hell, from everything he knew about her now, she'd never experienced a real relationship. Not the important kind.

Business crap she had down pat.

But honest caring? Not so much. It was like being with an emotional virgin. Everything was new and different for her. Her reactions were priceless, and sometimes heartbreaking.

He needed to take things slow and easy so he didn't overwhelm her. Slow and easy, though... It didn't come naturally to him. He was a doer. Jump in and get it done.

Well, except with sex. He could take all night enjoying her and not be anywhere near done.

And thinking about that made him want her even more.

"Damn." Muttering to himself, he strode to the other side of his car, admiring it, using the edge of his shirt to polish off a smudge of dust. Red was the perfect color. She looked great.

Howler, maybe sensing his frustration, looked up from his sunny repose a few feet away. His loose jowls overlapped his front paws, where he rested his head. He gave a lazy "Woof" that sounded a lot like commiseration.

He probably missed Mary, too.

"Sorry," Brodie said. "I didn't mean to wake you."

Yawning widely, Howler rolled to his back, scooted his spine a little in the dry dirt and went back to sleep.

The dog now had plenty of room to wander thanks to a run Jack had helped him install. They'd hammered in one pole right outside Brodie's door, the other several yards out, with a cable running between them. A ten-foot leash slid along the length.

Sunshine beat down on Brodie's head, making his temples sweat. The blue sky seemed to go on forever, but it wasn't as pretty as Mary's eyes.

Those eyes had been filled with concern when she'd left.

He hadn't missed how it had shaken her, being with his family. Even after she'd rallied, the rest of them had noticed. It'd take a blind idiot not to see Mary's reservation, and his family was anything but.

Running a hand over his face, he bit back a growl.

"The car looks great."

Taken unawares, Brodie glanced up, then dropped his hand and tried to play it cool. Though he was parked right outside the office, he hadn't heard Jack approaching. "Yeah. Thanks."

Hands in his pockets, Jack moseyed over in a casual way that belied his purpose.

Was he that far gone? Brodie crossed his arms and asked with a touch of belligerence, "What?"

"Just wondering what's up." Jack started to lean on the car, but changed his mind.

"Go ahead. She's for driving, not just showing. With Howler getting in and out, there's no reason to treat her with kid gloves." To prove his point, Brodie propped himself against the driver's door. He didn't know how long he could stay there, though.

He needed to be active enough to burn off the restless energy.

Like…if he could wrestle an alligator or something, that might help. But standing around yakking? Not a good day for it, not when he burned with a…a fucking *helpless* need to go to Mary.

Jack opened his mouth.

"Nothing's up," Brodie barked, "so don't feel like you have to give me a pep talk."

Jack held up a hand in surrender. "We've stayed so busy the last few days getting things set up for Howler and installing the security everywhere, we haven't really had a chance to talk."

"We talked. You told me I was putting that security shit together wrong and I told you to fuck off."

"You *were* doing it wrong," Jack insisted, then added with a grin, "But I knew you didn't mean to be surly."

"Did, too." He almost groaned at his own juvenile obnoxiousness. "Look, it all works, right?"

Jack shrugged, then went on to ask, "What are you going to do?"

Damn it. Playing dumb, Brodie cocked a brow. "About?"

"Mary. We all figured she'd be hanging around more now, and instead you're out here with your ass dragging the ground."

His brother didn't own an ounce of subtlety.

Apparently he *was* that far gone because he almost laughed. "What, exactly, do you want me to do?"

Without missing a beat, Jack said, "Go after her." Then, as an afterthought, he asked, "You do know where she lives, don't you?"

"Yes, I know." Not that he'd ever been there.

"Mary is reserved."

"You don't have to explain her to me."

That didn't stop him, though. "I think we overwhelmed her. And she looked guilty, too, even though there's no reason. You need to reassure her."

Yeah, he had. “She told me not to worry about it.”

Jack nodded as if he had all the answers. “She’s the type who wouldn’t share her burdens, you know?”

“In fact, I *do* know.” But she had shared with him, parts from her past, some of her future hopes. He’d been making progress, and now...now she had her walls up again.

“Use the excuse of showing her the car.”

Yeah, he could almost see himself knocking at her door and saying, *Matilda is all dolled up now. Come see.* “That’s a stupid idea.”

“Don’t use an excuse. Just tell her you missed her.” Jack elbowed him. “It’s the truth.”

“Yeah.” No reason to deny it. “I’ve talked to her.” He called each day and she always answered, chatted a few minutes, then let him go.

Jack gave him a pitying look. “So you’re hanging on the phone with her instead of going to see her?”

“I asked her over.” She’d already made plans. Whatever the hell that meant.

“God, you’re a lost cause. Did you at least offer to pick her up?”

He hadn’t, only because he’d known she would refuse.

Spearing the fingers of both hands into his hair, Brodie paced away. This was ridiculous. Since when did he need love advice from his... He stopped so suddenly he almost tripped himself. He stared off into the distance without seeing anything.

Love?

Well, hell. Yeah, he loved Mary Daniels. It wasn’t just that he wanted her—though he did, a lot. It wasn’t simply liking her and sympathizing. He also respected her and admired her.

He wanted to keep her close, talk with her, make love to her.

He wanted to stake a claim, then declare it to the world.

A little flummoxed, he turned to Jack. “I love her.”

Deadpan, Jack said, “Uh, yes, I know. Why the hell do you think I’m out here pumping you up?”

"I assumed Charlotte sent you."

They both turned to see Charlotte standing at the window, watching them. She smiled and ducked away.

"She suggested it, but I was already planning on it anyway. It was too disturbing, watching you out here fussing over Matilda, looking all glum and beat down."

"I don't *fuss*." He hoped.

"Call her," Jack suggested. "Tell her it's important."

Brodie shook his head. "She needs time to do things her own way. She's smart. *Scary* smart. She'll figure out what she wants without me pressuring her." And God willing, she'd want him.

Jack looked past him, shading his eyes with a hand. "Huh. Maybe she already did."

Turning, Brodie saw her car approaching. "Do me a favor and look after Howler."

"You'll owe me."

"Screw you." Brodie walked toward the dog with Jack's laughter behind him. Howler had already gone alert, ears perked and gaze glued to Mary's car.

With a happy bark, he jumped to his feet.

Brodie looked back at Jack. "He gets five minutes to say hello."

"I'll come back out then." Whistling, Jack headed to the office.

Man and dog stood together, waiting, while Mary pulled up and put the car in Park. Thinking of everything he wanted to say to her and how to say it, Brodie prepared himself.

Then she stepped out and he almost fell over.

Mary, *his* Mary, wore a sexy, beige dress that fit her body to perfection. Gone was the boxy outfit, replaced with a dress that showed off every lush curve. The modestly scooped neck drew his attention to her cleavage. God, the woman had a fine set.

Letting his gaze track farther down, he took in the nip of her waist, the gentle sweep of her belly, the flare of her hips. The hem ended just above her knees. Barely there sandals showed off her shapely calves.

His nostrils flared, and his chest labored. "Holy smokes."

Dark sunglasses hid her eyes, but her lips curved in a smile.

Her hair was up again, but this style was different, looser with long twining curls hanging free in key places, like over one temple, in front of one ear. It gave her a slightly messy, "just tumbled" look that he heartily approved of. Oh, hell yeah, he approved.

Expanding his chest on a big breath, Brodie announced, "I just got hard."

The smile froze, then twitched into a laugh. "You did not."

He *loved* how she laughed. "Made you look."

"Nothing new in that." She knelt down by Howler, and yeah, that looked sexy, too. The dog gently nuzzled against her while his tail went wild. "I can't keep my eyes off you."

Nice. "You can do more than look, you know."

"I was hopeful." Her small hands moved over Howler's neck and back. "I've missed you, sweetie."

Brodie stood over her. "Me or the dog?"

Pulling her sunglasses away, she looked up his body until she met his face. "Both."

Her on her knees was giving him ideas. Hot ideas. Much more of that and he *would* be hard.

He took her elbow and urged her back to her feet, then against him. God it felt good to hold her again. "You look incredible." Arms looped around her, he rested his hands at the delectable place where the small of her back met the plump jut of her ass. He kissed her forehead, her cheek, her jaw. "I'm glad you came by."

She caught his face and captured his mouth for a slightly longer taste, then released him with a sigh. "I wanted to talk. Do you have time?"

"Only if you're going to tell me you want me, too."

"I do—oh!" Eyes widening, she looked past him to the car. "Oh, Brodie, is that Matilda?"

He'd almost forgotten about his beloved car. "Turned out great, right? I told you red would be the perfect color."

"You were right. It's stunning."

Howler followed them as they walked to the car. Mary circled it, and dressed like she was, he enjoyed the show.

"You could do that a few more times if you like."

Reverently grazing her fingertips over the hood, she asked, "Do what?"

Brodie twirled a finger. "Walk around the car. Slowly." He didn't know if she'd believe him, but he said it anyway. "The way you move is like foreplay."

Again she smiled. "You are such a flatterer."

The office door opened and Jack came out, trailed by Charlotte. They each looked a little stunned.

Like him, they were probably wondering what had inspired the change. Brodie decided he could wait until she told him. Until then, they all stared.

Charlotte spoke first. "Doesn't she look great?"

Brodie and Jack both nodded.

Mary said, "The color suits her."

"Perfectly," Charlotte agreed.

Oh, they were talking about the car? Huh.

Brodie and Jack shared a look. Jack gave a silent whistle and Brodie nodded.

"Ahem."

They turned to see Charlotte watching them, brows raised. She smiled sweetly. "I'm going to take Howler in for some lunch."

At that magical word, Howler went berserk, leaping around and barking. He knew most words that had to do with food.

"Remember the routine," Brodie said.

"I remember." Jack unhooked the dog. "As long as I don't have to actually eat the stuff, I can—" Knowing he was free, Howler lunged for the door, nearly pulling him off his feet.

Brodie laughed.

"You had breakfast," Jack complained as he regained his balance, which only made Howler more excited because he knew *breakfast* also meant food. "And a few treats since then. Why do you have to make people think we starve you?"

Charlotte waved. "We've got it covered. You two go relax." She paused with the door open. "You look great, Mary."

"Thank you."

After flashing a thumbs-up, Charlotte let the door close behind her.

Alone. At last.

Brodie looked up at the sky. "It's got to be ninety out here. Let's go inside." He held out a hand, palm up.

"All right." Mary tucked back one of those long, teasing curls and put her hand in his.

Brodie knew she had strength, more than any woman should have to possess, but as he closed his larger hand around hers, she felt small and fragile. She didn't need his protection, but he wanted to give it anyway. Protection against physical harm and emotional. He wanted to pamper her, and he wanted to love her.

He wanted that more than he could ever remember wanting anything.

Cooler air greeted them as they got into his place. He closed and locked the door. She set her purse on a chair and stepped out of her sandals.

The gesture was familiar, comfortable, in a way she'd never been before. He hoped it was a good sign.

"Know what? Even your bare feet are sexy."

Looking down at them, Mary wiggled her pink-painted toes and grinned. "Really? I got a pedicure."

"Not sure that has anything to do with it." Even without the polish, he'd admire her narrow feet…and trim ankles. And those *calves*. "It's that you're here, more skin showing than usual, and removing your sandals makes me think about you removing everything else." He hitched his chin at her. "What do ya have on under that dress?"

Grin twitching, she struck a pose, hand on her hip and her expression beckoning. "Just a flesh-toned demi bra and matching panties."

Envisioning that, Brodie tugged at the material over his fly. "Damn."

The grin settled into a gentle smile. "I think maybe you missed me, too?"

"Very much." He moved closer. "I called, hon. You were busy."

With a nod, she said, "Doing this." She gestured at herself. "Finding something that would show you…" The words trailed off, then she made her gaze direct and tried again. "I think we've had some misunderstandings."

"Misunderstandings?" That didn't sound great.

"Yes. Well. I mean…" She stopped, gave a roll of her eyes, drew a deep breath and gave it another go. "I'm pretty sure I understand *you*. You're up-front about things, what you want and how you feel. When you're ticked off or happy. I like that I can read you, that I don't have to guess at what you're thinking."

"If you're ever unsure, just ask. I'm happy to share."

Those soulful blue eyes held his. "I'm not like you, though, so I figured it had to be more difficult for you to understand me."

Being honest, he admitted, "Sometimes."

"I wanted to clarify."

Brodie resisted the urge to touch her. "Should I sit down?" He had no idea where she was going with this, and he wasn't sure he wanted to know.

She bit that full bottom lip, blue eyes intent with determination—and something else. Maybe a hint of…wickedness?

God, he hoped so.

"Let's go to the bed instead."

Concerns melted away and he slowly smiled. "Hell of an idea." As long as Mary wanted him, he could work with everything else.

Because Brodie was so agreeable, Mary had him in bed, on his back with her sitting on his abs, in no time. After hiking the dress up high to settle over him, she bracketed his hips with her bare thighs. He rested his hands on her there, keeping them still, but the contrast of his rough palms against her smooth skin excited her. Knowing Brodie, she assumed that was on purpose.

Before he took over, she said, "Strip off your shirt."

"No problem." He moved under her, shifting enough to tug the shirt up and over his head. He tossed it off the side of the bed.

Leaning forward, she spread her hands on his chest. The heat of the day had dampened his skin and intensified his scent. Inhaling deeply, she breathed him in and felt parts of her respond, parts that were currently against his abs.

She liked this, being open over Brodie Crews, her legs spread wide around him. It made her feel both vulnerable and in charge, an enticing combo.

Stroking his chest hair, darker now with a light sheen of sweat, she swept her palms out over those rock-hard shoulders, down to stretch her fingers around his biceps. Even using both hands, she wouldn't be able to completely encircle him.

And he was at ease, his muscles relaxed. When those muscles bulged, he was impressive indeed.

A strong, caring man was a wonderful thing.

"I can lose the jeans too if you want."

"So accommodating." She drew her hands down his chest. "No, this is better for now. I get very distracted with your body."

"Yeah?"

"Very." She drifted her fingers over his small, flat nipples. "Very." Down his ribs and onto his abs. "Distracted."

"I like you this way, Red. Confident women are sexy." He raised his knees behind her back and clasped her waist. "Annnd... I'm hard."

"I know." With a small wiggle, she confirmed the bulge under her, obvious even through his denim jeans. "I'm glad."

"Tease."

Liking the sound of that, she leaned down to kiss him. The position pressed heated parts of her more firmly to him and gave her breasts contact with his chest. "I was never a tease before." Making sure it didn't sound like a complaint, she added, "You've corrupted me."

He cupped the back of her neck to keep her close. "Good." She went breathless with the way his tongue played with hers, how his bristly jaw lightly abraded and how his hands held her so carefully.

Mary knew if she didn't get back on track, she wouldn't get any of it said. For that reason, she pressed her hands to his chest. He resisted only a moment before groaning and letting her go.

Balanced on her elbows, she sighed. "I get around you and it's so easy to just lose my head."

"Same." Gently, his palms swept up and down her back, up again, then down all the way to her backside. "It's not always this way, you know. Things are different with us."

"Chemistry," she said, nodding. She'd already figured that out. She straightened again to avoid the temptation of his mouth. "I wanted you to understand why I always dressed as I did, and why I'll usually dress differently now."

Dark eyes searched hers. "Okay."

"Before, I didn't want attention." Not from anyone.

His expression softened. "I knew that."

"Now I want *your* attention."

The corner of his mouth curled. "You've had it from the second I first saw you."

Very true and it still amazed her. "Therman assumes that I don't know how to dress, that I have no style. I didn't want you to think the same thing."

That statement brought on a scowl, and when Brodie scowled, he looked downright fierce. The dark hair and eyes, the slight crook in his nose, the shadowed jaw—it gave her shivers, but in a good way.

In her heart, she knew he'd never hurt her.

And that was the most wondrous thing: being able to trust someone else completely, not just in things sexual but in *everything.* It might spook him if he knew the depth of what she felt, so she didn't yet share.

She wanted to quietly hold that faith close to her heart and cherish it for as long as possible.

"Therman told you that?"

"Not in so many words." She soothed him with a soft stroke through his thick hair. In contrast to his heated body, it felt cool sliding through her fingers like silk. He could probably do with a haircut, but she liked it like this, a little long, a little unkempt. "Therman would never deliberately insult me. But he did offer me a new wardrobe for the job. He said Jolene would make the arrangements."

Brodie gave a low curse. "Guess that was his attempt at being subtle."

"He meant well." She traced his stern brows, down the bridge of his very masculine nose, to that firm, sensual mouth. "The problem, of course, was that I'd gone to a lot of trouble choosing clothes that..." Saying it was harder than she'd expected. "Hid me."

"Didn't work." His thumbs drifted back and forth, almost touching the undersides of her breasts. "Not with me."

No, he'd seen through her right off, but he'd never disparaged her choices.

Fingers spread, he slid a hand over her hip. His gaze never left hers. "Your style turned me on from the get-go. It was this in-your-face attitude."

"Really?" Her intent had never been to entice.

He nodded solemnly. "You had this whole 'take me serious or else, because I'm a hard-core professional and I don't need you ogling my boobs' vibe going on."

She laughed. "I guess it was."

"Confession, Red." He tugged her down so his mouth could briefly play with hers again. "I ogled anyway."

"I'm glad you did or we probably wouldn't be here right now."

"Here, with you sitting on me looking so smokin' hot I expect an alarm to go off any minute?"

"Here..." She drew a breath. "With me telling you that I want you."

His expression stilled, then he murmured, "Thank God," and reached for her.

"Not just for sex," she rushed to say. He had to know her intent.

Brodie settled back. "Okay."

"I want us to have a real relationship."

He treated her to another endearing smile. "We already do."

Mary shook her head. "Not just a sexual relationship. Not just a business relationship. I don't want those to change, but I want us to...well, date. Be a couple." It sounded so lame now that she tried to explain it out loud. "I like you. A lot."

Smiling, he started to speak.

Mary smashed her fingers over his mouth, not ready to hear his reaction to her declaration. She'd put him on the spot while also enticing him. Unfair, but she wasn't sure of another way to do it—mostly because she had zero practice in declaring herself to a man.

"Don't misunderstand, Brodie. I'm not rushing things. In fact, just the opposite. I want to savor every minute."

He lifted his brows to encourage her.

"I'm not a shy person." Surely he'd already noticed that. "You can't leave home at seventeen and make your own way if you're shy." Her fingers against his mouth started to tremble, but she needed to say it all. "You can't fumble your way through mediocre jobs for much of your adult life, then dare approach Therman Ritter—*the* Therman Ritter—and declare yourself perfect for a career that's completely out of your league if you aren't confident."

His tongue traced between her fingers, making her pull back with a start.

"I agree you have loads of confidence. In *some* things."

How could that quick lick of his tongue be so erotic? It made no sense, except that it was Brodie and he could excite her with a single look. A touch of his wicked tongue and she was a goner.

Mary shook her head. "If you're talking about the other day when your mother caught us together—"

"I'm a grown man, honey. She doesn't *catch* me. She just interrupted."

"That sounds rude, though, and I can't imagine your mother being rude."

He laughed and shook his head. "You're going to be shocked when you really get to know her."

Did that mean he wanted a relationship, too? She wasn't sure of the protocol in these situations, so she hesitated to outright ask.

"I knew as soon as I saw her that she was your mother, so of course I was embarrassed. Anyone would've been."

"I could never be embarrassed for being with you, but I understand why you were. It's unfamiliar territory."

"True, but that's what I need you to understand. I don't let unfamiliar territory intimidate me. Not for long anyway. Once I decide to do something, I want to do it right."

"There's no *wrong* way—"

Of course there was. Mary leaned down to quiet him with a brief kiss, but Brodie caught her there, and the way he took control of the kiss... She got a little lost in his taste, the heat of him and that indescribable scent that made her forget her own name. By the time she got it together and pulled back, they were both breathing hard and the air had started to simmer.

Steadying herself, Mary braced her hands on his shoulders. While Brodie looked down the neckline of her dress, she concentrated on the point she wanted to make. "Be forewarned. Now that we're doing this, I won't hold back."

"This?" he asked hopefully, lifting his hips and grinding against her.

The pleasure was so sharp that she had to close her eyes a moment. "Yes, that." She licked her lips and focused. "This. Us?"

"If that's a question, it shouldn't be." He stroked the backs of his fingers along her cheek. "I don't want anyone but you, remember?"

"I don't want anyone, either." It would take a while to get used to being a priority for Brodie, but she liked it. A lot. Now that she had their mutual feelings confirmed, she was ready for the rest. "It's still new for me. Before I met you, my closest relationship was with Therman."

"You kept that mostly business."

Because, until Brodie, she'd been afraid to want anything more. She'd been content to settle on Therman's respect, and hadn't wanted to chance losing it. Yes, she was a confident person, but also overly cautious, and that was why she said, "No rushing. No making assumptions, okay?"

He was quiet a moment, his brows slightly drawn, his expression...sympathetic?

Oh no, no, *no*.

She'd had enough of that in her lifetime. She didn't want it from Brodie. Verbally stepping away from his disconcerting reaction, she stated, "It's your family, too."

"My family?"

"I like them." Having him like this, half-undressed, under her and agreeable, made it harder to talk. "I want them to like me."

"They already do."

"Good." She didn't know much longer she could hold out. "When I started the job with Therman, I had no idea what I was doing but I was determined to do my best." She shifted, moving over his lap, anxious to be done with clothes. "That's how I feel about your family, especially your mom."

Suddenly Brodie flipped her, pinning her down with his weight, somehow between her sprawled legs.

From her new position looking up, Mary blinked. "Hey." He'd done that awfully fast.

"One." He kissed the tip of her nose. "I can't discuss family when you're sitting on me and I'm hard."

"Oh." Perfect example of things she needed to realize. She wrinkled her nose. "I guess that would be weird."

"You only need to know that they like you a lot. You don't need to do anything different for them."

She doubted that was true, but nodded anyway. "Okay."

"Two." He nuzzled her throat, managing to tease a lot of sensitive nerve endings. "Therman is damned lucky to have you."

"I agree." She tipped her head to the side to give him better access. "*He* agrees."

"Perfect. Then for now, how about we get naked and I'll show you one of the big benefits of being in a relationship?"

Mary grinned. Even through his jeans, she could feel Brodie's erection throbbing. "It is rather *big*, isn't it?"

He laughed as he pressed his mouth to hers, making it tickle at first, then slowly drawing her into a hot, heated, hungry embrace.

She thought she'd covered all the important points, but if not, it could wait. This, she decided, could not.

CHAPTER SEVENTEEN

Five o'clock rolled around and still Brodie didn't want to leave the bed. Mary slept snuggled against his side, one smooth, pale thigh draped over his hairy leg, one small hand resting on his chest. Knowing he'd exhausted her satisfied him on an elemental level.

After the days apart, she'd come to him looking different, with a specific goal in mind, but in the most important ways she was the same. *Thank God.* He didn't want her to change, unless that change included happiness.

With him.

Once I decide to do something, I want to do it right.

He wouldn't mind waking her and loving her all over again. And again—until she realized that anything and everything between them was *right.* Her past. Her worries. Her uncertainties.

He could handle all of it. He *wanted* to handle it.

She didn't have to be strong with him, but her strength didn't threaten him, either.

When she felt vulnerable, he'd gladly share his strength.

His family would love her, not only because they loved him, but because *she* was very lovable.

Even in sleep, her chin looked stubborn, but then, that stubbornness had brought her through a hellish childhood so they could be here now. She'd been so earnest about her intentions, almost like she thought her determination might scare him off.

Not happening.

If she hadn't added in that part about taking things slow, he probably would've declared himself then and there. Hell, he still wanted to. He'd never been in love before and keeping it contained wasn't easy.

Only for Mary.

Keeping her here in bed for the rest of the night would be perfect...except that Howler would be missing him, and Jack would need to head out. His brother spent most free evenings working on the renovation of his house, which would be easier to do without a ninety-pound dog underfoot.

To wake her, Brodie stroked back her hair. At some point while she'd been riding him with enthusiasm, her topknot had come loose, spilling that gorgeous hair down around her shoulders. The sight of it had damn near made him spill, too.

Mary stirred, her chin lifting, one arm reaching out while she stretched.

So sexy without even realizing it.

Knowing she was more than a handful, he cupped a full pale breast. Her nipples were soft now, pink and pretty.

He brushed his thumb over her. "C'mon, sleepyhead. There's a big dog missing us."

Lashes lifted lazily. Her lips curled the smallest bit. "Mmm. Sorry I fell asleep."

"Don't be." Her eyes now were sated, clear of concern. Such distinctive eyes. "Want to see where I'll build my house?"

That got her a little perkier. Pushing her hair back, she sat up and looked around, as if orienting herself. "We can go now?"

"We'll get Howler and make a picnic of it. What do you think?"

"I think that's the most perfect way to end the day."

It wouldn't be the end, not if he could help it. He had high hopes of convincing her to stay the night again, but he'd work on that later.

Knowing Jack was waiting, Brodie dressed in his discarded jeans and a clean shirt. He sat on the end of the bed to pull on his shoes while Mary hooked her bra.

Though it seemed a shame to put those beauties away, he enjoyed watching her. "You're not burnt anymore."

"I wasn't burned that much to begin with." She lifted each breast to settle it in the cups, making his cock twitch with interest. "By the second day it was fine."

He touched his forehead. "Same here. All gone."

"Not exactly true." She pulled her dress over her head and smoothed it down. "I still see some bruising."

After mussing his hair so it covered his brow, he held out his arms. "Now you don't."

"Clever." She bent at the waist, flipping her hair forward and combing it with her fingers, then twisted it and fastened it with a clip.

She straightened, pulled a few curls loose and headed out of the room.

Fascinated by her process, Brodie followed her. There was a new ease in her gait, a sensual reckoning that before now she'd kept under wraps. Feeling a burst of pride, he watched her step into her sandals and hitch her purse strap over her shoulder.

It occurred to him that she hadn't carried in a briefcase. It was one the few times he could recall seeing her without it. She did, however, have her phone.

After she checked for messages, she glanced up and caught him watching. "What?"

He hesitated to let business intrude on the personal evening, but he needed to know. "Have you heard anything else from Therman?"

"Yes. He's come up with a theory about the problems, but it's a bit complicated, so maybe we should get Howler before I go into it."

He didn't want to wait, but knew she was right. In agreement, Brodie took her hand and together they walked the short distance to the office.

Before they ever reached the door, Howler was there watching for them. As soon as he spotted them, he took several berserk spins, blending a bark with a howl for the most dramatic effect.

As they came in, Howler threw himself against Brodie's legs, almost knocking him over.

Laughing, Brodie dropped to his haunches and allowed the dog to lavish him with love in the form of wet doggy kisses. "Such a good boy," he said in his baby-dog voice. "Did you miss me? Did you?"

He heard Jack say, "Nauseating, isn't it?"

"I think it's sweet."

"So sweet," Jack said, "my teeth are hurting."

Brodie hid his grin. "Calm down, now," he urged softly, patting Howler until he was no longer so frantic. "That's a good boy. Easy." He ran long strokes down his back, from his neck to the base of his tail. "I know, I missed you, too. Shh, shh."

Calmer now, Howler turned to Mary and demanded equal affection. She didn't hesitate to give it, hugging Howler's neck and patting his side.

"Somehow, I don't believe you were actively missing that horse." Jack was already on his feet, ready to go, but before he could move away from his desk, Howler charged back to him, sitting down as if waiting and blocking the way.

"Are you kidding me?" Jack asked the dog.

He got a deep "Woof" and a swishing of tail for reply.

Brodie lifted his brows. "What's this?"

With a huff, Jack opened his desk drawer and pulled out a bag of dog treats. "He stayed at the door watching for you no matter what Charlotte or I did, so I got a bag of treats and tried to get him to refocus."

"So far, so good," Brodie said.

"I called him over here, by my desk. Having him at my feet seemed better than letting him act abandoned. But after half an hour, he was back at it, so I called him over again."

Starting to catch on, Brodie laughed. "He turned it against you, didn't he?"

Mary tipped her head. "I don't understand."

"This." Jack gestured with the treat, tossed it in the air and Howler snatched it into his great jaws. "Now, watch."

The dog walked back to the door and sat down.

"He's done that every thirty minutes or so now. He waits there, looking inconsolable, then walks over for me to reward him. Like I've taught him a trick or something."

"That's incredibly clever." Mary turned to the dog. "You're so smart, aren't you?"

Still licking his chops, Howler leaned against her and accepted the praise.

"I have to go." After slapping Brodie on the back, Jack pulled Mary in for a brief, one-armed hug.

Surprise stiffened her spine and widened her eyes, but just as quickly she smiled in delight. Over Jack's shoulder, she met Brodie's gaze with a look of wonder.

Jack stepped back. "I'll see you again soon?"

Actually blushing, she nodded. "Yes."

With genuine warmth, Jack said, "Glad to hear it."

They all walked out together, Jack going to his yellow Mustang, Brodie leading Mary and Howler to his red one.

Once they were on their way, Brodie couldn't resist teasing her. "My family is big on hugging."

"Jack never hugged me before."

He shrugged. "We weren't together before."

That earned him a blinding smile. "I'll try to remember."

On the way to his property, he stopped to pick up food and drinks. A few minutes later, after spreading out a blanket he kept in the truck and leashing Howler to a small tree, he and Mary feasted on fried chicken, biscuits and colas.

They'd shared some very fine meals with Therman, but they couldn't compare to a picnic with Mary.

"This is really all yours?" She kept looking around, admiring it much as he did.

Brodie pointed toward the creek. "You can just see Mom's place through the trees."

"Really?" She got to her feet, moving closer to where water trickled along in the shallow creek bed. "I do see it. Pretty."

Sitting cross-legged, Brodie watched her. Because she'd left her sandals on the blanket, she walked with caution, picking her way.

And even that turned him on.

It'd be so easy to lure her back to the blanket, to strip her panties out from under her dress and show her again how much he enjoyed her.

Unfortunately, they had other things to deal with, too. "You want to tell me about Therman?"

Looking up at the treetops, she shaded her eyes and turned a circle. "It's beautiful here."

"Yeah." And she was procrastinating, but he enjoyed the show too much to press her. He wondered if being here, seeing the land where he planned to build made her think of the house where she'd grown up. She wanted to level it, as if that would level her history, too. He knew, whether she realized it yet or not, that destroying a building wouldn't destroy the memories. They'd always be there.

He hoped, eventually, they'd be at peace, though.

And then, with him, she could build new memories.

"Do you hear the birds?" Arms out, she turned her face up

to the sunshine filtering through the leaves. "So many of them singing."

"Blue jays, cardinals, crows, blackbirds, robins..." If she enjoyed birds, she needed to live here with him. Hell, now that he knew he loved her, he wanted them to plan a future together. "The house would go just about here, where we put the blanket. It's a natural clearing so I wouldn't have to cut down too many trees. My back porch would face the front of Mom's house but with plenty of woods between us." He pointed at a boulder on the edge of the creek. "I'd probably build a little footbridge right there."

"That way the two of you could easily visit."

He formed a picture in his mind. "We could sit out here, drinking coffee with her."

If she caught the "we" part of that image, she didn't comment on it. Instead, she bent to gently touch a tiny yellow wildflower, then picked up an acorn. "It smells good out here."

"Cooler, too, with all the shade." Goddamn, the small talk was about to kill him.

She bounced the acorn in her hand. "I used to have a pretty good arm. Sometimes, when I didn't feel like sitting in the trees, I'd practice throwing acorns instead. I always loved the woods anyway. They're peaceful. But I'm not good with idle time, you know?"

"Yes." He did know, because he wasn't great with idle time, either.

"I'd pick a target, like maybe a knothole on a tree or a specific rock, and I'd keep throwing until my aim was true." Casting him a sly glance, she asked, "Want to compete?"

Actually, he wanted to howl.

She couldn't know how it affected him, thinking of her as that young girl, trying to occupy herself while her mother entertained men. In his mind he saw her with those big innocent blue eyes and the freckles she didn't like, her hair crazy from her mother's newest experiment, all alone in the fucking woods.

Pitching acorns.

He pushed to his feet. "You're on." Trying to keep his tone light, he said, "I have a fair aim myself."

"Ah, but throwing an acorn is different from throwing a ball."

To his surprise, she took a stance, barefoot there in the fallen pine needles, that damned dress closing tight around her hips and thighs as she drew back her arm…then let the acorn fly. And *fly*. It kept going, clearing a hole in the trees and soaring over the creek.

Brodie whistled. "I'm impressed."

She looked around, found a few more and tossed one to him. "Let's see what you've got."

His first effort would have gone a lot farther, except he hit a tree. His second curved too much. He was laughing when he threw his third, with the help of her instruction, but at least it matched her effort.

"There you go." Mary bounced on the balls of her feet, which made other parts bounce, too. "Good job."

Brodie caught her upper arms and pulled her in for a kiss, holding her close until he felt the beating of her heart, until her breath sighed out and her smile softened. "Any other demonstrations of talents learned in the woods?"

"Hmm." She glanced around. "Well, I'd show you my tree-climbing skills, but not in a dress. And if that creek was deeper, we could skinny-dip." She bumped him with her hip. "I'm a good swimmer. I can skip a rock five times over the surface of a lake. Catch a crawdad in my bare hands." She gave it a little more thought. "And I can make a mud man that looks something like the Pillsbury Doughboy."

Brodie laughed. "You're the whole package, a refined professional and a survivalist, too." He hugged her. "The creek is deeper farther up, so don't think I'll let you forget about skinny-dipping." He glanced at Howler, but the dog was busy watching a squirrel, so he picked up Mary and carried her back to the blanket. "Now."

"Now, what?" She laughed as he went to his knees and lowered her to the ground.

"This." He kissed her, at first light and easy, tugging on her bottom lip, licking her upper. When she made a small sound and tightened her hands on his shoulders, he sank in for more. Mouths open, tongues stroking, breaths hot and fast. "I will never get enough of you."

At his murmured words, she pressed him back. Her wide eyes searched his face. Whatever she saw must have satisfied her because she relaxed. What she said, though, had nothing to do with his declaration.

"Therman thinks he knows who was following us."

The switch took him off guard.

"It's so nice here, and I was enjoying the time with you so much, I hated to get back to business." Mary put a hand to his jaw. "But we do need to talk about it."

What a confession, considering the woman was usually all about business. "I understand." He stretched out on his side next to her, close enough that his thigh pressed hers, his groin to her hip. He rested one hand on her stomach. "You want to tell me now?"

"I think I have to." She sighed. "Apparently Therman and this other man have each started a collection of weird artwork."

"Most of Therman's shit is weird."

She conceded that. "This is weirder, though, because it's done by a prisoner."

Yeah, didn't see that one coming. It took Brodie a second to say, "I assume this dude created the work before getting locked up?"

She shook her head. "No, actually, according to Therman, the most valuable pieces are straight from prison cells. Some are created on small canvases that got smuggled in. But Therman said he has a few pieces made from cigarette packs, one from a toilet paper roll and one…"

He prodded her. "Don't leave me hanging."

She wrinkled her nose. "With human hair and toenail clippings."

"No fucking way. Like a kid's macaroni art?"

She shrugged.

"Damn, that's gross."

"Agreed." Despite the serious and bizarre subject matter, when Mary inhaled, his gaze went to her chest. He couldn't imagine a moment when he wouldn't want her, but God willing, the need would blunt with time. He wasn't sure he could live with an urge this sharp.

"I didn't ask for particulars, but Therman said the artist is locked up for murder."

"And yet people buy his art?"

"Actually, they can't. Not legitimately. The prisoner isn't allowed to profit from it. From what I understand, he has a rep who bribes a guard to sneak the stuff out. It's hot on the black market."

"And Therman, of course, wants it."

"Along with several other collectors, yes."

It sounded so sick. Brodie slid his arm around her, needing to hug her closer, needing to keep her safe. "Don't get pissed, okay?"

She eyed him. "When people say that, it's usually because they plan to do something guaranteed to piss off the other person."

True enough. He did it anyway. "I don't want you involved in acquiring that shit." Before she could feel insulted, he added, "Hell, *I* don't want to be involved."

"I'm not crazy about it myself." She turned toward him so they rested face-to-face. "Therman doesn't see anything wrong with it, and neither does his competition."

"Who's the competition?" Knowing that would likely answer a lot of questions.

She waved a hand in dismissal. "These collectors use aliases online. Therman didn't tell me the name he uses, but this other person goes by Assassin."

Well, hell. Brodie worked his jaw. "That says a lot."

"I had the same reaction, but then Therman told me some of the other names. How do you like The Prodigal, Bone Collector and Wraith? Those are his main competitors for this collection."

"Grown men—and I assume women—playing masquerades. It's absurd." And so obviously dangerous.

"There's a popular message board where most of the collectors find what they want. Soon, a new piece is supposed to be offered. It's Therman's theory that Assassin is trying to scare him off so he won't bid on it, then he can claim it for his own collection without having to pay as much."

"I say let him have it."

"I said that as well." Mary went to her back again, her gaze on the sky. "Therman was pretty upset. He gets obsessive about completing a collection."

"So I gather. What was the final decision? Will he let it go?"

"He didn't say he wouldn't, but he didn't say he would, either." She closed her eyes. "I like my job, Brodie."

Damn. He lightly traced the contours of her mouth. "I know." Her lips drew him and he couldn't resist tasting them again. Her mouth was so damned perfect…

"I don't want it to be a problem between us."

He promised, "No problem." He wouldn't let there be any problems, not with Mary. After one final press of his mouth to hers, he said, "How about I talk to Therman?"

One eye peeked opened and she said firmly, "With me."

What could he do but agree? He gave a reluctant nod.

Through the quiet of the woods, they heard the sound of a

car on gravel. Mary sat up with a frown. "Did someone follow us here?"

"No, that's probably someone coming to visit Mom. Sound travels. Let me take a look." As Brodie stood, he noticed that Howler was also on the alert.

He strode toward the creek to peer over. He couldn't make out individual faces, but he recognized the car.

Gina had come to see his mother.

Every day, maybe every hour, his craving grew stronger, less manageable. *Had his father known how he'd feel being caged like this? Did he not care?*

Helton paced the seedy rented hotel room, the recklessness stirring from deep inside. He needed this fucking collection complete so he could get on with his life.

A life he no longer enjoyed.

His trip to Red Oak a few days ago… Ah, that had felt real. Intimidation. Manipulation. He flexed his hands, loosening and tightening his thick fingers. Now if only he could get in a brawl, bust a few heads. *Then* he'd feel like himself again.

He strode to the window and back again, his thoughts churning.

If all goes as planned, fighting won't be necessary.

He wasn't sure which he wanted more: success or failure.

One way or another, he'd complete his father's beloved collection. If it came down to it, violence would be so rewarding—but his father had disapproved of that. He'd wanted Helton to change as he'd changed, to moderate his ways and accept the leash willingly.

Rubbing his temples, Helton thought back to when his father had been a hale, mean son of a bitch, powerful enough to live forever. Denying him had been easy.

Funny that it had taken his death to bring Helton to heel.

Needing a distraction before he punched a hole in the wall, he glared at his cell phone on the dresser.

And the damned thing buzzed.

Huh. But no, he wouldn't pounce on it like an eager kid—he wasn't that far gone yet. He waited until the third ring, then answered with a deliberately bored "News?"

Lem mimicked that tone, the self-contained prick. "The girl finally made a move." He spoke as if informing Helton on the fucking weather.

"It'd be a big mistake," Helton growled, "if you're waiting for me to guess." He didn't yet let his shoulders relax. Would Brodie call or not? Would he get to crack some heads or would he have to return to the boring office?

"Sorry." With new, crisp respect, Lem said, "She's gone to his mother's house."

Helton's brows dug furrows in his forehead and his shoulders clenched even more. "The fuck you say?" He'd been very clear with Blondie: go to Brodie, pitch the plan and then forget she'd ever met him.

He did not tell her to visit Rosalyn Crews.

In the three days since Helton had found her in the diner, Gina had gone to the bank and the salon. That was it. Lem and Todd took turns watching the girl, but she hadn't gone anywhere near the Mustang Transport offices.

He'd started to think she'd been too wasted the morning he'd explained things to her. Maybe the coffee hadn't sobered her at all. Maybe she'd passed out again after he'd left and completely forgotten his threats.

Of course, she'd kept the money. That'd been his clincher. Fuck it up and he'd come to reclaim what was his. He'd softly informed her that she didn't want that, that if she was lucky she'd never lay eyes on him again.

At the time, she'd looked so horrified he thought she might faint. Not that he'd really hurt any woman.

He considered that the worst sort of cowardice.

But the girl didn't know that. Hell, other than his victims, few did. Wasn't like he'd announce a soft spot, right? To those who came into his realm, he was cold-blooded enough to eat puppies for breakfast.

No man with a brain would announce a weakness.

"We can follow her when she leaves," Lem offered.

"Yeah, you do that." When Helton had handed her the envelope of cash, she'd accepted it with wide eyes and obvious greed that overrode her fear. He'd walked away, confident that she'd follow his orders to the letter.

Now she finally made a move, but she'd gone to Rosalyn Crews.

He wouldn't mind going to Ros as well, but that wasn't the point. "Maybe Brodie is with his mother?"

"No, sorry." Lem cleared his throat. "We caught sight of him having a picnic with Ms. Daniels."

A surprised guffaw burst out. "A picnic? No fuck?" He hadn't figured Brodie for a picnic type of man.

"Wait." A note of excitement sounded in Lem's voice. "Crews and Ms. Daniels just showed up. They're at the house now, too."

Maybe Gina was following instructions after all. That familiar satisfaction mixed with disappointment burned in Helton's gut, sending him pacing around the room again.

The newest piece would go up for sale soon.

It'd be the last...*ever.* He'd seen to that.

Thanks to his contacts, there was one less artistic prick in the prison system. He'd just saved taxpayers a lot of coin by having the fuck gutted in the shower.

A fitting end for the man who'd murdered three women.

Helton continued to move, past the dingy little bathroom, around the bed, to the window and back again.

Plans were coming together. He'd already picked off the other two collectors. Without Therman Ritter's money and means, they'd been easy to intimidate.

Now he needed this one last thing to end his obligation to his father. After that, if he chose to, he could sell the fucking empire, maybe buy a nightclub instead, get back to basics…and finally start to live again.

An abrupt decision filled him with purpose. He grabbed up his jacket from a chair, his wallet from the dresser. "I'm going to join you."

Lem's shocked silence preceded a strangled "Join me?"

"Yeah." Saying it felt good. He could finally draw a deep breath. Instead of his muscles itching, they twitched with anticipation. "I'm twenty minutes away." He'd left Red Oak but hadn't gone far. He'd sensed this moment, *craved* it.

He needed to be in the thick of things. He needed to use his hands for more than pushing papers.

Finally he had his chance. "Tell me where to meet you."

The sense of being watched grew with every step that brought them closer to Ros's house. Mary didn't know if she should share that with Brodie. It could be her imagination based on her uneasiness with this interruption.

She wanted to see Ros, true. The woman completely fascinated her. But with Gina there? The girl made no secret of wanting him so it was bound to be awkward.

Unfortunately, after spending much of her life under the microscope, she knew all about being watched—and it felt exactly like *this*.

Glancing around, she looked at the trees, the hillside. The main street in Red Oak wasn't that far away as the crow flies. And Ros had a few neighbors, not close, but near enough to spy on Mary? Maybe.

The feeling intensified when she saw that Howler, too, kept

looking off toward the nearest neighbor. All Mary could see was a barn…with an open loft window.

"What's wrong?" Brodie's hand tightened on hers.

She didn't want him to misunderstand, or to consider her weak. He already had a massive protective streak and if he thought she was nervous about seeing Gina, his mother or both, he'd amp it up even more.

She didn't need or want that from him.

This, then, would be one of those reasons why she didn't want to rush their relationship.

Mary didn't want to talk out in the open, not with the escalating apprehension. "Promise me you won't stop."

"Stop?"

She kept him walking, a little faster now. "Here in the yard."

"Why would I stop?" Of *course* he stopped to ask that.

Tugging at his hand, Mary admitted, "I think we're being watched."

Scowling, he obligingly matched his stride to hers even as he looked around. "What do you mean?"

They'd almost reached his mother's porch. "It feels like someone is spying on us. Howler feels it, too."

He looked at the dog and nodded. "Let's go." Picking up the pace even more, he hustled her along the walk and up three steps to a covered porch. "I don't want to look around and alert anyone that we're onto them."

"You feel it, too?"

"Only now that you've mentioned it." He rapped twice on his mother's door, then opened it. Howler tried to hold back, his body stiff, his gaze on the area of the barn. "Come on, boy." The dog resisted, Brodie insisted, and finally they all stepped into an empty living room.

Brodie closed and locked the door. "Mom, I'm home," he called out.

She immediately poked her head around an arched doorway.

"Perfect timing," she whispered and beckoned him in. "Gina has a story to tell you." Ros disappeared again.

Sighing, Brodie said to no one in particular, "What now?"

Mary heard the girl sob.

So did Brodie. His mouth flattened and his eyes narrowed. "Let's get it over with."

Mary agreed, though she thought it might just be starting.

CHAPTER EIGHTEEN

Mary had never seen another woman look so miserable. Oh, Gina had fixed her hair and makeup, but the current crying jag had ruined the usual effect.

Drinking iced tea, sitting around a wooden table in the spacious eat-in kitchen, Mary waited—not too patiently—to find out what was going on.

Brodie was even more annoyed. He'd locked the back door, too, then found a large chew bone for Howler to keep him occupied. Ros, apparently, considered herself something of a grandma to the dog and, according to Brodie, spoiled him rotten.

She also claimed Howler would chew on something, so better a bone than one of her shoes.

Howler liked the treat, but it didn't keep him from repeatedly looking out the windows from various angles in the house. He'd go from the patio doors, to the dining room window, to the window behind the couch in the living room and back again.

That, more than Gina's sobbing, alarmed her.

Ros reached across the table and took Gina's hand. "Enough of that, now. Take a breath and tell them what you told me."

Gina shot a mean, red-eyed look at Mary. "Why does she have to be here?"

Why, indeed? Mary started to push back her chair. "I'll wait in the other room."

Both Brodie and Ros refused. They sat beside each other, sharing the same stubborn, determined look. It was almost enough to make Mary smile.

Somehow the order of the table went Gina, Ros, Brodie and Mary…which, yes, put her next to Gina.

"You're staying put," Brodie said.

Mary lifted a brow. "Not if I want to leave."

Grinning, Ros elbowed her son—which told Mary where Jack had gotten the habit—and said, "I really do like her."

"Yeah, I more than like her."

Gina stiffened.

Mary tried not to react. *He more than likes me?* What exactly did that mean?

Sitting back in his chair, Brodie folded his massive arms over his chest. "She's staying." He added to Mary, "If you don't mind?"

After what he'd just said, of course she didn't mind. Besides, the curiosity *was* about to kill her. "All right."

Gina stared daggers at her. "You changed your look."

Surprised by the comment, Mary admitted, "A little."

"A lot." Gina's petulant gaze moved to her hair. "It'd look better down."

Maybe it would, but with temps in the upper eighties? "It's too hot today to wear it down."

As if she didn't understand that, Gina repeated slowly, "But it would look better down."

Because fashion was never her first concern, and she'd spent too many years trying to blend in, Mary shrugged. "I'm not into making myself uncomfortable." Now that they'd taken a step away from the antagonism, Mary felt the need to apologize. It wasn't her usual way to be mean to another woman, whether that other woman deserved it or not. She knew what it was to hurt, to be miserable from the inside out.

Currently, Gina was miserable.

"The other day, when we were in Brodie's car, I'm sorry I was so rude."

The younger woman stiffened in surprise. "You weren't rude. You *gloated*."

Yes, she had, and this time she wouldn't blame the wine. "You were coming on to him right in front of me."

"I didn't know the two of you were..." Her face pinched. "Together. I mean, you were supposed to be working together, that's all. Besides, you aren't exactly his type."

Sympathy be damned, she wouldn't accept direct insults, either. "Apparently I am."

Brodie smiled. "I have been pretty apparent."

"Still," Mary continued, "I should have resisted the urge."

Gina grabbed for another tissue. "That's what started it all, you know." Ros had already set a small wastebasket next to her. It was currently half-full with tissues.

"Started what, exactly?" Brodie asked.

The tissue crumpled in her hand. "You're supposed to hold back on a job." She flagged a hand. "Drive slow or be late or don't show up at all. Something like that." More tears welled. "If you don't, I could be in trouble."

Ros cleared her throat. "That's not exactly the beginning. Should I give it a try?"

Covering her face with her hands, Gina nodded.

In another show of motherly sympathy, Ros patted Gina's hand before continuing the story. "You know that Gina blasted you both on Facebook. Well, apparently a man tracked her down because of it. She not only used your name in her posts, Brodie, she tagged her location, repeatedly, so he knew where to find her."

Brodie scowled. "What man?"

"I don't know." Gina swallowed audibly. "He was big. Really big. Even bigger than you, but older and ugly. He looked so…so *mean*. But he told me I'd won the lottery and I was still a little drunk and she'd made me so upset!"

Anger tightened Brodie's expression, but Ros spoke before he could.

"We've already discussed this. You're not going to blame anyone else for the bad decisions you made."

Her calm, firm tone sounded just as Mary had always suspected a caring mother would speak.

Gina shot Mary another hate-filled look.

"Did he leave a name?" Brodie demanded.

"No." Gina dug a crumpled paper from her pocket and pushed it across the table with a shaking hand. "He told me to share the message with you, then call that number to let him know what you said."

"A phone number? That's a start." Brodie took the paper, looked at it with grim satisfaction and shoved it in his own pocket.

Gina gaped. "Oh…but you can't keep that. I need to call him."

"I'll take care of it."

Oh no, Mary wouldn't let him get away with that. She knew exactly what he was thinking. "You're not cutting me out, Brodie Archer Crews."

"Don't act like my mother, Red. It annoys me."

Ros raised her brows but stayed silent.

"It annoys *me* that you think you should take over." She wasn't falling apart, wasn't almost hysterical and didn't need to be pampered.

Hadn't she proved that for most of her life?

Keeping her expression as reasonable as she could manage, she said, "We need to call it *together*."

Turning his hand, he laced his fingers with hers. "First, I figured we'd check with Therman to see if he recognizes the number."

Oh. *Oh.* Yes, that made sense. "All right."

"If you two are done bickering," Ros said, "there's more."

They all looked at Gina.

She cowered under the scrutiny, and that, too, made Mary empathize. Fearing the worst, especially with all the theatrics, she asked, "Did he hurt you?"

Gina shook her head and, in a small voice, whispered, "Not the way you mean."

"Then tell us how."

"He…he gave me a thousand dollars."

Silence swelled until Brodie muttered, deadpan, "Cruel bastard."

That set Gina off and she rushed her words together. "I still owed on my car. They might've repo'd it without a payment. Plus I hadn't been to the salon in forever! He gave it to me and then…just left. It felt like *free* money, not a big deal. What did you expect me to do?"

Dear Lord. Mary sat forward. "Are you saying you already *spent* it?"

"That's exactly what she's saying." Brodie ran a hand over his face. "Gina—"

"No! Don't you give me hell for it. It was a thousand dollars in cash."

Probably a lump sum she didn't see often. Mary sighed. "Pointing fingers will get us nowhere."

Brodie watched Howler circle to another window, his body tense.

"Someone is watching us." Mary felt sure of it.

"What?" Jerking around so fast she almost fell out of her seat, Gina demanded, "Who? Where?" Hand to her heart, she shot to her feet. "I need to go."

"You shouldn't go alone." Brodie folded his arms on the table, his expression lethal. "If someone is stashed in the barn, I have an idea."

"No." Mary didn't know what his plan might be, but it terrified her. "Absolutely not."

Ignoring her refusal, he said, "I could edge my way over there—"

"No."

"—staying out of sight in the woods—"

"I said no." She wouldn't give on this.

"—and when I was close enough, I'd text you. Then you could call the number. If someone answers, I'd hear them and we'd know if we have the right person."

Mary shoved back her chair. "Absolutely not."

Still seated, Brodie looked up at her. "Why not?"

Why not? Because she loved him and wouldn't risk him, that was why not. She couldn't tell him that here and now, though, so she fudged the truth. "We just started a relationship. We're supposed to listen to each other, right?"

Gina made a rude sound. "Brodie doesn't listen to anyone."

"He listens to me," Ros countered.

Smiling, Brodie took Mary's hand and tugged her toward him.

She resisted him. "How in the world can you smile right now?"

Rolling one shoulder, he said, "I have you." Then he gave one more tug and she ended up in his lap.

Mary seriously considered smacking him. "Damn it, Brodie—"

"Damn it, Red." Still amused, he kissed her, a brief, firm kiss that made her cheeks hot since his mother and Gina were in the room with them. "You're right, you know. We're supposed to listen to each other. But that doesn't mean you call all the shots."

Was he laughing at her? She narrowed her eyes.

"Whoever was there is gone now anyway."

Twisting, she looked toward the window that faced the barn. "How do you know?"

"Howler went to sleep."

Ah. The dog now stretched out in a ray of sunshine in front of the patio doors, his chin resting on what remained of his bone, doggy snores making his loose lips quiver.

Looking toward that barn again, Mary made a decision. She hated to alienate Therman, but it was the right thing to do. "We have to call the cops."

"But..." Gina looked at each of them. "I'll be in trouble, too. They'll want me to figure out who he is when I don't have any idea." She turned to Ros. "You know how the township police are. They'll show up with sirens and lights and I'll be a spectacle."

"Actually," Brodie said, "I agree with Gina. Tommy Felder gets wood anytime he gets to turn on his lights. The locals are just that—local. Besides, what would we even tell them? Gina was drunk when this all happened."

Gina nodded vigorously. "And the money's gone," she reminded him.

Brodie ran a hand up and down Mary's back, speaking to her as if they were the only two in the room. "We can't prove anyone was at the barn, right? We should at least talk to Therman first, and then call the number before we make a big deal of it."

Unconvinced, Mary tried to think it through. She did owe Therman loyalty after three years of employment. And maybe Gina had exaggerated some of it.

"Collectors are notoriously eccentric people," she mused.

"And Therman already has someone in mind, right? This Assassin character."

"Dear God." Gina pulled her purse strap up over her shoulder. "I need to go."

"It's a message board name," Brodie told her. "He's not actually an assassin."

Mary hoped that was true.

"It's all too weird. I want to be home with the doors locked before it gets dark."

Ros stood. "Will someone be home with you?"

"My whole family."

"Good." Ros pulled her into a hug. "If you need me, call. But until this is resolved, I think you should be careful." She turned away to put their glasses in the sink.

Mary scrambled off Brodie's lap, he stood, and the two of them walked Gina to the door.

After Brodie watched her drive away, he said, "We're leaving in just a minute, okay? I agree with Gina, I want to get to my car before it gets dark."

"Is that safe?" Ros asked, coming in behind them. "Maybe I should drive you."

"I want you to stay put." Brodie put a shoulder to the wall and withdrew his phone. "And please, Mom, don't complain, but I'm going to call Jack."

"To go with you?" Ros nodded. "Good. Why would I complain about that?"

Phone to his ear, Brodie said, "To keep track of *you*, not me."

The way Ros scowled, Mary figured they might need a moment. She went into the kitchen to finish tidying up, but she could still hear them debating.

After wiping off the table, she paused at the sink and stared out the window at the yard.

She heard Brodie's insistent voice, Ros's defiant tone, and through it all, she heard…respect. Concern.

Love.

Even when faced with trouble, maybe *because* they faced trouble, they pulled together.

Yes, they bickered occasionally, but even that was based on affection, each wanting to take care of the other.

It swelled her heart with happiness that Brodie had such a close bond with his family—so the emotion suddenly burning her eyes didn't make sense. Mary gripped the edge of the sink, unseeing as she tried to swallow back the tears. The tightness in her throat made it impossible.

Oh God, she couldn't let him see her like this. What would he think? Or would he think anything at all?

Her mother had never cared that much about her tears, not really. She'd note them with a pat or a brief hug, then move on to other things.

Other people.

Men. Sex. Drugs.

Mary felt a sob swelling up and…

Brodie's arms came around her. "Shh."

No. She didn't need him to—

"Just for a second, okay?" He tucked his face against her neck and his arms—those arms she admired so much—pulled her back tight to his chest as he rocked slightly from side to side. "I need it."

A cleansing breath filled her lungs. *He* needed it? That didn't make sense, but it did make it better. Mary crossed her arms over his and concentrated on blinking away the humiliating moisture blurring her gaze.

After a moment, he said, "Mom's annoyed, but she agreed to call Jack if anything at all happens. She'll keep the house locked, and she's in for the night."

Still not trusting her voice, Mary nodded. She worried about a great many things; she didn't want to add Ros to her list.

"Gina," he said, hesitant. "She's immature and scared."

"She's young."

"Thanks for not giving her hell, and not letting me give her hell."

"You're welcome," she managed to answer.

"Did I tell you lately that you're amazing?"

The smile came, pushing the rest of her turmoil away. "I'm not, but thank you anyway."

"Actually you are," Ros said. She leaned in the doorway, her dark gaze filled with understanding but, thankfully, not pity. "It takes a strong, confident woman to be that compassionate. Thank you."

With a last pat to Brodie's arms, Mary moved away. "Gina got in over her head. I think she cares for Brodie more than she'll admit."

"I hope not," Brodie said, watching her, smiling and looking very possessive. "She'd be doomed to disappointment, because I'm already taken."

Mary acknowledged her own possessiveness. "Yes, you are."

Howler didn't seem at all wary as they went back to his car. Other than chasing a bee, trying to eat a stick and piddling twice, the dog paid no attention to his surroundings as Mary folded up the blanket and he stored away the remains of their picnic.

That, more than anything, told Brodie they were clear.

Still, his mother watched through the window, threatening to call the police if she saw anything shady. Once they were back on the main road, Brodie called to let her know not to worry.

As soon as he was off the phone with her, Mary called Therman, putting the phone on speaker so Brodie could listen in as she updated him.

While they talked, the sun began its descent, splashing shades of gold, crimson and purple across the sky. A beautiful sunset on a memorable day…

If only they didn't have some loony asshole going by the name of *Assassin* threatening trouble.

To his credit, Therman seemed suitably alarmed by it all. No, he didn't recognize the number, but he agreed they should come to his house before Brodie called it.

Of course, Therman wasn't keen on them contacting the police, which would probably lead to the entirety of his collections being scrutinized.

He did, however—without prompting—vow not to bid against Assassin on the upcoming piece.

Mary glanced at Brodie in surprise. Yes, that was a huge concession for Therman, but then, Brodie had always known, despite his oft unethical behavior, the older man cared for Mary.

"We appreciate that," he told Therman.

"I'll go on the message board right now to let Assassin know that the piece is his. With any luck, that'll be the end of it."

Mary didn't look convinced. "If he wants the whole collection, but you still have part of it—"

"I'll sell him what I have." Softer now, Therman said, "No collection is worth you being hurt."

Stunned, she shook her head. "I wouldn't ask you to do that."

"You don't have to."

Silently, Brodie cheered. *Score one for Therman.*

Appearing flustered, Mary whispered, "All right...thank you."

"Drive safe. I'll see you both soon."

For the remainder of the drive, Mary stayed lost in thought. Occasionally she'd frown, then sigh and stare out the window.

He thought about seeing her in his mother's kitchen, her proud shoulders slightly trembling, that awful catch in her breathing that meant tears were imminent.

How hard she fought it.

Holding her had been necessary, especially since he knew why emotion got the better of her.

And why she didn't want to give in to it.

To Mary, being strong, overcoming obstacles, *proving herself,* meant everything.

She didn't need to prove anything to him, not ever, but he

understood now that she was at her most defensive when emotional. He hadn't wanted to say anything that might push her over that edge.

Holding her had been his only option.

The contrast of his family to hers was pretty damned stark. Yeah, his dad had been more absent than not, but he'd always had his mom. Always.

Mary hadn't had anyone.

One person could make all the difference, and he wanted to be that person for Mary.

When she'd stopped straining away from him and instead let her body relax against his… Yeah, in that single moment he'd felt like he'd won a war, all triumphant and jubilant, but also spent.

She'd need time to adjust. He couldn't just smother her with his feelings, easy as that'd be.

This one sexy, stubborn, bossy woman meant the world to him. "It's going to be okay." He needed her to know that.

"I assume." Distracted, she continued to look out the window as they pulled down the narrow lane that led to Therman's private entry. "How many serious collectors can there be? Therman might be able to figure out who Assassin really is by whatever conversation he hears—"

"Yeah, that, too." The sun had settled behind the trees lining the lane on both sides, leaving the sky a dusky gray. "But I meant with us."

"Us?" Smiling, she turned her head to face him—and her eyes flared in panic. "Brodie—"

Too late, he heard the roar of an engine, then the screech of tires as an SUV shot forward from the entrance of the gate, nearly ramming him in the effort to cut him off. Reflexes kicking in, Brodie braked and turned the wheel, sending Matilda skidding sideways until her front tires left the road.

It had been an instinctive reaction to avoid a collision, but now the SUV blocked him from backing up, and he couldn't pull forward because of the trees. Darkened windows kept him from seeing in the SUV, but he had a gut feeling about it.

His heartbeat settled and determination took over. "Call the police. Lock the doors behind me, then unleash Howler, but don't let him out." If necessary, the dog would protect her long enough to give her a chance to run.

Jolted awake, Howler was already frantic, growling and straining against his restraint as he stared out the side window.

"Yeah, I see them," he said softly. "That's a good boy. Be easy now."

Two men stepped out of the big, utilitarian Mercedes that looked like it could navigate deserts and jungles alike. The damn thing probably cost over a hundred and fifty grand, meaning he wasn't just dealing with a collector but something more.

Maybe a real…assassin. But why?

Brodie recognized the men as the same fucks they'd encountered at the rest stop.

The positioning of the vehicles put them to the side of Mary's door, only a few yards away.

One of them carried a gun held loosely at his side, and they both looked cocky.

Muscles tensing, Brodie reached for the door handle.

"What do you think you're doing?" Mary scrabbled to grab his arm but only caught his sleeve. "Get in here and we'll drive away!"

He hated to disappoint her. "Can't. They have us blocked." He briefly met her gaze. "I love you, Mary Daniels." She had to know that, no more waiting, no more patience. "Now, do as I told you." He hit the locks himself as he stepped out, and then closed the door on her gasp.

Determined to put himself between Mary and the men, Brodie circled the hood and started forward. "Big mistake."

They both smiled.

"That's far enough," the one with the gun called out before

looking at the car and smirking. "Ms. Daniels, if you don't get your ass out here right now, I'll shoot him."

They knew her name? Brodie took another aggressive step forward—and heard the car door open.

Goddamn it. He heaved a breath and reached for calm. "Get back in the car, Mary."

Behind him, he heard Howler's muffled fury, meaning the dog was still contained.

"Hurry it up," the gun holder ordered her.

In a composed voice that belied the fear she had to be feeling, Mary said, "I had to slip out without the dog getting loose." Her voice trembled but she forged on. "I opened the driver's window enough for him to get air and that distracted him long enough, but he's not happy about it."

"Stop babbling." The bastard with the gun gestured. "If he gets loose, I'll put a bullet right between his eyes."

Despite everything, Mary's patented defiance came through. "Yes, I assumed a bastard like you would shoot a sweet innocent dog."

The *sweet innocent dog* was probably destroying his car, given the noise he made.

Brodie felt her nearing him, but he didn't take his gaze off the men. He said again, very distinctly, "Get back. In the. Car."

"No." She stopped a few feet from his side. "What is this all about?" she asked the men.

The unarmed guy said, "I have someone who wants to talk to you."

"Fine, where is he?"

"The back of the SUV."

Brodie thrust an arm out to his side, forestalling her from moving forward. "She's not going anywhere."

"Fuck it, Lem." The chattier of the two took aim. "I'll shoot him and be done with it."

"No!"

Brodie said, "Mary, you can't—"

"You won't do anything." The unarmed man shot a glare at his cohort. "Now, shut up and let me talk."

"You talk to *me*," Brodie insisted. "Not her."

Aggrieved, Lem stepped forward. "Ah, but I think you'll be more manageable if we do it the other way around."

"That's far enough," Brodie warned.

"Todd," Lem said, still approaching, "if he moves, go ahead and shoot him."

"Oh God." Mary stirred beside him.

"Hush," he told her, needing to think. The way the two of them shared names, Brodie assumed he wasn't meant to survive. He could accept that, if it kept Mary safe. He didn't *want* to die, but more than that, he wanted *her* to live.

As if she knew his intent, Mary whispered, "Please, Brodie, I don't want you hurt."

He hated hearing her fear, but he couldn't reassure her just yet. Lem wasn't backing off and that was a real problem for him.

"Touch her," Brodie promised softly, "and you won't walk away."

Snorting, Lem reached for her—and Brodie pivoted, kicking out the man's knee.

The leg buckled with a sickening snap and Lem collapsed to the ground, screaming in pain. Another kick to his face shut him up real quick.

"Fucker!" Todd shouted, but Brodie was already on the move, charging him.

Three long strides were all he needed…

Todd raised his gun hand—not at Brodie, but at Mary.

God, no.

With his heart caught in his throat, Brodie drove his shoulder into the leaner man's gut, jamming him hard up against a tree with a satisfying thump that shook leaves loose. The gun exploded at the ground near his feet, making his ears ring, but all Brodie could think was that at least it wasn't anywhere near Mary.

Grabbing Todd's wrist with his left hand, Brodie used his right forearm to smash the prick's face, once, twice.

Todd viciously brought up a knee, barely missing his nuts but still with enough force to traumatize the thigh muscles. Brodie absorbed the pain and instead of loosening his hold, he ruthlessly twisted Todd's wrist.

"I'm going to kill you," Todd panted, his whole body straining. "And then I'm going to kill your bitch."

"Fuck you." Brodie head-butted him hard, and as Todd's eyes crossed, he broke his wrist.

When the gun fell to the ground, Brodie kicked it away, sending it several feet into deeper grass.

Stepping back, fury still burning through his blood, his chest heaving with rage, Brodie said, "You're not going to—"

A loud retort sounded behind him. At almost the same time, blood sprayed from Todd's chest and he slumped, deadweight, to fall sideways to the ground.

Thinking only of Mary and this new threat, Brodie jerked around, and there by the SUV stood a massively built man, shirtsleeves rolled up over bulging forearms, thick lips curled in a gleeful grin. "Prick had it coming, am I right?"

What. The. Fuck? Brodie's attention jumped from the man's face, which showed him to be a few decades past Brodie's own age, to the gun in his hand, to the open back door of the SUV.

A third goon? *Fuck me sideways.*

Thanks to the headlights of the SUV, Brodie was able to glimpse Mary standing by the Mustang. In the split second that he took to look, it appeared she was trying to soothe Howler through the partially opened window. She seemed distressed but otherwise unharmed while keeping her attention on him.

God willing, she'd at least called the police when he'd asked her to.

With resignation, Brodie asked, "You are?" He moved slowly, maneuvering so that he stood between the man and Mary.

"I *was* his boss." He spit toward Todd. "He shouldn't have threatened her. He knows I don't abide hurting women."

Okkkaaay. Still casually sidestepping, Brodie said, "So I can assume you'll let her go?"

"I have nothing but respect for Mary," he said in a nonanswer. "I've been aware of her since she started working for Ritter. She strikes me as the loyal sort."

Brodie didn't know what might set the man off, so he didn't confirm or deny that. "I take it you're Assassin?"

"Ha, no! That sniveling puke has no balls, no balls at all. I shooed him away like an annoying fly. Ritter, though, that old bastard refused to be intimidated."

Maybe because it hadn't been Therman's ass on the line. Unwilling to make a wrong move, Brodie waited.

Holding out those tree trunks where arms should have been, the man said, "I'm The Prodigal. Get it? Prodigal son, dragged home for his duty." He tossed the gun into the back seat of the SUV and slammed the door. The auto-locks clicked into place. "Poetic, right?"

"If you say so." Brodie's thoughts churned. Todd wouldn't be bothering anyone else, but Lem was starting to make sounds of life. Brodie needed to get a handle on things. "What are we doing here, if you don't mind me asking?"

Cracking his knuckles, then his neck, The Prodigal said, "Now that it's just you and me, let's see what you've got. Mano a mano, eh?" He beckoned Brodie forward. "I got an itch that can't be scratched unless I draw some blood."

What an image.

With a nudge of his head, Brodie indicated Todd, then lifted his brows as if to say, *There's your blood.*

"Nah, that doesn't count. Too easy. I'm thinking you'll be

more of a challenge." And with that, The Prodigal started for-ward, immense fists already up, mountainous shoulders bunched and a maniacal gleam in his eyes.

CHAPTER NINETEEN

Mary prayed for the police to arrive, though she hadn't called them.

She'd called Therman instead, babbling hysterically to him about the situation and getting his promise to send help right away. Why she'd chosen him for her call, she couldn't say for sure. A gut reaction to her panic, maybe?

She couldn't breathe, couldn't slow her stuttering heartbeat. The worse sort of near-crippling fear had grabbed hold the second Brodie had left the car.

I love you, Mary Daniels.

That statement said more than the obvious. It said he'd protect her.

He'd die for her.

She'd known it in her heart and that, along with the fear, had obliterated her usual calm reason. It was as if every bottled-up need, fear and desire had suddenly exploded, leaving her utterly rattled and desperate.

Luckily Therman had taken control, telling her that Jolene was already making the call, promising he'd have people there in minutes and saying…

She swallowed hard.

…saying in a broken voice that she was important, that she mattered.

That she was family.

He'd begged her to use every caution.

"It's okay, baby," she told an enraged Howler, needing to hear her own voice. "Please, I don't want you in the middle of this mess. We need to trust Brodie, okay?"

Trust, real trust. Such an elusive thing, but with Brodie, she'd found it and by God she wanted to keep it, now and forever.

Despite Lem's pitiful groans and the awful bend of his leg, she'd been doing pretty good with trusting Brodie to handle things. Amazingly, against the odds, he seemed in complete control.

Until that blast had sounded, echoing everywhere—especially in her heart. For a single moment she'd thought Todd had shot Brodie and everything in her had died.

A second later Todd crumpled and the behemoth came from the car.

Brodie was okay…but good Lord, the third man was enormous. He topped Brodie's height by a few inches, his shoulders wider, thicker. Even his skull looked bigger.

Was this, then, the man who'd spoken with Gina at the restaurant?

Remembering Gina gave her a desperate idea and she acted even before thinking it through.

"Mr. Prodigal?" she called out, making the giant pause just as he'd started toward Brodie. "I thought all you wanted was a phone call?"

Behind her, Howler went berserk.

In front of her, Brodie wasn't much better.

"For the last time, Mary—"

"That was you, yes? Who, um, visited Gina at the restaurant?"

"It was me," the ape agreed, speaking over Brodie. "But that was a few days ago. Gina dragged her feet and now—" he shrugged "—here we are."

Mary nodded, but asked, "Where, exactly, are we?"

He eyed her, then Brodie.

Mary knew Brodie, knew he was gauging the best angles, coming up with a plan of attack. She needed to prevent that. Yes, he was good. Amazingly fast. *Scary* strong.

But he wasn't a murderous behemoth.

"I'm about to mess up your driver's face."

Barely covering her gasp, Mary said, "I wish you wouldn't."

The Prodigal pinched the air. "Just a little, okay?" Sweetly apologetic, he said, "I need this."

"This?" She took a few steps forward, which made Howler even more ferocious. "Violence?"

"Yeah, see..." He rubbed the back of his squat neck. "It's what I'm good at. The rest of this shit, all these idiotic collections, they don't matter to me."

Brodie threw up his arms. "Then why are we even here?"

A steely gaze shot his way, ripe with irritation. "It was important to my father. I inherited it all and I need to finish this collection."

"It's yours," Mary promised fast, moving yet another step. *Closer and closer to Todd's gun.* "Mr. Ritter has agreed to let you have it."

"Therman Ritter can't give me shit!" A mailbox-sized fist thumped his mammoth chest. "I *take* what I want."

"Then take this," Brodie growled, swinging his locked fists together in an arc that connected with the bigger man's chin.

The Prodigal stumbled back, blinked in surprise and laughed as he shook his head to clear it. "There you go." He aimed a punch at Brodie's face.

Mary screamed, then realized Brodie had ducked. Oh, thank God. The man could have taken off his head! She sidled quickly to the tree, doing her utmost not to stare at Todd's sightless eyes or the blood and gore that splattered his chest.

She heard a horrible noise and glanced up to see Brodie sprawled on his back.

"C'mon," The Prodigal goaded, standing over him. "I finally have you alone, so at least show me some sport."

With a groan, Brodie drove the heel of his shoe into the other man's groin.

Wincing, Mary searched for the gun while keeping one eye on the men.

For a second, the big man stood there looking blank, his hands over his groin, before he doubled over.

Brodie rolled back to his feet and kneed the man in the face. Unfortunately, as he went down, he dragged Brodie with him.

Mary flinched at every pounding, grunting, painful sound she heard. How much could Brodie take? He was already limping, already bleeding.

Where was the gun? There!

She dove for it, so afraid for Brodie that she could barely see straight. She'd never shot before, but that didn't mean she couldn't.

The problem was that the men were rolling around too much, up one moment, down another, clenched, apart, stumbling…

"That's enough!" She held the gun in both hands, her finger on the trigger, her breathing choppy. "Swear to God, I'm going to shoot someone."

Brodie straddled The Prodigal, fist cocked, but at her threat they both froze.

Blood, dirt and bruises covered them. *Both.*

Even now Brodie held his own. Well, sort of.

His left cheek bore a split that trickled blood. His right eye was nearly swollen shut. He'd definitely taken the brunt of the abuse, yet he was currently on top.

The Prodigal peered around him to see Mary. "You won't shoot."

She shifted her stance, tightened her jaw. "Wanna bet?"

Softly, as if trying to soothe her, Brodie said, "Babe, take your finger off the trigger, okay?"

Mary shook her head. "No, it's not okay." A siren sounded in the distance. *Finally.* Those ten minutes had felt like ten hours. Ten *days*. "Back away from him, Brodie."

"You don't want to kill anyone."

"You don't know that." She thought of Todd's dead body and acid crawled up her throat. If she puked, then she puked.

But she wasn't lowering the gun.

She lifted her chin, and because Brodie needed to understand, she stated with conviction, "I'd do anything to protect you."

Both men stared at her.

In another display of speed, Brodie moved off The Prodigal and to the side. His gaze never left her. "Because you love me?"

She couldn't get the words out so she nodded.

"Ahh," the ape said with sarcasm. "That's sweet." Then with underlying steel, "Now, how about you get that fucking gun off me?"

"Don't curse at her," Brodie ordered. "She's upset."

"No shit. She's shaking so bad she's liable to shoot me without meaning to."

"Oh, I'll mean to." Mary partially lowered the gun. Honestly, her whole body had started to quake. At this point if the gun went off, she might even hit Brodie. She looked at him helplessly, feeling the edges of her vision start to close in. "Will you come take this, please?"

"Yeah." His grin went crooked thanks to the swelling in his face, and he limped when he walked. As he eased the gun from her hand, The Prodigal got to his feet. Brodie didn't aim at him, but the intent was there anyway.

He was ready, and unlike her, he didn't shake.

Leaning against his other side, grateful for the arm that held her close, Mary peered around at all the destruction. "Well, Prodigal, are you happy with yourself?"

The man laughed. Actually *laughed*. "Since it looks like I'm busted, you may as well call me Helton. And the answer is yes." He stretched. "It's been a long dry spell, but now, I feel pretty damn good."

Brodie grinned, too.

Mary considered throwing a punch of her own. "You think this is funny?" She glared her accusation at Brodie. "You think *he* is funny?"

"He's a psychopath and this situation is as far from funny as we can get."

"So what amused him?"

"He thought it was just him and me. Mano a mano, remember?" Brodie gave her a squeeze. "He forgot about you."

His smile, even crooked, was the sweetest thing she'd ever seen. Feeling her lip start to quiver, Mary bit it.

Helton shook his head. "She'd seemed like such a sweet girl."

"She's a woman," Brodie corrected. "And actually, she's the strongest fighter I know."

Tears burned Mary's eyes and no amount of blinking would clear them away. Police cars pulled into the drive, one after another until three sets of lights and sirens mingled.

Needing something to do, besides being an emotional wreck, she ran over to the first officer and gave a stammering explanation. Luckily, Therman had already detailed much of the situation, saving her some trouble. The police at least knew that she and Brodie weren't the bad players in this drama.

Once that was done and the police had taken over, she went to Brodie's car.

Howler needed reassurances, and she needed a moment to think. It took a little coaxing to calm the dog down enough for her to slip into the car with him. After he'd snuffled all over her, whimpering and crying—making *her* cry again—she got his leash on him. Stupidly, she told him he had to promise to be good.

He gave her the most innocent look she'd ever seen from him, and she bought it. Adopting Brodie's absurd baby talk, she crooned to Howler, repeating over and over, "You're such a good boy."

He played along, she'd give him that. Yet the second they stepped from the car the dog literally hauled her, without pause, straight to Brodie.

Mary stumbled and barely kept up.

When Howler reached him, he jumped up, paws on Brodie's shoulders, to bathe him in uncontrolled love. Laughing, wincing a little, Brodie accepted the affection and gave it back in return with long strokes down Howler's back, a few hugs and lots of baby talk.

Standing back just a bit, the leash now loose in her hand, Mary watched him and thought again about how much she cared for him. She hadn't really known what to expect of love, but *this*?

It overwhelmed her.

In a good way, she supposed, though it also scared her.

She didn't like feeling needy, but she knew she needed Brodie.

She didn't like the turbulence of her emotions, and yet new tears gathered on her lashes.

Any cold control she'd once felt was blown. Warmth and sentiment and sexual attraction had taken its place, filling her up, all but choking her.

And the trust—that was the newest emotion of all. She truly, one hundred percent trusted him. In everything.

Because she knew he loved her, too.

She was wondering what they'd do next, where the love would take them, when movement on the driveway drew her eyes.

Therman rolled into view in his wheelchair.

Good heavens, it was a *long* drive. Vera, Burl and Jolene hustled behind him and for once, Jolene didn't look as dignified, not with tears tracking her face. Vera openly sobbed with a hand to her mouth. Worry lined Burl's face.

And Therman… Therman locked his gaze on her and kept coming. His stricken face took her breath away. Suddenly he looked small and frail—and yet, he'd come for *her.*

These people cared about her, they always had.

Dear God, now that she'd opened her heart, she felt so much. Almost too much. Blindly, she reached out. "Brodie?"

Following her gaze, he said, "Breathe, honey."

She gulped in air.

"Let's meet him halfway." Brodie took her arm and, holding Howler's leash in the other hand, they all moved forward until she and Therman met in the middle.

All around them, noise filled the night air. People talking, giving orders. Paramedics seeing to Lem. Helton arguing as he was put into a vehicle. It all seemed to fade away.

"Mary." Therman swallowed heavily—and opened his arms. Tears glittered in his eyes and it broke her.

Going to her knees, Mary embraced him while Vera, Burl and Jolene closed in around her.

"Thank God you're all right," he said over and over while hugging her tight. "Thank God."

"This is nice."

Brodie. She turned, swiped a wrist over her eyes and stared up at him. *Oh, his poor battered face.* She gave Therman one last pat, then stood with a purpose. "You need to go to a hospital."

He shook his head. "It looks worse than it is."

It looked pretty damned bad. "Are you sure?"

"You love me. I won't let you take it back, so yeah, I'm fine."

Crazy, wonderful man. Fighting back tears of joy, Mary said to their collected group, "He loves me, too."

"We already knew that," Jolene said with a smile.

"And we love you." Vera leaned into Burl. "All of us."

Humbled, Mary swallowed heavily. "Thank you for not giving up on me."

Therman stated, "You're family," as if that explained everything.

And maybe it did. *Now.*

Mary gave another watery sob. Brodie pulled her against his chest, letting her hide her face for just a moment. No longer than that, though, because Howler started to fret.

Against her temple, Brodie said, "Howler loves you, too, you know. You're just that damned lovable."

Yes, for the first time in her life, she believed it. She *felt* it.

"You're all wonderful." She stroked Howler, then encompassed them all in her gaze. "Thank you. I love you so much, and I'm glad to have you for my family."

Even with the craziness around them, she couldn't have been happier.

That was how it was with family, she realized. They made everything better.

"Speaking of family..." Brodie dug his phone from his pocket. "My mother will skin me if I don't clue her in."

"Bring her to dinner tomorrow," Therman said, his tone firm. "Your brother, too."

"And Charlotte," Mary added. She was also family.

"Great idea." Burl rubbed his hands together. "I've got a standing roast that'll be perfect. Now, I just need to decide on a dessert. Something special." After quick hugs, he and Vera moved off together.

Jolene put her hands on Therman's shoulders. "I should get him back to the house."

Therman resisted her efforts, his head down, his hands tight on the arms of the chair. "I want you to know, I burned it all."

Not understanding, Mary looked at Brodie.

He shrugged and asked, "Burned what?"

"The art from the prisoner." His bushy brows clenched together. "I've never displayed it. I started out buying it to ensure no one else could. I didn't want it glamorized." After clearing his throat, he met Brodie's gaze. "I got caught up in the competition of acquiring it. No excuses. It was wrong, especially when other buyers tried to threaten me away." He shook his head. "That happens sometimes. I thought it was fun and games. I never imagined..."

Mary took his hand in hers. "We spoke with The Prodigal. I think he's insane, but you couldn't have known that."

Gratitude softened his expression. "Still..."

"It's over and done," Brodie interrupted. "I'm happy to remain your driver if you'll have me."

A slow smile came over Therman. "Boy, I'm not about to let you go."

"Neither am I." Mary moved against Brodie again, loving how his arms came around her. Loving *him*.

And especially loving her future, now that she had everything she'd ever wanted and more.

EPILOGUE

Once the dinner dishes were cleared away, Brodie spread out the house plans on his mother's table. They'd started with a basic floor plan, then added to it based on things he and Mary wanted, along with suggestions from his mother, Therman and even Jolene.

Next to him, Jack nodded. "I like it." He pointed at the master bedroom. "Opening to a deck out back? Nice."

"That was Mary's idea. She loves the woods." He'd had a hell of a time adjusting to that, since he knew she'd spent too much of her childhood killing time in isolation.

But now it had new meaning.

According to Mary, *most* things had new meaning.

She'd stated that *these* woods belonged to them. Together.

Brodie stated that she'd never be alone again.

Mary came in from the living room, where Therman and Jolene sat with his mother, chatting over coffee and a cake that Burl had brought along. Vera had tried to insist on cleaning up after dinner, but in turn, his mother had insisted that Jack and Brodie could do it.

And they had. Hell, he was so pleased to have everyone together that he wouldn't mind doing dishes the rest of the year.

"It's going to be beautiful," Mary said as she breezed in, wearing a warm glow. Happiness, that was what it was, and it suited her as well as the adorable freckles did. "In another month or so when the leaves start to change, it'll be so colorful. And the birds." She hugged herself. "I love hearing them sing."

In so many different ways, she'd opened up the last few weeks. She'd changed her clothes, her hair, her makeup.

And she was still the most gorgeous woman he'd ever seen.

Brodie had to kiss her. Hell, it happened a dozen times a day. She'd say or do something, and he couldn't resist.

Hard to believe he'd first met her in July, only a few months ago, because now he couldn't imagine her not being in his life.

With his mouth against hers, he whispered, "You look hot in those jeans." They fit her lush body perfectly, as did her sweater. She'd slowly changed her wardrobe, adding new pieces while eliminating old. And always, no matter what she wore, her sexy confidence shone through. That, thank God, hadn't changed.

Ros came in to refill coffee, but paused to look at the plans. "How long before you break ground?"

"Soon." He gave Mary another kiss. Then one more.

Laughing, Mary put her hands to his cheeks and held his face away. "You're embarrassing me."

"Am not." He kissed her nose. "It's just family."

That made *her* kiss *him*, before she snuggled close. "I think we can start building a little sooner than we'd planned."

They'd worked out the finances together and decided that if they got the house under roof before winter, they'd be happy with that progress. But if she wanted to adjust that, he'd make it work.

"Whatever you want, Red."

"Spoken like a man in love," Jack said.

Charlotte laughed. "Don't say that like it's a surprise. He's been in love since he first saw her."

"He was in *lust*," Jack corrected, then said to his mother, "Though you probably shouldn't hear that."

"Being a mother," Ros said, "didn't make me blind or stupid. Plus, I know my son."

Mary laughed. "I'm so glad Brodie was part of a package deal." She stepped back and dug a check from her pocket. "I was talking about this. Therman just gave us an early wedding gift."

Brodie took it from her, then whistled. "Seriously?" The amount was a little staggering, but that was Therman. Now that Mary had accepted them all, Therman had gone all in, treating her like a daughter in nearly every way.

They still worked for him, and he continued to add to his collections, but the relationship had changed a lot and Brodie felt like they were all better off.

Charlotte crowded in to look over his shoulder. So did Jack. They were each suitably impressed.

"I told him it was too much, but he said it wasn't a bonus for work. It was for family."

Therman crowded into the kitchen. "Damn right." His busy brows narrowed as he eyed them each in turn. "You are family. I'm going to give her away at the wedding after all."

Way to go, Therman. Brodie slowly grinned as he turned to face the older man. "I think that sounds perfect. You'll look real swanky rolling down the aisle."

On her way out, Charlotte bent to kiss Therman's cheek. "You are just the sweetest guy ever."

Jack followed her, pausing to pat Therman's shoulder. "I don't know about sweet, but definitely generous."

For his part, Therman looked a little nonplussed, then his face split with a big grin. "I do like your family, Brodie." He wheeled around and followed the others.

After that awful incident, Mary had given up her apartment

to move in with him and they'd started wedding plans. The big day was a month away. Nothing too fancy, just his Mary in a white dress, lots of flowers and their families—both sides—as witnesses.

"There's something else." With a deep breath, Mary reached into her other pocket and drew out a second check. "I sold my house."

The air froze in Brodie's lungs. Other than the day she'd told him about the house, she hadn't mentioned it—and he hadn't asked. It was her decision and he wanted her to be comfortable with it. If she wanted it demolished, he'd take it apart for her, brick by brick with his bare hands if that was what it took.

Ros raised her brows. "You never told me you had a house."

They'd grown close, just as Brodie had known they would, but especially so as his mother helped her with wedding plans. Mary loved hanging out with the women, and the women loved her.

"I grew up there," Mary explained. "The memories…weren't great."

What an understatement. She'd survived hell and was still the most beautiful person he knew.

"For the longest time after my mother passed away, I had planned to level it to the ground. It made sense to me—before I met Brodie." A smile teased her lips. "Now it's not important."

Brodie was so damned proud of her words practically stuck in his throat. "You're sure, babe?"

"I better be, because it's a done deal." She smiled toward Howler, who'd started to snore. "The memories are still there, but they're not that important anymore. This—" she held out her arms "—you, our families, our future, that's all that really matters."

Smiling, Ros gave her a hug, gave him a high five and left the room.

"I adore your mother," Mary said.

"She's not an angel," he reminded her. "But I agree, she's pretty awesome."

"I'm so glad we'll live close to her." She smiled down at the house plans. "My past used to take up rent in my head far too often. I realize that now that I'm dwelling more on the future."

Her future with him. "You know, the memories won't go away. Not completely."

"Probably not. But they've lost importance."

"Just know that when they come back, I'm here. I'll always be here."

"With me." She looked up at him, devouring him with those incredible, bluer-than-blue eyes. "I love you, Brodie Archer Crews. I love your family. I love *my* family." She smiled. "I love your dog, and I love loving you."

Brodie hugged her off her feet, then whispered in her ear, "Think anyone would notice if we snuck away?"

Mary laughed.

It was a sound he'd never tire of hearing. "I guess we should go thank Therman first."

"It is a lot of money," she said.

"The money's nice, but that's not what I meant."

"Then what?"

Brodie grinned. "In the beginning, he insisted on me when you wanted to swap for Jack. And for that, I owe him everything."

★ ★ ★ ★ ★

Read on for a sneak peek at the next sizzling
Road to Love book,
Slow Ride,
from New York Times *bestselling author Lori Foster!*

CHAPTER ONE

Ronnie wouldn't have walked into Freddie's, a dinky little honky-tonk bar in Red Oaks, Ohio, if she'd known a local's birthday party was underway. But hey, she'd sought a distraction and this served.

Seated on a stool, she lifted her beer to the loud toast made by a fellow in dusty overalls. Something about the birthday boy supplying corn to an upcoming festival. Ronnie wasn't sure. Small towns usually eluded her.

And this town was smaller than most.

The main street began with farms, melded into small, tidy houses lining each side, along with a few establishments, then abruptly ended with Freddie's.

God willing, she wouldn't have to be here long. Her employers had recently decided that she needed a professional courier to help acquire their purchases—even though Ronnie was more than capable on her own.

Worse, the man they wanted to hire was, by all accounts, a superslick suit-wearing choirboy—and she wanted nothing to do with him. Tomorrow she would present the offer as directed, but with any luck he'd turn it down—and then she could get back to work.

Alone.

Until then, she needed to shake off the tension, or at the very least find a distraction, thus her visit to this dive.

"Come on in," someone shouted. "There's still plenty of room."

Ronnie glanced up to see the newcomer—and was instantly caught. *Well, well, well.*

This new customer stood better than six feet tall. Messy light brown hair contrasted with heavily lashed, dark eyes. Two different paint colors splattered his T-shirt, and his faded jeans hung loose and low.

Hello, distraction.

She'd hoped a beer would take the edge off, but perhaps there was a better way to help her sleep tonight.

Swiveling to face him, Ronnie smiled. This was what she needed. *He* was what she needed. Her heart beat faster just thinking of the possibilities.

Allowing her gaze to skim down his body, she lingered in key, tantalizing places.

Straight shoulders.

Trim waist.

Delicious biceps.

Down to a flat stomach, narrow hips and…a nice bulge in his softly worn jeans. Whoa.

A curl of heat teased through her system. Yes, she had a definite type, favoring rugged, rough men. *Real* men.

This one fit the bill to perfection.

Her gaze shifted to his hand. She noted the lack of a wedding band, but then, a lot of guys didn't wear them. She never, ever, got involved—even for one night—with men already in relationships.

Now, how to proceed?

When she looked back up to his face, she found him standing

still, arms loose at his sides, feet slightly braced apart, staring at her with a very slight smile on his sexy mouth.

Terrific. They had a mutual attraction going on.

Playing coy, Ronnie slid her gaze away and faced the bar again, forearms folded on the counter. Awareness sizzled as she sensed his casual approach.

"Drinking alone?"

Mmm, that deep voice. So far, everything about him stirred her.

He kept a slight distance, not invading her space but still making his interest apparent.

Rubbing her thumb along the neck of the bottle, she glanced up at him. "Not if you join me."

Her invitation warmed those dark brown eyes. He settled on the stool beside her and turned slightly so that his thigh touched hers.

And just that, such a light touch, sent excitement coiling through her. As he ordered a cola and pulled-pork sandwich, she studied his profile: the masculine nose, sensual mouth, strong jaw and high cheekbones. Oh, those darker-than-sin eyes and lush lashes…

His gaze cut her way. "Have you eaten?"

She lifted the beer. "Moved on to dessert." No, she wasn't a heavy drinker, but he wouldn't know that. Let him think what he wanted. She didn't care.

"New to the area?" he asked.

"Just passing through." Somehow she'd make that true. But what if he was a local? On the off chance Slick took the job tomorrow, she'd be in and around the area a lot—meaning she shouldn't complicate things with neighbors. She sipped her beer again, gauging how she'd ask, then settled on, "You work here as a painter?"

His mouth slightly curled. "No."

"Ah, somewhere else, then." Relieved, she let out a tense breath. "That's good."

He'd started to say something, but asked instead, "Good because…?"

Ronnie waved a hand. "I don't want to start anything with the locals."

One brow cocked up. Eyes direct, he asked, "But you want to start something with me?"

Oh, she liked his confidence, the bold way he asked that—and she liked how he held her gaze.

Why hedge? It was already getting late and the beer wasn't doing it for her. She dreaded the idea of sleeping alone. That was true for most nights, but as it sometimes happened, tonight was worse.

So she turned, slid her knee along the inside of his and said with suggestion, "I do. Something that could last the night?" Then she clarified, "*Only* through the night. What do you think?"

His attention roved over her, from her short pale hair in styled disarray, to the front of her sweater, where her less-than-stellar boobs wouldn't impress a single soul, down her waist to her legs to her ankle boots. Those sinful eyes slowly rose back to her face. "There's a hotel a few miles down the road."

She knew that, because she'd rented a room there. "Perfect." Tipping up the beer, she finished it off and started to stand.

He grinned. "Mind if I eat first? It's been a long day."

Well. Well, *hell.* Here she was ready to rush out the door and he wanted to eat first?

Plopping her behind back on the plastic-covered stool seat and resting her elbows behind her on the bar, she waited as the steaming sandwich with a side of chips was set before him.

"You could get it to go," she suggested. "Eat it on the way, maybe?"

For an answer, he picked it up and took a big bite.

What. A. Jerk. Did she need a diversion this badly?

Her heart ached as she accepted the truth that, sadly, yes, she did.

She crossed her legs and swung a foot. "If I have to wait, you damn well better be worth it."

Nonchalance personified, he nodded. "I'll do my best."

Ronnie sighed out her frustration. She had the feeling his best would be pretty damn good.

Jack couldn't remember the last time he'd been this attracted to a woman...or when he'd had so much fun teasing her. The little beauty next to him was all but steaming, but still she wanted him.

A real boost to the ego.

And he wasn't at his best. He'd gotten a day off at the office, but he'd worked all morning on the yard, done a few roof repairs and then painted two rooms. Hunger had driven him to Freddie's without showering, shaving or changing into clean clothes first. Not his usual style.

Judging by *her* style, his present state of "worked all day on a rehab house" suited her. He cast another glance over her and forced himself not to gulp his food.

Petite women didn't usually turn him on—but God love her, she did.

She had this edgy style with platinum hair cut short in the back but long in the front. The wispy bangs nearly hung in her eyes—soft gray eyes lined with kohl—until she ran her slender fingers through it, pushing it to the side. When she turned her head, it fell forward. No matter how it lay, she looked sexy as hell.

The pale blue sweater hugged her upper body, but not as tightly as those jeans hugged her trim little ass and crazy long legs. For a woman so small, she was put together really fine.

And she wanted him.

For *tonight*.

She wasn't local and probably wouldn't be around here again. Even knowing it was better that way, he couldn't deny the twinge of disappointment. He had a feeling he was going to enjoy her. A lot.

Suddenly she asked, "You're not involved, are you?"

"Romantically?" He took another massive bite. Freddie's had amazing sandwiches.

"Romantically, sexually, whatever. I don't want to step on any toes."

He swallowed. "Uninvolved on all counts." But he thought to ask, "You?" because he didn't trespass, either.

"Free and clear." She fidgeted, toying with a dangling silver earring in her right ear.

In her left she had a stud.

Three fingers on her left hand sported silver rings, along with her thumb on her right.

Fascinating.

He watched her survey the bar, not with any real interest but just to track the movement of the party.

She had amazing skin. Peachy. Smooth. Natural skin, he thought, despite the loud eye makeup. Her brows were a medium brown, not that he needed to notice that to know she'd bleached her hair. Altogether, she gave off a confident, distinctive, sexy vibe.

He liked it. "What's your name?"

She immediately shook her head. "No names." Bringing her attention back to him, she scowled. "Hurry up already."

"What's the rush?"

Tucking in her chin, she gave him a killing glare. "Look, if you're not interested—"

"I'm interested." Jack shrugged. "I'm also hungry after working all day. Will five more minutes hurt?"

She seemed to be debating it, then with a deliberately flippant attitude, she said, "Whatever," and slipped off the bar stool.

For a second, Jack thought she was leaving and he had to fight the urge to catch her arm, to dissuade her, to…convince her.

Since when did he have to *convince* women? Not for years.

When she merely dug some change from her pocket, he relaxed. Sort of. But he did eat a little faster.

"The jukebox work?"

Jack nodded, swallowed. "But it's all country music."

"Of course it is." Wending her way around the crowds until she finally reached the old-fashioned jukebox, she studied the songs, slipped in the change and smiled as music joined the din of conversation.

Jack studied her body as she started back toward him, the graceful way she moved while still being very aware of the press of bodies around her. She touched no one as she slipped this way and that, not even a brush of arms. Her sweater barely met the waistband of her jeans, and twice he got a glimpse of her smooth, pale stomach.

Fuck the food. He'd had enough.

Standing, he put some money on the bar and waited for her. If he wasn't careful, he'd get half-hard just imagining what was to come.

Right before she reached him, someone said, "Hey, Jack. The house is looking good."

He gave an offhand "Thanks," not even sure who'd said it. Everyone around here knew him, his brother and his mother, and they were all friendly.

She stopped, her made-up eyes flaring. "Jack?"

He didn't have a problem with names, so he held out a hand. "Jack Crews. Feel like sharing now?"

Instead she slapped his hand away and surged forward in one big step, going on her tiptoes to glare up into his face. "You're supposed to be slick."

"I am?" This close, he could see her individual lashes and he detected the faint perfume of flowers—an odd contrast to her sharp appeal.

"Yes!" Dropping back, she gestured at him. "You are not supposed to be messy or rugged."

With no idea what was going on, Jack folded his arms and leaned back on the bar. "Is it against the rules if I'm all of the above?"

She appeared to be sawing her teeth together. "Thanks for nothing." Turning on her heel, she started out the door.

What the hell? Jack bolted after her, following her through the door and out the walkway. "Where are you going?"

To the tune of furious stomping, she said, "To the hotel."

"I have a truck."

"Alone."

He easily caught up to walk beside her. "So…that's it? You changed your mind and I won't see you again?"

She muttered something low and mean.

"What?"

Halting, she stared down at her feet a moment, and when she raised her face, she looked *almost* calm again. "I'll see you tomorrow, as a matter of fact." Her smile could wound. "At your office."

Jack still didn't get it.

"We have an appointment first thing."

"I have an appointment with Ronnie Ashford."

She held out her arms. "That would be me. And if you don't mind, I'd like to forget about this. Tonight. That we might have… Just forget it." And with that, she continued on her way, her behind swishing, her legs eating up the pavement.

Very slowly, Jack smiled. Forget about it? Like hell.

And damn it, now he *was* getting hard.

Don't miss Slow Ride
by New York Times *bestselling author*
Lori Foster!